Merry Christmas 2009
Brittany from
Grandma Co

OFFICIAL SKE

OF

JACOB HENRY KIMBALL

— POTTER —

IF FOUND, PLEASE RETURN TO
HUDSON UNIVERSITY CERAMICS LAB

JK

"AND THE POTTER SAID TO THE
CLAY — BEWARE —
... AND IT WAS."
GEORGE OHR

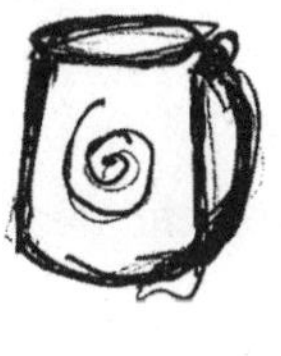

reminded me that a town like Niederbipp can exist when we remember to care for each other and take time to enjoy life." *–J. Parish*

"I just finished reading it and loved it! I loved the characters so much I was sad when it ended. I miss hanging out with them. There are so many great messages in the story. I'd like to buy more copies for my kids and some friends." *–L. Boyer*

"I just finished reading Remembering Isaac by Ben Behunin. I'm still awash in the wonderful feelings left behind by the experience... Well-written, joyful, meaty (but not heavy-handed), with whimsical illustrations by the author sprinkled throughout, this is a compelling book that both delights and imbues wisdom in a most subtle way. I couldn't put it down...I can't wait for the sequel!" *–L. Steele*

"Through the book I couldn't help but wish that I had known Isaac and that I could visit Niederbipp. This is a book that for me was inspirational, entertaining and joyful. I loved it." *–Kate*

"I got wrapped up in the characters and had a hard time putting this book down. I am waiting for the sequel(s)." -W. James

"This book is a work of art!" *–M. Markham*

"I thoroughly enjoyed getting to know Jake, and felt very at home in Niederbipp. This was one of those books I didn't want to put down. My only complaint is that I have to wait to find out what happens next - I'm looking forward to the next installment. Thanks for a great read." *–A. Orchard*

"An intriguing writing keeping you glued til the very end and wishing there was more. I found it hard to leave even to eat or sleep. I anxiously await the next book by Ben Behunin." *–C. R. Scott*

Remembering Isaac
The Wise and Joyful Potter of Niederbipp

First printing, March 2009
Second printing, September 2009

Published by
Abendmahl Press
P.O. Box 581083
Salt Lake City, Utah 84158-1083

ISBN -978-0-615-27606-9

Artwork by Ben Behunin
Photography of pottery sequence by Al Thelin
Designed by Ben Behunin and Bert Compton
Layout by Bert Compton- Compton Design Studio

REMEMBERING ISAAC

THE WISE AND JOYFUL POTTER OF

NIEDERBIPP

VOLUME ONE IN
A SERIES BY
BEN BEHUNIN

REMEMBER, DISCOVER
~ BECOME ~

To Lynnette —
My best friend,
My cheerleader,
and the
mother of
my
children.
—BB—

ARISE, AND GO DOWN TO THE POTTER'S HOUSE, AND THERE I WILL CAUSE THEE TO HEAR MY WORDS.

JEREMIAH 18:2

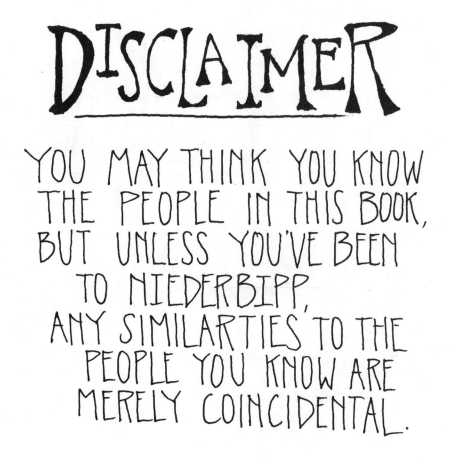

DISCLAIMER

YOU MAY THINK YOU KNOW THE PEOPLE IN THIS BOOK, BUT UNLESS YOU'VE BEEN TO NIEDERBIPP, ANY SIMILARTIES TO THE PEOPLE YOU KNOW ARE MERELY COINCIDENTAL.

PRELUDE

~~PROLOGUE~~

I didn't plan on writing a book, but the voices wouldn't leave me alone. I am a potter. Twelve years ago, I began making my living exclusively by playing in the mud, making stuff. I dropped out of college nine years ago to follow my passions. And I still am.

I was minding my own business when the voices came. I don't remember the day, but I remember where I was. I was working on the wheel when Isaac started talking to me; telling me his story. Over the next few years, he brought his friends and they had tea parties in my head, refusing to leave me alone.

I am not a writer, but I am a dreamer and I've heard they might be cousins. As these voices continued to visit me, I began taking notes. The things they were telling me were beautiful and instructive and meaningful. But I am a potter. They should know better. I spin mud into vessels, not words into tales.

But they kept coming and bringing more friends.

Five years ago, I was again sitting at my wheel when my hands stopped working. At least they didn't work the way I had been used to. I was confused. I am a potter, after all. I need my hands to make stuff. The voices danced about me, telling me they needed a voice others could hear. I reminded them I was a potter, but they wouldn't leave me alone.

So I began.

In the evenings, I started to write. The notes I started so many years ago were jumbled and crazy, but the voices straightened me out. Their stories needed to be told. The people of Niederbipp needed to be heard.

I am a potter with busted hands, but my ears still work. They told me they could work with that.

They don't pay much. In fact, I have yet to receive a dime. (They tell me the check is in the mail.) I realize I didn't do this for money, or for fame. I did it so the people of Niederbipp would have a voice.

I hope it helps.

Ben Behunin 2009

TABLE OF CONTENTS

CONGRATULATIONS!
YOU JUST BOUGHT THE BOOK,
BUT YOU MAY NOT HAVE NOTICED
THAT IT COMES WITH A FREE
SELF-PROPELLED MOVIE ENTITLED
"THE LITTLE POTTER MAKES A BOWL".
(YOU PROVIDE THE SOUNDTRACK)
THE PHOTOS ON THE OTHER SIDE PRODUCE
A FAMILY FRIENDLY FLICK WHEN YOU SLOWLY
FLIP THE PAGES.   HAPPY VIEWING

1
A DEATH SENTENCE

Two weeks before graduation, the front foyer of the Hudson Student Union building teemed with overfilled tables, piled with a year's worth of pottery from hundreds of students. The Annual Student Pottery Sale that began that morning met with a flurry of anxious patrons hoping to find the diamonds among the common stones. The crowds were gone now, leaving a few folks browsing for a good deal on coffee mugs or cereal bowls.

Jake Kimball sat behind the central table, thoughtfully drawing in

his sketchbook while guarding the cash box. As the studio assistant, Jake had spearheaded this event for the last three years. Other students always helped, but he tried to spend as much time there as he could. He wanted to be there to meet the people who bought his pots and eavesdrop on the conversations of those who had come to buy and admire. He always learned things from these observations: what made a good handle on a coffee mug, what glazes were the most popular, why people chose one form over another. Opportunities to show and sell his wares were few and far between and he relished these occasions for both the money he could earn and the insight he could glean.

With the funds he earned from past sales, Jake had financed vacations to different places around the world: Italy, France, England, Germany, Morocco and Spain, as well as domestic locations including Seagrove, North Carolina and the Hopi Mesas of New Mexico. Each of these destinations had one thing in common: pottery! He couldn't get enough of it. His job at the ceramics studio on campus put him in a position to learn every aspect of the art. When he wasn't making pottery, he was firing kilns, mixing glazes, recycling clay scraps and cleaning up after the students and the three professors he called "boss". In all, Jake had spent four years of his life at Hudson University in Albany, New York, most of that time within the four walls of the studio.

Jake had already made enough from the sale of his pottery to meet his financial goal. Just days before, he had purchased a roundtrip ticket to Athens, Greece and paid for it with his credit card, counting on the show being successful enough to pay for his bill. A ticket booked on Priceline. com set him back just shy of a thousand dollars and he had spent many hours surfing the internet at the campus library, reading and re-reading every bit of information about the potters of Peros Island. Several of the sites listed requests for accomplished assistants and Jake responded, sending his information to two of them, hoping to secure at least an online interview before he left.

This summer's trip would be different from those of the past. He always had school to return to, to pick up where he left off. Graduation meant the end of an era...an end to a time where he knew what he was doing. School had seemed like a huge wall that he couldn't see around or over and now that he stood on the top of this wall, he was disappointed, still feeling uncertain of what his future would be. Apprenticeships in the pottery field were becoming increasingly difficult to find. With no family or obligations to hold him back, Jake hoped that the summer in Greece might be a springboard for other adventures and opportunities to expand his ability with clay. His thoughts were scattered and distant as he sat at the table, sketching in his sketchbook while imagining what his future held.

"Excuse me." A voice from the other side of the table interrupted his thoughts.

Jake looked up to see a short, gray-haired woman carrying a stack of bowls. He stood immediately when he recognized the bowls were his.

"I'd like to purchase these," she said, placing the bowls on the stacks of open newspapers Jake had been using to wrap the pottery.

"Of course." He lifted all but the bottom bowl, setting the stack to the side so he could wrap each bowl individually.

"I was glad to see there were still some good bowls left," said the woman. "I've been coming to this show for many years now and I've developed quite a fondness for this potter's work."

Jake looked up as he continued to wrap. "What is it you like about these?"

She took one of the bowls that had yet to be wrapped and handed it to him. "Feel this," she said.

Jake cradled the bowl, examining it as if for the first time. He looked into the bowl and smiled at the star pattern inside. These were new bowls, fresh out of the kiln and some of his more successful attempts at a new technique he was teaching himself. He ran his hands over its belly,  admiring its striped pattern. He looked at the finely trimmed foot and ran

 his thumb over his stamp that had been pressed into the clay when it was still wet. JK, a stamp he had used for the past four years to identify all of his pottery.

"It's very nice," he said, handing it back to her.

"Yes, but did you feel how light it is?" She returned the bowl to him for further examination. He took the bowl again in his hands and with an exaggerated nod repeated his accolades.

"Do you collect a lot of pottery?"

"Oh, I've been buying pots from students here for more than twenty years. My husband is retired now, but he was president of the University for many years. I usually get here sooner, but I forgot what day it was. I bet I missed a lot of really nice stuff."

Jake nodded. "We had a good crowd this morning, but there are still some good pieces out there." He pointed to a table behind the woman, but she didn't turn.

"I came specifically for this potter's work. You felt that bowl. There aren't many potters who can throw a bowl as thin as he can. I've bought his work for the past three years and know, whoever JK is, he is probably getting ready to graduate and will be moving on to get a real job somewhere."

"A real job?"

"Yes, well, it seems it happens to all the potters, no matter how gifted they might be. I told you I've been buying pots here for the past twenty-something years and I can't think of any of those potters who are still making pots today, at least not full-time. It seems they graduate and then just fade away, probably get married or get a mortgage or something and realize they can't make a living doing this kind of work. I knew it was late, but I figured I better get down here and find some of this potter's work before he too fades into oblivion."

Jake finished wrapping the last bowl, but remained quite speechless. He felt as if he had just been handed a death sentence and he couldn't think of a response. He enjoyed the woman's comments of admiration and would have normally pursued further questioning to see what else he might learn from her, but her unabashed honesty about the future life of a potter—his future—was more reality than he cared to hear.

He always knew it would be tough, but he had prepared himself well, learning all that he could about the art and process of pottery. He knew from his travels that making a living as a potter required more than just the ability to make pretty pots. Marketing and business skills would also be required.

Knowing his tenured ceramic professors would have little or no real world experience with marketing, he tried to prepare himself by taking a couple of marketing classes and learning the basic principles of economics. He was starry-eyed and optimistic, even though he knew how tenuous and uncertain a future in pottery could be. This straight talk from the woman in front of him was like rain on a picnic and he didn't want to hear any more.

"That'll be $180."

The woman reached into the black patent leather purse hanging from her elbow, produced two crisp hundred dollar bills and handed them to Jake. "Do you know this potter, the one who made these bowls?"

"I do."

"Do you know how he makes them so thin? I was just thinking it would be good for some of the other pottery students to learn a thing or two from him."

"All of the students have to pay for their own clay. This potter is pretty poor and has had to learn how to make the biggest pots he can with the least amount of clay. I'm not sure you can learn to make thin pots any other way." He opened the cash box and put the money inside, handing the woman $20. He thanked her and put the bowls into a recycled grocery bag, anxious to be done with her so he could get back to more positive thoughts of his future.

"Tell me," she said, "for the past three years I have wondered about this young man every time I have used his pottery or given one of his pieces as a gift. All I know about him are his initials, JK. I have wondered what that might stand for: John Kemp, Jared Knight, Jeremy Kidd. Is there anything else you can tell me about him?"

Jake studied the small woman in front of him. He had pegged her as a cynic from her earlier comments, but as he looked into her eyes, he saw something different, something more humane and kind.

"He's a senior. His name is Jake Kimball and he wants to be a potter when he grows up. For the past four years, he has worked as the studio assistant at the ceramics studio and he just started experimenting with the glazes on the bowls you just purchased."

"Is he a friend of yours?"

"You could say that."

"Do you think he has what it takes to make it as a potter?"

Jake smiled thoughtfully. "I can't imagine him being happy if he didn't at least try."

"Do you know what his plans are?"

"I think I'm... that is he... he's just trying to figure that out. He plans to spend the summer in Greece, but other than that, I don't think he has any definite plans. It's kind of scary thinking about the future when you're used to twenty-four- seven access to the studio and the kilns and all the equipment the university has to offer. I don't know many kids who have the money or know-how to open a studio of their own after graduation. Sometimes I wish I'd chosen a medium that didn't require as much equipment, like painting or even printmaking."

"So you're a potter too then, I take it?"

Jake nodded.

"Then I ought to tell you this," she said, putting the bag back down on the table. "There's something special about using a hand-made bowl. I've never been much of a cook. I try hard, but cooking has never been my passion. But I've found over the years, that when I make something for a party and take it in one of my hand-made pottery dishes, my food is always the first to be consumed and I get more compliments than I ever deserve. People somehow connect to the pottery in a quiet, yet remarkable way. It's almost as if it can somehow breathe life and passion into a meal like a genie escaping from a magic lamp."

Jake's eyes narrowed and he leaned closer. The woman's words echoed his own thoughts about his craft.

She continued, "You can't use a piece of pottery without communing with it, without feeling somehow connected to the potter who made it, even if you have to imagine who that person is because you've never met him. Our world needs that connection. We need to connect with people on a daily basis to remind us of our own humanity. Our world is dying because humans have somehow forgotten how to connect with each other."

"So you think the world still needs potters?"

She looked thoughtful. "Since the age of plastics, the world doesn't *need* potters. You can make things out of plastic that are lighter, more durable and cheaper than you ever could with pottery. But there is simply no human connection. No artist took pride in a mass-produced plastic bowl. The world needs people with passion and I have yet to meet a potter without more than his share of it."

Jake smiled broadly. "For the past three summers, I've been roaming the world looking at pottery and meeting potters. I've met all sorts of them and though I've never met a rich one, I have yet to meet an unhappy one. It's too bad that more of us who get started with clay can't find a way to stick with it, but I'm determined to make it somehow."

The woman looked deeply into his eyes as if she were a soothsayer reading his future. "That's the kind of passion I'm talking about. I think you must have a bright future ahead of you. I feel like you're on the cusp of a daring new adventure."

Jake squinted and looked back into her eyes, not knowing what to think. He was certain, though, that he shouldn't laugh even if he wondered if she might be crazy.

"Camilla Sorelli," she said, extending her hand.

He took her hand in his firmly. "Jake Kimball. I should have told you earlier, but I've found I can learn more what people think about my work if they don't know they're talking to the potter."

She squeezed his hand more firmly. "You're just about what I imagined you to be, sitting across from me during all those meals."

"It's nice to meet someone who admires my work. I often wonder who'll buy it and use it. It sounds like at least some of it has found a good home."

She nodded. "So, where are you going to end up? I'd like to keep track of you so I can buy more of your work over time."

"I really don't know what I'm doing. I always thought I'd have it all figured out by the time I finished college, but here I am, two weeks left of school and wondering what to do with the rest of my life. I don't really want to teach; it seems like a bit of a sellout and would take three more years of school."

"Three more years of school?" Camilla looked surprised.

"Two for an MFA and one more for a teaching certificate. But there are lots of other ways to get an education. I already know that I really just want to be a potter. I want to make pots—functional pots—pots with purpose and meaning that people will embrace and use in their daily rituals of nourishing themselves.

"What you were saying about feeling a connection to me through my work was exciting. I've spent the last four years fighting with my professors about the stuff I want to make. To them, there is little value in functional pottery. It's ok for beginning students to make it, but if you're still making functional work by the end of your second year, they begin to give you a lot of crap. They believe pottery needs to be obscure or radical in a way that only other artists might pretend to understand.

"I've jumped through their hoops and made the stuff they wanted me to make, just to get a grade. I call most of that work, 'Landfill Art', because it's now decorating a landfill somewhere. It's nothing I'm proud of or even interested in. Late at night, after I finish my work and the professors have gone home, I stay up making the pots I love to make—bowls, plates, cups, platters—stuff that's accessible and useable and doesn't require an artist statement to help people understand what it is or why it was made. I was accused of selling out after the student pottery sale my freshman year and I've been branded a rebel by the teachers and most of the advanced students. But my travels to Europe have shown me that functional pottery can be important. I often feel like I was born a century too late, especially when I hear people ask the question."

"What question?"

"Oh, I've heard it phrased a dozen different ways, but they all boil down to one root question... 'Can I, like, use this for food and stuff?' It seems we've forgotten that hundreds, maybe thousands of generations have used pottery to store, prepare and serve their food. Just a generation or two ago, the village potter had a place in society. The villagers ate off his plates and bowls and drank from his mugs and tea pots. Now, it seems, if it's not shrink wrapped, homogenized, standardized and unvarying in size, color, or pattern, it's somehow shoddy or inferior."

"Wow!" she said shaking her head. "It sounds like you've spent a lot of time thinking about this."

"He has," came a voice from behind her.

Camilla and Jake both turned to see Dr. Eric Lewis, a pudgy man dressed in a flannel shirt and blue jeans worn white on the knees.

"I just have to say that this young man doesn't speak for the university or the college of ceramics." He winked at Jake. It was nothing the professor hadn't heard before. Jake returned each fall from his excursions to far flung destinations in his quest for the last remnants of the functional pottery world, more indoctrinated and convinced that he wanted to be a potter when he grew up.

"We've tried to talk him out of it every step of the way, but this young man won't hear a word of it. We're just glad to be getting rid of him before he convinces any of the other students that there's a future in functional ceramics. He just won't let go of the dream."

"I hope he never does," said Camilla in his defense. "Eric, this boy has more talent and passion than I've ever seen in a young man. I've been buying his pottery for four years now and he's the best potter your program has ever produced."

A smile spread across Dr. Lewis's face as he put his arm around Camilla's shoulder. "I know you're right. I just have to keep him humble. I've tried to convince him of the folly of his decision to become a potter, but his skin is tough and he's so damned headstrong that he won't hear anything contrary to his silly aspirations."

Camilla looked back at Jake to find him smiling. "You put up with this nonsense?"

"That was nothing compared to most of the stuff I hear. Dr. Eagen is much worse. I can't repeat most of what she says in polite company."

Camilla looked aghast. "Surely you have someone who's on your side?!"

Jake nodded. "Dr. Lang tells me it's good for me to hear all of this now before I go and do something stupid."

Camilla looked back at Dr. Lewis and then again at Jake, like she was wondering if she might have missed a joke. "It seems things have changed a bit since I was here last. Eric, I can't say I approve of the negative morale you are promoting in this young man. Fortunately, he seems to be able to resist your negativity. But shame on you!" She looked quite put out.

"I really don't mind," said Jake. "It's worked for me."

"He's quite a case," said Dr. Lewis, "but all of us are going to miss him. He knows the nuances of the studio and the kilns better than any of us. We've seen a lot of pottery students come and go, but none will ever be missed more than Jake."

Despite the bantering, Jake considered Dr. Lewis one of his best friends. He had worked around him for four long years and the two knew each other like brothers.

"I didn't mean to interrupt you two," he said, turning his attention to Camilla. "How's Bob enjoying retirement?"

"He's doing just fine now that he's learned how to blog and spends his days sputtering off his opinions to cyberspace. It's been a godsend and has finally given me some peace."

"You know it was he who hired me nearly thirty years ago."

"My, how times have changed. You came to us looking more like Jake: trim, athletic, handsome."

Jake smiled at the subtle jab at his professor's expanded waistline and the buttons pulled tight on his shirt.

The professor smiled good naturedly, turning his attention to Jake. "Have you seen the May issue of Ceramics Monthly?"

"No, I didn't know it was out yet."

"Mine just arrived this afternoon." He reached into his back pocket and produced a folded magazine with a brightly colored sculpture of a ceramic military tank covered with flower decals. "You might want to check the classifieds."

He handed the magazine to Jake before turning to Camilla. "It was

nice to see you. Please give my regards to Bob." And then without another word, he walked away.

Jake watched him go. When he was gone, his eyes shifted back to Camilla. She was looking at him again the way she had before. "You have greatness in you. I hope you know that."

Jake blushed and felt uncomfortable. "Thanks for buying my bowls."

"Thanks for solving the mystery."

Jake couldn't think of anything to say. He had never been good with compliments and learned to prefer the goading and relentless harassment his professors gave him.

Camilla reached into her purse again and withdrew another hundred dollar bill. "Cheers to your Journey, young potter," she said as she handed him the bill. "May God bless you in your trials and triumphs. Oh, and if you ever set up shop somewhere, please let me know." She handed him a business card with her name and address.

"Thank you." Jake managed.

"Thank you. Your pottery has enriched my life." And with that, she took her bag and left.

(2) OPPORTUNITIES

Jake watched Camilla go, energized by their conversation and empowered by the compliments she had given him. When she was gone, he turned to the crisp bill in his hand. Money had always been tight for him, even though he had received a scholarship which paid for his tuition. His job as the studio assistant paid much more in knowledge and experience than it did in dollars. Six dollars an hour at twenty hours a week kept Jake on a tight budget. A hundred dollar bill represented nearly a week of hard labor and Jake slid the money into his back pocket, grateful he had been in the right place at the right time to meet undoubtedly his biggest fan.

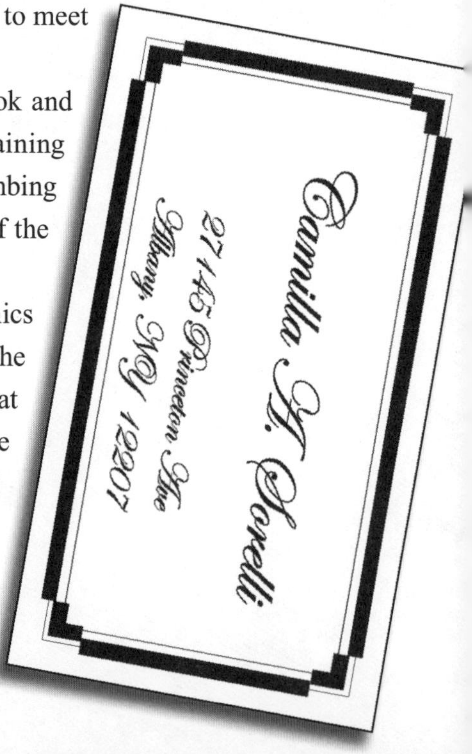

He slid her card into his sketchbook and returned to his seat, surveying the remaining pots. A few buyers lingered, combing through the pots during the last hour of the sale.

He turned his attention to the Ceramics Monthly magazine. After looking at the cover for a few moments, Jake did what he always did with each new issue: he flipped to the back where the classified ads were printed. This was normally a small section, no more than two pages with items that often excited him. There were always the three or four

Camilla H. Sorelli

27145 Princeton Ave

Albany, NY 12807

real estate listings, offering houses and studios for prices far beyond his reach, but they still aroused dreams.

The Buy/Sell section advertised inventions whose inventors were too cheap to buy a regular ad. There were ads for new and used kilns and rare or discontinued clays.

The Employment section advertised jobs, for which he was generally under qualified, except for the positions at summer camps for kids and Jake could only imagine the torture that would be.

He skimmed the ads, many of them familiar from previous issues, until his eyes rested on one under the Opportunities section. In bold lettering, it read:

Opportunities

Potter Wanted: Town seeks potter to replace former, now deceased. Tasks include making, glazing, firing and selling pottery. Must be friendly and patient. Must have passion for life and clay. Position includes studio and apartment and extensive pottery collection. Pay is determined by marketability of one's work and motivation. Review of portfolio will be required. Send letter of interest and three photos of work to review board. Serious inquiries only. Must be received by April 22nd. Village Bergerhaus, 34 Hauptstrasse, Niederbipp, PA 09754.

Jake read it again. And then again. He wondered if this was what Dr. Lewis had seen that prompted him to drop it off. He scanned the rest of the classifieds just to make sure.

He had never heard of Niederbipp but figured Google could find it. The deadline was just a week away and Jake's palms sweated as he thought about it. He had learned in his short life that if something sounded too good to be true, it probably was. But still, he couldn't help but dream. There was no mention of a price—it didn't sound like they were selling anything, and the fact that it was in the Opportunity section and not the Real Estate section seemed to indicate something other than the sale of a business, studio and apartment.

He read it again. Though he had always been a shy person, he had never been considered unfriendly. In every way, he qualified. He began considering the pictures he had of his work. Would they be good enough? He also began composing his letter of inquiry in his head. How long had it been since he had written a real letter?

Jake had already received many breaks in his life—a scholarship to Hudson, the job at the studio, earning enough money from the student pottery sales to pay for some great travel—but he wondered still if he wasn't foolish to get his hopes up. Surely, there would be hundreds, no, thousands of people reading this ad today or tomorrow. His would be lost in an avalanche of inquiries. Yet he felt compelled to throw his name into the hat, knowing that if he didn't try, he would never win.

By the time the tables were cleared away and things put back in the studio, Jake had definitely decided to apply. In his mind he had chosen the pictures he wanted to represent him and he was dreaming about his future in a town he had never heard of and wasn't sure how to pronounce.

After locking up the cash box in Dr. Eagen's office, he walked to the library to visit the computer lab. A Google search for Niederbipp produced 648,000 links. He wondered at first how he had never heard of a place with so many links, but as he read on, he learned that it was a town in the canton of Bern, Switzerland. He began wondering if the ad might be a hoax. He narrowed his search by typing in "Niederbipp, PA."

Only three sites were listed. The first two said the site had moved. The third gave Jake reason to sit up straight. "The official website of the municipality of New Niederbipp, Pennsylvania." He excitedly clicked on the listing and was taken to a site with a picture of a crowded cobblestone street with shops on both sides. Jake was excited. The place existed. He read on.

"Founded in 1717 by German and Swiss religious refugees, New Niederbipp was built as an extension of William Penn's 'Holy Experiment', a place of religious tolerance and unity. Its founders, hardworking farmers, tradesmen, craftsmen and merchants, built our town on the banks of the Allegheny River after searching out a place that reminded them of their homeland, the Rhein River Valley of Southern Germany and mountain valley of Niederbipp, Switzerland.

"When they arrived, this area was on the edge of the frontier and primitive in every way. With fortitude and conviction, the early settlers carved our town out of the wilderness. The town was built as if it was transported from 16th and 17th century Europe and many of the shops remain in the custody of the families who started them seven and eight generations ago.

"Farms and orchards cover the surrounding hills. A flour mill still functions in town and a saw mill runs during the summer months on the outskirts. The town bakery is a must-visit for fresh breads and pastries. Pottery Niederbipp has wares available year round. Our town is on the National Registry of Historic Places and boasts more than a dozen bed and breakfasts, miles of hiking trails, five museums, festival grounds and a lovely churchyard.

"Come for a visit or stay for a lifetime. Niederbipp welcomes you."

Jake scrolled down further and saw a listing of events including the May Day Festival, a few concerts, and The Harvest Festival, all for the year 2003. He scrolled to the bottom of the page where a sign read, "Site under construction. Last updated April 2003."

He clicked around on other buttons and found listings for local businesses: a branch of a computer business, a car dealership, a tailor, a bakery, a department store, the grocery store and a pottery shop. Jake's excitement rose when he found a button that, once clicked, ran a short slideshow of ten pictures. There was a panoramic shot of the town from far off, a picture of a farmer's cart filled with produce, a picture of a bungee jumping platform that seemed entirely out of place, and then a picture of a grey bearded man dressed in a blue apron, sitting at a potter's wheel, making a bowl.

Jake pushed pause on the slide show and stared at the picture of the old man. The picture was small and a little fuzzy, but what he saw intrigued him. He opened the magazine to the ad again and reread it. He wondered to himself if this was the man who had died and left it all behind for some lucky potter.

The lights in the computer lab blinked on and off before a voice came over the P.A. announcing that the lab would be closing in five minutes. He clicked on the print icon and logged off the computer before approaching the front desk to retrieve his picture from the printer. The black and white copy was even fuzzier than it had appeared on the monitor, but Jake thanked the girl at the desk and left the library to walk home.

Jake took his time, walking slowly in the cool, spring air. The sun had set two hours earlier, and as  he passed under street lights, he strained his eyes to look at the dark image of the old potter at work. He wondered who he was. He wondered what kind of potter he was. He wondered why the old man's shop was now available. Did he not have any family? He tried to imagine himself there, walking through the old man's shop, examining his wares. He thought about the other pictures he had seen of the town and wished he had printed them too, even if they were hard to see on the copy.

When he entered his apartment, Jake found his roommates draped over the sofa and floor, engrossed in a rerun of ultimate fighting. When no one acknowledged his greeting, he went to the kitchen and made himself a peanut butter and honey sandwich, then retired to his bedroom, in search of silence.

He lay down on his bed and reread the ad, wanting one more time to be sure he had read it correctly. Then he took the copy of the potter's photo and stared at it while he finished his sandwich. The fuzzy, black and white image seemed like an ancient dream. He reached for a yellow legal pad and began to draft his letter.

THE PHONE CALL

Since Pennsylvania was a neighboring state, Jake figured the letter he dropped into the corner mailbox on Saturday morning would arrive no later than Tuesday. He kept himself busy all week, trying not to think too much about it and get his hopes up.

On Thursday he went to the library after work to look at the slide show on Niederbipp's website for the third time. He was also pleased to find a reply to his email from Andreas Stephanopoulos, one of the Greek potters he contacted about a job. Andreas's English was broken, but he expressed interest in Jake and asked how soon he would be arriving on the island. As Jake began his response, he felt uneasy. He was going to Greece. He'd already bought his ticket. He was set to leave just four days after graduation. He would be arriving on Paros Island in less than two weeks. But as he tried to respond to Andreas's email, he couldn't. After sitting in front of the monitor for several minutes, he clicked out of email and back to the websites where he learned of the opportunities available to him in Greece.

The previous summer, Jake had met potters from the Greek Island of Paros in Germany at the Amersee Töpfermarkt in Diesen, an annual festival of potters from all over Europe. Jake was immediately in awe of their work. The men made pots larger than themselves out of native clays, mostly terra cotta. The Greek potters set up a makeshift workshop at the show and demonstrated their techniques. It was there that Jake first began thinking about spending some time in Greece.

The websites continued to excite him and he turned to his sketchbook to write down the addresses for some of the potters on Paros. Flipping through the book to find a blank page, he opened to the black and white photo of the potter of Niederbipp.

Jake picked up the photo and looked at the old man again. He wrote the addresses in his book, but the image of the old potter drew his attention. He stared at the photo for several moments, deciding to wait another few days before responding to Andreas.

On Saturday night, with his roommates off at parties, Jake found himself at home trying to decide what possessions, if any, he would keep from his college days. There was very little that wouldn't fit in his over sized-duffle bag and he prided himself on the fact that his life was simple and uncluttered.

Just before 10:00, the phone rang, rousing him from his thoughts. He looked at the caller ID and didn't recognize the number or name: Sproodle, Jerry, with an 814 area code. He was tempted to let the answering machine pick it up, but after the fourth ring, decided to answer.

"Hello."

"Good evening," came the response. It was a woman's voice. "I'm hoping to reach Jake Kimball."

Jake wondered if it might be a telemarketer or military recruiter and considered his response before answering. "Can I tell him who's calling?"

"Yes, this is Beverly Sproodle calling long-distance from Niederbipp, Pennsylvania."

"Just a minute," he said, "I'll get him." He covered the receiver with his hand and let out a whoop. He could hardly believe it.

"This is Jake," he said after waiting for what he thought would be an appropriate length of time.

"Jake, this is Beverly Sproodle, calling from Niederbipp, Pennsylvania," she repeated. "I'm calling to let you know that your letter has been received by our review committee and we're interested in setting up an interview with you."

Jake swallowed hard. "When?"

"Well, we've decided to interview a few others. So far, we have appointments for Monday and Wednesday next week. I was hoping to schedule you for Thursday if that works for you."

"I'm actually graduating next Thursday, but I think I could be there by Friday." He could feel his heart thumping and his hands beginning to sweat.

"I think we can make that work. Say, around six, for dinner?"

"Uh, sure. I think that should be fine."

"Wonderful. Do you need any directions?"

Jake let out a little laugh. "As a matter of fact I do. I've been on your website, but I haven't yet looked you up on the map."

"Will you be traveling by car?"

"Unfortunately, no. I don't suppose Greyhound comes to Niederbipp."

"It won't get you all the way here, but as far as Warren. The city bus can bring you the rest of the way. The train service ended twenty years ago, but the train station is still used as the bus depot and buses come through from Warren five times a day. You'll have to check the schedule from there, but you should be able to find a bus to get you here by six."

"And where will I find you?"

"I don't suppose you speak German?"

Jake coughed nervously. "No, is that a necessity?"

"Oh no, but it helps. Niederbipp was founded by Germans and the street signs are still written in German, at least in the older part of the town. When you get off the bus, you'll be at the top of Old Town. From there you will have a great view of the town as it rolls down the hills to the river. Just follow the sidewalk to where it meets the cobblestone. This is a friendly town. I suggest you ask for directions once you get to Hauptstrasse. If you get lost, the pottery shop is on Zubergasse. You'll find us at the top of the back stairs, just off of Hinterstrasse. Any other questions?"

"Uh, yeah, how do you spell Zoo-ber-gahss-uh?" he asked as he scribbled the notes in his sketchbook.

Beverly snickered under her breath. "Listen, there's only one pottery shop in town and it's been a landmark for a couple hundred years. Even the tourists will know where it is. It really will be easiest just to ask. Anything else?"

"None that I can think of right off, but I'm sure I'll think of something after I hang up."

"Then let me give you my number. Please feel free to call me with any questions."

Jake added the number to the notes in his sketchbook and thanked her for the call.

"We look forward to meeting you, Jake. Your letter and your photos really impressed us."

He thanked her again and hung up the phone. This was the phone call he had been waiting for, but for some reason he wasn't entirely at ease. Everything he had learned about the town excited him. But somewhere in his stomach, he felt like there was an undigested bit of matter knocking around and causing discomfort.

He already had plans for the summer. His flight for Greece was set to leave JFK at noon on Monday, just nine days away. He turned to his roommate's laptop on the table. The top was smeared with raspberry jam, but he opened it and got online to book a ride on Greyhound.

Jake was no stranger to Greyhound. He had used it every time he traveled home to Burlington and back over the past four years. He went to the familiar homepage and typed in his departure and arrival locations. The last scheduled bus would be leaving Albany at 10:30 pm and arrive the next afternoon at 12:25 pm, a thirteen hour and fifty-five minute journey. He moaned at the thought of the long ride. The bus ride home to Burlington was only ten hours and that seemed like an eternity. Fourteen hours would be extremely painful. At least it would be dark and he would be able to sleep for part of the ride. A one way ticket cost $96.00,

$96.00

ALBANY TO ERIE, PA. 10:30pm — 8:25 AM

ERIE TO WARREN 8:35 — 10:05

WARREN TO NIEDERBIPP ?.

but he knew of no other affordable way to get there, so he copied down the information in his sketchbook and went to his room to make a plan.

Commencement exercises were set to begin on Thursday evening at 6:00 at the basketball stadium. Even if they went long, he would be done by 9:00. Walking to the bus station would take another half hour. As he lay on his bed, contemplating his future, he realized the trip to Niederbipp complicated matters. It sounded like everything he had ever dreamed of, but the dream of being a village potter was always a long ways off, something he would do in his thirties.  Money had always been the biggest obstacle to making his dream a reality. Without equipment, supplies, or capital to pay for a studio, he knew he would have to work hard to get where he wanted to go.

The trip to Greece was planned, in part, to help continue his education. He knew he ultimately wanted to make utilitarian pottery, but hoped that learning other methods would enable him to refine his skills. He had chosen a course that he hoped would lead eventually to where he wanted to be. The certainty he felt when he booked his flight was now muddy. Niederbipp was not a convenient stop along the way, and yet he felt compelled to take a look, even if it meant going out of his way. He had to know.

His summer trips had taught him several things about himself: chiefly, he had an insatiable wanderlust and secondly, he definitely wanted to be a potter. He decided he would go to the interview and if nothing came of it, he could ride the Greyhound back to New York on Saturday or Sunday and be ready for his flight on Monday. It would cost a bit more, but the pottery sale had been successful and he had the $100 bill from Camilla Sorelli. He reasoned that if he could get a job in Greece for the summer, he might not have to dip very far into his savings. His future remained uncertain, but he fell asleep dreaming of its possibilities.

4
THE OFFER

"Jake, I'd like to see you in my office in five minutes." It was Dr. Lewis. The firing had been going for three hours and Jake was adjusting the damper on the kiln to begin the reduction. Jake nodded to his professor without a word.

When he arrived five minutes later, he found the door ajar and his three professors sitting on the desk and chairs, engaged in a hushed conversation.

"Come in," said Dr. Lewis, rising to his feet. "We've just been talking about you."

Jake immediately felt uncomfortable, wondering what to expect. Over the years, he had developed a friendship with Dr. Lewis, but his relationships with Dr. Lang and Dr. Eagen were still very formal and businesslike.

"What can I do for you?" asked Jake without hesitation, hoping to avoid a long, uncomfortable conversation.

"We've just been discussing your work here and decided we'd like to make you an offer," said Dr. Lang.

Jake looked confused.

"We know you're a world traveler in the summer, but knowing that you're graduating, we thought that maybe we could entice you to stick around this summer and help us with the summer workshops. We feel you're qualified to teach the wheel throwing classes and it would give you a free studio for another few months. We could double your pay for the extra work load and offer you some other benefits as well. We think it would be great for your resume, should you choose to go into teaching."

Jake knew he was qualified to teach the classes. Of his three professors, only Dr. Lewis had better skills than he did on the wheel. Twice the pay was hardly a temptation considering how meager it was to begin with.

"I appreciate your generous offer," he said resolutely, trying to hold back his feelings of frustration, "but I have other plans this summer."

The two women looked at each other, obviously disappointed. After another minute of small talk, they excused themselves from the office, leaving the two men alone.

"They just don't want to teach the wheel throwing class," said Dr. Lewis with a haughty grin. "I've taught the summer workshop for the past three years while they run off and play and I just told them today I wouldn't do it again this summer. What are your plans anyway?"

Jake looked up with a smile. "To be honest, I'm not entirely sure. I bought a ticket for Greece a couple of weeks ago, but I also answered that ad in Ceramics Monthly and I have an interview on Friday."

Dr. Lewis looked triumphant. "When I saw that ad, I thought it sounded just like you. I guess you figure it's worth taking a look at if you're going to go all the way to Niederbipp for an interview."

"You know about Niederbipp?"

"Only by reputation. I'm from Pennsylvania, remember, and some of the oldest and most valuable crockery comes from Pottery Niederbipp. Every once in a while you see their stuff on The Antiques Roadshow. My mom had an old earthenware whiskey jug with the shop's stamp on it. I remember being fascinated by it when I was a kid; in fact, it was that jug that first piqued my interest in pottery. Its whimsical name caused my imagination to run wild. It's hard to believe you've been all over the world meeting potters and you've never been to Niederbipp."

"I'd never even heard of it before last week. I only found one semi-active website about it when I did a Google search."

"Yeah, well, I don't think it's very big. I remember looking for it on the map when I was younger. I think it's a couple of hours north of Pittsburgh, out in the sticks. It might be a Quaker town. If you're not careful, you might end up looking like the guy on the Quaker Oats box and driving around in a horse-drawn buggy."

"I thought it was the Amish who drove the buggies."

"You're right. It's hard to keep all those eccentric religions straight. I actually won't be too far away from there this summer. My folks aren't doing very well and asked me to help them get their legal affairs in order. They live just outside of Pittsburgh so I'll be just a couple of hours down the road if you need to escape."

"Yeah, or maybe you could stop by for a visit. I don't have a car and don't anticipate that changing any time soon."

"It sounds like you already have the job."

Jake shook his head. "Maybe it's just wishful thinking. I know I have to get the job first, but even if I don't, I really don't want to come back here. No offense. It's been a good experience, but I feel like it's time to move on. That offer to teach the workshops really proved that to me."

"And if you don't get the position?"

"Then I leave for Greece on May 1st. You remember those photos I showed you of the giant pots at that market in Germany?"

Dr. Lewis nodded his head.

"I want to learn how to make those. They're looking for potters with experience and I figure I should see a bit more of the world before I put down roots."

Dr. Lewis pursed his lips and nodded again. "We're going to miss you around here. I've had a couple dozen studio assistants over the years, but none of them have had the passion you have. I've given you a lot of grief about making functional work, but I know that's what you want to do. You've got the skills to make a living at it and we all know you're pig-headed enough to not let anyone tell you can't or won't."

Jake grinned, more comfortable with Dr. Lewis' friendly jabs than with his praise. "Sounds like you've figured me out."

Dr. Lewis looked thoughtful. "I'm glad you never let us talk you out of it. Someday we'll say, 'We knew him when he was just the kid who fired the kilns and swept up around the studio.'" He looked at Jake. "Whatever you decide to make of your life, Jake, I want you to know you have my confidence. I expect great things of you. You have my email address and wherever you end up, I'd like to hear from you."

Jake reached out his hand to shake Dr. Lewis'. "I appreciate your friendship. It's kept me afloat."

Dr. Lewis pulled him in and gave him an awkward hug. "Now get back to work," he said with a wink. "And take that box with you."

Jake turned to the table by the door and saw a brown cardboard box with an envelope on top.

"I thought you could use this, wherever you end up. It's a graduation gift. Congratulations."

Jake lifted the box. It was much heavier than it looked and he wondered what it could be. "Thank you," he said and left the office to check on the kiln. He opened the card and read Dr. Lewis' words of congratulations, but it was the long-awaited words of encouragement that Jake relished most. He had spent the last four years of his life striving to make the best pots he could and finally he received the praise he had been seeking: the words that made it all worthwhile. He opened the box and pulled out the cast-steel banding wheel, a small table top wheel with a heavy base. In recent months, Jake had borrowed Dr. Lewis' more times than he could count, but now he had his own. He set it on a table and spun the wheel, thinking about his new designs and techniques that required this tool in the decorating process. It was a thoughtful gift, but very heavy and bulky. Jake considered the space it would take up in his

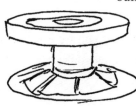

limited luggage, but he knew wherever he ended up for the summer, he would be able to continue with his decorating experiments and make good use of it.

5 GRADUATION

The last days of school went quickly. Attendance at class seemed less than important, with even some of the professors failing to show up. Spring was in the air and the campus was alive with excitement.

Jake was happy to have the freedom and used his time to sell his textbooks and unload the rest of his useless stuff. He visited friends and teachers, giving away his pottery to those he cared about. His ceramic professors each got one of his best bowls that he knew they would appreciate for the craftsmanship regardless of how they viewed functional work.

Ten minutes into the commencement, Jake wondered why he hadn't caught the earlier bus to Niederbipp. The speaker, a one-time busboy turned multi-millionaire spoke of "dreaming the dream and fighting the fight and winning the war," which was meaningful the first time it was spoken. But after a dozen times, he heard his classmates mumbling the mantra under their breath as they collectively awaited the finale, which took much longer than everyone hoped.

By the time the president of the school stood, dressed in his various robes and sashes, to congratulate the graduates, most of the audience had grown restless and some had even left. After explaining that the diplomas would be mailed after the final grades were in, he instructed the graduates to move their tassels from the right to left side of their caps, and then it was over. It was one of the most anticlimactic events of his life.

He turned in his rented gown on his way outside. The courtyard was dotted with tables, each offering some kind of brightly-colored punch and store-bought cookies. He stopped to look at those gathered around the tables. Proud parents were taking pictures of their children. Others were shaking hands with professors and the president of the university. Jake felt like an outsider looking in. He waved to his roommates who were surrounded by family and turned to walk back to his apartment to get his bag.

Thirty minutes later and two hours early, Jake sat in the bus depot, ticket in hand, ready for a new life to begin.

6
Niederbipp

Jake awoke the next morning with a stiff neck, the side of his face stuck to the bus window. When his eyes first opened, he didn't recognize his surroundings. Soon enough, though, the view out the window of the mist rising from the forest floor and the gentle chugging of the bus's engine reminded him where he was. The sun had not yet risen but there was enough light to see the interstate as it cut its way through the woods. He watched the trees pass, wondering sleepily if Niederbipp would have woods this beautiful.

"Good morning," a voice chirped from over his right shoulder.

He turned to see the wrinkled face of an old woman, looking at him over her large glasses. He was surprised. When he had fallen asleep, a few hours earlier, he had been alone on the row.

"I got on in Syracuse," the woman offered. "You were fast asleep and looked harmless compared to some of the folks on the bus. I hope you don't mind me being your seat mate."

"Not at all," he muttered. "I just hope I didn't snore."

"Only a little, but you stopped when I poked you in the ribs," she smiled with teeth too straight and white to be her own.

He wasn't sure if she was serious, but she continued before he could ask.

"I'm off to visit my granddaughter. She just had a baby last week and the poor girl's mother won't be back from her European cruise for another week yet. I'm going down to see if I can lend a hand."

"Are you going to Pittsburgh?"

"No. Just as far as Erie. Her husband is going to meet me at the bus depot and drive me down to McKean where they live."

Jake had never heard of McKean, but wasn't sure he wanted to ask. He was reluctant to get stuck in yet another conversation with a long-winded eccentric on an eternal bus ride.

"Do you know where we are?" he asked.

"I figure we've got to be somewhere this side of Westfield."

Jake nodded, but still had no idea where he was. "So, how long do you figure it'll be before we get to Erie?"

"Oh, maybe three-quarters of an hour, give or take a few minutes. As soon as we see the Barcelona Lighthouse, we'll know we're within a half hour of Erie."

Jake nodded again, still unsure of what to think of the woman from Syracuse who marked her path to Erie with a lighthouse named after a Spanish city.

"So, where are you off to?" she asked.

"A little town called Niederbipp. Have you ever heard of it?"

Her eyes lit up and sparkled in the ever-growing sunlight. "Sure I have. My father was a lumberjack and floated his logs down river to the sawmill there. I haven't been there for ages. I grew up in Hemlock, just up the Allegheny from Niederbipp. When the folks were clearing the land to build farms, there was a lot of money to be made in logging. The work dried up before I was out of school and my folks moved us up to Syracuse in search of work. It's a charming town. It must have grown up a bit if Greyhound stops there now."

"It actually only goes as far as Warren, but I guess there's a bus from Warren to Niederbipp a few times a day."

"Do you have family there?"

"No, I'm interviewing for a job."

"Oh, that's nice, dear." She reached into the carpetbag resting on her lap and pulled out an overstuffed patent leather wallet. Jake groaned inwardly as she fumbled through it until she came to several pictures, the corners bent and colors faded. He thought to himself wryly that surely they been handled by dozens of busloads of people. He wished he had kept his ipod with him so he wouldn't have to do this.

"These are my grandkids," she said, thrusting the pictures into his hands. Jake sighed resignedly, grateful that this leg of his journey would soon be ending.

Somewhere during the story of the woman's gallstone surgery, the bus left the interstate and was soon parked outside a round, red brick and glass building. Jake looked up at the clock at the front of the bus and then at his ticket. It was already 8:25 and his connecting bus was set to leave in just ten minutes. He handed the pictures back to the woman and ended the conversation as politely as he could, stepping into the already clogged aisle.

The driver opened the doors to the luggage compartments before disappearing into the Erie Intermodal Transportation Center. Jake was left alone to find the giant green duffle bag that served as his only piece of luggage. He found it buried under two layers of suitcases, yanked it out, and hurried off to find his bus.

It wasn't until he had taken his seat that he realized the bus was parked on a pier. The dock slips were filled with boats of all sizes and the tall, white masts of the sailboats looked like a forest stripped of its foliage. He thought to himself how strange it was that he had visited the other side of the world several times, and yet this was the first time he had ever seen Lake Erie. He wished there was time to look around but was anxious to get to Warren and find something to eat before continuing on to Niederbipp.

The nearly empty bus stopped briefly at Edinboro University, just a half hour from Erie, and picked up a few students before continuing on. Jake enjoyed the silence as he looked out the window, watching the forest become thicker and the landscape turn from flat land back into rolling hills.

He looked out with intrigue as the bus passed an Amish horse drawn buggy. He remembered a trip to Montgomery County, not far from Albany, his freshman year, to visit an Amish potter. He was inspired by the simple pottery and tools, but the maple sugar candy made the trip even more worthwhile. As Jake remembered the delicious candy, he hoped there would be Amish folks near Niederbipp.

Farms turned into suburbs and the suburbs turned into a quaint little town. The bus pulled into the Warren station just after ten. After retrieving his bag, he walked to the ticket counter to inquire about the bus to Niederbipp. As Beverly indicated on the phone, there were five buses a day to Niederbipp. He had already missed the first one, but the second would be leaving at noon. Jake bought a ticket and wandered out onto the streets of Warren, burdened by his heavy bag. He paid too much for a bagel and a juice at a swanky café and sat on a bench to eat. Looking up and down the street, he was surprised by the wide mix of architecture. Colonial, Art Nuevo, Victorian, Craftsman: it seemed the city had grown up piece by piece throughout the last two hundred years. After finishing his food, he took his time walking back to the station, admiring the quaintness of the town.

Jake was glad he had chosen a front seat so he could see out the windshield. The highway paralleled the river as it snaked forward. The sun broke through the clouds, sending sunbeams over the landscape just as the bus crested a hill. He was blinded by the reflected sparkles coming from a thousand cars in the Bargain-Mart parking lot. The bus slowed and pulled to a stop at an enclosed shelter at the edge of the parking lot. Five people stood from their seats and left the bus. Two older women boarded the bus, toting large blue plastic bags with yellow smiley faces printed on the sides, and made their way to the back of the bus.

Jake watched the bus driver raise his eyes in the rear view mirror to see the women had found their seats before he pulled out of the stop. He took the opportunity to ask the driver some questions. "Excuse me, I'm new to this area, and I was wondering how much further it is to Niederbipp?"

"Two more stops," said the man.

Jake nodded as they pulled away from the curb.

"Is Bargain-Mart always this busy?"

"It's still new and the novelty hasn't worn off yet. This county is full of small towns and this is the biggest store we've ever had. The weekend it opened, people were parked out here on the highway. And I hear that it's become the new hangout for teenagers from all over Kinzua County.

Jake nodded and looked away. He wondered how a town and larger community that frequented Bargain-Mart would respond to hand-made pottery. He knew that he would not be able to compete with prices and wondered if the reputation of the pottery shop would draw enough tourists to make the business viable.

The next stop was in front of a tall bungee jumping platform that obviously hadn't been used in years. The platform was rusty, the parking lot overgrown with weeds, and the sign old and faded. As Jake peered at the sign more closely, he noticed it had been shot with a shotgun. The paint was fading, but he could still make out the words: Rita's Bungee-Bipp.

"That's the old hangout for the kids of Kinzua County," said the driver, pointing at the structure. "Some old lady from Niederbipp opened it fifteen years ago and made a small fortune before the fad faded out."

The stop also serviced the Dairy Freeze. A sun-faded sign in the window advertised that the dilapidated building was for lease or rent. A church on the opposite side looked like it had been turned into a junk yard. Outdated cars with smashed windows filled the parking lot.

After passing farmhouses and several blocks of newer homes and businesses, the old town Jake had seen on the internet rose from the banks of the river and up the side of the hill. The hamlet before him looked like many of the small villages he had visited in Europe, with old world architecture and a church overlooking the town. The pictures on the website had given hints of the town's beauty and charm, but they were nothing compared with the real thing.

The bus approached a sign and Jake squinted to read it.

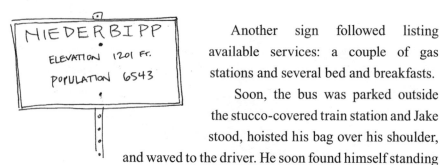

Another sign followed listing available services: a couple of gas stations and several bed and breakfasts.

Soon, the bus was parked outside the stucco-covered train station and Jake stood, hoisted his bag over his shoulder, and waved to the driver. He soon found himself standing on the deserted, weathered boardwalk, looking up at the wooded hills and whitewashed homes. It reminded him of his trip to Europe the previous summer and a small village he had visited in search of potters. Tiengen, Germany, on the banks of the Rhein and on the edge of the Black Forest, had given Jake a taste of what life as a small town potter could be. He had stayed and worked with Irene Adeler for a week after being offered lodging and food in exchange for helping out in the studio. He might have stayed longer if he had not needed to return for his last year of school, but it was while he was in Tiengen that he became enamored with the idea of becoming a village potter.

Hoisting his heavy bag higher on his shoulder, Jake walked around to the other side of the station where he could see the town cascading down the hillside in a river of orange tiled roofs. In front of him stood Hotel Sonnenberg, a four story building with a granite façade, the front door flanked by two giant, gnarled trees. Red, white and pink geraniums filled the flower boxes outside each window, offering an explosion of color to the otherwise drab building.

Across the street from the hotel stood a hospital and elementary school. From behind the hospital, Jake could see the steeple of a church. He crossed the street and began walking down the sidewalk, feeling lopsided under the strain of his bag. When he reached the corner, he put down his bag and opened his sketchbook to the notes he had written during his phone conversation with Beverly. He looked up at the street sign. One arm pointed to his left with the word Hauptstrasse written on it. He closed his book. But before hoisting the bag to his shoulder again, he stopped

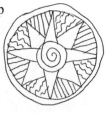

a middle aged couple who were about to cross the street and asked them for directions to the pottery shop. The couple explained that they were tourists, in Niederbipp for the first time and didn't know. He thanked them anyway and was picking up his bag when an elderly woman approached him.

"You're looking for the Pottery?"

"Yes, I am. Do you know where it is?"

"Of course, but I'm afraid you'll be disappointed."

Jake looked at her. Her face was wrinkled and extra skin hung from her neck and cheeks. She only came up to his chest, and appeared to be well into her nineties. But she stood straight and proud. When she didn't continue, he looked into her eyes. Their luminous blue color, as bright as the sky itself, shocked him.

"I'm going that way. If you'd like, you can walk with me. But the Pottery shop has been closed since the potter passed away over a month ago."

"Yes, I heard about that. I'm actually here to apply for the job. My name is Jake."

Her eyes opened wider as she extended her hand.

"Ruth Stein," she said. "I assume you're a potter then."

"Well, I've been making pottery for eight years. I just graduated from college in New York."

"You look like a nice enough boy, but the last potter made pots for almost fifty and eight years. We've heard that a committee is working on finding a replacement for Isaac. The problem is, no one will ever replace him. You might be able to turn his wheel and fire his kiln, but I don't believe there is a soul alive that could take his place."

Jake nodded. He opened his sketchbook and pulled out the picture of the potter he printed from the website.

"Is this Isaac?" he asked, handing her the photo. She took the paper in her gnarled fingers and held it close to her face. Jake watched as she looked intently at the photo.

"Where did you get this?" she finally asked after a long moment of silence.

"I printed it from the internet, from the town's webpage. I tried to learn as much as I could about the town, but there's not much on the internet."

"There aren't many of us old timers who have computers, and unfortunately, half this town is made up of folks that are older than dirt." She smiled wryly. "If you don't mind walking with an old, slow woman, I'll take you where you want to go."

Jake nodded and slid the photo back into his sketchbook. He picked up his bag and offered Ruth his elbow for support.

They crossed the pavement and stepped onto Hauptstrasse where the pavement ended and the cobblestones began. Ruth gave Jake a slow, walking tour of the town, pointing her cane at one building after another and giving a brief history. Many of the buildings were painted with murals and Ruth pointed out the year that each building had been built, noted by the carved stone at the base of nearly every building. All of them had been built before 1720. The whole town seemed to have been dug up in Europe and transported across the Atlantic, one cobblestone at a time. The sights and sounds excited Jake and distracted him from Ruth's words. Storefronts opened onto the street while shutters and flower boxes adorned the windows of the apartments above. Baskets full of geraniums hung from the lamp posts and the street was abuzz with activity.

Before long, they came to a stone fountain and Ruth let go of Jake's elbow, resting instead against the side of the fountain.

"This is as far as I go," she said. "I've got some shopping to do at the bakery next door and your pottery shop is just up the street." She turned and pointed a crooked finger. Jake looked up to see the street sign: Zubergasse.

He read the sign slowly, sounding out each syllable, trying to remember how Beverly had pronounced it. He looked back at Ruth who studied him with a broad smile.

"Those old Germans came up with some crazy names for their streets. The mayor before our current mayor tried to change the names and was voted out of office. In a town like ours, tradition is important and change is slow. I've met some of the others who have come to be interviewed. I don't think many of them could ever make it in this town."

Jake looked at her, surprised. "Why do you say that?"

"Oh, well, this is a charming town, to be sure, but it's a bit remote. There aren't many people who can handle the quiet. Lots of folks come here for a visit, to stay at one of the B&Bs, but they all leave when the weekend is over. For some, I think the stars are too bright and the crickets too loud. For others, there just isn't enough going on to keep them excited. When you live in a small town, you have to be ok with quiet."

Jake nodded thoughtfully, considering her words.

"So, young potter, I wish you well. If you get the job, and decide to stay, I will come for a visit. If you don't, well, then, I wish you a good journey."

Jake thanked her for her directions and the tour of the town. He swung his bag over his shoulder and trudged up Zubergasse. Straining under the burden of his big bag, he kept his eyes to the cobblestone, reviewing in his mind the words Ruth had just spoken. He thought it curious what she said about deciding to stay and tried to remember her exact words.

Deep in thought, he walked past the windows of the pottery shop and stopped when he reached the archway that separated Zubergasse from the perpendicular street. He turned around and walked back to the shop's windows, dropping his bag next to a huge ceramic planter filled with new, green life.

The windows were dark. Cupping his hands around his eyes and leaning against the glass, Jake tried to peer into the shop. A light in the back corner seemed to come from a rear window and door. The widow display was filled with pottery: bowls, vases, plates and mugs. Pulling back from the glass, he read a hand-painted sign on the door: POTTERY CLOSED INDEFINITELY DUE TO THE DEATH OF THE POTTER.

⑦ REALITY

It seemed only natural that a European-looking town would have a European-looking sign for the pottery shop, much like the other signs in town. There was no glitz or neon, just a round disk hanging from an

ornate, rusty iron lattice. The disk itself was faded and worn and colored green from lichen and moss. "Pottery Niederbipp, Established 1717" circled the outside of the disk, written in an old style font. A stylized picture of a potter at his wheel was carved into the center.

Jake's attention was drawn to another sign in the showroom window, this one dusty and sun-faded, but he smiled to himself when he read it. "Apprentice Wanted".

Apprentice Wanted

He looked again to the sign hanging above him and noticed the mural painted on the wall above the archway. Jake recognized the mural from the town's website. Viewing it online, it had been difficult to know exactly what it was because of the angle from which the photo had been taken. But now he saw it clearly. A huge ship with billowing sails, its deck filled with people, sailing headlong into the adjacent building. A banner flew from the tallest mast. Jake squinted to see the people on deck, many of whom had tools in their hands. They were dressed in simple black clothing, similar to those Jake had seen in depictions of the pilgrims.

On the right side of the ship, a scroll had been painted on the wall, embellished with these words:

Persecuted because of their faith in God, the men and women who built this village left their homelands of Germany and Switzerland in 1715 in search of a better world. With love of God and truth, they carved this town out of the wilderness to rival the villages they left behind. Dedicated to Sir William Penn, our friend and patron who granted us this land and thus preserved our faith and hope.

Jake looked closer at the people on the boat. One man carried a loaf of bread, several others held tools: a compass, a hammer, a sickle, and a weaver's shuttle among others. The women wore white bonnets, similar to those he had seen worn by Amish women. Everyone looked forward with resolution in their faces.

In the distance, Jake heard a bell ring and he moved through the archway and onto the perpendicular street, Müllerstrasse, as marked by the street sign. Soon, children dressed in uniforms flooded the street with noise and laughter

He came to a corner where the narrow street opened to his left onto a courtyard of sorts. Looking up at the street sign on the side of the building, Jake read "Hinterstrasse." He opened his sketchbook to review Beverly's directions and knew he was getting close. Several cars were parked near the old buildings. A beautiful chestnut tree with new leaves stood in the middle, sharing its shade with four stone benches that encircled its trunk. He noticed that one set of stairs had a ceramic planter on each step. The handmade pots were filled with young, tender plants. He dropped his bag at the bottom of the stairs and turned to the adjacent door whose polished brass knob glowed in the sunlight.

Peering through the dusty windows, he saw a potter's wheel in the center of the room and a kiln in the far corner. The small studio looked cluttered and disorganized. Jake knew he was in the right place, but he wasn't sure how he felt about it. He tried to remember how he had imagined it. Many of his imaginings were in tune with reality because of the pictures he had seen on the website, but the shop itself was different. Without pictures to inform his ideas, Jake had imagined something newer, cleaner, and more … faultless. In reality, the shop looked old and tired. Feeling disappointed, he took a seat on the steps to rest and sort through his thoughts. He wondered if he had wasted his time coming here. He was tired from his travels, hungry and confused. He remembered his initial thoughts when he first read the advertisement. "If it sounds too good to be true, it probably is." He shook his head, considering how reality was sucking the life out of his dream. So far, the thought of taking over this little dump felt more like a burden than a blessing.

He opened his sketchbook and began to write.

I'm here on the back steps of pottery Niederbipp, Niederbipp, PA. AReHHHH — it has been almost 24 hours since I graduated from Hudson University and already I am a world away from Albany. I took the bus last night to Warren, PA and then on to Niederbipp this afternoon. The town is beautiful — reminds me of that town in Germany last summer, but it's not entirely what I expected. I came here hoping that —— well, hoping for something different than the run down, dumpy little place that this is. I haven't been inside yet, but I'm wondering if I wasted my time and money coming out here. I'm glad I still have my ticket for Greece. I'll probably take the bus out of here tomorrow and be back in New York for the flight on Monday. I think this has been a lesson to me about wishful thinking.

Jake read what he had written before closing the sketchbook, then leaned back against the stairs to rest.

The church bell tolled four times, waking Jake from a shallow sleep. He stood and stretched. It was still two hours before he was supposed to arrive for dinner, but he was already hungry. He picked up his sketchbook and stowed his bag under the stairs he had been sitting on. That done, he wandered off to discover the town.

Jake walked back to Müllerstrasse and looked at the cobblestone street ascending the hill before him. He walked past several houses and stopped when he heard water splashing on stone. He turned to see a waterwheel on the side of an old stone building. A plaque on the whitewashed façade explained that this had once been an active mill, pressing nuts and seeds for their oil. A crude drawing of the inner works explained how it was done. Then it listed the museum hours: open Saturdays from 1:00 pm - 5:00 pm or by appointment. Jake smiled at the cushy operating times. He wondered what it would be like to be a tourist in Niederbipp and if he might ever come back to take a tour of the Oil Mill Museum.

He continued his ascent up the hill. In a nearby house, a would-be musician picked out scales on the piano. Two children played badminton in the street. Müllerstrasse ended at the top of the hill where three large cement blocks had been placed to keep cars from traveling any further. From there, another courtyard expanded before him. A church rose on one side and a dozen trees checkerboarded the cobblestone. The young and vibrant green leaves grew from branches that looked as though they had been trained to spread far and wide, offering a large canopy to the benches below.

The sky darkened as storm clouds rolled in on a blustery wind. He considered taking a closer look at the church, but instead decided to go back to the bus station and check on the timing for the return trip to Warren.

A narrow pathway out of the churchyard led him back to the street he had followed into town. The wind was picking up and blew dust into his eyes as he neared the station. The doors were locked, but a faded schedule, taped to the window, listed the times of departure. The last bus was set to leave at 10:05 pm and the first one in the morning left at 8:20. Just in case, he copied down all five departure times into his sketchbook.

NIEDERBIPP TO WARREN

10:05pm LAST BUS

8:20 AM - FIRST BUS

10:30 AM

3:00 pm

6:15 pm

Walking past an alcove, he saw two teenage boys huddled together with their backs towards him, writing on the wall with fat magic markers. He stopped when he saw them and cleared his throat loudly. The boys turned, looked at him and ran off without a word. Graffiti had always bothered Jake, but as he watched the boys run away, he wondered why it bothered him here. This was none of his business. This was not his town, nor would it likely ever be.

He walked past the hotel and stopped at a bench on the corner that offered a view of the river below. He had missed this before under the strain of his bag, but this time he was taken by the beauty of the view. Though the river was probably a mile away, Jake could see the sparkles on the water from the sunbeams that broke through the dark clouds. He sat down on the bench and watched the shadows from the clouds race across the valley.

Even with the weather brewing around him, Jake was surprised by the feeling of peace he felt here. Niederbipp was definitely quieter than Albany. Quieter, even, than his home town of Burlington. As he sat on the bench, he began to imagine himself living here. Since his time in Germany the previous summer, he believed that this was what he wanted: to be a village potter. But thinking about it now, he wasn't so settled. The idea of coming to Niederbipp was in many ways a dream come true, and yet he could already tell that dream was not going to be exactly the way he imagined.

A panicky feeling arose within him when he realized he didn't have a place to stay for the night. Normally he would not have been opposed to sleeping on a bench or in the park as he had so often during his summer travels, but the weather concerned him. He was not excited about spending a soggy night outdoors without a tent. He wondered when the last bus might leave Warren for Erie, remembering the size of the hub there and its probability of having a dry place to spend the night.

As Jake contemplated these things, he remembered his first summer trip to Europe. Mitch Mumford, a friend from school, had accompanied him, but they parted ways after only three days. Mitch liked to plan ahead and have things settled more than ten minutes in advance. Jake did not. He believed too much planning eliminated the potential for magic to happen, so he largely spent his vacations living on the fly. This generally worked well for him, even though he had spent a few nights out in the rain. Knowing there would be little opportunity to dry his stuff before his flight to Greece caused him to begin calculating his moves much sooner than he normally would.

Despite his independence, his thoughts turned to his mother, as they often did at times like this. Surely she would have some bit of wisdom to share. What would she tell him to do? He had been a sucker many times in his life. Would she say, "I told you so?"

He was glad he had made plans to go to Greece. It would lessen the pain of being disappointed here. The loss of money for the bus fare hurt, but he knew if he had not come, he would have wondered about it for the rest of his life.

Again his thoughts turned to his mother. He asked himself what she would do and in a moment of genius, the answer came. She would go and get some flowers to take to dinner. Jake stood from the bench and walked toward the hills in search of wildflowers.

DINNER

Jake knocked on the door just as the church bell tolled six times, his duffle swung from his shoulder while his other hand held a huge bouquet of wildflowers. A woman answered the door and warmly invited him into the apartment. He handed her the flowers before putting down his bag.

"Am I in the right place?"

"You are if you're a potter," said the woman. She handed the flowers to a chubby man with a handlebar mustache and extended her hand to Jake. "I'm Beverly. I spoke to you on the phone last week."

"I'm Jake."

"Welcome to Niederbipp," she said, pulling him further into the apartment.

Three men came forward to meet Jake. The man with the handlebar mustache handed the flowers to another chubby man and extended his hand to Jake. "I'm Sam," he said with a wry smile. "I'm the baker in town."

Jake nodded.

The second chubby man passed the flowers on to the third man before stepping forward. "I'm Jim, but most folks just call me Mayor."

Jake shook his hand and nodded, trying to remember the first man's name before he added another to his memory.

The third man, who was dressed in the black clothes of a priest, left the flowers in the sink and turned back to Jake. "My name is Thomas," he said with a warm smile. "Welcome to Niederbipp."

Jake had never been graceful in social situations and he immediately began to feel uncomfortable with four sets of eyes on him. He was also distracted by the pottery. Never had he seen so many pots in such a small space. Shelves lined with pots stood against every wall and above the window on the other side of the table. His eyes were having difficulty focusing as they jumped from one object to the next.

"Would you like to take a closer look at the pots before dinner?" asked Sam.

Jake nodded enthusiastically and reached high on the top shelf, pulling out an old stoneware bottle with a cork stopper. He wiped the thick dust on his gray t-shirt and rubbed his thumb across the maker's mark. The neck of the bottle was slightly bent and looked whimsical, glazed with a bumpy brown glaze that had long been out of fashion.

"Who is ZE?" he asked when he had finished the examination.

"Why do you ask?" queried the Mayor.

Jake turned to him and pointed to the maker's mark.

"Well," said the Mayor, putting his finger to his chin, "The E would have to stand for Engelhart. That was the name of the pottery family who first came to this town. As for the Z, I'll have to do some research and get back to you on that one. We only know Isaac Bingham and his father-in-law, Henry Engelhart. There are probably still a few folks in town who knew the potter before Henry, but they'd have to be in their nineties."

"You could find out at the graveyard," interjected Thomas. "All the potters are buried there and they all have distinctive grave markers. I've seen other bottles like that one. If I were a betting man, I'd bet that was an old ginger ale bottle."

"Not one from the old Meier brewery, is it?" asked Beverly.

"It could be," responded the priest.

The mayor shook his head. "Thomas is the only one of us that isn't originally from here, and yet he knows more about the history of Niederbipp than we do."

Sam reached for the bottle to take a closer look. "I think Thomas might be right. I used to look for these, down by the river when I was a boy. In the spring, when the river ran high, it often washed away the bank near the old dump, exposing all sorts of treasures." He looked up at Jake and then at Thomas. "Thomas, you probably ought to set the boy straight about the brewery before he starts thinking something that isn't true."

Thomas nodded and stepped forward, taking the bottle in his hands. "You may have heard that this town was settled by religious refugees from Europe."

Jake nodded.

"Part of their creed was a disapproval of alcohol, so when I say brewery, I mean a rather harmless operation: root beer, ginger ale, sarsaparilla and a variety of medicines. In the early days, before glass was common, the potters produced thousands of jugs for the Meier family as well as some old bottles like this one. The Meiers closed up shop when the logging boom hit and the loggers wanted something a little stiffer to wet their whistle. That couldn't have been any later than 1850 or so."

He handed the bottle back to Jake who handled it much more gently, knowing it was over a hundred and fifty years old. He put the bottle back where he had found it and turned his attention to several other pieces while the others finished up the preparations for dinner.

"Dinner's ready," said Thomas, a few minutes later. He placed a ceramic trivet on the table before setting down the hot platter filled with baked trout, the butter still sizzling. Jake asked if he could wash his hands and walked to the kitchen sink. The dishes left in the rack to dry by the side of the sink caught his attention. So did the soap dish. He picked it up and examined it closely. When he finally turned around, drying his hands on his pants, four pairs of eyes were  watching him. He felt self-conscious, wondering what impression he might be making.

Everyone took their seats and Thomas said grace.

"Thank you for working around my schedule," said Jake when Thomas began to serve them. "I graduated last night; otherwise it would have worked out yesterday."

"That's right," said the Mayor. "Your parents must be proud of you."

Jake smiled. "I hope so."

"Do they live nearby?" asked the Mayor.

"Not anymore. My Mom passed away last year and I haven't seen my father since I was three."

"Wow," said the Mayor, looking sorry that he asked.

"That must have been hard for you to lose your mother," said Beverly.

"It was. We were really close. She was the first one to encourage me with my pottery in high school. I was a pretty good student, but it was pottery that kept me excited about school."

"Do you have other family?" asked Beverly.

"No. I wish I did sometimes. I was an only child, as were both of my parents who married a little later in life. All of my grandparents were gone by the time I was twelve."

The four friends nodded respectfully, but Jake recognized the need for the subject to change.

"You mentioned something about a family of potters; how far back does this family go?" he asked.

The Mayor looked up. "This town was founded back in the seventeen hundreds and the Engelhart family was one of the first to arrive. The shop and this apartment have been passed down from one generation to the next."

"That's amazing," said Jake, enthusiastically. "How many different potters have lived and worked here?" Again the friends looked at each other.

Thomas spoke up. "In the graveyard at the church, there is a monument to each of the potters. As I understand it, the potter who took over for the deceased made a bench in memory of the previous potter. So far there are six of these benches, but Isaac's bench hasn't been made yet. That's a job for the next potter."

Jake was stunned. "So that means that the next potter will be the eighth potter to live and work here?"

Thomas thought for a quick moment. "That's right."

Jake shook his head in amazement. "So what happened? Why did the line of potters stop?"

Again the four friends looked at each other. Beverly took this one. "Henry Engelhart, the potter before Isaac, had only one child, a girl named Lily. She was just a few years older than most us, and a wonderfully charming person. She married Isaac, but less than a year later, influenza swept through town, taking with it both father and daughter. Isaac had been in the town for only a year, but he decided to stay and carry on the tradition that had been handed to him."

Jake furrowed his brow. He had many more questions, but didn't feel that now was a good time to be asking all of them. In the silence that followed, the attention turned back to him.

"Tell us about you," said Beverly. "Your letter said you were just graduating with a degree in pottery. Tell us why you chose that field of study."

Jake thought for a moment before he answered. "My path to pottery has not been an easy one," he began. "I took my first pottery class as a freshman in high school. I was nearly as tall then as I am now, but only weighed a hundred pounds. I was weak and my muscles weren't trained. I made quite a fool of myself. I was more concerned about getting good grades than learning anything and I thought that pottery would be an easy A. Unfortunately, it didn't take long to find out how wrong I was. My teacher made it look so easy. The problem was that I couldn't do what he did, no matter how hard I tried. After a month of practicing every day, I was nearly always able to center the clay on the wheel. But it took several more months to get to the point that I could form anything bigger than a dog bowl.

"Just before the end of that first year, my teacher pulled me aside. He told me that I was a lousy potter, but he admired my desire to keep trying. He said he would accept me into his intermediate class if I promised to continue to try as hard as I had.

"At the end of my second year, my teacher told me I was a lousy potter, but that if I continued to work hard, he would allow me to advance to the next class.

"During my junior year, I worked harder than ever. I stayed after school and even came in on Saturdays sometimes. By the end of the year, I was feeling good about myself and my progress. My teacher pulled me aside and said, 'Jake, you're a lousy potter, but you work hard, and if you keep working hard, I'll let you keep going.' I knew he was wrong by then. I was actually starting to make some nice stuff, but I wanted his approval, so I kept working at it. One day, I was cleaning up before my next class and I found a key on my books. It had the room number of the studio stamped into it."

Jake pulled a key ring from his pocket to show them the key he still carried with him.

"He never spoke of it, but I knew it was his way of giving me the approval I had sought from him. I used the key as often as I could. I discovered that the little bit of confidence he gave me was enough to push me through my challenges.

"I think it was during those last few months of high school that I made my biggest improvements. My hands finally knew what they needed to do. With the encouragement of my teacher, I decided to apply for a couple of scholarships. My mom didn't have much money, so she also encouraged me.

"To my surprise, Hudson University in Albany offered me a great scholarship that took care of tuition and books. I only had to worry about housing and food, so I took a job on campus as the studio assistant at the ceramics lab. At first I wondered if I was just another janitor. Soon, though, one of my professors recognized that I had some talent with clay and he gave me other responsibilities. He got another kid to mop the floors and take out the garbage. I learned how to mix glazes and fire kilns and kept making all the pots I could. I saved my money so I could travel during the summers and visit other countries and other potters. I learned some things from these trips that had a profound effect on me and helped me to decide that I wanted to be a potter for the rest of my life."

"What did you learn?" asked Thomas.

Jake thought for a moment before responding. "I've met a lot of potters over the years," he said with a twinkle in his eye. "I realized a while ago that I have never met a rich one, but I have yet to meet one who is unhappy. That was a defining moment for me. I'm not sure yet how that works. Maybe there's something in the clay, maybe it's working with your hands or being in touch with the earth, maybe it's just plain hard work that has made those potters happy. Without fail, old and young, male and female, all the potters I know are happy.

"I have friends that spent four years in college studying to do things they now hate doing. I have other friends that will be in school for another ten years to become doctors and scientists. I hope they'll be happy when they finish, but they don't seem very happy now."

Jake turned his attention to his dinner and didn't notice how the four friends looked at each other, nodding and winking and communicating without words. They smiled at each other again as he helped himself to more rice, his third helping, eating like he hadn't eaten in months.

When their plates were finally empty, Beverly asked Jake if he would like to see the studio. As they marched down the stairs, Sam smiled when he saw Jake noticing the pottery planters filled with young peppermint plants that sat as sentinels on each of the eleven stairs.

The door was opened to the studio and Jake walked in behind the others. It was much as he had seen through the window, small, dirty, and cluttered with tools and buckets. The floor near the wheel was littered with dried clay scraps. He walked to the kiln and pulled open the door. Leaning inside, he looked down the portholes to the burners. He stooped down underneath and examined the gas line, nodding his head.

"Do you know what that is?" asked Beverly.

"It's a straight-updraft, cantenary arched, hard brick kiln," he said with confidence.

"Do you know how to fire it?" asked Sam.

"Not exactly, but I've fired a lot of kilns that are similar in design. Every kiln is a little bit different and it takes a while to learn how the dragon breathes and how the kiln gods like to be caressed."

They nodded, but had blank looks on their faces.

He turned next to the old wheel. Sitting down on the stool, he switched it on and pressed down on the pedal, watching the wheel spin.

"I think it's pretty old," said the Mayor.

Jake nodded. "Yeah, but it's a good one. It ought to be good for another twenty years."

"Would you like to see the showroom?" asked Beverly.

Jake nodded, stood and began walking towards the showroom before his attention was drawn away by the old fashioned wooden cash register on the counter. He pushed some buttons and pulled some levers before discovering the crank on the side. This he turned twice until the bell rang and the drawer popped open.

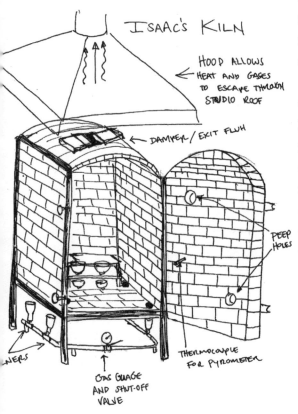

ISAAC'S KILN

HOOD ALLOWS HEAT AND GASES TO ESCAPE THROUGH STUDIO ROOF

DAMPER / EXIT FLUH

PEEP HOLES

NERS

THERMOCOUPLE FOR PYROMETER

GAS GUAGE AND SHUT-OFF VALVE

He turned and looked into the showroom, moving quickly towards it. "I got into town earlier this afternoon and looked through the windows. I have to admit I was a little disappointed, but it looks a lot better from the inside with all the lights on."

He picked up a pitcher and pretended to pour out of it. "It's well balanced," he told the others. He moved to the next shelf and picked up a pie plate, running his fingers over the rippled lip.

Meanwhile, the Mayor picked up the pitcher and did what Jake had done, discovering for the first time the science of a well placed handle.

Beverly approached, silently taking the pitcher from him and repeating the motion, looking surprised.

Their attention went back to Jake who was now sitting on the dusty floor, looking at the bowls on the bottom shelf. He turned one over and caressed the smooth foot. He ran his thumb over the maker's mark. He liked the design. It was a "B" with six rays coming away from it, three on top and three on the bottom.

He moved on to look at the larger bowls on the adjacent shelf. They were simple and functional, yet their craftsmanship was excellent. Again he ran his finger over the foot of the bowl.

"I'm curious what you're looking at," said Beverly, walking to where he stood over the bowl. He looked up at her.

"I was just admiring the foot he carved," he said, pointing. "Do you make the same kind of foot?"

"Yes, but not every potter does. It takes extra time and effort and there are many potters who believe it's a waste of time because so few people ever see the bottom of the bowl. To me, it's not really a bowl until it has a foot. I love the care for details that some people put into their work. There are lots of ways to save time and money making quick and dirty pots, but the work suffers, as does the integrity of the potter.

"What do you mean?" asked Sam.

Jake looked thoughtful as he got to his feet to face them. "Something magical happens when you mix clay and fire. It hardens, becoming more dense and nonporous." He reached into his pocket and pulled out three small items. The four friends huddled closer so they could see what he held.

"These look like stones, but really, they're remnants of old pots." He picked up a red one and flipped it over to reveal a black side. "I found this one on the beach in Italy," he said. He picked up an orange one. "I found this one in a field in England. This last one, I found in the New Mexico desert. I have a bag of shards like these that come from all over. All of them have one thing in common: the potters who made them are all dead. Many of them have been dead for hundreds, maybe even thousands of years, but their work, in one form or another, lives on.

"A couple of years ago when I was in Italy, I visited the beach in Monterosso, one of the Cinque Terres. Walking along the shore, I noticed some of the sand was colored. As I looked closer, I found hundreds of pieces of pottery and glass. This shard was one of the biggest. I sat down and ran my fingers through the sand, imagining generations of Italians, throwing their broken pottery and bottles into the sea, not knowing that it would one day wash up on shore as polished shards. I realized then that my pots are going to be around far longer than I will. I'm not sure what will happen to them after I'm gone, but I'd like to think they will be used and loved and enjoyed for generations. Most of them, though, will probably break and be tossed into the sea or buried in the fields.

Maybe when the spring floods come and wash away the remnants of the dump and some young potter stumbles upon my shards, he will know that someone took the time and care to do it well.

"I don't know the potters who made these, but they've left a record of themselves. These pots," he said, pointing to the pots on Isaac's shelves, "these will be remembered and treasured."

Beverly and the Mayor passed a quick smile between each other.

Thomas cleared his throat and looked at Jake, wanting to speak, but unsure of how to begin. "We have all been unsure how to approach this with the others we have interviewed, and fortunately for you, none of them have made it this far, so I guess I'm sailing on uncharted waters here. I don't really know how to ask this to a near stranger. The others," he said pointing to his three friends, "they decided this question would be best asked by me because I have some experience with sensitive religious matters. Part of our charge as outlined in Isaac's will was to leave the shop to someone who is a God fearing individual. In recent years it has become politically incorrect to ask questions of faith, but the people who started this shop were faithful people. They believed that all they had was a blessing from God. They kept the traditions of the bible in paying one tenth of their increase back to their God to care for the church as well as the poor and needy. We have been asked to choose someone who would be willing to continue the tradition of paying one tenth of their income to the church."

Jake nodded in understanding.

"Sounds fair to me. I learned about tithing when I was about fifteen or sixteen, when I began attending church. I can't say it's been easy for me to always pay tithing, but I know about it."

"So you're a Christian then?" asked Thomas, obviously relieved.

"I am, but I don't really have a church. I've kind of gone where the spiritual winds have blown me."

The four friends smiled at his response.

"I think you'll get along just fine here," said Thomas, without another word.

"I'm ready for some dessert," said Sam.

"Sounds good to me," said Jake.

"I can't imagine you're still hungry," chided Beverly.

"I'm sorry. I hope I haven't made a pig of myself. I haven't had a good meal in a long time."

"Then you'll get the leftovers," said Thomas. His comment suggested to all of them that Jake was going to be around longer than the evening. Jake was surprised by his sudden feeling of uneasiness.

 TRUTH

Jake followed the others upstairs, trying to figure out what he was feeling. He was much more impressed with the shop than he had been that afternoon. But he had a ticket to Greece and wasn't sure he was in the mindset to make a decision that could have implications for the rest of his life.

"You mentioned in the ad that you wanted to see my portfolio," said Jake once they were back in the kitchen. He was trying to stall, trying to give himself more time to think.

Jake dug through his giant duffle bag and pulled out the binder. It had clay dust permanently ingrained into the black plastic cover. He handed it to Beverly who carried it to the table and opened it. She smiled when she turned to the first picture, a large brown bowl with steep sides. She flipped to the next page, a cobalt blue pitcher with four matching mugs. The next was a teapot, beautifully executed with a bamboo handle. Pictures of platters, bowls, and tiles followed. The friends seemed very pleased.

"Why don't we talk about this over dessert," Sam suggested. He placed a fruit torte in the middle of the table and cut it into six pieces, giving Jake the biggest slice. Thomas poured tea for all of them and handed Jake a mug full of the amber liquid.

Jake took a big gulp of the peppermint tea. "That's good tea."

"That's Isaac's special blend. He was known far and wide for his tea," said Sam.

Jake nodded and took another long drink.

The mayor cut to the chase. "I think you are just the man we've been looking for. I, for one, would like to believe that Isaac would have hired you himself if he had been here tonight."

Jake looked up, not believing his ears.

"We have been given a charge through Isaac's will to award this apartment, the pottery studio and everything that is within their walls to the person we deem worthy and deserving of the honor of continuing the pottery tradition in Niederbipp."

Jake sat up and wiped the crumbs from his mouth.

The mayor continued, "Over the course of the last month, we have reviewed Isaac's will, sent out solicitations, and entertained those we felt merited an interview. None of the others have been a good fit, but we think you are. We'd like to offer you the job, which includes pretty much everything you've seen tonight."

Jake smiled and raised his eyebrows, but remained silent for several moments. "Um, this is really crazy," he finally uttered. "I...I don't know what to say."

"We'd like it if you said yes," suggested the mayor. "Perhaps it would help you if I explained the conditions of this agreement, should you choose to accept the job."

Jake nodded.

"As we have told you, this shop and apartment are what remains of the lives of seven potters. They've been passed down from one generation to the next until today. You'll be the first potter that is not related by either blood or marriage, but the same obligations must apply to you as they have to all the others."

Jake nodded again, but his mind began to cloud.

The Mayor removed Isaac's will from his breast pocket. Placing a pair of glasses on his chubby nose, he began to read.

"As outlined by Isaac, the house and the Pottery are yours for the course of your lifetime, as long as you remain in Niederbipp and continue to make pottery. At the time of your death, the articles and properties of the house and shop must be passed on to your replacement.

"Second, you have already become somewhat familiar with the collection of pottery here in the apartment." Jake nodded again. "This collection, we have been told, is the single most valuable asset associated with the estate. Yet the monetary value is very small compared with the lessons that can be learned from each of the pieces in the collection. We were told that only a potter could appreciate why the pieces were part of the collection."

Jake looked at the shelves all around the apartment, filled with hundreds of pots in all shapes and sizes. He was confused. He wondered what more there was to see in the collection beyond the pots themselves.

"Third," said the Mayor, interrupting his thoughts. "The pottery in the shop is yours to sell or to give away. Might I suggest that it would be a wise business practice to sell them instead of giving them away." He winked at Jake, who smiled back.

"Fourth, the revenue from the sale of those items should be taxed and tithed, and some of the revenue set aside for the property taxes that are due in December."

"Fifth, there are log books for the kiln and recipe books for the glazes. These books will be found on the shelf above the wedging table. These too are lessons that have been passed on from father to son and should be preserved for the generations that follow." Jake nodded again.

"Sixth," said the Mayor, examining his papers. "Well, it appears that's all. There is no sixth." And with that, he reached deep into his pocket and pulled out a key ring with several keys. "This," he said, holding the biggest key, "is the key to the apartment. This one goes to the studio. This one is for the little motor scooter under the stairs." He handed the key ring to Jake with a wink. "Welcome to Niederbipp," he said. "I feel like I am giving you a key to the city."

Sam smiled broadly as did Thomas and Beverly.

"Should you ever lose your keys," said Beverly, "we all have copies. Isaac made sure of that after he lost his keys at the clay pit several years ago."

Jake smiled, completely unsure of what to say.

"So, what do you think?" asked the Mayor.

Jake leaned his elbows on the table, looking very uncomfortable. "I think this is very generous of you. I guess I'm thinking that someone is going to come out of the back room and point to the hidden camera somewhere and tell me this is all a big joke."

"I assure you, this isn't a joke," said the mayor. "We have interviewed four others and received correspondence from dozens of folks about this offer. We knew what we were looking for before this all started, and I believe I speak for all of us when I tell you we are all pleased with what we see."

Jake looked at the others who were all smiling, looking anxious.

"Tell us what's troubling you," said Thomas.

Jake looked at him, relieved that Thomas could see something the others didn't seem to notice.

Jake pursed his lips and smiled softly. "I guess I'm just a little overwhelmed by all of this. I make a lot of spontaneous decisions, but I'm not really sure how to take this one. I mentioned before that I've spent my summers roaming the world, but I should have told you I have a ticket for Greece and I'm supposed to leave on Monday morning from JFK. I made these plans before I saw your ad. I am very interested in your offer, but I don't know if the timing is right. I'm only twenty-two. I don't feel like I can make a lifetime commitment to a shop and a town I wasn't even sure how to pronounce until just a few days ago."

The mayor looked at the others before he turned to Jake, obviously disappointed.

"What would it take to change your mind?" he asked humbly.

Jake felt the eyes of the others looking at him, expectantly. "I feel like I need some time to figure this out. This is a lot to think about. I mean… this is what I always wanted. But now that it's staring me in the face, I wonder if this is really where I'm supposed to be."

"So, what if we gave you some time to think about it?" asked the mayor, looking surprised if not a little put off.

Jake took a deep breath. "Then I'm interested in trying to figure out if this is for me. I just don't think I'm ready to commit the rest of my life to this yet."

"And what about your ticket to Greece?" asked the Mayor.

"That's the tough part. I bought it on Priceline. If I don't show up to that flight, there's no refund. I had no reason to think anything like this would come up when I bought the ticket so I didn't buy the travel insurance. Even when I saw the ad, I had no idea it would turn out like this."

The mayor reached in his back pocket and produced a check book before continuing. "Jake," he said leaning forward and looking intently into his eyes. "It is in my personal interest to make sure this pottery shop has a potter. I made a commitment to Isaac that I know I must keep. If you will commit to staying until September 1st, and end up deciding this isn't for you, I will buy you a ticket to anywhere in the world." He filled out a check, tore it from the book, and placed it in front of Jake.

Jake looked at the check. It had his name on it and on the amount line, it said simply, "For one ticket anywhere in the world." Jake stared at the check for a long time before looking up at the four friends who sat in silent anticipation. "I guess I have nothing to lose," he finally uttered.

James Franklin Goldmund   06/76   4784

Pilatusstrasse 11
Niederbipp, PA 09754

Date

Pay to the Order of   Jacob Kimball $

For one ticket anywhere in the world   Dollars

NIEDERBIPP
BANK
AND
TRUST

Niederbipp Bank and Trust
Niederbipp, PA
09754

For

1125784 1000 168742456112451 04784

The friends let out a collective sigh, as if they had been holding their breaths for a long time.

"Do you have plans to stay anywhere tonight?" asked Beverly.

"No. I was just planning on heading back on the bus."

"Well, if you're going to live here for the summer, you might as well start tonight. Choose whichever room you want. I've washed the linens and there are clean towels in the bathroom. Make yourself at home."

Jake blinked hard, wondering if he was dreaming. He had just graduated the night before and now he held the keys to a dream he figured would take a lifetime, or at least the better part of ten years, to achieve. How had this happened? In the matter of a few minutes, his trip to Greece had been put on hold indefinitely. He hoped the trade-off would be worth it.

The four friends stood and began gathering up their things.

"Tomorrow, the town is celebrating May Day," said the Mayor. "We know it's not really 'til Monday, but we move things around to the weekends when we can. We hope you will be our guest of honor. There are lots of folks who have been anticipating our decision tonight."

Jake nodded, but wondered what that meant.

"My bakery is just around the corner," said Sam. "I owed Isaac a lot of bread when he died. He started a tile mosaic for my floor that still needs to be installed. If you'll help me with that, I'll make sure you have all the bread you can eat for the summer."

Jake smiled and nodded.

"Drop by tomorrow and I'll give you some for the weekend," he added.

"My husband is the town barber," said Beverly. "We'll treat you to the first haircut."

"Thank you." said Jake.

"Church is on Sunday at Ten." added Thomas. "We'll hope to see you there."

"I'll be there," said Jake, not sure what he was committing himself to.

"I had my secretary make you a copy of Isaac's will," said the

Mayor, handing Jake a large manila envelope. "We threw away most of the applications we received, but I thought you might want to look at the applications of the others we've interviewed. They're in there too."

"Welcome to Niederbipp," said Sam, extending his hand to the new village potter. Jake took his hand and shook it vigorously before doing the same to the others.

"I almost forgot," said Beverly. "I've been taking care of the potted plants around the shop and on the stairs here. Now that you're in charge, I trust you'll take care of them."

Jake nodded.

"If you have any questions," she added, "you can find me at the apartment above the barber shop."

Thomas was the last to leave. He extended his hand to Jake and gave him a friendly smile. "Jake, I'm glad you're here. This is a special place to many people and I am pleased to see the legacy continue."

"Thank you for your confidence," said Jake.

The priest was out the door before he turned back. "If you run into any trouble, please, don't hesitate to ask me for help. I'll drop by often to check on you."

Jake closed the door and sat down at the table. A minute later he heard it. It had begun to rain.

10
THE POTTER'S WILL

Jake walked to the door and pulled it open. The rain danced on the cobblestones by the light of the street lamps. His tired eyes became trance-like as he reviewed the events of the evening. The keys he had just been given were resting on the table. His bag was leaning against the wall where he left it after pulling his portfolio from it. He looked again at the hundreds of pots stacked on the shelves. He had never done drugs, but at that moment he wondered if he might be hallucinating. Were the events of the past twenty-four hours just a crazy dream?

He didn't know where to start. It was late, but he knew he wouldn't be able to sleep, so he turned to the dishes. He scooped the left over trout and rice into a chipped covered dish and put it in the fridge for another meal.

When the dishes were done, Jake decided to explore his new apartment. It wasn't any bigger than his apartment at school, but the fact that he had it all to himself made it feel palatial. He looked into both bedrooms. He had been used to seeing bunk beds and wall to wall junk. The clean and neat surroundings and the queen sized beds were a welcome luxury. He opened the closet and found several old t-shirts still hanging on wire hangers. He considered the audacity of wearing a dead man's shirts, but then reasoned that most of his clothes had come from thrift stores anyway. So, he unpacked his duffle and hung his own shirts next to Isaac's. The dresser was still filled with Isaac's overalls. These would not fit. Jake stacked them up on top of the dresser to make room for his own clothes.

He moved his toiletries into the bathroom and looked at himself in the mirror of the medicine cabinet over the sink. He smiled at himself, full of emotions too big to name or comprehend. Everything seemed surreal, and yet somehow familiar, somehow right.

Unable to put off his curiosity any longer, Jake went to the bedroom and opened the envelope the Mayor had given him. He sorted through several letters and pictures of pots until he found a Xerox copy of the potter's will. Several thin pages, neatly typed outlined the distribution of all his earthly goods. Jake began to read.

Neiderbipp Bank & Trust
Est. 1896

The Last Will and Testament of Isaac Aaron Bingham, Potter

Thank you friends for gathering at my request. If you are reading this, I must be dead.

Knowing that I cannot live forever, I am putting together some notes that will serve as my will when I finally am allowed to leave this world. I have entrusted Mayor Jim as the executor of my will with the knowledge that he knows the laws of the land and can, with honesty and humility, carry out my will with your help. I have asked you here for many reasons. The first is that you are among my very dearest friends, but more than that, I trust your judgment. You will need that judgment to help you in making a decision that I have failed to make.

As you all know, I was not the first potter who came to this town. I stand on the shoulders of six potters from the past. These, you may or may not know, were all from the same family, the Engelharts. The Pottery and its legacy have been passed down for six generations. Henry Engelhart was my father-in-law. He had no sons and only one daughter. When Lily and I met, I was a businessman, living in New York. I was successful, respected and on my way to becoming a wealthy man. But I was not happy. I discovered your town one spring day on my way home to visit my roots. I was looking for something that was missing in my life. On the way, I got lost, and in so doing, I found myself.

Walking the streets of the town that day, I noticed the "apprentice wanted" sign in the Pottery's window. On a whim, I walked in and applied for the job. I had never made pottery before, but I was good with my hands and I decided I would disappear from my old life in the city and reinvent myself as a potter in your town. There were reasons for this of course, not the least of which was the potter's daughter, Lily, whom I loved from the moment I saw her. She agreed to a date after a few weeks and we were married a few months later.

My folks died when I was twenty-three years old and being the only child in my family, I was left without anything to tie me down. Henry Engelhart took me in and treated me like the son he never had, teaching me the potter's art. It was not easy. There were days I wanted to go back to the city and pursue my career, but the love I felt here kept me from leaving. Before long, Niederbipp was the only place I could call home.

Just over a year after I arrived, influenza swept through the town taking many people, including Henry. Lily cared for him night and day until he died. Within a week of her father's death, Lily contracted pneumonia and died. I became a widower at thirty-three years old. I was angry with God for leading me to this town and then abandoning me, taking from me all that I held dear.

Time passed slowly as I looked for answers, but in time, the answers came as I got back to work. I studied the notes and the pots of the potters before me. With the things they left behind and a lot of work, I developed the skills I needed. My work at the wheel put me in a unique position to hear the stories of the town folk. These stories healed my soul and gave me a reason to live. I realized that though my pains and sorrows were big, they were often small when compared to those around me. My anger towards God melted into humility and understanding. Though my life was not what I hoped it would be, it has been most rewarding. Working with my hands enabled me to get to know myself, to learn my weaknesses and gave me opportunity to get to know each of you and so many others. I have many regrets in my life, but coming to this town and following the potter's art will never be listed among those.

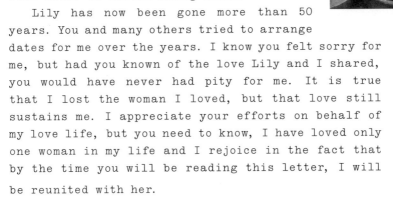

Lily has now been gone more than 50 years. You and many others tried to arrange dates for me over the years. I know you felt sorry for me, but had you known of the love Lily and I shared, you would have never had pity for me. It is true that I lost the woman I loved, but that love still sustains me. I appreciate your efforts on behalf of my love life, but you need to know, I have loved only one woman in my life and I rejoice in the fact that by the time you will be reading this letter, I will be reunited with her.

Jake stopped to wipe his eyes before continuing.

In the past several years, I have had many young men and women come to my shop for employment and apprenticeships. Many of them exhibited great talent and skill, but none of them wanted to stay to replace me. I know many of the folks in town have experienced this in their own professions as they have sought to replace themselves. I have no kin to whom I could leave my shop. I feel I have failed the potters of the past by not training my replacement. And so I come to you with a task that requires immediate attention.

As I have watched some of the other trades die out, I've worried about the same thing happening to my shop. The shoemakers and the blacksmiths are gone now, and with them has gone a piece of our history. For years I've had a recurring dream that once I'm gone, the Pottery I inherited from six generations of potters, will be taken over by a company from the city. They will throw out the pottery collection, tear down the walls, and build a big box store in its place to sell trinkets made by machines in third world countries. I would hate to face my forbearers if this was ever to happen.

This dream has been inspired by reality. In January, I was visited by a lawyer from Pittsburgh. He showed me a copy of an agreement that was signed over a hundred years ago by Alvin Engelhart. I had never seen the document before and was completely unaware of its existence.

The lawyer had been sent by the children of Elizabeth, my father-in-law's sister, who stumbled upon the old document while doing genealogical work. The document states that the assets of the studio and apartment are to remain in the custody of the potter, but that if at any time, the studio is left uninhabited by a potter for the length of sixty days, then the assets and property may be sold and divided among any remaining kin. It seems this lawyer was sent to check on my health and return to report on an estimation of when the family might expect their inheritance.

Jake looked up from the will. Suddenly he knew why the mayor had gone to such measures to keep him there. The ticket to anywhere was a generous offer, but it also bought the town time to find another potter who would be willing to make a longer commitment. He continued reading.

I know that I am only a custodian of this shop and the collection of pots in the apartment. I hate to be the one whose death brings about the demise of the tradition. I am getting older. In June I will be 88 and I feel myself slowing down.

I have wondered many times what would happen if I were to die without anyone to take over. The heirs to the estate would certainly be disappointed with the collection of pots in the apartment, and not understanding their value, would probably throw them away. The kiln would be dismantled, the shop would be sold to the highest bidder and the treasured secrets of the trade would be lost forever.

And so I plead for your assistance. I hope you will help me by selecting a person to fill my shoes, turn my wheel and fire my kiln. I understand this is a difficult and unusual request, but I know of no others who would be better suited to complete it.

Sam, you were one of the first friends I made in Niederbipp, so many years ago when I was hit with your flour bomb on that first day I came to town.

You have experienced your own disappointments with finding apprentices and I believe you know what it takes to find a good one. I trust your judgment and wisdom. I also owe you a mosaic for your floor and figure it would be good to have someone who has a vested interest involved in the process of replacing me. I hope he or she will do a better job for you than I have done.

Mayor, beyond your knowledge of the law, I have chosen you because you have long been a protector of the town. I know of your desire to see Niederbipp continue to flourish. I trust you will seek a potter who will be an asset to the town for many years to come.

Thomas, the luckiest man I have ever met. You've been a loyal friend and I know you're a good judge of character. You're the only one of the four who isn't a native of Niederbipp and are therefore more sensitive to the feelings of an outsider. I leave it up to you to help the new potter settle in. You also know history, both my history and the history of the town and I urge you to share your knowledge with the new potter. Help him learn that the beauty of this place is deeper than the river and taller than the hills. Help him to learn the secrets that make this place so special.

Beverly, beyond being one of my dearest friends, I asked you to be a part of this because I know that if I left this up to the boys, it might never get done. You know how to make things happen and I know that after all these years, the Mayor and Sam are still intimidated by you. I trust you will keep the boys on task, but I also trust you will be open and honest with your opinions.

Some qualities that I think are important for a potter to have are:

1. It is important that the person be kind to the customers and thoughtful in his work. I have developed a rapport with my customers over the years and I count them as friends. I hope the new potter will also treat them as friends.
2. The potter will need to have experience with clay and fire, be a self starter and a hard worker.
3. For the past two hundred and eighty years, the potters of Niederbipp have lived in the apartment above the shop. I would like to see this tradition continue.
4. I know it is a lot to ask you to find someone who is religious in today's culture, so if you can't, I would hope you can at least find someone who fears God and has understanding of spirituality. You all know of my faith. It is the core of who I am. It was the most important thing in the lives of all the potters who came before me. Please, find someone who can be sensitive to these things.

If you are reading this will and I am in fact dead, I have set aside some money to help you in your selection process. With this money, please place a classified ad in the local and regional papers and Ceramics Monthly magazine. This ad should simply read:

POTTER WANTED: Town seeks potter to replace the former, now deceased. Tasks include making, glazing, firing and selling pottery. Must be friendly and patient. Must have passion for life and clay. Position includes studio and apartment and extensive pottery collection. Pay is determined by marketability of your work and your motivation. Review of portfolio will be required. Send letter of interest and three photos of work to review board. Serious inquiries only. Village Bergerhaus, 34 Hauptstrasse, Niederbipp, PA 09754.

I hope that the offer of a studio, apartment and an established business will interest many applicants. I pray that you will all agree on the one to replace me.

I suggest setting an early deadline to allow you to select a new potter before any attorneys get involved.

You may be asking yourselves why I have not done what I am asking you to do. The answer is complicated. Two years ago I was diagnosed with silicosis, a lung disease caused from years of inhaling silica particles from the clay. It started with a cough that wouldn't go away and I finally went to see a doctor. They told me I should stop making pottery immediately and move to a dry climate.

At the time I was nearly eighty-six and not interested in retiring. I was told that if I continued my work in clay, my life would be significantly shortened. This required a lot of thought, but in the end, I decided that if I wasn't in Niederbipp, among my friends and those I love, doing what I love to do, I would surely die a more painful and miserable death.

There were times I considered telling you, but I decided I didn't want to be treated any differently. I did my best to hide my cough from you, not wanting to be coddled. I wanted to continue to live with dignity and enjoy whatever time I had left. And so I drank a lot of peppermint tea and prayed for my health to be preserved for as long as the Good Lord needs me to stay.

I began thinking that though I would like to approve of the potter who replaces me, you are the folks who have to live with whoever is chosen. Each of you wants to see Niederbipp flourish for the generations to come. There may come a time that our town will no longer have a potter, but I pray that time will not come for many years.

I have a few requests. I hope you will do what you can to honor them.

1. Please keep the collection of pottery that is in my apartment together. This is an unusual collection and is most valuable as a whole.

2. If a potter is found to replace me, please let him have full run of the house and studio. He should not feel like a guest, but should also understand that the studio, home and pottery collection are only his for his lifetime or the time he remains in Niederbipp as a potter. Ownership should be treated like a baton, to be passed on to the next runner.

3. All of my financial assets should be given to the church. The potter who replaces me should be able to make his own way. At the time of writing this will, I have replaced the supplies for glazes and the clay cellar is full. This should buy the potter some time to get his feet on the ground as he waits for his work to sell.

4. The pottery that is in the shop is to be sold alongside the work of the new potter. Money earned from those sales should be tithed but the rest of the money will stay with the potter to help to pay the taxes for the first year of operation.

5. You should all go to the shop together and pick out a piece of pottery for yourselves as my gift to you.

6. Please water the plants on my steps so they don't die.

7. Keeping with the tradition of the potters, the person who replaces me will be in charge of creating my grave marker like the others in the graveyard. As each of these benches reflects the life of the person who lies beneath them, it might be helpful for the new potter to hear something about me. If you feel so inclined,

share with him the lessons I shared with you about finding joy in life.

8. Do not mourn my passing. I have been blessed in life and I have faith in the world to come. See you soon!

Sincerely, Isaac

PS. You have made my life rich. I love you all. Thanks for being such great friends.

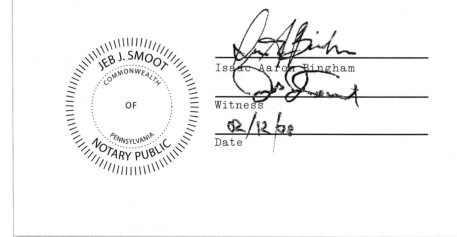

Isaac Aaron Bingham

Witness

02/12/68

Date

Jake ran his finger tip across the embossed seal of the notary public. It was signed by both Isaac and someone named Jeb Smoot. He put down the will and wiped the tears from his eyes. He wished he could have known the old potter on whose bed he now rested and whose legacy he was now charged with perpetuating. The task ahead was both exciting and daunting. Though he had just graduated, he felt as if his education was just beginning.

He sorted through the letters of the other applicants. Each of them expressed interest in being the next potter in Niederbipp. He flipped through the photos. Some of them were very nice. Others were less so and he wondered what he had said or done that had inspired the committee to choose him.

Jake returned the items to the envelope and placed it on the dresser. His head ached from fatigue and was made worse by the flood of emotion he was feeling. He walked to the kitchen to get a drink of water. Leaning against the sink, he looked at all the pots stuffed into the shelves. There were easily five hundred pots here. He wondered what could be so important about keeping them together.

He approached a shelf behind the table and pulled five pots from their dusty resting places. Balancing them in his hands, he returned to the table and sat down. He picked up a tall, black vase with white stripes and studied it closely. As he turned it in his hands, he noticed one side was rough and the glaze was bubbled. He thought it curious that the obviously flawed pot had found its way into a collection at all. It was still a nice piece in every other way, but the flaw seemed blatant to him. He would have sold this one on the cheap or given it away.

He moved on to a smaller vase, glazed with green and yellow. The vase was cold to the touch, but it was smooth. He cradled it in his rough hands, rubbing the dust from its neck and shoulder. As he got to the bottom, he found that a piece of the foot was missing where the glaze had run and sealed itself to the shelf. The flaw had been sanded smooth, but it was still obviously flawed.

Jake looked at the other three pieces and was surprised to find flaws in each one. Each piece was still beautiful in many ways, but each was far from perfect. Curious, he stood and pulled the bottle from the high shelf that he had looked at earlier. The bottle seemed perfect in every way, except for the crooked neck. When he pulled the cork from the top, he realized the lip of the bottle was more oblong than round. A round cork could never fill the void adequately and maintain a decent seal.

He looked at the shelves again, brimming with pots. Junk, all junk, he thought to himself. Most potters he knew would have relegated these pots to the shard pile. Instead, seven generations of potters had brought their junk home, displayed it nicely and passed it on like the family jewels. Jake shook his head, questioning what other delusions he might find here. He went to bed, wondering if he had chosen too quickly to abort his trip to Greece.

A NEW BEGINNING

Jake awoke the next morning to the sound of church bells. The hot shower washed away the grime from the bus and the sweat from his adventures of the day before. By the time he entered the kitchen in a clean pair of clothes, he felt like a new man, ready to start his new life. He decided against eating trout for breakfast when he noticed the apartment lacked a microwave. Then he remembered Sam's offer of bread. The bright morning sun danced on his shoulders and wet hair as he returned to the corner of Hauptstrasse and Zubergasse where Ruth had left him the day before.

It was still early, but Hauptstrasse was already filled with vendors setting up for the May Day celebration. Dozens of spectators milled about, anxious to see and buy what the vendors brought. Jake climbed the few stone steps and entered Sam's gallery of baked goods. It had been over a year since Jake had been to such a bakery. Waiting in line, he reminisced about the bakery in Henrichmont, France, just outside of LaBourne—one of Europe's best pottery villages with more than 100 potters in a ten mile radius. He had spent a week visiting the potters of the French countryside and eating French bread.

His mouth watered as he breathed in the smell of the bakery. Sam looked up and smiled. "You found me," he said, turning his attention to Jake and allowing his employees to help the others in line.

"Yep. It's a small town, I guess."

Sam smiled. "So, what'll it be?"

"Pfff, what do you suggest?" His eyes darted back and forth to all of the choices, making his stomach growl in anticipation.

"The sunflower bread is one of my specialties," Sam said as he grabbed a long loaf. "And why don't you try some of this sourdough." He dropped the loaves into a brown paper sack with the bakery's logo printed on the outside.

"Hey," Jake protested, "it's just me in the apartment you know."

"Yeah, but we're closed on Sundays and I've seen you eat," he said with a wink. "I'll give you half loaves next week if you can't finish them."

"Thanks!"

"That's not a gift," said Sam. "It's a bribe. I need my floor finished. I'll give you a chance to get settled, but I'd really like to get that done soon." Sam had already returned to his customers so Jake took the bag and walked out onto the street.

He threaded his way through the vendors' booths and wagons. There were all sorts of things for sale: hand-carved birds, home-made brooms and shoes, homemade jams, soaps, and silly hats made from colorful felt. Children played with wooden whistles and yo-yos. One booth sold nothing but colorful hand-knit socks that had no exact match.

Amused by the socks, he picked up two that looked as if they were his size. One of the socks had one inch stripes from top to bottom, while the other was covered with multicolored polka dots. He took out his wallet and handed the money to an old woman with crooked fingers. She smiled a toothless grin and thanked him for being the first purchase of the day. Jake had long believed it was good luck to support other artists and craftsmen. He had no idea where he would ever wear his new socks, but he thought they were really cool and the woman's smile alone was worth the price.

The last booth at the top of the street was an old wooden wagon.

"Adams Family Orchards" the sign read. Jake smiled when he saw what must have been the Adams family children wrestling with each other while their father struggled to secure the awning. Jake rushed to his aid.

"Thank you." said the man.

"You're welcome." said Jake. The two men looked at each other.

"I'm sorry. I don't know you."

"Jake Kimball," he said extending his hand.

"Are you new to town?"

"Brand new. I just arrived last night. I'm the new potter."

"Of course. I heard they were looking for someone to replace Isaac. I'm Josh Adams, the apple man." He smiled brightly and his blue eyes sparkled in the morning light. "Isaac was a good friend of mine. I've spent many hours watching him work. The man had magic hands."

Jake nodded, but said nothing.

"You say you just got in yesterday?" asked Josh. He pulled back his straw hat to mop his brow and revealed a receding hair line.

"That's right."

"Well, then let me be one of the first to welcome you to Niederbipp," he said, grabbing a green bottle and thrusting it towards Jake.

"What's this?"

"The best apple juice in the world. And this is one of the last bottles until fall."

"Well, how much do I owe you?"

"It's a gift," said Josh. "It's the least I can do for Isaac's replacement, and the man who helped me put up my awning."

"It's no big deal," said Jake, not wanting to be paid for the small act of kindness.

"Nonsense. I'll tell you what, let's call it a trade. As soon as I get my pruning finished up, I'll come for a visit and you can trade me for a cup of Isaac's tea."

"That sounds reasonable to me," said Jake, assuming there might be more tea in the apartment somewhere. He took Josh's hand again, and then the bottle of juice.

"Come meet my kids," said Josh. He led Jake by the elbow to the end of the wagon where one of them had climbed onto a bicycle. The others were still wrestling. "These are four of my kids, but I have three more at home.

"I told you, you're gonna have to take turns," he yelled out at the kids, who only stopped wrestling for a minute. "I invented this new juicer," he said, summoning Jake to come closer. The bicycle was missing its rear wheel and the chain had been extended and hooked up to a converter that attached to a steel shaft and changed the direction of the motion. The steel shaft was connected to two dozen wooden mallets that dropped onto the apples in a trough, pulverizing them. A gathering tank, hooked up at the far end, collected the juice while a pipe diverted the pulp into a wheelbarrow.

"We have three more of these at home," explained Josh. "I invented it one afternoon when the Mrs. told me she was going to drown the kids in the pond if I didn't find a way to get rid of their energy. I have quicker ways of juicing the apples, but none of 'em are as much fun for the kids."

Jake smiled. He liked Josh. "I'd better be going. I need to get the shop open."

"We'll be seeing you then," said Josh.

"That's right. I guess you know where to find me."

Josh waved before turning back to his kids to break up the wrestling match that had begun again.

Jake was anxious to get into the studio and begin discovering what was there. The shop had been closed for over a month, and he knew that few people would expect it to be open today.

He went in the back door and walked through the studio, turning on the lights. The electric glow chased away the shadows and the air of abandonment. He propped open the door with an old jug filled with sand to dispell the stale and musty air. To Jake, the studio already looked more inviting than the dusty cavern he had seen through the window the day before.

The showroom floor was three steps above the street level and the studio was one step above that. The old wooden floor creaked and slanted slightly towards the street after nearly three centuries of settling.

Jake picked up the dusty rag rug from the floor in front of the door and stepped into the street to shake it. When he returned, he realized the rug had been hiding a beautiful mosaic on the floor. It looked very old and was chipped and cracked in areas, but its design was classy. "TÖPFEREI NIEDERBIPP" written in black glaze encircled a plump, white chicken in a folk art style. He wiped away some dirt with the corner of the rug. Above, bold black letters spelled "WILKOMMEN." Jake knew from his experience in Germany the previous summer that Töpferei was the German word for pottery shop. He also knew that many English words were derived from German. Welcome was originally wilkommen.

Deciding it was a shame to cover this with the rug again, he recruited a bucket and sponge. Within a few minutes, some warm water and hard scrubbing, he cleared away years of grime.

Jake's attention next turned to the stairs. They had been laid with old tile. He cleaned them to reveal ornate carving and inlay, the likes of which he had seen in old European cathedrals. He swept and mopped the wooden floor in the showroom, then returned with some soft cotton rags and dusted the pots. Bowls, platters, mugs, plates and vases in all ranges of colors and shapes filled the shelves. By noon he had managed to clean the entire showroom and, in the process, became more familiar with Isaac's style and work.

Next, he moved to the studio. Looking over the sea of chaos, he wondered where to begin. It was a mess. And worse, it was somebody else's mess. Once he started making pots he would be less likely to care about the mess, but for now, he needed to start fresh. And knowing that this was now his shop, at least for the summer, motivated him. He decided to tackle one small section at a time.

By the time his stomach began to growl two hours later, he had made a small dent in the clutter. Instead of taking a real lunch break, he sat down on the back stairs and tore pieces of bread from the loaves Sam had given him. The sunflower bread was amazing and he had nearly downed the entire loaf when he heard voices coming from the showroom.

"Hello," he said, rounding the corner and frightening two elderly ladies.

One nearly dropped the bowl she was holding.

"Excuse me," he said. "I didn't mean to frighten you."

The taller one smiled. "Don't worry. We're just a couple of jumpy old birds. We were happy to see the door open. We've been hoping another potter would come and take Isaac's place."

"Thank you," he said, extending his hand to the women. "My name is Jake."

"Oh, how do you do?" asked the tall one. "I am Mrs. Klein and this is Mrs. Webber."

"We were just walking by and were curious. Isaac used to share our pew at church. Oh, what a love he was. Will we be seeing you there?"

Jake knew her question was more out of nosiness than to ask if they should save a spot for him on their pew.

"I'll be there," he said with a grin.

"Then we'll be seeing you tomorrow. We both just live around the corner. You'll be seeing a lot of us."

Jake smiled at the ladies as they walked down the stairs and out the open door. He spent the rest of the afternoon sorting and dusting, trying to make sense of the tools and other miscellaneous stuff that cluttered the studio. He mopped and washed and organized until the dumpy little shop began to look quite different.

At 5:45, the Mayor stopped by, dressed in a three piece pinstripe suit. He reminded Jake that dinner was going to be served at six, with music and dancing to follow.

Jake looked up from his work, tired, dirty and in no mood for a party with a bunch of strangers.

"We're glad this party coincided with your arrival. There are lots of folks who are excited to meet you. I need to be on my way, but I'll wait for you up at the church courtyard. Dinner is on me."

Jake reluctantly put down his sponge. He locked the front door and climbed the stairs to change his clothes.

When he arrived at the courtyard a few minutes later, the Mayor looked him over with a grimace.

"I'm guessing that's the nicest set of duds you've got."

Jake looked down at his clean white t-shirt and faded canvas work pants. "I've never owned a suit, if that's what you're asking."

"You potters are all alike," said the Mayor, shaking his head.

Jake wondered what he meant, but was happy the conversation ended at that.

The Mayor took Jake's elbow, walking him past the ladies selling tickets for the food. He sat with Jake at the center table in the courtyard and sent for two plates filled with barbequed chicken and potato salad.

Men in sports coats and even ties accompanied by women in pretty sun dresses walked past his table, extending their hands to meet Jake. He watched as people pointed at him and whispered to others. After the Mayor's comments, he wondered if it was his clothing that was drawing their attention or if it was because he was the only stranger in town. He hated feeling like the center of attention and began plotting his escape before the dancing could begin.

When darkness fell, someone lit the colorful lanterns that had been strung from tree to tree, illuminating the courtyard with magic. Beverly arrived and introduced her husband. Sam introduced his wife and the Mayor broke through the crowd gathered around Jake to introduce his wife.

When the clock tolled eight, the band stepped on to the bandstand and began tuning their instruments. The dinner tables were moved away to make room for the dancing. Jake recognized that it was a Polka band and grinned to himself as he listened to their happy music. The music had a strange effect on him and he noticed his mood changing as he watched the first couples move to the middle of the courtyard and begin dancing. Soon, the whole crowd was alive and moving with the music. There was laughter and happiness and Jake felt unexpectedly at home in a very strange place. He stayed and even danced when he was pulled onto the dance floor by a few women who were more than twice his age.

At 10:30, the band announced they were playing their last number and the crowd booed with disapproval. Jake stayed until the end of the party and was walking home when the band's encore began.

He climbed into bed, exhausted, but happy, hoping his decision to stay was a good one.

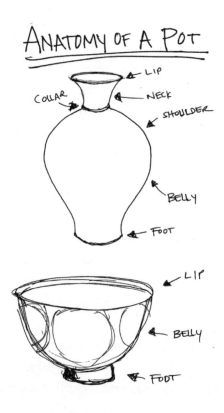

ANATOMY OF A POT

COLLAR

LIP

NECK

SHOULDER

BELLY

FOOT

LIP

BELLY

FOOT

12

THE INVITATION

Light was filtering through his shutters when the ringing of church bells woke Jake the next morning. He rose groggily from his bed and decided to eat breakfast outside on the small porch at the top of the stairs.

The sun warmed his face as he climbed the hill to the churchyard. The streets were abandoned, the shops all closed for the Sabbath. It seemed a bit eerie to Jake, like he was the last person left alive in Niederbipp. The night before, he had noticed that the cemetery was adjacent to the church and he decided since it was still early, he would visit the small cemetery and try to learn more about the potters.

The gate to the cemetery squeaked and moaned like a sad song as it swung open. The sound was somewhat unsettling to Jake's nerves. But as he passed through it, he was surprised to find so much life; the flowers and even the weeds seemed to be happy in the morning light. A beautiful tree in the corner of the yard drew his attention. It was on fire with pink flowers. He walked towards it, catching a trace of its aroma on the breeze.

He sat down on the bench that stood underneath the tree and leaned his head way back, smiling at the patches of blue sky that broke through the blossomed branches. Feeling overwhelmed by the beauty of the day, he had nearly forgotten why he had come when he felt the surface of the bench beneath his fingers. This was one of the potter's benches; he could tell by its mosaic surface. Even though it was old, weathered, and chipped in places, with some of the tiles gone completely, Jake could still make out the writing. He stood to examine the bench and there, in the center, beneath where he had just been sitting, he found the name of the departed.

Zebulon Peter Engelhart,
May 2, 1770 - April 6, 1859.
Son of Gabriel and Zola Engelhart,
Husband of Patrice Joder Engelhart,
Father of Josef, Paul and Katja.

Jake scratched at the dirt and lichen that encrusted the words that followed until he could read them.

'Sweet is the peace the Gospel brings.' [1]

He sat down on the bench again. It was simple, but it was elegant. He thought about the words and wondered if they were chosen by Zebulon or by his children, who likely made the bench. Of all the things they could have written, they had chosen to express their faith. Jake knew from his own experience with losing his mother that the gospel of Christ was a message of hope and peace. He ran his finger across the saying. It spoke truth to his soul and he felt a closeness to a man he had never met, but whose pot had drawn his attention when he first entered the apartment.

Jake sat back down and looked out at the cemetery. He noticed other mosaic-covered benches scattered among the headstones. Suddenly, in a burst of excitement that sent a chill down his spine, he realized he was part of something bigger than himself. He was not just the newest potter in Niederbipp, he was the next potter in Niederbipp! If he chose to stay, he would carry on a tradition that was older than the trees, older than this bench, older than the church and streets and the whole village. Though he was an orphan, he felt in that moment that he was part of a family that

was bigger than he ever could have imagined. Jake was confused by the feelings.

The clock tolled the half hour and a minute later, all the bells began ringing, summoning the congregants to church. He moved towards the church, hoping to catch a word with Thomas before the congregation arrived. Jake imagined he would find Thomas pulling on the ropes to ring the bells but when he pulled open the doors that stood underneath the clock tower, he was surprised to find it empty. No sign of the priest or even of any ropes. He walked around to the side of the church opposite the graveyard and found the priest rushing out of the little whitewashed house, looking flustered.

"Good morning," he said, surprising the priest.

"Oh Jake! I overslept. Is everyone here?"

"Just me. It's only nine-thirty."

Thomas slowed his pace, looking relieved.

"Who's ringing the bells?" asked Jake as they entered the church and walked under the clock tower.

Thomas smiled. "They're all computerized now. I haven't rung a bell in twenty years."

Jake looked disappointed.

"I know," said Thomas, with a look of understanding. "It's one of those modern conveniences that takes the fun away from the old ways."

Jake nodded.

"If you'll excuse me, I need to run over my sermon one more time."

A minute later the doors opened and a short woman with poofy gray hair came scurrying in, her arms filled with sheet music stacked haphazardly in a bundle. She made her way quickly to the organ and pushed up the roll top cover to expose the keyboards. He heard the muffled sound of a motor starting somewhere in front of him. The woman removed her shoes and donned a crazy looking pair that looked more like stilts.

Suddenly, a burst of sound came out of the pipes, startling Jake. He looked at the woman who was pulling and pushing knobs. When the sound came again, it was much softer. He watched as she moved her feet over the pedals under the bench. The tall platform shoes suddenly made much more sense.

She played a melody that was unfamiliar, but he was hypnotized. He closed his eyes and listened to the sweet music, remembering his first time visiting a church with his mother and some of her friends. He had been fifteen at the time and the music had affected him then in the same way it affected him now. When he opened his eyes again, the chapel was filled. He had fallen asleep.

The congregation rose as the conductor motioned. An elderly man had sat down next to Jake while he was asleep, and now handed him the left side of a hymn book while he held the right. They sang a hymn as the stilted woman played the organ.

> *From every stormy wind that blows*
> *From every swelling tide of woes,*
> *There is a calm, a sure retreat-*
> *'Tis found beneath the mercy seat.*
>
> *There is a place where Jesus sheds*
> *The oil of gladness on our heads,*
> *A place than all besides more sweet-*
> *It is the blood of the mercy seat.*
>
> *There is a scene where spirits blend,*
> *Where friend holds fellowship with friend;*
> *Though sundered far, by faith they meet*
> *Around one common mercy seat.*
>
> *There, there on eagle's wings we soar,*
> *And time and sense seem all no more,*
> *And heaven comes down our souls to greet,*
> *And glory crowns the mercy seat.* [2]

They took their seats. Thomas stood at the pulpit and after greeting the congregation with a smile, he opened a giant Bible resting on the lectern. "Let us turn together to Paul's second epistle to Timothy, to the first chapter and the seventh verse."

Jake looked around as the rustling of pages whooshed through the stone chapel. The man at his side offered to share his Bible and pointed to the verse on the open page. The page had been marked and underlined with notes written in the margins. He looked over the shoulder of the woman in front of him and saw that her Bible had also been marked and underlined. These people seemed to know their Bible and he made a mental note to bring one next week.

"For God hath not given us the spirit of fear; but of power, and of love, and of a sound mind."

The man took the Bible back from Jake, but as he did so, Jake glanced down to see a note scribbled in the margin. "Spoke to Isaac, the potter today...," but it was too late. The man seemed to sense that he had read the note and kept it hidden from his view, as if it were intensely personal.

Jake turned his attention back to Thomas.

"If it is not God who gives us fear, then who is the father of fear? Fear, that great inhibitor that keeps us from moving, from growing, from becoming. It holds us bound, keeps us from opening our eyes and truly seeing not only the world around us, but most importantly, the love He has for each of us. I find it compelling that Paul presents fear on one hand and on the other, the opposite of fear: namely love.

There is a power that conquers fear, perhaps there are many, but I know of no power stronger than that of love. It is the source of all goodness in our lives. We are here because of love, and we are here to learn how to love. Our parents, given the gift of creation by God himself, created for us a tabernacle of clay in which our spirits now reside. And together, our spirits and our bodies face this world blind to who we really are, to who we can become.

"Throughout time, poets and scholars have tried to make sense of this world and our place in it, but this scripture, this nugget of golden wisdom and truth offers us insight and understanding in just a few words. Volumes, maybe even entire libraries, filled with the learning of men cannot give us such clarity.

"Fear, that evil chain that binds us down, whose author is he who would have us fail, must be overcome. We, the children of a Father in Heaven who loves us and desires our happiness has given us all the tools we need to free ourselves from entrapment. He has given us love. It is because of love that He created our first parents. It is because of love that He sent His Son to die for us. It is because of His love that He offers to forgive us and make us whole as often as we desire.

"Fear has no place in that love and if we allow it to be a part of our lives, it will serve only as an impermeable shield against the life-sustaining love He showers upon us freely."

The rest of the sermon was a bit of a haze to Jake as he slipped into thoughts of his own life and the choices he'd made. He acknowledged that some of his choices in life had been made out of fear. He was empowered with the idea of making future decisions based on love, truth and wisdom, but recognized his deficiency in all three.

It was the most unusual service Jake had ever attended. During the past four years, he had regularly attended mass at The Cathedral of the Immaculate Conception and Holy Eucharist services at the All Saints Cathedral, both in Albany and an easy walk from his apartment near campus. He was neither Catholic nor Episcopalian, but had gone in search of peace and truth. He had found some of what he sought at both of the cathedrals, but had become distracted by the buildings themselves or the details of the ceremony and often went away with more questions than he had when he arrived.

This church was different. It was largely unadorned. The windows were plain, leaded glass. A hand-carved statue of Christ stood above the simple pulpit, nestled among the organ pipes. There was no blood or cross or signs of pain and despair. Instead, Christ stood with a shepherd's staff in one hand, his other hand holding onto the feet of the lamb draped about his neck. His face was clear and pleasant and looked as if he was almost smiling.

The service was short and understandable and even the few children in the congregation seemed to be enjoying it. Jake was almost sorry that it was over and lingered in his pew while the others filed out.

Outside, Jake was stopped by several people as he made his way across the courtyard. The Mayor shook his hand and said he was happy to see he had made it. Sam waved from a distance, as did Beverly and Thomas who stood chatting together on the steps. Mrs. Klein and Mrs. Webber, the ladies from the shop the day before winked at him as he made his way through the crowd.

"Yoo-hoo, young potter," came a woman's voice from behind. He turned to see an older woman who he recognized from the party the night before, shuffling over the cobblestones. She extended her white gloved hand with great formality. Jake took her hand and tried not to smile when he saw that her bright pink lipstick was smeared on her front teeth.

"I wanted to be the first to invite you to Sunday dinner. My granddaughter is coming and she's about your age. I was hoping to introduce the two of you."

Jake grimaced. "Uh...," he said, sounding like a dope. "Uhh...," he said again, desperately searching his head for any excuse. All ideas failed him. "Uh, sure. That's very nice of you," he finally mustered.

"Wonderful!" she said with a haughty little laugh that seemed strangely out of place. "Dinner will be at five. I live just around the corner from you at Schulstrasse 45. Do you think you can find it or should I send my husband to pick you up?"

Jake assured her he could find it and thanked her again for the invitation. He had nearly made it to the edge of the courtyard when he heard the rushed clicks of high heels on cobblestone and turned to see another woman, about the same age as the first, rushing towards him.

"Young man, YOUNG MAN," she yelled, nearly out of breath. Jake turned to face her. She put her hand to her chest in an effort to catch her breath before speaking. "I hoped to catch you earlier. I'm Clea Faber, I met you last night."

Jake nodded, taking the hand she offered him.

"I was hoping you'd join us for dinner this evening."

Jake couldn't believe it. He couldn't think of the last time he'd been invited to dinner. And now twice in one day! "I'm sorry, but I've already been invited to dinner tonight."

She looked very disappointed. "So, who beat me to it?" she asked indignantly.

Jake looked over her head, back to the courtyard. "The woman over there in the peach dress," he said, pointing her out.

"Oh, that's Betty Finkel," she spat in utter contempt. "She's been trying to get her granddaughter married off for years. We'll see about that."

"I don't have any plans this week," he said, surprising himself with the hope of extending his good fortune for another free meal.

She looked up with disappointment. "No, my granddaughter only visits on Sundays. I'm sure you two would get along splendidly."

Jake tried hard to keep from smiling, watching the wheels turn in her head.

"Well, what about next Sunday?" she asked. "Do you have plans for next Sunday yet?"

Jake shook his head.

"Fine, then next Sunday it is. I'll drop by the shop this week with directions to my house."

Jake thanked her for the invitation and turned to go. After a few steps, he turned back to see the two women engaged in animated conversation. He thought they looked like two witches casting spells at each other and couldn't help but smile to himself. Never in his short life had so much attention been paid him.

Jake spent the rest of the day relaxing. He took a nap, fumbled through a dog eared volume of poetry that he found on Isaac's bookshelf, and ate the left over trout before taking another nap. He couldn't remember the last time he had had a full day of rest.

At four, he went for a walk to gather some flowers to take to dinner and was knocking on the door at Schulstrasse 45 when the church bell tolled five.

Three hours later, Jake emerged from the house exhausted. The meal was great, but the company was less than interesting. As it turned out, the granddaughter was pushing thirty years old and laughed like a hyena at things that weren't very funny.

The table had been set with dishes made by Isaac, as were the mashed potato bowl and pitcher. Mrs. Finkel explained that she had ordered the set glazed in pink, to match the drapery in her dining room. Jake knew the shade was impossible to create at stoneware temperatures. She said she was disappointed when the color turned out to be more of an oxblood and had nearly refused them until Isaac told her that Mrs. Faber had just seen them and was interested in purchasing the whole set.

He walked home the long way in an effort to see more of the town and clear his mind. He had been in Niederbipp for only fifty-something hours, but it had already been eventful.

It was nearly 10:00 when he finally made his way back to his apartment. He put a load of laundry into the washer before lying down on the bed to rest. A few minutes later, he opened his sketchbook and began to write.

— NIEDERBIPP —

So I DECIDED TO STAY. THE SHOP ISN'T AS DUMPY AS I FIRST THOUGHT. I SPENT YESTERDAY CLEANING IT UP AND I THINK IT MIGHT WORK OUT O.K. I AGREED TO STAY AT LEAST UNTIL THE END OF AUGUST AND THEN MAKE MY DECISION.

THERE IS SOMETHING WEIRD ABOUT THIS PLACE. I HAVE BEEN HERE JUST OVER 48 HOURS AND I THINK I LIKE IT. PEOPLE SEEM TO BE GLAD

I'M HERE. I GUESS I NEED TO EMAIL THAT POTTER IN GREECE AND TELL HIM I'M NOT COMING. I NEED TO FIND A COMPUTER. I JUST REALIZED I HAVEN'T SEEN ONE YET.

TODAY IN THE CEMETERY, I FOUND ZEBULON ENGELHART'S BENCH. THE FACE OF IT SAID "SWEET IS THE PEACE THE GOSPEL BRINGS." I COULDN'T HELP BUT THINK OF MOM.

IT SEEMS I'VE BECOME THE MOST ELIGIBLE BACHELOR. I GOT TWO INVITATIONS TO DINNER TONIGHT. I SPENT THE EVENING WITH THE FINKELS. I HOPE THEY DON'T INVITE ME AGAIN, BUT THE FOOD WAS GOOD.

I'VE BEEN THINKING A LOT ABOUT ISAAC — THE GUY WHO DIED AND LEFT ALL OF THIS FOR ME TO SORT THROUGH. HE MUST HAVE BEEN A PRETTY COOL GUY BECAUSE I THINK HE KNEW THE WHOLE TOWN. HE WAS A GOOD POTTER, BUT HIS GLAZES WERE KIND OF BORING. I'M HOPING TO SHAKE THINGS UP A BIT.

Jake read what he had just written and then tossed his sketchbook onto the dresser. A piece of paper slipped out and caught his attention. It was the travel itinerary for his trip to Greece. He looked it over, hoping he made the right decision. He put the itinerary back in his book and went to bed.

LUFTHANSA FLIGHT # 411
JFK - 12:00 PM
ARRIVE MUNICH, GERMANY 7:55 PM

CONNECTION TIME (45 MIN)
LUFTHANSA FLIGHT # 3388
DEP. MUNICH @ 8:38 PM
ARRIVE - ATHENS 12:14 AM

CHECK OLYMPIC AIRWAYS
- 6 FLIGHTS DAILY (OR THE BOAT
FROM PIRAEUS) ON ANTIPAROS)

13
THE GOSSIPS' TALE

Jake woke the next morning, excited to begin his first full week in Niederbipp. The shop had traditionally been closed on Mondays, giving the potters a day off to shop for groceries, do the laundry and take care of other chores. Recognizing the work he had ahead of him, Jake opted to spend the day in the studio.

By noon, he had grown tired of cleaning up someone else's mess and decided he'd spend the afternoon throwing on the wheel. He got to work, preparing the clay for the wheel. The clay was softer and grittier than he was used to and he spent the afternoon missing the clay from school. The studio was cramped before he even began and the more he produced, the more cramped it became. He knew he needed to figure something out if he was going to endure the summer in this small space.

Despite his frustration with the space, Jake spent Tuesday doing much of the same. He trimmed the bowls and vases he had made the day before and set them aside to dry while he continued his cleaning.

While straightening things on a shelf, he stumbled upon a set of tattered log books that recorded the firing schedules for the past ten years. On the top of each page was the date and a short note about the weather. Sunny and calm. Snowy. Windy and cold. Because the kiln had a chimney stack that vented outside, weather could have a big impact on the firings and Jake studied the nuances of things like the additional time required to reach temperature when it was windy or cold outside. As he studied, he appreciated the hours spent in trial and error to get so much detailed information. He hoped this record would enable him to pull off a firing in the old kiln without too much trouble.

At 3:00, he heard the clanging of the bells on the front door, followed by women's voices and laughter. "Hello," he said, looking up to find four well-dressed women. They stopped, startled, and stared at him.

The tallest, a redhead flamboyantly clad in a purple dress suit, stepped forward and formed a great smile across her perfect teeth.

"Oh my, girls, he's much more handsome than they said!"

Jake blushed as she continued walking towards him.

"Welcome to Niederbipp," the redhead said, smiling cheerfully with lips even brighter than her hair.

"Thank you," Jake managed to stutter, still embarrassed. He had never been one who could graciously accept compliments.

"My name is Sally," she said, and extended her hand to meet the potter.

Jake took her hand and shook it. "Welcome to the pottery shop," he said lamely.

The other three women giggled in a way that seemed way too juvenile for their middle-aged, refined selves.

"Oh, we've been here before," Sally said assuredly. "We practically grew up here. Isaac was my uncle. We came here after school to hang out. He gave us money for candy or ice cream in exchange for dusting the pots in the showroom."

One of the others spoke up. "He also helped us understand how boys think. We used to bounce our ideas off of him. If it weren't for Isaac, I might have married Larry Waltzer, who has already been through four wives."

"Isaac seemed to have room in his heart to love everyone," said another woman. "I have never seen so many folks at a funeral."

The fourth woman walked towards Jake. She was the plainest of the bunch—pretty, but in a more natural way. Her clothes were not as rich and her colors, more subdued. She stood next to Sally and put out her hand to take the potter's.

"Welcome to your new home, Jake." The woman held his hand for a long moment, looking deeply into his eyes with such intensity and kindness that Jake felt his face flush again. "My name is Marjorie," she said, finally dropping his hand.

"We all just call her Marge," the redheaded Sally replied, laughing again. She turned to the other two. "This is Mary and Emily."

"Nice to meet you," Jake said. "What can I do for you ladies?"

"We've been in town to visit our mothers. Everyone's talking about the new potter so we decided to stop by to meet you," said Sally with a flirty wink. "We have a lot of memories here." She raised her hands, turning to look at the studio, as if she was casting a net to catch all the memories.

The other women nodded.

Mary, the only blonde, moved toward the studio. "I hope you don't mind if I check something." She brushed past Jake, not waiting for a response, stopping in front of the back wall, which was covered with old, fading post cards. She lifted one, hinging it from the tack that held it in place. Smiling, she turned to the other ladies and said, "It's still here."

The others surged forward, passing the threshold that separated the showroom and the studio. Jake stood where he was, but turned his body, following the women with his eyes. He felt as if the shop belonged more to them than it did to him. Mary pulled the rusty tack from the wall and the post card came with it, exposing a scribble of black ink on the plaster wall. "Mary Loves Larry." Three simple words with a heart drawn around it all. The ladies laughed out loud.

"I am so glad you didn't marry that jerk!" spouted Emily. "The only thing you two had going for you is that your names rhymed and that made everything even worse." The women laughed even louder.

Jake tried to imagine how Isaac  could have ever accomplished anything with four silly girls in his studio. They had only been here a few minutes, but he knew somehow that they had not planned a short visit.

Jake walked towards the women, curious of what else might lie under the postcards hanging on the wall.

Sally turned to him wiping her mascara-smeared eyes with a white hanky, trying to calm herself from her fit of frivolity. "Jake, there must be a million secrets in this place. We know that you never knew Isaac. You missed knowing an amazing man. As we ate lunch together today, we talked about Isaac and the way he touched our lives. We cried and laughed and then we cried some more. He was one-of-a-kind, a friend to all who knew him. He was a father figure for all of us and many, many more."

"You also said he was your uncle?" Jake asked, looking at the red headed leader, wondering if she might be one of the long lost family members mentioned in Isaac's will.

"That's right," she responded. "Uncle Isaac. He must have a dozen or more nieces and nephews scattered around the world. He was a man of great love and patience. He always knew when to step in and offer to be an uncle or friend to a child who needed attention. That's the way it was for me, anyway. I found Isaac when I needed him most and I will love him forever for the love he gave me."

Jake nodded thoughtfully. "I have been trying to piece together who Isaac was, but the problem is I don't have many pieces. Tell me, how did you come to know Isaac so well?"

Sally's eyes widened with joy and also mischief. "I'll make you a deal. I'll tell you about Isaac if you'll let four old ladies watch you make some pots on the wheel."

"You've got yourself a deal," Jake said, with a smile. "I'll get some clay from the cellar. If you ladies would like to dust off the chairs in the corner there, you'll have a more comfortable place to sit."

The women sprang into action. Jake returned from the cellar with a plastic bag full of clay and placed it on the wedging table to begin dividing it into smaller pieces. When he had twenty round balls, he loaded them back into the plastic bag and placed it on the floor next to the wheel.

He went to the sink and filled an ancient-looking batter bowl with water. Portions of the shiny brown glaze peeked through the smears of dried clay. He placed the bowl on the table in front of the wheel and sat on the old stool. The four women faced him, anxiously awaiting the show.

Without words, Jake reached into the bag and removed a ball of clay. He moved his right foot to the pedal and switched on the wheel. In a sweeping motion he plopped the ball onto the middle of the wheel and pushed the pedal to the floor, making the wheel spin at top speed. The ball became a blur as he dipped his hands into the water, splashing a small amount onto the spinning clay. Then he cupped his hands around the spinning mass.

As if the clay was suddenly endowed with life, it rose to a point between his thumbs and fingers before being pressed into a centered dome in the middle of the wheel head. It looked like a small buff colored muffin. Jake dipped his hands again in the water and returned them to the sides of the spinning clay, driving his thumbs down into the mass. Then he moved the fingers of his right hand into the cavity his thumbs had created. With his left hand, he cupped a bit of water into the cavity. As the wheel continued to spin, his fingers moved smoothly across the bottom of the vessel, creating the floor. Then with his left hand on the inside and his right hand on the outside, he pinched the clay between his fingers, lifting and raising the walls of the vessel.

He repeated this motion twice more, each time the vessel growing taller and wider. He held a sponge to the rim, smoothing an uneven area as the wheel continued to spin, but at a slower speed. He next took a kidney-shaped, flat piece of wood from the table in front of him and gently pressed it against the sides of the cavity. This formed a wobble at first, causing one of the women to gasp, but Jake confidently continued the motion until he reached the bottom of the vessel. He repeated this a few more times until, in the middle of the wheel, there stood a delicately formed bowl. He cut it from the wheel with a wire strung between two wooden dowels. In a smooth and practiced motion, he lifted the limp bowl from the wheel head and placed it gently on a ware board next to him.

The four women had not spoken since he had taken his place behind the wheel, all having been hypnotized by the spinning motion and the work of creation before their eyes. The completion of the first bowl freed them from their trance and brought them back to the present.

"I always loved to sit here and watch Isaac's magic fingers," admitted Emily.

"You do that just the way I remember it," added Mary.

Jake grabbed another ball of clay from the bag at his feet and held it above the wheel.

"I'd like to continue throwing," he said, smiling, "but I was wondering when your part of the bargain was going to begin."

"Oh yes, of course," smiled Sally. "Where to begin….," she said, looking thoughtful.

"Tell me how you met Isaac," Jake suggested as he threw the next ball of clay onto the wheel.

"Ok, that won't be too hard. It was one of the most terrible days of my life." Jake looked up in surprise.

She continued with a wry smile. "I was twelve years old and my parents had just announced they were getting a divorce. I watched as my father loaded up his stuff in our old station wagon and drove away, leaving my mom sobbing on the sidewalk.

"I couldn't handle the pain and fear I was feeling, so I turned and ran until I came to the benches under the big tree in the courtyard behind the shop. As I calmed down, I heard someone whistling a happy tune and was drawn to the open door, looking for the person who could be happy enough to whistle while my world was falling apart. Isaac was sitting at the wheel, trimming bowls. He looked up and invited me to come in and have a seat.

"He welcomed me to his studio, poured me a cup of peppermint tea and asked me if I would like to watch him work. I was grateful he didn't ask me any questions; he just worked and whistled. After watching him trim a dozen bowls, I finally introduced myself. I remember him looking at me with his kind eyes and telling me that he was glad to meet a new friend. I had never had an older person as a friend, but there was something about him that caused me to trust him from the very beginning.

"As I told him about the events of my day, I began to cry again. He spoke softly and gently, rising from the stool and moving towards me. I remember him putting his strong hands on my shoulders while I cried.

"When he spoke to me, his words were calming and full of love. He reasoned with me as if I were an adult, explaining that I couldn't control what my parents were doing or the choices they were making, but that I could decide how I was going to deal with those choices. He taught me that day that happiness was the result of deciding to be happy and told me I was old enough to make that decision for myself.

"Somehow, he invited himself to dinner," Sally said, with a little laugh. "He walked me home and on the way, we stopped by his garden behind an old lady's house and picked some vegetables for a salad. While we ate dinner, he told my mom he was looking for a girl about my age to come by his shop every afternoon to dust the pots in the showroom. He told me that I would have to put up with a grumpy potter but that he'd pay me a dollar a week and all the peppermint tea I could drink. The entire mood of our home changed from one of despair to one of hope.

"My mom got a job that week at the dry cleaners, which allowed us to stay where we were and she picked me up from my job every evening on her way home." Sally trailed off, still smiling at her memories.

Jake looked up from the wheel. "So, how do the rest of you fit into the picture? I can't imagine that any potter would ever hire four dusters."

The women giggled. "You're right," said Sally, "the rest of them came later. I worked in the shop by myself for a year or two, but when Mary and

Emily learned that I was earning a dollar each week, they started coming too, to see what they might do to earn some money."

"I think we overwhelmed him at first," said Emily. "We were so silly and full of giggles and gossip. He called us his girls and we treated him like our favorite uncle."

"And he always had the greatest advice," added Mary. "He taught us how to attract the right kind of guys and avoid the toads."

"Like Larry," Sally said, laughing.

"That's right, like Larry," Mary repeated.

"I was the last to come to the gang," Marge said. "I came to help care for a very sad chicken." All the women erupted again in giggles.

"There has to be a story behind that one," Jake said with eager curiosity.

The women looked at each other, trying to decide who would begin. Marge suggested that she did not know all of the details and that one of the other girls might be better at explaining the course of events. The ladies tossed looks back and forth to each other and finally it was decided that Emily would take a shot at it, insisting that if she got off track, the others would have to bring her back around.

"I guess this all started when we were in the 8th grade. The three of us had been friends for a few years already. Just before school started, a new girl moved in next to me. That girl was Marjorie. We were the same age and so my mom encouraged me to invite her to walk to school with the rest of us. Marjorie was different though. Her dad was a

veterinarian and she had been raised with more animal friends than human friends. Her clothes were always covered with animal hair and it seemed at least one of her shoes had always been chewed on by some beast or another."

Marge smiled at this and looked at her sweater, producing a sample of pet hair as a visual aid to the story.

"Anyway, she was different. We were interested in boys and makeup and the latest gossip. My mom kept at me to befriend Marge, but the more she pushed, the more we rebelled. We began avoiding Marge."

"We were a bunch of brats," added Sally, with a frown.

Mary shook her head. "If it had ended there, our consciences might be clearer, but it went from bad to worse." Sally and Mary both bowed their heads, not wanting to admit the guilt they still felt, even after more than thirty years.

Emily continued. "What started innocently enough as avoidance quickly turned to gossip and faultfinding. Within a few days, we had sufficiently smeared Marge's good name around the school so that no one wanted to be seen with her for fear of being somehow contaminated. I remember one afternoon converging here at the shop to discuss our next plan of attack. We were quite pleased with ourselves and the trouble we were causing Marge. If Isaac heard what we had to say, he didn't show it. When we had finished our dusting, he asked us to escort him out to Farmer Hill's place on the edge of town to deliver a few pickling jars and some cider jugs. We never knew Isaac to own a car, so we helped him load his wares into a borrowed cart and packed the whole thing full of straw for the trip.

"We walked ahead of Isaac for a while, continuing our cruel talk. I remember glancing back at him, wondering what he thought, but he seemed to be engrossed in the sights and smells of the autumn day.

"While Isaac attended to his business with the Hills, we rested on a bench overlooking the farmyard and continued our plans. None of us were farm girls and though we were not far from home, we had never had occasion to watch chickens.

"Soon after we sat down, our attention was drawn to a most peculiar sight. There was a rather ugly looking chicken whose tail feathers were missing. Her front half looked nearly the same as the others, but from behind, it looked as though she had been plucked and was ready for the frying pan. The other chickens were chasing her, and when they got close enough, they would peck at her, pulling out more and more of her feathers.

At first we just sat and watched, but then we began yelling at the other chickens to leave her alone. We became quite passionate in our shouts and it wasn't long before the good farmer came to our aid, finding us standing at the fence yelling foul at the fowl. Isaac was not far behind. He introduced us to the farmer between our shouts and hollers and the two of them stood next to us watching the injured chicken run from her torturers.

"Farmer Hill explained that what we were watching was what chicken farmers called 'the pecking order' and that there was little he could do to save the poor bird. He told us that if he stepped in now, it would only be a matter of time before another bird began to get picked on and that it would be better just to let nature take its course.

"Sally became quite passionate when we learned that the poor bird would probably only live for another few days. She burst into tears and the rest of us quickly followed. Sally was especially affected by what we were watching and, being the most outspoken of all of us, even back then, determined she had to do something about this great injustice. She grabbed onto the poor farmer's overall straps and pulled his surprised face down to her level, demanding that something be done.

"When the farmer explained that the only way to save our bird was to separate it from the others, she scolded him for not already having done so. He shook his head, telling us that he was running a farm, not a pet shop and couldn't possibly quarantine all the chickens in separate cages.

"Sally ignored him and pulled the silver dollar from her pocket that Isaac had paid her earlier that day. With tears in her eyes, she asked if it was enough to buy the chicken and enough chicken wire to build a cage.

"The farmer said it would be enough, but that a chicken would have to eat. At this, Mary and I went through our pockets and found some change. The farmer said he would fetch a few pails of feed.

"While he was away in the barn, Sally detailed how she was going to build a cage and nurse it back to health. Isaac explained that a sick and injured bird would need to be out of the rain and wind if it was to ever regain its strength.

"We all watched the wheels turn in her head. She insisted that the only place that would work was underneath the stairs that led to Isaac's apartment. Her suggestion was made so matter-of-factly that I'm sure it took Isaac quite by surprise.

"He told us he had grown up on a farm and knew that domestic chickens couldn't take care of themselves. Sally stood firm with her hands on her hips as he added that chickens were messy and stinky and required a lot of work.

"Undeterred, she held her ground and told him that the three of us would help take care of the bird and would visit it every afternoon to feed and water it and clean up after it. She promised it wouldn't be any trouble to him.

"While this discussion was taking place, the poor bird continued to be tormented by her pursuers. Seeing the work of slow destruction continue, we began to cry again.

"About that time, the farmer returned carrying a burlap bag over one shoulder and a roll of chicken wire on the other. He placed these items in the cart and stood at the fence watching the gladiators in the barnyard.

"He shook his head, opened the gate and pushed us all into the yard. We hadn't considered that we would have to catch the chicken before we could take it home. After some instruction from the farmer, we set about to try and isolate our chicken from the others. We ran one way and the chickens ran another, sliding through our legs and arms. After some effort, we were able to isolate our chicken in a group of twenty others in one corner of the farmyard. We stood around them, forming a human fence.

"He instructed us to move forward and hold the chicken down against the ground until he could help. It hadn't occurred to us that we would have to handle the wild animal and we all shrunk from the challenge. We began to cry again as the farmer goaded us on, but the tears seemed to work. He went into the crowd of chickens and masterfully yanked ours from the middle of them. He held the squirming bird upside down by its feet and told me to run and get an onion crate from the barn. Soon the crated chicken was in Isaac's cart along with the wire and feed and we were on our way back to the sanctuary of civilization.

"We dried our tears and started making plans for our new pet. As we neared town, Isaac asked if any of us had any experience caring for sick birds. None of us had experience with anything sick. When we didn't respond, he suggested that it would be good to find someone who knew something about birds or animals.

"Mary got excited and told us that her uncle kept horses on the other side of town and that he might have some good ideas. Isaac reminded us that a horse is much bigger than a chicken and has neither feathers nor wings. He suggested that we find someone who knew something about small animals and would work for cheap.

"By the time we arrived back at the Pottery we were very humbled. We had a sick chicken on our hands and no idea how to care for it. Our sympathy for the poor animal had overpowered our common sense and we knew we needed help. Within a few minutes, Isaac had stretched and tacked the wire to form a cage. We took the straw from the wagon and laid it over the cobblestone as Isaac lifted the crate from the cart and introduced the bird into its new home. We all stood against the wire fence and watched her strut back and forth on the straw, unmolested by anyone or anything.

"I remember that Isaac stood behind us and reminded us that we still didn't know how to care for a sick, half-plucked bird. He asked us if we knew anyone who had a parrot or parakeet that might be willing to lend a hand. Sally and I shook our heads, but Mary bowed her head and was suddenly very quiet.

"She admitted that we all knew a girl who knew a lot about animals, but doubted she would be willing to help us because we had been mean to her.

"As she said it, it began to dawn on us how our actions towards Marge had been similar to how the rest of the chickens picked on our refugee. It wasn't long before we were all in tears again.

"Isaac was patient with us, but told us that the life of our chicken was far more important than our pride. He suggested that an apology might go a long way and told us we better make it quick, or risk losing our new pet. He pointed out that if we put as much effort into being a friend to Marge as we had in trying to destroy her, we might be able to save our chicken and make a new friend in the process. With humble hearts, we hurried off to find Marge.

"Due to our handy work, Marge was not difficult to find. She had no friends. We found her at her father's clinic, feeding a kitten from a bottle. It was really awkward at first, facing the girl we had gone to great lengths to injure. Sally finally got to the point and told Marge about our very sad chicken and convinced her that if she didn't come immediately, the chicken would surely die.

"Marge agreed to come with us and take a look. She opened the new pen and held the poor bird in her arms. After inspecting the mangy chicken, she suggested that it would live if we, as its new family, could somehow convince the bird that we loved it and could offer it the attention it needed.

"She taught all of us how to hold the chicken and our fear of it quickly left. She agreed to help us if we would help her feed the kittens at the clinic until they were old enough to drink on their own.

"The chicken, who we named Rosie because of the color on her backside, soon grew feathers again. In the process, our friendship with Marge also grew and from then on, our plans always included her."

"Because of Marge, all of us have experimented with pets over the years," added Mary.

Marge laughed out loud, "I think I have at least 3 pets that once belonged to you girls."

All four women laughed and admitted she was right.

"I've often thought about the lessons we learned from Rosie that day on the farm," said Emily. "A year ago, I found my daughter and her friend spreading gossip about another girl. At first, I was angry with them, but then I remembered that I had been there before. I loaded the girls into the car and went looking for a farm. Not wanting to take a chicken home for a pet, I did my best to teach the girls the trouble with nature and the pecking order as we watched it on the farm. They cried the same way we did thirty years ago, and I cried with them. They changed their attitudes and started including the girl in ways they had previously left her out. Now our home is filled with the laughter and energy of teenagers."

"Ya know," said Sally, "there are many ways to teach a lesson. Every time I find myself lecturing my kids with words, I stop and remember how Isaac taught me. If they were words, they were words of love and encouragement. But more often, his lessons were taught through his actions. I think he taught us all to be more observant, to listen to the wind blow, to take time to be silent and to ask as many questions as we could. Uncle Isaac was a man with no equal in my eyes."

All of the women nodded in silent agreement.

"Those are some great stories. I'd be happy to hear some more," said Jake.

Sally smiled broadly. "I'm sure we would love to stay and chat, but unfortunately we have responsibilities at home. Besides, we've already taken up too much of your afternoon."

Jake nodded, disappointed.

Sally stood from her chair and the other ladies joined her. "I'd like to buy one of Isaac's pots before I leave," she announced. She walked to the showroom and the other women followed. The chatter with which they entered the shop began again. Jake moved to the counter to wait on them, observing their selections. Sally chose a large salad bowl. Marge picked out a dusty dog bowl from the bottom shelf. Emily chose a serving platter. Mary picked a colander.

Jake wrapped their pottery and rang up their purchases, feeling funny about taking money for Isaac's pots from women who knew the old potter better than he ever would.

"We'll be back in a few months to discover your work," said Emily.

"Thank you," Jake replied.

"Goodbye for now," Sally said, extending her hand once again. "Others will come and, I have no doubt, will be anxious to share their stories with you. We will be back, and maybe then you can share with us what you have learned about the old man." She looked at him squarely in the eyes again as the bells on the door jingled and her friends stepped out. "Best of luck to you," she said and turned to follow her friends.

Jake turned and looked at the bowls he had thrown while the women wove their tales. He took off his apron and closed up the shop before climbing the stairs to his apartment to record what he had learned in his sketchbook.

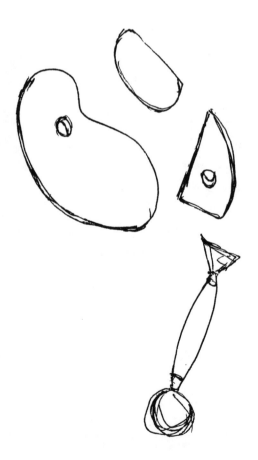

14
DISCOURAGED

A handful of visitors stopped by during the week. The Mayor and Thomas each dropped by, but didn't stay long. Sam dropped some bread off on Wednesday afternoon as a "bribe to get moving on the mosaic." Jake accepted the bread gratefully, but told Sam he wanted to figure out the kiln before he made any promises.

By day, Jake worked in the studio, continuing to clean, organize, and make pots. In the evenings, he busied himself exploring the contents of the apartment. The bookshelf in the bedroom was filled to overflowing. Well worn poetry, art, and science books lined the shelves. He also found two Bibles in the apartment: the first, written in English and heavily marked; the second, written in German and filled with old etchings.

Jake spent several hours carefully flipping through the older, leather bible. Its words were impossible to read, written in old German script, but the etchings and engravings were beautiful and captivating. The paper was thick and deckled on the edges. A family tree inside the cover charted the Engelhart family line from Abraham Engelhart's birth in 1675 until Josef Engelhart's in 1814.

On Sunday, following church, the Mayor introduced Jake to Jeb Smoot, the president of the bank. Mr. Smoot apologized that he had not made contact earlier, explaining that he had been away on vacation. He asked if he could stop by to discuss some business. Jake agreed, recognizing his name as the notary on Isaac's will.

He enjoyed a good meal at the Faber's house on Sunday evening, but disappointed Mrs. Faber by being less than interested in her granddaughter, Julie. Mr. Faber seemed to recognize immediately that Jake and Julie were poorly suited for each other and spared Jake the discomfort of an awkward evening by challenging him to chess as soon as dinner was finished.

When he returned home that evening, Jake was surprised to find that two dinner invitations had been slid under his door. He had never considered himself a very eligible bachelor and wondered if these new invitations were also made in an effort to line him up with granddaughters. Whatever the reason, he decided a good meal might be worth a little discomfort so he made some phone calls and accepted the invitations before going to bed.

Mr. Smoot dropped by on Monday morning, catching Jake at work on the wheel. He explained that he had come to see what services he might be able to offer Jake as the shop's new owner. They discussed business loans for renovation, merchant services for credit cards, as well as savings and checking accounts. He explained that Isaac had probably lost out on a lot of sales by not accepting credit cards from the tourists who frequented Niederbipp. He left a stack of pamphlets and brochures to peruse and told Jake he could always find him at his office at the bank.

Jake looked through some of the paperwork Mr. Smoot left and learned that though setting up a merchant account was free, both a checking and savings account were necessary and required a minimum of a one year contract if the monthly statement fee was to be waved. Jake spent the rest of the morning wondering what he had gotten himself into.

A one year contract! As he thought about it, he realized he had no idea where he would be in a year. There were few things that fueled the fires of Jake's wanderlust more than facing commitment, especially commitment that complicated his simple life. He imagined the blue-green waters of the Mediterranean and the village of Paros where he would be now had he not agreed to spend the summer here. He imagined himself working in one of the studios on the island, making pots and learning new techniques. He began to wonder if he had stepped into a trap.

By 2:00, the fires of his wanderlust seemed to be burning him alive. He closed the shop and went looking for a computer with an internet connection. A small woman with a beehive hairdo looked up from her paperback when Jake came through the front doors of the Niederbipp Public Library—a small building next to the hospital, not far from the bus depot.

She slid her cat-eye glasses higher onto her wrinkled nose and smiled warmly. When he told her he was looking for a computer, she directed him to a small table where two computers sat. One was already occupied by a strange-looking grey-haired fellow dressed in plaid polyester pants and a baby blue dress shirt with butterfly collars. The woman at the desk handed Jake a kitchen timer after setting it for fifteen minutes. He looked at her, wondering what this was all about, but she had already returned to reading her book, a romance novel with a lusty cover that she held close to her nose.

Jake walked to the table where he noticed a sign taped to its surface.

These computers are for the use of our patrons for 15 minute intervals. Please be respectful. Thank you, The library staff.

Jake looked around. Besides himself, the lady at the desk, and the strange man next to him, the library was empty. He sat down to look up the familiar sites of Paros. He had just typed in the web address when the strange fellow's cooking timer went off. Jake watched as the man stood, walked out the front door and came back in again, standing in front of the woman at the front desk. She put down her book, set a kitchen timer and handed it to him before returning to her reading.

Jake shook his head and tried to keep from laughing. When he looked back at his computer screen, he could hardly believe his eyes. A progress monitor on the screen indicated that his search was 15% complete. He glanced at his timer. He only had eleven minutes left. The internet was a dial-up connection! His frustration began to rise as he waited for the connection to be made. Finally, with seven minutes left on his timer, the web site appeared on the screen. Jake clicked a button and waited another full minute for the computer to respond. He could feel his face growing hot as he glared at the screen, waiting between clicks.

He glanced over to the other computer. The screen was filled with pictures of ornate pudding molds. He shook his head, wondering what kind of crazy person would spend his time looking up pudding molds on a painfully slow, dial-up internet connection. With one minute left on his own timer, the pictures Jake had come to see were finally open. He gazed longingly at the pictures of white, flat-roofed houses juxtaposed against the lapis-colored water.

When his timer went off, he stood from the table, went out the door and came back in again, just as he had observed the strange man do. The woman repeated her greetings, set the timer again, and Jake returned to the computer.

A few minutes later, growing even more frustrated with the slow computer, he felt warm hands on his shoulder. He turned around to see Father Thomas looking at his computer screen.

"Hello, Jake. Are you planning a trip?"

Jake shook his head. "I'm not sure what I'm doing."

Father Thomas nodded thoughtfully. He pulled a chair next to Jake and sat down.

"Glück ist ein fernes Land," he said

"Excuse me?"

"That's something Isaac used to tell me from time to time when I first came to Niederbipp. I think it means something like "happiness is a faraway place."

Jake smiled and shook his head. "So, what brings you here?" he asked, trying to turn attention away from himself.

"I've volunteered here for a hundred years, re-shelving books in the afternoons. I'm just checking in for duty."

Jake nodded and turned back to the screen.

"Is that the place you were going to spend the summer?" asked Thomas.

"Yeah. I've been thinking about this island for almost a whole year."

Thomas nodded, looking thoughtful. "It looks like a beautiful place, but it's probably not all you expect it to be either."

Jake raised his eyebrows and looked at Thomas, wondering if he knew how unsatisfied he was becoming with Niederbipp.

"Jake, I've been here for long enough to know that is town is not paradise, but it's a pretty great place to live. We've got our problems, but so does every other town. In the years I've been here, I've learned that paradise is not a place, but rather an attitude."

Jake's timer went off and he turned to the computer to click out of the website. Thomas stood, patted Jake on his shoulder and wandered off to the back shelves to begin his work. Jake picked up his sketchbook and left the library more frustrated and forlorn than when he had come.

He was hungry, tired, and feeling like he made a huge mistake in committing to stay for the summer. He stopped by the bakery, but Sam was gone for the day, so he had to pay for his pastries and bread. This upset him even more. When he opened the studio door, he found the floor covered with mail that had been shoved through the slot. The gas bill was on top, followed by the electric bill and the phone bill. The rest of it was junk mail, including three weeks' worth of ads from Bargain-Mart and a grocery store named Bruce's. He threw the ads away and opened the bills.

Since the shop had been closed for several weeks, the bills were small. But they still upset him and added to his feeling that the world was combining against him. He left the bills on the counter and went to his apartment to mope. He walked past the shelves filled with junky pots and into his bedroom. After eating both pastries, he opened his sketchbook to write.

MAY 4 –
DISCOURAGED IN NIEDERBIPP...

He looked at the words for ten minutes and then twenty as he considered what else he might write. Tired and cranky, he finally lay down to rest and fell asleep feeling discouraged.

15
THE FIRST FIRING

Jake was in the studio early the next morning, having slept off much of his discouragement and determined to try to have a better attitude. The kiln had already been partially loaded with Isaac's greenware when Jake arrived in Niederbipp and he added his own greenware to the shelves inside the kiln in preparation for a bisque firing.

After reviewing the kiln's logbook, he opened the damper before lighting the burners. He adjusted the gas so that blue ribbons of flame rose into the kiln like neon serpents. He knew the process of slow heating or "candling" would allow the greenware pots to dry out completely before reaching the boiling temperature of 212°F. Because of a firing fiasco his sophomore year, Jake had learned to reverence the physics of heat when mixed with damp clay. The pots had been too wet and the rise in temperature too swift. In that one firing, he learned the cruel consequences of impatience. Ninety percent of the pots were destroyed in the ensuing series of explosions inside the kiln.

He checked the log book once again and then set about preparing the clay for the day's work on the wheel. He threw several small vases, but felt unmotivated to do anything else. The morning was gray and overcast and by noon it had begun to rain. He pretended to be busy by checking on the kiln every ten minutes or so and in between, he straightened and cleaned up around the counter, setting the bills aside for another day.

Finally at 3:00, he decided he'd better do something other than sweep the floor for the third time. But as he sat down at the wheel, he knew his heart wasn't in it. He turned over the vases that he had thrown earlier so they would dry evenly before taking his fourth tea break of the day.

The rain came down harder and he knew he would be lucky to have anyone stop by on a day like this. A few minutes later, however, the bells on the front door rang as the door opened. The unexpected visit woke Jake from his funk and he stuck his head around the corner that separates the studio from the showroom.

"Hello," he said, genuinely happy to see another human. He was greeted by a friendly face, a woman of about sixty five, he guessed.

"You must be the new potter," she said, folding her wet umbrella and hanging it on the hand rail.

"Yes ma'am. I'm Jake."

"It's a pleasure to meet you," she said. "My name is Nancy Pfeiffer. I was sorry to hear about your predecessor," she said looking up into his eyes. "I assume you must be a relative of Mr. Bingham?"

"No ma'am. Unfortunately, I never knew him."

"I didn't know him well, but he was always a friendly fellow. I live outside of town and don't come in much anymore. I understand that his funeral was the largest one ever held at the church."

"That's what they tell me," Jake said, nodding his head. "So what brings you to town on a rainy day like today, Mrs. Pfeiffer?"

"I'm looking for some flower pots. My poor old dog has gone blind and knocked over the flower pots Mr. Bingham made for me years ago. I don't suppose he has any more lying around here?" she asked, looking around on the shelves.

Jake moved forward to a lower shelf where a few small flower pots sat under a thin coating of dust. "It looks like these are the last of them," he said, holding one in each hand.

She came closer and inspected the pots. "They're nice, but they're far too small for what I need. You don't know where I could get some larger ones do you?"

"Well, that all depends on when you need them. I could make you some, but it would take a couple of weeks."

"Isn't that a lot of trouble?"

"Actually, I haven't made flower pots for a couple of years, but I'd like to give it a shot. How big were you thinking?"

She held up her hands to indicate the size. "About this big," she said.

"I can do that. What color?" He moved to the front desk to write the details down in the order book.

"Well, at my age, it seems nothing really matches anyway. I wouldn't ask you to try to match my sofa."

"Thank you," he said with a little laugh.

She turned from him to look at the colors that were represented in the showroom.

"Oh, I don't know. Why don't you just surprise me?"

Jake looked up from the order book. To him, these were magic words! He could put his creativity to work rather than try to recreate someone else's idea. He loved opportunities to try new things and a couple of big flower pots would offer him a canvas big enough to get excited.

"Fine," he said, jotting down a few notes next to the order. "Should I call when they're ready?"

"You said two weeks, didn't you?"

"Yes, I think I can do that."

"Then why don't I stop back by when I return in two weeks."

"Very good," he said.

"Would you like some money up front?"

Jake was still new at this. He was not sure what to say. "Was that customary with Mr. Bingham?"

"I think so. It seems only fair."

"Ok, then. How about half now and half when they're ready?"

"Fine," she agreed, unclasping the purse that had been hanging from her elbow. "How much is half then?"

Jake was again stumped. "I'm not really sure."

He looked around the shop for something of similar size with which he might compare prices, but soon realized there was nothing even close. "How about fifty dollars apiece?"

"Sounds reasonable," she said, fumbling through her purse and retrieving the cash. Jake took the money and placed it in the old fashioned register on the counter.

"I'll see you in two weeks then, Mrs. Pfeiffer."

"Very well. Good luck, young potter," she said as she turned to go.

He moved ahead of her to open the door. He grabbed her umbrella and stepped out into the cold rain to open it for her. She thanked him and walked back towards Hauptstrasse.

As he watched her go, he was reminded of his mother and the rain walks they often went on when he was a child. Standing under a big umbrella, they would hop from puddle to puddle, going home only when they were too soggy and cold to continue. Nostalgia quickly faded into loneliness when he felt the chill of the rain on his arms. He went back into the shop and closed the door, taking a deep breath, trying to chase away the loneliness that seemed to crawl under his skin.

He walked back to the counter and began sorting through the order book. It was a cheap spiral notebook with lined pages that dated back several years. He flipped through its pages, reading descriptions of pots and looking at crude thumbnail sketches of bowls, cookie jars, and platters. Many of the names were repeated throughout the book. At the side of each of the orders was a check mark indicating that it had been completed. Towards the end of the book, just before the order he had just taken, he noted several orders without a check mark next to them. "Josh-

24 honey jars" was scrawled on the top of one page, followed by an order for six batter bowls and another for ten vases. The last order before the flower pots was for two cat dishes for Hildegard with bold letters "ASAP!" He wondered who these people were and if they might be coming back to pick up their orders.

He closed the book and turned to put it back on the shelf behind the counter. There was no sign of the cat bowls, honey jars, or batter bowls and he wondered if he should start making them.

The rain continued to fall and Jake looked out onto the street feeling tired and alone. He checked the kiln again, then made himself another

cup of tea and sat down near the kiln to wait for it to reach the correct temperature. When his tea was gone, he checked the vases he had thrown earlier. They were still too wet to trim. He considered covering them with plastic so they wouldn't be too dry to trim in the morning. But feeling lazy and reasoning that the high humidity would keep them damp, he decided to let them be. When the kiln reached 1860°F, he turned off the burners and closed the damper.

He turned out the lights and locked the door before climbing the stairs to his apartment. Still feeling the discouragement and ambivalence that had dogged him for the last two days, he cooked himself a cheese sandwich and went to bed early, hoping a good night's sleep might help him feel better about his life and circumstances.

16 THE TAILOR'S TALE

The sun was bright when Jake awoke the next morning. His situation seemed a lot less bleak when he examined it in the sunlit morning. Determined not to dwell on negative thoughts all day, he pulled on his pants and shirt and made his way downstairs to get started on the planters. He hauled up several bags of clay from the cellar and began wedging them into ten pound balls. Figuring he would be able to sell any extras, Jake decided to make six planters and allow Mrs. Pfeiffer to decide which two she liked the best. After the balls were wedged and ready to go, he carried them to the wheel before filling up the batter bowl with warm water from the sink.

Jake had just finished his first flower pot when the bell on the front door jangled and the door opened. He rose from his stool and looked over the counter to see a tall, thin man with a graying goatee, coming through the door with a package.

"Good morning," said Jake.

"Good morning to you. You must be the new potter," said the man, looking at Jake's hands and arms which were covered in clay slime up to his elbows.

"Yes, I am. My name is Jake."

"Very good." The man was dressed in a blue half coat with a measuring tape draped around his neck. "My name is Albert Schreyer. I'm the town tailor."

"Very nice to meet you," said Jake.

"And you as well. I'm sorry to bother you so early in the morning, but I didn't want to wait any longer to bring these to you. Isaac ordered them a week before he died and I figured they would be better used here than they are sitting on my shelf."

"What is it?" asked Jake. He studied the brown paper package tied with twine. He didn't have the slightest idea what Albert was talking about.

"Shall I open it?" Albert asked, looking at Jake's clay covered hands.

Jake nodded and the tailor pulled on the strings, unwrapping the package, to reveal two canvas aprons.

"Cool. I always got teased in college for wearing an apron in the studio, but they made it so I didn't have to do laundry as often. I've been using this one since I got here, but it's wearing pretty thin."

"Well, I'm the only tailor in town and would be happy to help you with any needs you might have. I don't usually do aprons, but I always made Isaac's."

"You were friends then?"

"We were," said the tailor. "I've been coming here to swap stories with the old man for longer than you've been alive."

"He seemed to have a lot of friends."

"Indeed, he did. He had a profound influence on a lot of people, including me."

"I met Sally the other day. She dropped by with three other women and they told me how Isaac helped them. They mentioned that others would probably stop by to share their stories too. I have to admit I've been pretty curious about Isaac since I got here."

Albert smiled and looked at his watch before setting the aprons down on the table. "I've known Sally since she was a kid. I'm a few years older than she is. I suppose I could tell you a few things, but I need to get back to the shop before too long."

"Great. Would you like some tea?" asked Jake.

"Don't mind if I do, as long as it's Isaac's peppermint tea."

"I think it's his. I found that old tin filled with loose tea last week while I was cleaning," he said, pointing to the tall, round cookie tin on the shelf.

"Then I'll help myself. No offense, but I don't want to be drinking anything your hands have been touching."

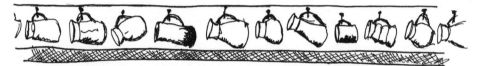

Jake smiled, looking down at his hands covered with slip. Albert reached up to unhitch a mug from a nail on the beam above him, and then went to the sink to fill the old teapot with hot water. Jake had never noticed the row of mugs hanging on the beam and was curious why they were there. He wondered how long it would have taken him to find them on his own.

"I assume you want some too?" asked Albert.

"A refill would be nice," said Jake, nodding to his cup as he began centering a new ball of clay on the wheel.

After Albert got the tea steeping, he returned to the stool in front of Jake. Jake had already centered the ball of clay and was beginning to open it up.

"I've enjoyed watching Isaac throw since I was a kid. I used to stop by and watch him work on my way home from school. I believed that Isaac was some sort of sorcerer who had mastered the laws of alchemy." He paused to watch Jake open up the ball, create the floor of the pot, and begin pulling up the walls. "It looks like you also know the magic."

Jake grinned. "I remember watching my first pottery teacher work on the wheel. He could make the clay dance in a way that I've never seen duplicated. He made it look so easy. All I made for the first several weeks was a lot of dirty laundry and some lopsided dog bowls."

"So you weren't a natural at it then?" asked Albert.

"Hardly. But maybe that's what kept me trying. I think back on the kids for whom it seemed to come naturally. They gave it up. It was too easy for them. A bunch of the others quit because it was too hard."

"So what kept you going back?" asked Albert.

"Stubbornness. That and the fact that I wanted to succeed at making pottery more than I wanted anything else. After a while, my dog bowls got bigger and thinner, and transformed into pots that looked refined enough to be used by humans.

"I look back at those early pots today with embarrassment, but I figured out a while ago that every potter has to make a lot of bad pots before he can make good ones. It still keeps me humble."

He finished the flower pot and moved it from the wheel by lifting the bat it was thrown on, setting it on a ware board at his left. He reached for another ball of clay as Albert stood, poured the tea and returned to his stool.

"So what about you?" Jake asked. "Have you always wanted to be a tailor?"

Albert, who had just taken a drink of tea, sputtered and coughed at his question.

"Well," he said when he had regained his composure, "in the beginning I thought I would be a fireman, like most kids do. It was actually in this studio that my dreams began to change."

"Did you want to be a potter?" Jake asked, looking over the ball of clay he was centering.

"Oh no, that was never in the cards for me, but it was here that I first learned to work with my hands. My parents were friends with Isaac. They grew up with his wife and after she died, my parents made sure they had Isaac over once a week for dinner. He had always felt like part of my family, so stopping by to visit him after school seemed natural.

"One day, I stopped by and Isaac was busy trimming bowls. I remember watching the ribbons of clay come off of the bowls and fall in coils on the floor. I picked up some of the scraps and began playing with them. I molded a piece to look like the tooth I had recently lost and then placed it in the hole where the tooth had been. When I got home, my mom noticed what I had done and praised me for my creativity.

"The next day, I stopped by to visit again and made enough teeth to fill a whole mouth. Isaac got a kick out it and offered to fire them for me. When they came out of the kiln as hard as real teeth, I wanted to make more. Over time, I began studying books on teeth and made friends with Doc Wagner, the town dentist.

"When I was fifteen, Doc Wagner hired me to make dentures and bridges for his patients. I was thrilled to be able to earn money playing with clay. By the time I graduated from high school, I had set my sights on becoming a dentist.

"After high school, I went away to college to pursue my goal. I enjoyed college, but no matter how hard I tried, I was never at the top of my class. After graduation, I came home to work for the summer with Doc Wagner while I applied to dental schools but by the end of the summer, I had received six rejection notices.

"I was disappointed, but decided it would be good for me to work for another year and save up more money for graduate school. I applied to ten schools the next year, but by the end of August, I'd been rejected from all ten schools. I felt completely dejected. I was angry that I had spent so much time working towards my goal without making any progress.

"Doc Wagner encouraged me to try again, so I sent out another ten applications. Later that spring after I had received my twenty-sixth rejection notice, I packed my bags, gathered up my money and bought a one way ticket to China. I was depressed and angry with God for letting me down. I felt all my prayers and hard work had been in vain. I had never been to China, but in a country of a billion people, I figured it would be a good place to get lost and forget about my troubles."

Jake looked up, surprised by the unexpected turn in the story. "China has been on my travel wish list for a long time. That must have been a great adventure. How long did you stay?"

"Almost two years. You could say it took me a long time to find myself."

Jake nodded thoughtfully as Albert continued.

"On my way out of town, I stopped here to bid Isaac farewell.

"He asked me to share a cup of tea with him and tell him about my plans. I wasn't in any mood to talk, but his kindness calmed me down before the tea was even poured. When I told him where I was going, he asked me to send him postcards from time to time so he could see some of the things I was seeing. I was grateful for his kindness and encouragement and agreed to write him as often as I could.

"Before I left, he asked if he could give me something to think about while I was away. He sat down at his wheel and opened a plastic bag filled with several balls of clay the size of a grapefruit. He took the first one out and, in a matter of a few moments, created a vase. He took a second ball and created bowl. A third became a plate, and a fourth, a bottle. The whole exercise took no more than ten minutes and by the time he was finished, I felt I had been hypnotized by his silent art of creation.

"When he was done, he asked if he could walk me to the train. As we stood to leave, I asked if I could take my mug with me. He refused, explaining that if he let me take my mug, I might not have a reason to return and he might never hear my tales from China. So I hung my mug back where it had been hanging for several years.

"I'll always remember Isaac standing alone on the platform as the train pulled away, his hands in his overall pockets, smiling at me. It was such a contrast to my parents who cried when I left, afraid I would be lost in China forever.

"After I got over my initial culture shock, I traveled to many provinces, picking up jobs where I could. Because my hands were nimble and I was willing to work hard, I was able to find employment wherever I went. I carved wood in Sang Ching, planted rice in Yunnan and worked as a fisherman in Ningbo. As I traveled, I often reflected on the things Isaac showed me before I left, wondering what he wanted me to understand.

I began to get excited about life again and my thoughts of dental school faded away.

"When the monsoon season arrived, I decided to spend some time in Hong Kong where the mud wouldn't be so thick. On my second day, I came back to my hotel room to find that all my possessions had been stolen: my clothes, my bags, my camera, even my shoes. Fortunately, I was carrying my wallet and passport. After reporting the theft to the police, I went looking for some new clothes. Around the corner from my hotel was a small shop that made clothing. The prices were very reasonable so I decided to order a couple pairs of pants. A beautiful young woman named Lin took my measurements and told me to come back in the morning.

"When I returned, Lin explained that her mother, the master seamstress, had left that morning to visit a sick relative in a far off province and would not return for a week. She showed me a mountain of work she now had to complete by herself and told me that my pants were at the bottom of that mountain. I asked her if I could help. She looked at me and my farm-worn hands and started to laugh. When she saw that I was serious, she looked again at the mountain of work and decided to reconsider. She told me I could watch her for one day and then decide if I really wanted to help. All that day I watched as she skillfully cut, sewed and hemmed.

"The next day, she showed me how to sew buttons onto pillowcases. By the end of the day, I was promoted to sewing fine shell buttons onto suit jackets and dresses. It came naturally to me and I was reminded of the creative joy I felt as a boy, making teeth, here in Isaac's shop.

"On my third day, Lin taught me how to do a blind stitch so the fabric hung naturally. By the end of my fourth day, I had hemmed one pair of my own trousers. Lin also let me help out at the front counter. Many of the customers were British and she didn't trust herself to converse in English, so I quickly learned to understand alterations and requests for custom designs.

"By the time her mother returned ten days later, I had learned to hem and sew and cut from patterns. Lin and I had become friends and her mother encouraged her to show me the city. So, during the day we went sightseeing and in the evenings, I helped in the shop. I decided to stay in Hong Kong and learn all that I could.

"One evening while I was working on a beautiful suit and feeling particularly proud of it, I started thinking back on my last visit with Isaac. In a moment of insight, it finally dawned on me what he was trying to teach me. I reviewed it again and again and the simple lesson filled my mind with peace.

"I believe he was trying to teach me that there is more than one path to happiness. Each of the vessels he made that day started as a small, unimpressive lump of clay, but all of them were transformed into their own unique vessels, full of beauty and purpose. I recognized that in my efforts to get into dental school, I had been blind to any other option. As I reviewed my memories of China, I recognized that I had found happiness in learning to carve wood, in farming, and in fishing.  But the happiness I found working as a tailor had easily eclipsed all the happiness I had experienced in my life. In a moment of humility, I saw that my prayers had been answered, just not in the way I believed they would be. I found the happiness I sought, but it required that I forget my single-minded goal and open my eyes to a broader picture.

"Looking back on it now, I wonder if I ever could have been happy as a dentist. I don't even like to visit the dentist."

Jake smiled, but looked thoughtful. "So tell me what brought you back here?"

"Homesickness. After living in Hong Kong for nearly a year, I realized it had been a long time since I had seen a bird, or walked alone down a clean street and these thoughts eventually brought me home.

"I invited Lin to come with me and help me set up a shop. My parents fell in love with her, and I soon realized that I had too. We were married a week before the shop opened and we have worked together for nearly thirty years. Our four children grew up learning to sew on buttons."

"Do they have any interest in the business?" asked Jake.

"No," said Albert, laughing and shaking his head. "My son Tom is in medical school. June is studying botany. Isaac wants to be a video game lab rat, and Alice is torn between becoming a poet and an acrobat."

The two men laughed again.

"I think one of the most important things I have taught my children is that the road to happiness has many on-ramps."

Jake nodded thoughtfully.

"Well," said Albert, "I better be on my way." He stood and rinsed his cup before hanging it back on the nail on the overhead beam. Jake watched as Albert turned to look at the post cards pinned to the wall near the door.

"This is a special place," said Albert. "I learned some of my most valued lessons about life right here, watching Isaac work and listening to his stories. I am glad you're here. It would have killed me to see the shop close."

Jake took a deep breath. "It's starting to grow on me."

Albert turned and looked at Jake for a long moment before he spoke. "I guess I didn't think about how this must be for you, trying to start fresh in a place with so much history."

Jake shrugged his shoulders. "I'd be lying if I said it's been easy. I guess it's just not what I expected."

"What did you expect?"

"I don't know," Jake said, shaking his head. "I'm still trying to figure out what wind blew me here and why. I was planning on spending the summer working at a pottery in Greece. I promised the Mayor I'd stick it out for the summer, but I'm not sure what I'll do after that."

Albert nodded his head, looking disappointed. "I suppose we all have to find our own place in life, don't we?"

Jake looked up. "Yeah."

"Hey," said Albert, pointing to the mugs on the overhead beam. "I know some of the others who own those mugs. Isaac helped all of us to find our path in life. Maybe hearing some of their stories might help you to find your path. If you don't mind, I'll tell some of the others to come and see you. I know a lot of them will be happy to hear the shop's open again, at least until the end of the summer."

Jake pursed his lips and nodded, but wasn't sure what he should expect.

"And if you don't mind, I'd like to bring my daughter Alice to meet you. She'd love to watch you work."

"Sure, said Jake. "Any time."

"Great! And we'll have to have you to dinner. We have a big collection of Isaac's pots as well as many from China. You might like to see them."

"I'd like that. And thanks for the aprons. I'll put them to good use," said Jake as he stood to walk Albert to the door.

Albert turned and looked at Jake. "Others will come. I'll make sure of it."

17
A THIEF'S TALE

That weekend marked two weeks that Jake had been working in the studio. After unloading the bisque firing on Thursday, he glazed the pots and a glaze firing followed on Friday.

On Saturday morning Jake rose early and made straight for the kiln. He held a piece of newspaper to the peep hole to check the temperature. It immediately turned brown and began to smoke, indicating the kiln was still well over 450°. He opened the damper a few inches to allow the heat to escape more rapidly and went back to his apartment to make some tea and get ready for the day.

Though it was still early, Jake returned to the studio to make himself useful. He went to the corner, lifted the door and descended the stairs into the clay cellar.

He had been in the cellar many times in the past two weeks, but still felt uneasy being there. It was dark and moldy and caused his active imagination to work overtime. He wondered how long it would take for his body to be discovered if he hit his head on the low rafters and died on the dirt floor. He grabbed two bags of clay in each hand and bounded back up the stairs. In his haste to escape the creepy cellar, he tripped on the last stair, sending himself and his load sprawling across the studio floor in a whirl of dust.

"Are you ok?" asked a deep voice from near the back door. Jake hadn't seen or heard anyone enter. His anxiety in the cellar, combined with the fright that someone had been watching him, was beyond what anyone should experience so early in the morning. Before he could respond, he was being lifted off the floor.

"That last step is a doosey," said the stranger. "I always hated that cellar. My name is Brian. Sam was just telling me about you." Jake shook Brian's extended hand, feeling his heartbeat return to a normal pace. Brian indicated the brown paper sack that he had tossed on the table when he came to Jake's rescue. "I brought over a couple of pastries and thought I'd take the chance of you being open early. I worked for Isaac for a few years as a kid and every year for Mother's Day, I've given my mom one of Isaac's pots. I was also hoping that while I'm here, I could pick up a piece of pottery for my mom."

"Of course," responded Jake, more than willing to make a sale. "Would you like some peppermint tea?"

"Absolutely." Brian sat down on the stool next to the potter's wheel, resting his elbows on the table behind him. He leaned his head back and looked at the exposed beam over his head, his eyes resting on the dusty mugs hanging there.

"Thanks for leaving the mugs there," said Brian, looking thoughtful. "Even though Isaac is gone, it still feels like home."

Jake allowed Brian a few quite moments for memories while he prepared the tea. "I just saw those mugs earlier this week when someone stopped by for a cup of tea. It probably would have been months before I noticed them. I should probably dust them off."

"Oh, please don't," responded Brian. "There's meaning in the dust. It helps us to know who has stopped by for a visit lately."

He stood and reached for the third mug in the row. It was a green mug, covered with a thin layer of dust. He walked to the sink and washed it off as a nostalgic look crossed his face.

"For twenty years I have been using this mug every time I've come to visit Isaac. He always had time to stop and share a tea with me, especially if I brought some of Sam's pastries."

"Who do the others belong to?" asked Jake.

"I only know a handful of them for sure, but I know some of them have been here." He pointed to a couple of mugs whose dust layer was very thin, stopping at Albert's. "In the interest of full disclosure, I should tell you that I'm also here because of Albert. He called me earlier this week to tell me that you're trying to figure out if this is the right place for you. He asked me to help spread the word that you're here and that the shop is open again."

Jake wondered what Albert had started. "I'm probably in better spirits than I was when Albert was here."

"That's good to hear. Isaac was my best friend and mentor and it's been tough dealing with the reality that he's gone. So much of who I am was influenced by him and the lessons he taught me." Brian moved the bag of pastries to the middle of the wheel and each of the men grabbed one.

"So, you used to work here?"

"That's right," responded Brian, taking another bite without offering more information.

"I am sorry, but you don't look like a potter." Brian was dressed in a tweed jacket and a pair of jeans that had obviously been ironed. His tasseled loafers were clean and polished and his socks matched his light brown turtleneck.

"Yes, well…that was in a previous lifetime."

Brian reached for the teapot and filled each of their mugs with the amber colored liquid before standing to get the sugar jar. Jake was impressed that he knew right where to find it.

"A lot of water has gone under the bridge since those days. I was 11 when I came to work for Isaac."

"That's great. I don't know anyone who started that early. I was 15 when I first discovered clay and it took a few years before I could make anything decent."

"Just because I started early doesn't mean I'm any good. When Albert called, I started thinking about all the time I spent here. I must have spent a million hours watching Isaac work. I have to admit that I'm a bit jealous of you. Knowing the wisdom he shared with me, I bet someone could write a bestselling book about all of Isaac's good advice if they could interview all the people who knew him. You may be the only person who ever gets to meet all of them."

"You're only the second mug owner I've met so far, but I've made notes on some of the things I've learned. I thought it might help me piece together who he was."

"Good for you," said Brian, his attention drawn to the bags of clay scattered across the floor. "It looks like you were in the middle of a project. I don't want to interrupt your work."

Jake looked at the bags. "No, you're not. I thought I'd throw some mugs today, but I'm in no hurry."

"I'd feel better taking up your time with my story if you were working at the same time. It's been a long time since I've touched the clay," Brian said, hesitating a minute. "Can I help you wedge?"

"Sure," Jake responded enthusiastically, standing and picking up a bag from the floor. Brian stood and removed his jacket before pushing up the sleeves of his turtleneck.

Jake removed the plastic bag and cut the block of clay into twenty-four pieces with a wire strung between two wooden handles. Brian grabbed one of the small cubes from the stack and began to roll it around with the palms of his hands until his body fell into a long forgotten rhythm that is unique to clay wedging and potters.

"I can't believe how good it feels to have my hands back in the clay. It must be nearly twenty years since I last touched it."

The two men quickly wedged the remaining balls of clay and Jake placed them back in the plastic bag before moving them next to the wheel. He filled the batter bowl with water and sat down behind the wheel to get started on the mugs.

Jake threw a ball of clay onto the wheel and began centering it. "I thought you had a story to share," chided Jake, aware of the hypnotic trance Brian had slipped into.

Brian raised his eyes from Jake's hands until they rested on his face.

"After Albert's call, I realized I've never told this story to anyone. It's not an easy story to tell."

"I'm all ears," responded Jake. He lifted the first mug from the wheel and placed it on the ware board at his side.

Brian took a deep breath before he began. "My mom and I had only been living with my grandparents a few weeks when my dad sent me $20 and a note asking me to pick out something nice for my mom for Mother's Day. That was a lot of money back then and I took my assignment very seriously. So, on the day before Mother's Day I set out to find the perfect gift. I had just started shopping when I ran into some of the guys from school.

"Mancini's had just opened their patio for the season and the guys were on their way to get some ice cream. They invited me to join them. When we took our seats, I told them that my father had sent me $20 to buy my mom a gift. When they heard that, my 'new friends' decided that I needed to be introduced to the 'Mancini Tornado.' The Tornado arrived a few minutes later, served in a gigantic plastic clamshell. It was piled high with 75 scoops of ice cream. It was amazing. I had never seen so much ice cream outside of a freezer before.

"By the time we were done, all of us were sick. My buddies excused themselves to use the bathroom.

"After twenty minutes of slouching in my chair, I headed to the bathroom to find my pals. The window was open to the alley, and their footprints were on the toilet seat, documenting their escape."

Jake looked up and smiled, shaking his head.

"Yeah, that was my one experience with dining and dashing. Unfortunately, the responsibility to pay fell on me since I was the only one left. The waiter relieved me of my money, leaving me with two dollars in change.

"I told my mom I'd be back early, so despite feeling sick, I resumed my search for a Mother's Day gift. I stumbled into one store after another in search of something really nice, but thanks to my gluttony and my friends, I couldn't afford anything.

"Finally, I ended up here. Isaac welcomed me as I entered the showroom. He told me that he was busy working and asked me to holler if I needed any help. I probably picked up every piece of pottery before my eyes fell upon a beautiful little pitcher. The neck has a pretty blue ash glaze and the belly was striped with six or seven different glazes. I knew my mother would love it. My heart sank, though, when I saw the price. It was eighteen dollars. I looked over my shoulder and saw Isaac working in the back room. In a moment of weakness and desperation I grabbed the pitcher, put it under my shirt, and left the shop without a word.

"When I got home, I wrapped the pitcher in a paper bag and took it to my room. I had never stolen anything before. I was not prepared for the way I felt. I went to bed early, hoping it would go away.

"The next day, I gave the pitcher to my mom after breakfast. She was thrilled, but when she praised me for my thoughtful gift, I felt even worse.

"I begged her to let me stay home from church, but my grandfather pulled me aside and reminded me that it was Mother's Day and that I needed to come to church and sit next to my mother and grandmother. I reluctantly obeyed.

"Father Thomas based his sermon on the things his mother taught him, with honesty and integrity at the top of the list. I had never listened to a sermon as well as I did that day, but it only exacerbated my guilt.

"After church, the courtyard was crammed with happy people. My mom and grandparents stopped to mingle with friends. I didn't feel like visiting, so I drifted off to a quiet bench under the trees.

"The next thing I knew, Isaac was standing in front of me. I squirmed with fear, but he disarmed me with his kindness. He apologized for not being more attentive the day before. I kept my mouth shut out of fear of incriminating myself.

"About that time, my mother approached us and Isaac introduced himself as the town potter. I froze, watching as she made the connection. She introduced herself as the daughter of Jon and Olivia Weiss. Unbeknownst to me until that moment, my grandmother had been quite a collector of Isaac's work and he had spent time in their home. When my mom commented on the pitcher and thanked Isaac for helping me select it, Isaac looked confused and an awkward silence fell between them. I wanted to vomit.

"To my relief, Isaac didn't ask any questions. Instead, he wished her a happy Mother's Day and winked at me before wandering off to mingle with the other congregants.

"If I had been sick before, it was nothing compared to what I felt then. I had stolen something from a nice man, squandered good money on ice cream, lied to my mother and allowed the lie to continue. The rest of that day dragged on endlessly for me, and that night was sleepless.

"The next morning, my mother came into my bedroom to thank me again for the beautiful pitcher. She said she was using it for the breakfast milk and encouraged me to hurry down and see. As you might imagine, I was in no hurry.

"At breakfast, Grandma praised me for choosing such a nice piece. She carried on about the merits of the new pitcher, Isaac the potter and the other great things he had created for their home. I began wishing I had stolen a box of chocolates, or a bouquet of flowers—something that would die or be consumed.

"I left for school as soon as possible, dogged by my guilt. I was miserable. Lunchtime found me sitting by myself under a tree in the school yard, thinking about what I could do to make the pain go away. I considered breaking the pitcher or throwing it away, but in a moment of inspiration, I knew I needed to go back and make things right. For the next few hours, I rehearsed what I was going to say and couldn't wait for the school day to end.

"When I found the front door of the Pottery locked, I came around to the back. Isaac was working at the wheel. The moment I saw him, my nerves and well-rehearsed apology abandoned me. I imagined spending the night in jail. However, Isaac's gentle smile put my mind at ease. When I admitted my crime, he stopped working and gave me his undivided attention. With great kindness he told me that he had asked God for the chance to help me. He told me that my coming to his shop was an answer to his prayers.

"I was speechless. He was a stranger to me, and yet I felt love pouring out of him.

"He explained that he'd been thinking about hiring a young man to help him around the shop. He told me that he would pay me fifty cents a day for sweeping the floor, taking out the garbage and bringing up the clay from the cellar.

"I was confused. I came to the shop to apologize for stealing and I was being offered a job by the very man from whom I stole. He went on to explain that if I would be in agreement, he would garnish my wages twenty-five cents a day until I had paid for the pitcher. I agreed, pending my mother's approval. I left with my burden lightened and grateful for the opportunity I would have to make things right.

"So that's how it began. After doing a background check with my grandmother, Mom agreed to allow me to work for Isaac. The next day, and every day after that, I came here to work after school. I quickly paid off the pitcher I had stolen and began earning money.

"Over the next several years, I learned many valuable lessons in this shop. This is the place where Isaac taught me how to be a man. I am honored to call him my friend and to know that my mug still hangs in his studio."

Brian's eyes were damp with tears brought on by the memories. The two men sat in silence for a moment.

"Tell me, why didn't you replace Isaac?" Jake finally asked. "You worked here. You probably knew better than anyone how he ran things. Why didn't you take the position?"

"I think Isaac would have liked that, and for a while, I considered it. But after several years of working by his side, I knew pottery wasn't my passion. Personal computers were brand new and our school had three of them. I got a hold of some books and learned all I could. I remember talking to Isaac about what I was learning. He later told me that he knew then he had lost any chance of me being his apprentice. He encouraged me to follow my passion. When I was elected president of the computer club at school, I continued to work for Isaac on Saturdays and whenever I could. Then one Saturday when I came to work, he asked me to go to the showroom and select my favorite mug. This is the mug I chose more than twenty years ago.

"He told me that it would be easier to lose me to a pretty girl than to a machine, but that it was time for me to follow my own dreams. Before I left that day, he drove a nail into this beam, hung my mug from it, and told me that I was always welcome. Then he swept me out the door to chase my dreams.

"I came back often. He always encouraged me and filled my soul with hope. When I graduated from high school, I left for college on a science scholarship and our visits became less frequent. But whenever we met, even if a whole year had passed, we were able to reconnect in a very unique way that made me feel as if I had never left.

"After I graduated from college, I came home for the summer to visit Mom and get my bearings before I began applying for jobs. I spent my afternoons helping Isaac wedge clay. We laughed about old times and I shared with him my fantasy of owning my own business, building computers and writing software.

"One day he asked me why I was going to work for someone else instead of following my desire to own my own business. The thought was exciting. I began to formulate a plan, using Isaac as a sounding board. Though his computer knowledge was limited, I found he was incredibly business savvy. He helped me put together a business plan and contacted a friend at the bank to review it.

"Within a week, I had a business loan. I ordered parts to make my first hundred computers and hired a couple of friends. In less than a month, we sold all of the computers and made a handsome profit. On my way to purchase a new car, I stopped by to thank Isaac for his advice. To my surprise, he asked if he could come with me.

"As we entered the showroom, my eyes fell upon a gold Camaro with racing stripes on the hood. Full of youthful exuberance, I believed I was destined for greatness and thought I needed that car as a symbol of my success.

"Isaac was quiet and unusually reserved as we sat in the front seat of the car. After a few minutes, he asked if we could go. I reluctantly agreed, having planned to drive my new car home.

"I walked behind him as we left the dealership, and for the first time in my life, I saw him as an old man in dirty overalls. In my pride, I felt sorry for him and his plain and simple life.

"Instead of walking home the way we had come, he led me to the old road. As we walked, he told me that this was the road that first brought him to town, long before the highway was built. The road was in poor repair by then, used primarily by farmers and their tractors in an effort to keep them off the highway. I was in a world of my own, thinking about my dream car when Isaac told me to follow him. We wandered off the road and across a ditch to the remnants of an old car. I had seen the car before. As a teenager, my friends and I often rode our dirt bikes out on the old road to throw rocks at it.

"He stepped over the door and took a seat on the rotten vinyl at the back. The axels sat half buried in the sod. The windshield had long ago been shattered, but pieces of glass still sparkled in the grass. I followed him, stepping on to the grass growing through the floor, and took a seat next to him on the dusty remnants of the convertible top. He seemed lost in his thoughts as he looked out over what was left of the dashboard and across the field to the old road.

"He told me that this car was the first and last car he ever owned. I learned it was a Porsche 356 Cabriolet. From reading my car magazines, I knew it was a highly sought after classic. I asked how he could have allowed a classic to fall into such a sad state.

"He explained that shortly after they were married, he and his wife, Lily, were on their way back from a Sunday drive when they ran out of gas and coasted to a stop. It was nearly dark, so they walked back to town, planning to return the next day with a gas can. He began laughing when he told me that the car seemed different when he arrived the next day, but he emptied the gas can before he realized the tires had been stolen and the car was resting on the brake drums and axels.

"The next night when he returned with a tow truck, the seats had been stolen along with the steering column and most of the stuff under the hood. Within a week, his very expensive toy was reduced to a shell. Knowing there was nothing he could do, he left the car to rust in the weeds. He told me that Lily said she would miss their Sunday drives, but that she had fallen in love with him in spite of his car, and not because of it.

"I had known Isaac for ten years, but I knew very little about his past. The fact that he had owned a fancy car and had once earned enough money to pay cash for it amazed me. As we sat on the back of his rusted car that night, he asked if he could share with me the lessons that had brought him his greatest happiness in life.

"I really didn't want to hear it, but I reluctantly agreed, hoping to get back to the dealership and buy my car before they closed. I will always remember his words as he turned to me and said, 'If I could have but one wish for you Brian, it would not be to see you succeed financially. My one wish is that you could know the love God has for you.'

"He went on to tell me that though he had grown up Christian, his faith wavered and fell dormant when he went away to college. By the time he moved to New York and started working, faith had become part of his past. He became too busy making money and pursuing his dreams to be bothered by it.

"After he had been in the city for several years, he was on his way home one day when he saw a crippled man propped up against the wall. He was singing a song Isaac recognized from the church of his childhood: How Great thou Art. The song pricked his heart and he began to feel ashamed of the person he had become, recognizing that his aspirations were merely vain and selfish ambitions.

"That weekend, he decided to take some time off and go back to his roots—a farm community somewhere in Ohio. He rode into Niederbipp on the back of a flatbed tow truck after getting a flat tire outside of town. While he waited for a new tire to arrive, Isaac became charmed by both the town and its residents. He often spoke of the first time he saw Lily, that he was smitten by the beauty  that radiated from her. When he found out she was the potter's daughter, he visited the Pottery, saw the "apprentice wanted" sign and applied for the job. He began working in the studio that week. He told me that there was something special about both Lily and her father that drew him in, like a bee to a flower."

"So that was it?" asked Jake, shaking his head in disbelief. "He just left his job and life in New York and started over as a potter?"

"That's about right. He told me that when he first saw Henry at work on the wheel, he felt like he had a chance to start life over, to become something better than what he was. So he traded in his high paying job to learn the potter's art. He often said it was the most important decision he ever made in his life, that the heavens led him here to make him a better man."

Jake nodded thoughtfully, considering his own reasons for becoming a potter.

"The Engelharts were faithful people," Brian continued. "Isaac said he was impressed from the very first day when they invited him to lunch and, before eating, offered a prayer on the food. He said their prayers were more than just a recitation of memorized words, but were spoken from their hearts. He became an observer, learning from their faith and humility.

"Over time, they taught him the tradition of tithing that had been passed down from Abraham Engelhart, the first potter in Niederbipp. He and his family made the roof and flooring tiles for the church before their home was even completed. Tithes and offerings donated to the church were used to care for the poor, widowed and fatherless as they believed God had commanded.

"Isaac told me it was Abraham who carved that tile," Brian said, pointing to the dark orange tile hanging above the back door.

Jake squinted at the tile, trying to read the old fashioned script.

"Unless you know German, you won't be able to read that one," Brian said, with a chuckle. Isaac told me that it says, 'As for me and my house, we will serve the Lord.' From Joshua 24:15. It was a motto that all the potters lived by."

Jake nodded, remembering Isaac's will.

"Isaac said he had never really known the scriptures before he met the Engelharts. As he began learning, he said he recognized that his meager contributions to church and charity had been whatever he thought he could spare, never giving God his best or sacrificing anything. He said that in his quest for success, he had done things quite backwards, and though he had found great success and wealth, his selfishness and pride had left him devoid of happiness and joy. Making God a greater priority in his life enabled him to redefine his treasure and purpose and find the happiness he sought."

Jake looked up, with a teasing smile. "So did you ever get your car?"

Brian grinned and nodded. "Yes, but it was different than I planned. I went away that night angry that Isaac was such a buttinski. I avoided him for a couple of weeks, but as much as I tried to ignore what he told me, I had to admit that I had always been better off when I listened to him. I decided to give tithing a try.

"That was a pivotal time in our business and I felt like we were directed to make some decisions that led us to where we are today. One of those decisions was to go back to Isaac and see what else I could learn from him.

"On the next visit, he taught me the importance of getting out of debt and encouraged me to operate the business on a cash basis, growing only when we could afford to do so without an outside loan. This required a lot of hard work, sacrifice, and budgeting, but we paid off our loan four years early and saved a bundle by not paying interest. As we grew, so did our need for transportation, but a used cargo van made a lot  more sense for the business than a Camaro. I paid cash for the van and had racing stripes painted on the hood. Not long after that, we bought out a competitor who was filing for bankruptcy because they had taken out big loans and were unable to repay them. We bought their business with cash.

"I continued to visit Isaac whenever I was in town. One day, after reporting on our success, he congratulated me and told me I was on my way to finding true joy. I was surprised, wondering what more I had to learn. I was paying my tithing. I was out of debt and operating a successful company on a cash basis. I wondered what else he had up his sleeve and how much it would cost me. I changed the subject and left before I got testy.

"That night as I lay in bed, my mind was filled with questions of what I still lacked. I recognized that my pride was keeping me from learning whatever Isaac had to teach me. I had to admit that my life was better, fuller, and freer from following his council. A few days later, I dropped by for another visit.

"I wanted to know what more I needed to do to obtain the joy of which he spoke, so I swallowed my pride and asked. His answer came without hesitation: to learn the difference between ownership and stewardship.

"He told me that understanding joy begins when we learn that ownership pertains only to things that we can take with us when we leave this world; the rest of what we perceive as ours is only in our stewardship for a time. He explained that many people he had known over the years had spent their lives amassing great wealth, only to die alone. Others, he said, made their fortunes and spent it on toys, trips, and homes all over the world.

"He spoke of a few of his friends who understood joy and instead of living lavishly or selfishly, gave their money to build hospitals and soup kitchens, training centers and schools. They funded research institutions to study and rid the world of disease, finding ways to use their money to better the lives and lifestyles of hundreds and sometimes thousands of people. He insisted that everyone, regardless of his station in life or the size of his bank account, could experience this same joy. He promised me that those who truly understand their role as stewards over God's gifts always have enough for their needs and their money is often returned to them tenfold, inspiring them to give more.

"He taught me that it is easier to develop a generous heart when you are young and poor, warning that once a man believes his wealth and position in life are due only to his own efforts, understanding joy becomes much more difficult.

"'Joy, in all its glory, can only be obtained through unselfishness,' he often repeated. As I've pondered that simple truth, I've recognized that the rules of joy are contrary to the wisdom of the world. The world teaches us that in order to be happy, we must have the biggest, the best, the newest and the most. In man's pursuit of these things, he forgets the widow and the fatherless. He passes by the beggar, and forgets his neighbor. In effect, he pulls himself to the top by standing on the corpses of those he's forgotten and neglected.

"When I asked how much this would cost me, his answer

was simple, yet meaningful. He recalled the parable of the widow's mite. The widow had quietly given everything she had with faith and humility as the rich men filled the coffers with their spare change, making a lot of noise so they could be seen by their neighbors. He taught me that attitude and gratitude were the fundamentals in charitable giving, that if I kept my heart open, my eyes would see clearly the people who needed my help.

"I left the Pottery that afternoon with a new spring in my step, but I also felt the mantle of the wisdom he had given me. I returned to my office and spoke to my partners about what I had learned. I figured even if they were not religious, they couldn't argue with the fact that charitable giving was great for tax breaks. I told them of my desire to share the wealth we were accumulating, telling them that I would be doing it with my own profits, but hoped they too would want to participate. To my
surprise, they agreed and from that time forth, we began setting aside money each month to give to a charitable organization. As our business has continued to grow, so have our donations. We developed a series of scholarships to educate kids. Funny thing is, years later, some of our brightest and best employees are the kids who received our scholarships. We've done what we can to give back to the world, and as we have, our reputation and business have grown. Isaac's promise has come true; we have never been able to give away more than we receive back.

"Jake, I've wondered many times if we could ever have had
this success without learning to be charitable. An accountant told us once that we were silly to do what we were doing and projected that if we kept the money in the business, it would double within five years. We decided instead to get a new accountant and continue what we were doing. Within five years our business had quadrupled. I'm not sure how this works, but I have to give God credit. I know He has trusted us with success, and as our stewardship has been proven, He has trusted us more. My partners and I are wealthy men, but the greatest wealth in my life is that I know the source of all good things. I have learned to know the

love of God, and that is my greatest joy. My joy has increased as I have taught these truths to my children. I'm glad I was at the right place at the right time so I could learn these things from Isaac. Hundreds of lessons that I learned here in the studio have been passed on to another generation. I can't think of a better way to honor him."

Jake nodded, feeling humbled. It seemed the stature of the man he'd come to replace grew with each new person he met.

Brian looked at his wrist watch. "I have taken way too much of your time," he said, getting to his feet and hanging his mug back on the nail.

"Do you think the others will come?" asked Jake as he looked at the mugs hanging from the beam.

"Oh, yes," Brian said, nodding his head. "Others will definitely come and they will have stories to tell. I don't know anyone who had more friends. Yes, others will definitely come."

Brian went to the showroom and selected a nice blue batter bowl for his mother. He thanked Jake for his time and wished him well. After paying for the bowl, he handed Jake his business card and invited him to call if he ever needed help.

The rest of the day was busy with customers looking for last minute Mother's Day gifts. As he wrapped each gift, he thought about Brian's story and how a stolen pitcher and the heart of a kind and wise potter had changed the course of a man's life forever. Before he went to bed, Jake opened his sketchbook and recorded what he had learned.

18 MOTHER'S DAY IN NIEDERBIPP

Jake had wanted to spend more time in the cemetery all week, but the rain interrupted his plans. On Sunday morning, he showered and ate his breakfast quickly and left his apartment a full hour before church would be starting. As he walked up the hill, he was inspired once again by the quiet streets. Never had he seen such stillness in Albany where Sundays were days of merchandising and recreating. He enjoyed having the day off to rest and gather his thoughts.

The beautiful tree in the corner of the cemetery was still in bloom, but it had begun to fade over the course of the week and browning petals littered the benches and the ground underneath. Two weeks before, Jake had discovered the bench dedicated to Zebulon Engelhart. Another bench stood nearby, sharing the shade of the same blossomed tree. Jake made his way towards it, drawn in by the sight and scent of the tree.

He knelt next to the bench and gently blew off the petals that covered the surface. This bench was brighter and more playful than its neighbor. In the middle was a tile that immediately grabbed Jake's attention. He sat down and began wiping away the dust in the recessed lettering. He unwrapped the leather thong from the button on his sketchbook and opened it to record the information.

DEDICATED TO
ALVIN ZEBULON ENGELHART
SEPTEMBER 12, 1854
OCTOBER 26, 1935
SON OF JOSEPH & PATRICE WILKES ENGELHART
HUSBAND OF ZINA FRANK ENGELHART
FATHER OF HENRY & ELIZABETH

He ran his fingers across Elizabeth's name, remembering the will, and then blew away the remaining petals on the edges of the bench before standing to look at all of it. Henry, his son and protégé, had done a good job with the bench. The tiles were well made and the grout was still tight. He stepped back when he realized that the tile continued neatly on the sides and front of the bench.

An inscription on the front section caught his eye and he moved closer, brushing the surface with his hands until he was able to read the inscription.

I HAVE NO GREATER JOY THAN TO
HEAR THAT MY CHILDREN WALK IN TRUTH
3. JOHN 1:4

Jake read the scripture several times before sitting down on the bench to ponder its meaning. There was that word again: joy. He thought about the conversation he had had with Brian the day before.

He flipped to the notes he had made and reviewed what he had learned. The things Brian shared with him were meaningful, but something made Jake feel uneasy. As he flipped back through the notes he had taken after his conversations with Albert and Sally and her friends, Jake began to realize that he held in his hand the lessons that had been preserved and passed down through seven generations. He recalled Brian admitting that he was jealous that Jake might be the only one who would ever hear all the lessons that Isaac had shared. Brian had spoken of the mantle of responsibility he felt when he learned the wisdom Isaac had shared with him. As Jake looked over the graveyard at the other four benches he had yet to examine, he rolled his shoulders, feeling the weight of that mantle fall upon him.

Dealing with the clutter and tradition of the shop had been daunting enough. This new feeling of responsibility made Jake feel like hyperventilating. He stood and closed his book, walking out of the shade of the tree. As the sunlight touched his skin, his body responded with a surge of goose bumps, making the hair on his arms stand up. He closed his eyes and faced the sun, allowing the heat to warm his body. Once again he wondered if he wouldn't be better off in Greece where his obligations and responsibilities would be limited, if any at all.

The bells began to chime in the clock tower and Jake turned to see that others were arriving for services. He heard the organ start up and smiled to himself as he imagined the short woman with tall platform shoes and thick glasses playing the keyboard. He watched women, old and young, arriving in their best clothes, bedecked with hats, jewelry and corsages and he remembered the significance of the day:  Mother's Day. This was the second Mother's Day without his mother and Jake felt a sudden pang of loneliness as he thought of her.

A large woman dressed in pink from head to toe crossed the courtyard, catching Jake's attention with her flamboyant pink hat with long feathery plumes that bobbled above her as she walked. She led a parade with the pride of a peacock, followed by an entourage of happy revelers: a husband, several children and a gaggle of what looked like grandchildren. Jake watched them enter the church before turning to look at the bench. His eyes were drawn again to the passage of scripture printed on its front side.

"I have no greater joy than to hear that my children walk in truth."

As he crossed the cemetery, his thoughts again returned to his mother. He imagined her smiling down on him and he smiled up at the heavens as he climbed the front steps of the church.

He was surprised to find the chapel nearly full. He moved quickly down the center aisle, taking a seat in the first available pew, greeting the woman next to him. After the hymn and invocation, Thomas took center stage with a friendly smile and wished all the mothers and grandmothers a happy day. Jake smiled to himself as he watched the response his words fostered in the congregation.

"Today, we will read from the Old and New Testament," Thomas said, once the crowd had become more subdued. "Let us turn together to Proverbs 31..." his voice echoed off the stone walls "...and begin with verse 10. 'Who can find me a virtuous woman? For her price is far above rubies.'"

Jake looked around and watched as women straightened and sat a little taller. Thomas smiled, apparently pleased that the verse received the understanding he hoped it would. "Let us move on to verse 25," he said. Jake was angry with himself for leaving his Bible at home again. He looked over the shoulder of the woman at his side.

"Strength and honor are her clothing, and she shall rejoice in time to come."

Jake looked forward to where the woman in pink with the feathered hat sat, thinking that it would require a lot of strength to wear an outfit like that.

"She openeth her mouth with wisdom; and in her tongue is the law of kindness."

"Achoo, Achoo," came the sound of a sneeze from behind him, followed by the hushed whispers of a dozen women saying "Bless you".

The priest continued, "She looketh well at the ways of her household, and eateth not the bread of idleness."

Again someone sneezed twice, louder than the first set, sending echoes throughout the chapel. Heads began to turn as another wave of blessings came from all around.

Thomas smiled and continued without hesitation. "Her children arise up and call her blessed; her husband also, and he praiseth her." Thomas looked up to see if a sneeze would punctuate that verse as well, but when it did not, he continued. "Many daughters have done virtuously, but ..."

"Achoo, achoo," sounded the sneeze, echoing off the ceiling and walls and turning all heads in the direction of a young woman sitting near the aisle, two rows behind Jake. He also turned and watched as she walked quickly to the back door, unsuccessfully stifling another set of sneezes. Jake strained to see her face, but could only glimpse ginger-colored hair. She pushed on the doors but before she could get them open, Thomas said from the pulpit, "Bless you," and the congregation erupted in laughter.

Thomas continued his sermon after that, speaking of Eve, the mother of all living and honoring her and the values that she passed on to her children. He spoke of Christ, who honored his mother, giving charge of her to his apostles as he hung dying on the cross. And finally, he looked out at the congregation, encouraging everyone to love their mothers and thank them often for all they do. There were smiles and happy tears on the faces of the entire congregation as the final hymn was sung.

Then the congregation poured out into the courtyard to visit and enjoy the spring day.

Jake stood at the doorway, scanning the courtyard for the ginger-haired girl. He spotted her standing with her back towards him, talking to Beverly and some other women. He walked toward them, unsure of what to say, but wondering who the girl was. He knew he hadn't seen her before; he would have remembered her beautiful hair. Perhaps she was just in town for the weekend, he thought. As he came closer, he felt an unusual sense of nervousness and slowed his pace.

Beverly caught a glimpse of him over the girl's shoulder and waved him over. She smiled brightly as she extended her hand to take his, and when he gave her his hand, she pulled him in to stand in front of the girl. When Jake looked at her, his nervousness increased. In four years of high school and four more in college, his social track record had been abysmal and though he had been increasing his experience with the many dinner invitations in the past two weeks, he still lacked confidence.

"I want you to meet my niece," said Beverly. She dropped his hand

REMEMBERING ISAAC

and put her arm around Jake in a motherly half-hug. Jake reluctantly looked up as he reached out his hand to meet the young woman, fearing his nervousness would become embarrassing. She gave him her hand while Beverly proceeded with the introductions.

"This is my niece, Amy Eckstein," she said. "She just graduated from Endicott College in Massachusetts and is spending the summer with me so she can paint." Jake smiled at her, feeling suddenly incapable of letting go of her hand. "This is Jake," said Beverly. "He just took over as town potter."

Amy smiled. "Then I bet we have a lot in common," she said.

Jake hung on her words, hoping they were true. "How long have you been here?"

Beverly answered for her. "Two weeks now. She came in the same weekend you did."

"I'm sorry we haven't met yet," Jake said sincerely.

"The poor girl has been sick since the moment she arrived," added Beverly, shaking her head.

"I got a cold that laid me flat," said Amy. "I just started feeling better this week, just in time for me to start my job last Tuesday."

"I take it you haven't been painting much?"

She shook her head. Jake was intrigued by the way the sun danced in her hair as she moved.

"No," she said with a look of disappointment. "I was hoping to get started on that this week, but I'm not sure when that will happen."

"I did a little painting in college. I'd like to see your work sometime."

"I wish I had some to show," she said with a little laugh. "I haven't painted since I graduated."

"You know," said Beverly, cutting in, "I was just thinking it would be nice if you joined us on our picnic."

"Sure," he said, looking at Amy with a smile. "I'd love to."

"I thawed a whole bunch of chicken yesterday to make my famous fried chicken. My son and his family were supposed to visit me today, but he called this morning to tell me they'd been up all night with a sick

- 164 -

daughter. I told them not to come. If there's one thing I can't handle, it's vomit."

Jake looked at Amy who grinned and lifted one eyebrow.

"That means I have more chicken than I know what to do with. I hope you're hungry," said Beverly.

"I sure am. I've been living on Sam's bread and pastries since I got here."

"Then we're off to do some frying," she said as she slid her arm through Amy's. "Meet us at the upper fountain at noon."

"Is there anything I can bring?" he asked, knowing it was polite to ask, but also knowing he had nothing to offer.

"Just yourself. Amy will bring her paints and maybe she'll whip up a masterpiece by the end of the day."

Amy looked over her shoulder as her aunt dragged her away. She smiled, but her eyes looked unsettled. He hoped this wouldn't turn out like the other dinners he'd been invited to attend, but something told him this one would be different.

He went back to his apartment and straightened up a bit. After only twenty minutes, he decided he'd rather be outside. He walked towards the fountain, figuring he could spend some time sketching while he waited. Jake had long been an avid sketcher. He had already filled several sketchbooks with his drawings and ideas, but this was also where he recorded his thoughts and gave voice to his feelings.

He was sketching the designs of the old cobblestone at his feet when Amy, Beverly and her husband arrived. Amy was carrying a basket. Beverly had a big bag over her shoulder and her husband was carrying a canvas bag filled with old blankets.

"I hope you haven't been waiting long," said Beverly.

"No," said Jake, closing his book. "I've just been drawing."

"You remember my husband, Jerry.

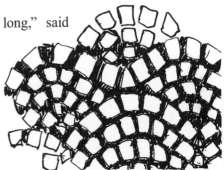

He's the barber in town. I'm sure you'll be getting to know each other soon."

Jake smiled at the less than subtle hint that his hair was getting long. He turned to shake Jerry's hand. Jake didn't remember Jerry, but figured they must have met at the May Day party.

"Nice to see you again," said Jerry. "Beverly has told me a lot about you. I sure was glad when you showed up. We hardly got a wink of sleep during those weeks after Isaac died. At first, Beverly kept us both up worrying if anyone would apply. Then she kept us up the next week reviewing the applications. The final week she spent telling me how bad the interviews were going. I think I probably owe a lot of folks a free haircut for the bad ones I must have given them during those weeks when I could have slept on my feet."

"We're all glad you're here," Beverly said.

Jake nodded and thanked them for their kindness.

"Can I carry the basket for you?" he asked, reaching for the handle Amy had hanging from the crook of her arm. She didn't resist and Jake soon found that the basket was heavier than it looked.

"Where are we going?" he asked.

Jerry smiled into the sunlight and closed his eyes.

"I wanted to go to the hills, but Jerry said he wants to lie in the sun. So, despite the fact that it's Mother's Day we're going down by the river," Beverly lamented, the obvious loser of the debate.

"Sounds good to me," said Jake. "I haven't had a chance to see much of anything yet, so I'm happy to go wherever."

"You'll like the river," said Jerry as they turned together and began their walk.

"Where are your paints?" asked Jake, recognizing an absence of art supplies.

Amy turned to him, but Beverly, who was walking in front of them, spoke first.

"Amy said she wasn't *in the mood* to paint. I guess we'll have to keep waiting to see how good she really is," Beverly said, shaking her head.

"I brought my sketchbook," Amy said softly, turning to meet Jake's eyes. "It's in the basket."

"Is that why it's so heavy?" he chided. She took his sketchbook from his hand and carried it without another word. Jake smiled at Amy and she smiled back.

They walked down the hill towards the flatland of the river. Before long, they left the paved streets and cobblestone walkways and found themselves walking along a dirt path that paralleled the river. Jerry pointed out a few landmarks, giving a brief history of each, but otherwise, they walked in silence, each of them enjoying the brightness of the day.

"This will do," said Jerry, walking through a field near the river. He started laying out the blankets on the young alfalfa. Less than a minute later, he was lying on the blanket, assuming the sunbather position. Beverly took the basket from Jake setting it down on the blanket.

"Why don't you kids go take a look at the river," she said. "I'll lay this out, if Jerry will move his caboose, and we can have ourselves a picnic whenever you want to wander back." Jake smiled when he noticed that Jerry was in no hurry to move his caboose.

"We'll be back soon," said Amy, as she began walking away.

"Take your time," said Beverly. "We've got all day."

They turned to look back at Beverly and Jerry when they reached another dirt path that meandered along the high banks of the river. They laughed as her aunt set a plate on her uncle's belly.

"They're a couple of crazy old birds," she said.

Jake nodded as he turned to look at them. "He sure puts up with a lot."

"You have no idea. I just try to stay out of their way. It's been fun staying with them. They're two of my most favorite people."

"Do you come to Niederbipp often?" asked Jake, as they strolled along the path.

"Yeah, we used to drop in to visit Bev and Jerry nearly every summer on our way to or from vacation. My dad grew up here, but left for college and never came back. Beverly is the only one who stayed. I think Uncle Jerry had already been cutting hair for a couple of years when they got married and he never had any desire to leave. They had four sons and they all left right after high school. Brad, the one who was going to come today, is the youngest and lives about a half hour away, in Erie. He's the closest cousin to my age, but he's still ten years older."

"So how did you end up coming here for the summer?"

Amy let out a long breath. "I needed a place to figure out my life. I needed a place to paint and dream and listen to the wind blow."

Jake nodded. "Is it working?"

"Not yet, but I hope it will. Now that I'm feeling better, I think I'll be able to get some stuff done," she said, looking distracted. "I can't believe it's still here," she said excitedly, pointing to a swing that hung from a tall tree branch.

Jake looked up, smiling when he saw it.

"I used to come here when I was a kid." She walked to the edge of the steep bank, looking down at the swing dangling above the gravel-lined river bottom less than fifteen feet away from the water's edge.

"Let's go," said Jake, scrambling to the edge and looking over at the roots and rocks that kept the bank in place.

"It seems like there was an easier way down," she said, looking down river to a place where the bank wasn't so high. Jake followed her line of sight and got to his feet. They hurried to a place where a ramp had been cut into the side of the bank, scrambling down it together like a couple of barefooted kids on a summer day.

The water ran close here, but the signs of its recession were evident on the gravelly beach strewn with driftwood. The rocks were smooth and Jake bent over to take a closer look.

"Are you coming?" she hollered, over the song of the river.

Jake looked up, his hands full of rocks, and nodded. He ran awkwardly over the uneven surface to catch up to her, and showed her the rocks he had found.

"I think I still have a whole jar of rocks just like these that I've gathered over the years," Amy said.

Jake put a couple of the rocks in his pocket and dropped the rest on the ground.

They came to the swing. The board that formed the seat showed signs of being polished by wind and water, and grass hung from the knots tied on the bottom side.

"It looks like the water was pretty high this year," Jake said, pulling the grass away from the ropes.

Amy stood, resting her hand on one of the ropes, looking out at the water as it rushed by. "It seems like it's still pretty high. I remember a lot more beach."

She dropped her hand from the rope and took a seat on the old gray plank, resting her hands again on the fraying ropes. "I love it here," she said, smiling out at the river. "I feel like a little girl again." She tilted her head back, looking at the canopy of young leaves that blocked out the sun and cast shadows splattered with sun spots all around them. "Will you push me?" she asked.

"Sure," he said. He came behind her and wrapped his hands around the ropes where they met the wooden seat. He pulled her back and let go. When she returned, he pushed her again and again and soon she was soaring out over the water, casting a shadow on the shallows that danced across the ripples before being yanked back over the gravel and getting lost in the denser shadows there. Again and again she soared, her summer dress flapping in the gentle breeze and her ginger hair trailing streaks of golden light.

Jake smiled as he watched her. It had been nearly two years since he had really looked at a woman. His heart had been broken by Candice Summerhays, his lab partner in chemistry. Chemistry had come easy to Jake and when she asked for his help in understanding a litmus test, he misunderstood her flirty nature and fell for her. It went on for several weeks and in the end, he found out she had at least three boyfriends and was only using him to get a good grade. He felt so dejected that he vowed never to look at a woman again.

Though he was now twenty-two years old, he still considered himself an imbecile when it came to matters of the heart. While his buddies were dating, falling in love and even getting married, Jake spent his weekends and evenings in the ceramics studio at school, finding his way with clay.

The clay had broken his heart too from time to time over the years. He still remembered the pain of losing a load of his best pots when a beginning student's pot had blown up in the firing, sending pieces of shrapnel throughout the whole kiln and ruining all of his work. But for the most part, the clay had responded much more favorably to Jake than any woman ever had.

As he stood watching Amy soar over the gravel, he realized it was his love of clay that had landed him here on the banks of the river with a beautiful girl whose fragrance was more intoxicating than spring itself. As her hair brushed against his face every time he pushed her, something in the air woke Jake from a lifetime of hibernation.

Uncomfortable with what he was feeling, he moved to the side of the swing and walked out towards the water, stooping down at the water's edge and reaching in **AMY** to retrieve a red rock. He pulled it out, his hand chilled by the frigid water, and turned it over. On the underside of the rock, he watched as a small water creature scurried around in circles, suddenly aware of the new light that surrounded its world.

"It's a mayfly larva," said Amy, who was now standing over him. He looked up at her and she eclipsed the sun, creating a golden halo around her head.

"How do you know?" he asked, his eyes returning to the wiggling creature.

"I studied them in my freshman biology class."

"You must have done pretty well if you can still remember that," he said, sincerely impressed. He stood and held the rock higher so they both could take a closer look.

"I nearly failed the class, but it was one of my all time favorites." She put her fingernail on the rock and scooped up the larva, allowing it to wiggle on her fingertip.

Jake thought it odd that a girl would do such a thing, but he admired her all the more for it.

"So why did you almost fail?"

"I was a freshman—and I was distracted by the freedom college life offered. I had done well for most of the semester, but when we started studying insects, I was inspired by their beauty. One day while passing the pond on campus, I noticed a bush completely covered with caddis flies. I watched as a bird landed on that bush, and within a second or two, a million green-winged caddis flies took to the air. I was so intrigued by the explosion of life that I began to spend more and more time at the pond, studying all the insects there. These little guys were some of the most interesting."

Jake looked at her, observing the sincere fascination she had with the little critter.

"I took some of the larvae home in a mayonnaise jar and over the next couple of days, I watched them mature and hatch on the sticks that I had poking out of the jar. I watched as their wings dried; and as they preened themselves, I admired their forked tails and big, green, beady eyes staring up at me. And then they were gone: flying off to live their short lives, mate, lay eggs and die. I began going to the pond every day to sketch and paint pictures of all that I found there. I painted dragonflies, damselflies and butterflies, but the mayfly was my favorite. I painted dozens of them in all their different stages of life and I neglected all my other schoolwork.

"When my grades were posted for the class, I was not too surprised to see I had failed. My teacher saw me outside his classroom, he pulled me aside and asked why he hadn't seen me. I apologized and told him that I was busy following my passions and thanked him for the things I had learned in his class. I gave him one of the little watercolors I had painted and tried to explain that I had been spending much of my time at the campus pond, painting the bugs they were studying in class. When I got my grades, he had changed the grade to allow me to pass."

Jake smiled and shook his head. There was much more to Amy than he had expected.

"I know it's not very feminine to care about bugs," she said.

"I guess I'm just surprised. I've never known anyone who liked bugs."

Amy looked thoughtful and as silence fell between them, Jake wondered if he had said something wrong.

"Jake, have you ever heard the saying 'the devil is in the details?'"

"Sure. Why?"

"Well, I've thought a lot about that saying since the semester I spent at the pond and I don't think that whoever came up with that ever studied bugs. I remember finding a dead dragonfly on my way to the pond one day. I sat down on the grass and lifted its tiny corpse to the sky, blocking out the sunlight with its wings and I was amazed at the structure and design of such a simple thing. It reminded me of a stained glass window, and yet it was more beautiful than any window I have ever seen. As I've studied the minutia of life, I've developed a sense of wonder for the universe."

Jake grinned, not sure if he was in love with her or intimidated by her.

She leaned over and returned the larva to its watery home. "We better be getting back," she said. "Aunt Bev is probably already wondering if we got lost."

"Sure," said Jake, finally recognizing his hunger pangs.

They wandered back the way they had come and found Jerry still asleep on the blanket. Beverly, who looked like she had been reading a book, was also asleep in the afternoon sun. They awoke as Amy and Jake sat down next to them and Beverly sprang into action, dishing up plates of potato salad and fried chicken for everyone while Amy poured juice and Jake helped Jerry sit up.

"Did you have a nice time down at the river?" Beverly asked, handing them each a plate.

"Yes," said Amy. "The old swing is still there."

"That's right," said Beverly. "I just saw it last week when I was out for my walk. Did you know that Brad is the one who hung that swing?"

"No," said Amy, looking surprised. "That's my cousin," she offered. "He's now a powerful attorney and probably incapable of such a stunt."

"That was a long time ago," said Jerry. "He used his money that he earned from sweeping up around the barber shop to buy the rope and then I went and watched him shimmy out on the branch to tie it up. Beverly didn't want any part of it. She was too afraid the boys were going to get hurt and we'd be sued. Come to think of it, maybe that's why Brad went on to study the law," he said with a wink.

Beverly changed the subject to art, a subject that quickly became apparent she knew little about. Amy looked at Jake after a particularly ignorant comment and rolled her eyes. Jake had to turn his head to keep from laughing. For his part, Jerry kept his mouth shut except when filling it with food. Jake learned that Amy had wanted to be a painter for many years and was talented in both watercolors and oils. He admired her thoughtful silence, watching her gaze at the landscape as if she were deciphering secrets from the light and shadows of the afternoon.

After a long lunch, Jerry rolled over and went back to sleep. Beverly picked up her book and Amy pulled out her sketchbook. She wandered off to a log and took a seat, looking out at the landscape of the river and forested hills on the other side. Jake went and stood by her, his own sketchbook in hand. But as soon as he saw what Amy was drawing, he lost all interest in his own sketching. He sat down near her and looked over her shoulder as her pencil recorded what she saw.

He admired how she made confident strokes with her pencil, forming the horizon and other horizontal lines and then moving seamlessly to sketch the trees and the flowers, the fields and the clouds. It quickly became a monochromatic sketch of what lay before them. Jake was very impressed.

"What?" she asked with a shy smile.

"I was just watching," said Jake. "I hope you don't mind." She continued her drawing without answering but angled herself slightly so he could see better. When she finished, she wrote in the corner, "Mother's Day in Niederbipp with a nosey potter."

"Hey," said Jake.

"This will help me remember this afternoon," she said, smiling brightly and disarming his mock protest. He had been nosey, but he had enjoyed watching her. She turned around on the log and looked at the town of Niederbipp climbing up the hill. The bell tower loomed over the other buildings, its orange roof tiles reflecting the afternoon light. From here they could still see the hands on the clock.

"What are you going to draw now?" he asked.

"I was just wishing I brought my paints. It looks like it is going to be a beautiful sunset."

Jake could imagine such a painting. "I guess we'll have to come back," he said.

"Do you like to paint?" she asked.

"I took some classes in college, but I also thought I knew how to sketch until I just watched you. I think I'd rather just watch you do the two-dimensional art."

"Sounds like a cop-out to me," she chided.

"Absolutely," he said with big grin. "I know when I'm out of my league."

She flipped the page over in her sketchbook and began to draw the view as it stretched out before them: Jerry and Bev on the blanket, the trees behind them and then the town rising up the hillside. On a distant hill she drew a patch of trees in straight rows.

"What's that?" he asked.

She shrugged her shoulders. "Looks like an orchard or something," she said, squinting at the distant hills.

Jake squinted too. "I didn't notice that before," he said, squinting to see it more clearly.

"I guess an artist just notices things like that," she teased. Jake feigned being hurt, and Amy laughed.

"That must be the Adams' orchard," he said. "I met him at the May Day market."

"I think I slept through most of that day, and the next."

"It was a good time," said Jake. "It gave me a taste of the uniqueness of the town. Can you believe they had a polka band?"

"Yeah," she said with a laugh. "I had to get up and close my window so I could sleep. I dreamt I was all dressed up in some native costume, and was forced to dance the polka by a group of Italian mafia men dressed in purple suits who threatened to cut off my hair if I stopped."

Jake laughed. "That's bizarre."

"I'm not sure you can live over a barber shop without it working into your subconscious somehow."

Jake began to laugh and she joined him.

"Do you know how to dance the Polka?" he asked.

"No," she said with a chuckle. "Do you?"

"Of course! You're looking at the three time reigning champion of Burlington County."

"You are such a liar," she said, and they laughed together again like old friends.

As evening began to fall and the shadows grew longer, Jerry and Bev came and stood over Amy's shoulder.

"Well, your father will be happy to know that the investment in his daughter's education wasn't a total loss," said Jerry.

"Thanks, Uncle Jerry," said Amy, with a wink.

"It's a very nice picture, Honey," added Aunt Bev. "If your dad's not proud of you now, he will be by the end of the summer."

"I'm not so sure about that," said Amy. The conversation between the relatives intrigued Jake, but no further information was offered and he didn't feel it was appropriate to pry.

"I'll go pack things up," said Beverly, taking Jerry's hand in hers and dragging him along. Jake stood and stretched his tired legs. He wanted to stay and watch Amy finish, but also felt obligated to help with the clean up. After another five minutes, he reluctantly left her to help fold the last of the blankets.

"We better get home," said Jerry. "Your mothers are going to be upset if they don't get a call from you tonight."

"That's right," said Amy, sounding and looking a bit deflated.

Jake didn't respond.

"Are you sad Brad didn't make it?" asked Amy. Beverly looked thoughtful.

"Are you kidding?" said Jerry. "And miss out on a nap in the sun? Don't get me wrong: I love Brad and Sara and the kids, but nothing can compare with a nap in the sun and a quiet picnic. I'm going home refreshed. If they had come, I'd be going home tired and ornery."

Jake couldn't help but laugh.

As they walked back to town together in the twilight, Jake wished the day would never end. He had never conceived of a perfect day, but if there was such a thing, he felt that this day had come very close.

When he returned to his apartment, Jake couldn't help but think about how the picnic had been so different from the previous invitations. When his thoughts kept him from sleep, he opened his sketchbook and recorded the events of the day. When sleep finally came, it came with a peace he hadn't felt since he arrived in Niederbipp.

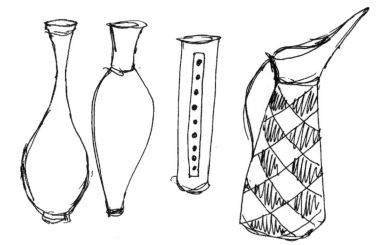

THAT WHICH HAS HIGHEST USE POSSESSES THE GREATEST BEAUTY!

SHAKER PROVERB

19
Hippies in Niederbipp

Jake awoke the next morning still reflecting on the magical events of the previous day and wondering if he would have to wait until the next Sunday to see Amy again. He had a wonderful time with her, but she had given him no indication that her feelings were mutual.

He showered and dressed for the day before he remembered the kiln and the firing he had completed the previous week. The kiln was made of hard brick, an old-fashioned type of brick that the ceramics industry replaced twenty years earlier with soft brick, made of lighter, less dense clay. With less thermal mass, the new bricks provided increased efficiency and heated and cooled much more rapidly than the old brick. The brick could be replaced; Jake had done it before at school, but he knew he was not in a financial position to make the change. A hard brick kiln would be difficult to get used to, but he knew he had no other choice.

He was happy to find the kiln cool enough to unload without the need for gloves. He stacked the new pots wherever he could find a place to put them. When the kiln was empty, Jake moved the pots to the showroom, filling in the holes on the shelves.

Thoughts of Amy continued to fill his mind. He wanted to learn more about her. The bright, warm day tempted him and finally, at 3:00, he closed the shop and went out to look for her. She had spoken the day before about working somewhere here in town, and he cursed himself for not asking more questions, making his search for her somewhat daunting. He considered going for a haircut and asking Jerry where Amy was working, but opted against it, deciding it might be fun to find her himself.

His first stop was a children's shop, just a few doors down from the Pottery. A bespectacled woman with graying hair looked up when he entered the shop, greeting him with a friendly smile.

"Hello," said Jake, as his eyes shifted from the toys to the brightly colored children's clothing and high tech strollers.

"Are you shopping for someone special today?" asked the woman.

"No," said Jake, caught off guard. "I don't even know any children. I'm the new potter."

"Oh, yes," she said, pushing her glasses higher on her nose and moving to the other side of the counter. "I thought I recognized you from church. I'm Juliana," she said extending her hand. "It's a pleasure to meet you. Isaac was a good man and we often had occasion to visit. I am glad to know the shop will be open again."

Jake invited her to stop by any time and made his escape quickly, not wanting to get tied up in conversation when his search had just begun. He ducked into the next store whose windows displayed an eclectic mix of books, posters, and army paraphernalia ranging from fake grenades to uniforms and war medals. The man at the counter was busy selling a model airplane to a pimple-faced teenager. Jake turned around without looking further and walked out. He thought he might stop by again to meet his neighbor, but it wouldn't be today.

The next shop was clearly a lingerie store, with posters of busty women posing in bras and silk robes. Jake felt himself blush as he walked past the door. He couldn't imagine Amy working there and he was unwilling to put himself into a humiliating situation by introducing himself to the proprietors.

The shop on the corner of Hauptstrasse sold vacuums. The store's windows were filled with the latest, greatest designs and a silly poster of a young woman wearing bright lipstick, hugging a particularly brightly colored vacuum. Jake stopped, looked at the poster, and smiled. He wondered if such a poster, with a beautiful woman hugging one of his pots, might bring more people into the Pottery. He was fascinated by the power of advertising and as he walked away, he began thinking about how he might draw more customers off of Hauptstrasse and up Zubergasse to the Pottery.

The next shop was a small café with doors that slid open to allow customers to order from the counter while still standing on the street. Jake watched as a tan man behind the counter took an order from a customer. He moved to a tall rotating cylinder of meat and began shaving off slices. Jake was very familiar with the Turkish kabobs from his travels to Europe as well as the small shop near campus in Albany. He made a mental note to return.

The next several shops were clothiers, selling a variety of men's and women's clothing. The mannequins were dressed up in the latest styles and Jake smiled when he saw his own reflection in the window, juxtaposed with high fashion. Work pants and t-shirts were all he needed and he was happy to find a job where he would never have to wear a tie.

The next store had huge bright windows that invited him in. He walked through the aisles of the store examining pots and pans and other fine housewares. He found an entire aisle containing nothing but small kitchen hand tools. He fumbled with the peelers and spatulas and looked through the rolling pins and whisks. Jake had always searched out such items for use in the studio.

"May I help you?" asked a young clerk wearing a white shirt and thin black tie.

"Uhh, I'm just kind of looking around," said Jake.

Jake returned to his browsing, but watched out of the corner of his eye as the clerk looked him over with an eye of suspicion.

It wasn't the first time Jake felt he was being suspected of wrong doing because of the coarseness of his clothes. He had once been followed by

a bank manager and asked for three forms I.D. when he came straight
from the studio, covered with clay, and tried to cash his paycheck. It had
bothered him at the time, but he was used to it now and was unwilling to
change for the sake of appearances.

He selected a potato peeler with a comfortable red rubber handle and
went to the counter to make his purchase. The clerk appeared, looking
a bit put out to have to fuss with such a small purchase. He took Jake's
crumpled bill and made change before placing the peeler ceremoniously
into a handled, printed, paper bag that was big enough to hold a thousand
peelers.

Jake smiled at the clerk, before extending his hand. "I'm Jake, the new
potter."

The clerk looked unimpressed, but took his hand.

"Michael," he said with a fake smile. Jake nodded his
head.

"Nice to meet you, Mike." And with that he took his
enormous bag and walked out the door.

Once he was back on the street, he pulled the peeler
from the bag and put it in his pocket before folding the
bag and hanging it from its handles on the wrought iron
structure that surrounded the garbage can in front of the store. He moved
to the next shop and looked in through the windows. It was a flower
shop. Jake was about to move on when he noticed a tall silver can with
Calla Lilies poking out of the top. He stopped in his tracks. He turned
to face the window and his mind raced back to his mother's funeral, to
a flower arrangement that had been placed on her casket. Jake had never
seen the flowers before that day, and as he looked through the window, he
remembered admiring their simple, unusual structure.

The door opened and a beautiful woman with strands of silver in her
jet black hair stood in the doorway looking at him. She wore a black turtle
neck under a green apron. He turned to look at her and noticed she was
smiling at him.

"You must be Jake." He looked closer, wondering if he should know her. There was something familiar about her smile. He was taken in by the kindness in her eyes.

"I am," he finally said.

She smiled brighter.

"Then please come in. We've been excited to meet you."

He might have felt uneasy if the woman had not been surrounded by an aura of kindness. He felt immediately drawn to her as she took his hand and pulled him into her cozy shop filled with the aromas of life.

"I'm Gloria," she said as she pulled him forward to the counter. "Let me go get my husband." She disappeared through the doorway behind the counter. A minute later, she reappeared with a tall, graying man. "This is Joseph."

He smiled and extended his hand to Jake.

"We've been excited to meet you," he said. "Sam told us about you just before we left town for a vacation. We just got back last night."

Jake had no idea who these people were or why they seemed so pleased to meet him, but their smiles and kindness made him feel welcome.

"So how's it been so far?" she asked.

"Alright, I guess." He wasn't sure how much he should say. "I've just been trying to get settled and did my first firing last week."

"That's great," she said. "We're so glad Sam and the others were able to find you. This town wouldn't be the same without a potter. People have associated Niederbipp with pottery for a lot longer than we've been around."

There was a jingle from the bells attached to the door and Jake turned to see a well- dressed older woman with a fur-collared jacket enter the small shop.

"Hello, Gerda," said Gloria, stepping forward to take the woman's hand and welcome her. A dog barked and Gloria looked down to the woman's purse at the tiny dachshund whose head was poking out.

"Hello, Killer," Gloria said with a laugh, leaning down to pet the little dog.

"We were just meeting the new potter," said Gloria, turning to present Jake. The woman shuffled forward and offered Jake her white-gloved hand.

"It's a pleasure to meet you, young man." Her accent was deep and charming.

"Thank you. And you as well."

"It's a pity about Isaac. He was a good man, but you look like a good man too," she said with a wink. "Welcome to Niederbipp."

The dog barked again. "Oh hush, Killer," she said in a faux angry voice that made Jake grin. "He's just excited to meet you."

"What can we do for you today?" asked Gloria.

Gerda took a deep breath, "I need an arrangement for my entryway."

Joseph pulled a pen from behind his ear and a pad of paper from the pocket of his apron. "Tell us what you'd like."

Joseph began taking notes as the woman rattled off wants and wishes and names of flowers Jake had never heard of, making him wonder what language she might be speaking. Gloria took his elbow and moved him closer to the door.

"Gerda is from South Africa. Her husband was a botanist and she insists on placing her orders using the Latin names. Joseph writes them down the best he can and we usually spend an hour looking them up in the field books."

Jake laughed. "Sounds like you have your hands full."

"You just wait. She frequented Isaac's shop too." And they both laughed.

"How would you like to come over for dinner?"

"Sure," said Jake.

"Good. Make it 6:00. We live above the shop. You can find the stairs off the alleyway."

"Sounds good," said Jake, as the conversation at the counter got louder and Gerda began speaking with her hands.

"We'll see you then," said Gloria, opening the door allowing Jake to escape.

After visiting several other shops, Jake stopped his search for Amy and wandered back to the Pottery, disappointed.

At 6:00, Jake climbed the stairs to Gloria and Joseph's apartment. Before he reached the door, his nose became excited with the aroma of garlic and basil. He began to salivate like a college student who hadn't eaten in days. Gloria answered the door and welcomed him into their small but charming apartment.

"We're running a little late. I was hoping you might be willing to busy yourself deciphering some of those Latin flower names while we finish up in the kitchen."

"Sure," he said.

She led him to the table where the handwritten list of Latin names sat next to a worn-out field book. He flipped it open to find its pages filled with photographs and descriptions of flowers.

"We'll be finished in about ten minutes," she said, leaving him to the task.

He had found the first two flowers on the list when he thought how easy this would be on the internet. He looked around, but saw no evidence of a computer, so he got back to work the old fashioned way.

Gloria returned ten minutes later carrying a ceramic bowl filled with pasta and another filled with red sauce. "I hope you're hungry. Joseph is half Italian and loves to cook."

Joseph followed a few moments later carrying a plate filled with huge slices of garlic bread and a bowl overflowing with green salad. Gloria thanked Jake for his work deciphering the code, and took the book and paper from him.

Joseph offered a blessing on the food. As he listened to the words, Jake was surprised to feel an emotion swell within him that he hadn't felt since his mother's death. He felt warm and welcomed, but it was more than that. He felt loved. Jake didn't hear the rest of the words of the prayer, but he felt the spirit with which they were spoken and he had to swallow to keep his emotions from coming to the surface.

"Amen," said Gloria. She winked at Jake as she reached for the salad tongs, serving him a generous portion.

"Do you have any children?" asked Jake, wanting to make friendly conversation.

Gloria looked at Joseph. "The Good Lord didn't bless us with any children," he said.

Jake was just about to feel sorry for asking when Gloria smiled at him in her kind and gentle way. "We just got back from visiting family in Tuscany for our thirty-fifth anniversary," she said. "We're old enough to be grandparents, but life doesn't always turn out the way you plan."

As they ate their salad, Joseph and Gloria asked Jake questions about himself. He told them about his mother, learning to make pottery, earning a scholarship and his studies in Albany. Gloria and Joseph seemed genuinely interested and Jake basked in their warmth and acceptance.

By the time they got around to serving the pasta, Joseph discovered it was cold. He excused himself and took the bowl back to the kitchen to reheat it. When he returned a few minutes later, Gloria and Jake were looking through a picture album. They laughed together out loud as they turned to a picture of the younger couple dressed as hippies.

"Was this Halloween?" asked Jake

Gloria looked up at Joseph and the two of them laughed out loud.

"No," she said, looking serious, "That's what we wore every day."

Jake looked at the corner of the grainy color photo. Orange digital numbers looked like they were burned onto the photo. 8, 19, 1969

"You mean you were real hippies?" he asked, looking up to meet their eyes.

"Hey, hey," responded Joseph, "Once you're a hippy, you're always a hippy. There are no has-beens in this family."

Gloria flipped forward a few pages and pointed to a couple of ticket stubs, preserved under the thin plastic cover.

Jake looked at the tickets and slowly raised his head as a smile spread across his lips.

"You guys went to Woodstock?"

Joseph nodded. "That's where we met. Where else could a guy from Pittsburgh and a girl from Ft. Lauderdale meet and fall in love? We were from opposite ends of the universe, but music and idealism brought us together with five hundred thousand of our closest friends."

Jake was amazed. "You mean to tell me you saw the Grateful Dead at Woodstock?"

"Yeah, and Jimmy Hendrix, Janis Joplin, Joan Baez, Jefferson Airplane, Crosby, Stills and Nash, CCR and a whole bunch of other cool guys too," reported Joseph. "It was an amazing weekend."

Jake looked at them with new respect. "Just seeing all those legendary bands is cool enough, but knowing that you ended the summer of love at Woodstock, fell in love with each other, and are still together today is incredible."

Gloria and Joseph looked at each other and smiled.

Joseph returned to the kitchen and came back carrying the bowl of pasta. He set it in the middle of the table and served everyone huge portions before taking his seat.

Jake continued to ask questions as they ate. He learned that they met on Friday, the opening night of Woodstock, when Joseph stopped his Volkswagen bus and picked up Gloria and her girlfriend who had hitchhiked all the way to Bethel and were walking their way out to the farm where the concert was staged. They spent the weekend together and then kept in touch after returning home.

Joseph finished his degree in English and Gloria studied the humanities and botany. They wrote to each other often over the course of the next few years, and finally Joseph got the nerve to drive down to Fort Lauderdale and see what would happen if they were in the same place. Within a week, they eloped to Atlanta and then just kept driving north, looking for the ideal place to settle down and raise kids.

Gloria pointed to a photo of them on the wall. They both had long hair, Gloria's flowing down to her waist and laced with ribbons and flowers. She also wore a crown of flowers on her head. Joseph was dressed in an awful sky blue, three-piece suit with butterfly collars and a huge belly-warmer tie. His sideburns were sculpted into lamb chops.

"We didn't know any better back then," said Joseph, laughing.

"When we stumbled upon Niederbipp, we fell in love with the town," continued Gloria. "We thought it would be a wonderful place to raise a family. We both got jobs and rented a little apartment and started putting down some roots. A year later, space became available on Hauptstrasse, so we gathered our money together and opened a flower shop. We were ignorant and crazy," she said, smiling at Joseph, "but somehow it all worked out. We had never really done flower arranging before, other than the stuff that most hippies did, but we were both creative and fortunately, people liked what we were doing. In the beginning, we picked as many of the flowers as we could in the hills and the forests so we could save money. Later we developed relationships with growers and greenhouses. We read a lot of books and spent a lot of time practicing and our business began to grow."

"You make it sound easy," said Joseph, as he listened. "The fact is, we nearly starved to death, but we were happy and we made it through the lean times together."

Gloria turned to Jake and smiled. "We've probably bored you to death."

"No, not at all," he responded. "I've never met real hippies before."

Joseph stood and gathered up the plates, taking them to the kitchen. He returned with three plates of strawberry shortcake topped with whipped cream.

"So, Sam tells us you're not so sure if this is the right place for you."

Jake looked up surprised. "It sounds like word travels fast in this town. Have you also heard from Albert and Brian?"

"Would it make any difference if we had?" asked Gloria, innocently.
"Probably not."

"Then the answer is yes. We've heard from a lot of folks in the twenty-four hours since we've been home. You ought to be aware that we're all somehow interconnected. Word tends to travel very fast. We've heard that you like Sam's sunflower bread and that several ladies from church have tried to line you up with their granddaughters. We've heard that you were planning on spending the summer abroad, but agreed to give us a try until the end of the summer. We've heard that you keep to yourself in the evenings and go to bed early. Oh, and Albert dropped by this morning to invite us to stop by and visit you. Did we miss anything?" asked Gloria, grinning at Jake.

Jake pursed his lips and shook his head. "I'm not sure I like people knowing so much about my life."

"We didn't either at first," said Joseph, "but when you're new in a small town like Niederbipp, people tend to know your business. We know how weird it is at first, but we've come to appreciate it for what it is. Because I'm Italian and have a big family, it was a little easier for me to get used to than it was for Gloria. There isn't much privacy, but we all look out for each other. I don't think you should be surprised if you start getting a lot of folks showing up to try to talk you into staying. We've heard the Mayor is bent on making sure you decide to stay."

Jake shook his head. "This is starting to sound like the Twilight Zone. Am I going to be able to leave if I want to?"

"It's not like that," said Joseph. "The doors are always open. We just don't have many young people settling down here anymore. That's troubling for the old timers who see the population falling every year. If it weren't for the tourists, our economy would fall apart. Folks are already suggesting that this summer's gas prices are going to put a damper on the tourist season. Bookings at the B&Bs are down and the whole town is worried that more and more of our young people are leaving for college and not coming back. You should know that you are an answer to a lot of prayers. We all hope that you'll decide to stay."

Jake looked thoughtful. "It almost sounds like if I stay, I'll be hitching myself to a sinking ship. That doesn't sound very attractive."

"Joseph made it sound a lot worse than it is. Business is down everywhere. It's going to get worse before it gets better. Many of us haven't even felt the effects of the economic slowdown yet. I, for one, am optimistic. Most of the businesses here are owned free and clear. If you ask me, your position couldn't be better. Your shop has great local support and a 300-year-old reputation. I have no doubt that you'll be able to make it and I haven't even seen your work yet."

Jake turned to his shortcake. It was more honesty than he had heard from anyone and it was both worrisome and refreshing. As they ate dessert, Gloria asked Jake what he thought of the shop and the town. Gloria and Joseph's honesty opened the door for Jake to share his feelings with someone other than his journal. As he opened his mouth, he was surprised by the relief it gave him. Another hour passed as he talked about the good, the bad, and the ugly happenings of his two weeks in Niederbipp.

Before he left, his burden had been lifted and he felt free. Gloria asked if she could stop by in the next few days to at least wipe the dust off her mug so Albert would know she had done what he asked her to do. Both Joseph and Gloria thanked Jake for coming and invited him to drop by any time if he needed to vent or had any questions.

As Jake walked back to his apartment he heard it for the first time since his arrival in Niederbipp; crickets singing on the evening breeze.

20
HELP

"Aren't you the woman from the library?" Jake asked. The woman had obviously been waiting for Jake to open the door when he got to the shop Tuesday morning.

"That's right," said the woman, as she walked through the door Jake held open for her. "How did you know?"

"I stopped in to use your computer last week."

The woman pushed her cat-eye glasses higher onto her nose and took a closer look at Jake. "Nope, can't say I've seen you before."

Jake looked away, trying not to laugh. "What can I help you with this morning?"

"I'm here because I need your help." She set her teal purse on the counter and turned to Jake with a big smile. Her lipstick was heavily smeared on her front teeth, as if she had entirely missed her lips. Jake had to bite his cheek to keep from smiling.

"What can I do for you?" he repeated.

"It's actually not for me, it's for my brother, Lamar."

Jake moved to the other side of the counter and pulled out the order book, flipping to a new page. He looked up, ready to take notes.

"You're the new potter, I presume."

"That's right, my name's Jake"

"Then Jake, I need your help. I have a very strange brother and I think you may be the only one in town who can help him. He was friends with Isaac and Isaac was the only one who was ever able to get through to him. You're a potter too and I think you probably have what it takes to help him."

"Uh huh," said Jake, wondering what could be coming.

"He's obsessed with opening another museum. He already went through *his* inheritance with the first museum and now he wants *mine*. I won't let him have it. Isaac always calmed him down, but since Isaac died, Lamar has been obsessed with resurrecting the museum. It's crazy, I tell you. No one came to the first museum and no one will come to this one either."

"What kind of museum is it?"

She took a deep breath and shook her head. "It's a museum dedicated to the preservation and cataloging of over 1000 rare and historic pudding molds."

Jake tried to hold back the smile, but lost. "This wouldn't be that strange fellow from the library would it?"

"You know him?"

"Uh, no, not really, but I think I might have seen him working on the computer when I was there the other day."

She slid her glasses higher onto her nose and took another look at Jake. "So are you going to help me or not?"

Jake looked at her, trying to figure her out. "I'm just wondering why anyone would want to pay money to see a collection like that."

"My point exactly, Jake. My point exactly."

"Why did the last one fail?"

"It depends on who you ask. Lamar's convinced that the location was all wrong. He set it up on the outskirts of town, out by the Bungee-Bipp. After Mom died, the trust was divided. I got the house and Lamar got the Bungee-Bipp along with the museum. Since the fire, he's been obsessed with moving the museum into old town. He believes the tourists will flock to see it if he can find a place on Hauptstrasse."

Jake shook his head, bewildered. "And what is it you want me to do?"

"Well, stop him of course," she said with a shrill voice. "He's crazy and it will bring nothing but suffering to all of us!"

WHY SHOULD I CARE?

"I'm afraid I don't understand," he said. "Did Albert send you?"

"Albert Who? What are you talking about? No one sent me. I'm here because I need your help. Aren't you a potter?"

Jake took a deep breath. "I am a potter, but I'm not sure what that has to do with anything. I don't know how I can keep your brother from opening a museum. Aren't there professionals who deal with this kind of stuff in Niederbipp?"

"Apparently not anymore!" the woman said loudly. She picked up her purse and huffed to the door. "Thanks for nothing!" she shouted, stomping out of the Pottery and hurrying down the street.

Jake shook his head and started to laugh. He wondered if this might be one of the things Thomas was talking about when he suggested he would be happy to help if Jake ran into any trouble.

Jake turned his attention to the studio. There was enough bisqueware to fill another glaze firing and the planters he promised Mrs. Pfeiffer needed to be glazed. He pulled out all of the glaze buckets, arranging them on the tables, the wheel, and the chairs, trying to make the most of the cramped space. He dropped a CD into the player and got to work glazing the planters.

Jake didn't hear the door open. The music was loud and his mind was occupied with his work and the crazy woman's visit. He was dancing to the music when he turned to see Thomas watching him with a smile on his face.

"Whoa," said Jake, stopping to look at Thomas. He felt his face flush as he moved to the boom box to turn down the music. "I didn't hear you come in," he said, feeling foolish.

Thomas didn't try to subdue his smile. "I'm glad to see it. Dancing is good for the soul and I'm guessing that means you're in good spirits, despite your crazy visit this morning."

Jake looked at the clock on the wall. It had been less than an hour since the woman left. "Word travels quickly," he said, recalling his impression from the night before that this town might be part of the Twilight Zone.

"Faster than you think. I wanted to come sooner, but I had to finish my work at the bakery. Sam sends his greetings and his pastries." He tossed Jake a brown paper sack. "I help Sam in the bakery several days a week and I was there when Roberta came in calling you a fraud and an impostor."

"Roberta," Jake repeated. "I guess I never got around to asking her name."

Father Thomas continued, "I suppose I should have warned you about the Mancini twins, but I came to try to put out any fires. I worried that you might be packing your bags, but from the looks of your dancing, it doesn't look like she ruffled your feathers too badly."

Jake smiled and shook his head. "I think I have thicker skin than that, but I'm glad you're here. I do have a lot of questions. What was that this morning?"

Thomas moved into the studio. "I don't suppose you have another cup of tea in that tea pot, do you?" he asked, pointing to the tea pot on the counter.

"Sure, but it's not very warm anymore."

"That's fine," said Thomas, plucking a red mug from the overhead beam. "When you're in a dry village, tea is the next best thing. I've often wondered if there isn't some kind of drug in Isaac's tea that helps calm my nerves."

Jake emptied the contents of the teapot into the mug while Thomas unfolded a chair from the stack against the wall. He sat down and took a long drink before he spoke again.

"At times like this, I'm glad I can't just drop by the grocery store and pick up a bottle of Jack. I used to deal with stress by checking out for a couple of days. This town has saved me in many respects."

Thomas's words surprised Jake, coming from a priest. He wondered what Thomas had been like before his ordination, he hoped he would confide in him sometime.

"It really wasn't that bad," said Jake, reassuring him. "I've laughed it off, but it's left me wondering what it was all about."

"That," said Thomas, "is an example of Isaac's good intentions gone bad." He shook his head. "Most of the time, the things Isaac did for people really helped. You've already had visits from some of those folks, but not all of his council and wisdom fell on equally capable ears. He tried to save everybody from themselves, but sometimes it just didn't work, no matter how hard he tried. The Mancinis are good examples of the latter."

Jake laughed and shook his head. "So, what happened?"

"How much time do you have?"

"I was just glazing. I have as much time as you need."

Thomas took a deep breath and mopped his brow again before looking up at Jake. "There is a lot of history here. The Mancini brothers came from Italy back in the twenties. Guido opened the Ice Café and Roberto opened a butcher shop. They both married women from the village and their businesses thrived. Roberto died early, leaving behind a wife and two young kids, twins—Lamar and Roberta. Apparently you've met them both."

Jake nodded and smiled.

"Well, Roberto's wife got a lucky break and sold the ancestral pepperoni recipes to some businessmen in Philadelphia, setting her up for life. The kids were in their early twenties when Isaac arrived in town. Lamar used to follow Isaac around, trying to learn about life in a big city. After losing her husband, the twins' mother kept the kids on a pretty short leash. They had never been out of the county and Lamar was itching to see the world beyond the river. Soon after, Lamar asked for his inheritance and wandered off to Philadelphia or somewhere to seek his fame and fortune. He wasn't heard of for nearly forty years.

"Rita, the twins' mother, blamed Isaac for her son's disappearance and Isaac spent the next forty years trying to make it up to her. He even spent a lot of his own money trying to track Lamar down. Over time, the ice melted and Rita and Isaac became friends.

"When she saw what Brian did with his life, Rita started asking Isaac for advice. I'm sure the advice he gave her was the same advice he gave Brian, but the outcome was quite different. Because of her pain at losing her son to the city, Rita decided to spend her fortune on developing opportunities for the youth of Niederbipp, hoping to keep them around. Her first 'philanthropic venture' was Rita's Bungee-Bipp. Kids came from all over Pennsylvania to jump off the tower. She was so pleased with herself that she took the money from that venture and dumped it into the new Rita and Roberta Mancini wing of the Niederbipp library. Roberta chipped in too, gifting her collection of some five-hundred books, mostly steamy romance novels. Rita's endowment stipulated that Roberta be named head librarian and hold the post for as long as she could manage."

Jake started laughing, remembering his first encounter with her.

"With that, Rita ran out of ideas, so she opened a competition. She invited the young people to come up with ideas for how they could improve their town. Grants were given to the ideas she and Roberta deemed most worthy. From this, the Dairy Freeze opened next to the Bungee-Bipp. One young man was awarded a suitcase full of money to open a fishing pond on the far end of town. My favorite, though, was a farm for abused and neglected snails. You can still see the bumper stickers on some of the older cars around town. The "Save The Snails" campaign helped put Niederbipp on the map and people from all over Pennsylvania drove to the farm to drop off their snails."

Jake looked up from his work, wondering if Thomas was joking, but Thomas continued without flinching.

"For a while, things really picked up in Niederbipp. Traffic increased and some of our young people made plans to stay. After a couple of years, Lamar the prodigal son, returned. He coasted into town completely broke, driving a U-Haul filled with his collection of pudding molds. Rita, who was in very poor health by that time, was overjoyed. She divided her estate, leaving the house and most of the money to Roberta and the Bungee-Bipp and the small house next to it to Lamar.

"Rita died about two weeks later and the sibling rivalry kicked into full swing. Lamar opened the museum shortly after that. He built onto the side of his home and he spent every dime he inherited on its construction. The house caught fire a few months later, damaging many of the molds and forcing Lamar to move in with his sister. The Bungee-Bipp went out of business not long after that because of poor management and employee embezzlement. With no traffic at the Bipp, the Dairy Freeze failed shortly after that.

"Isaac spent a lot of time with Lamar, trying to help him figure out his life, but he couldn't be helped. One night, he invited Lamar to join us for a swim at the river. While we were swimming, Lamar lost his most valuable pudding mold when the string that kept it around his neck broke. He was furious and threatened to sue all of us."

"For what?"

"Oh, don't ask. It started out with a charge of reckless endangerment, but when his attorneys got more information and found out he was broke, they dropped him. Roberta insists that her brother's collection is cursed. He insists that she's a witch. They're probably both right. For the past ten years, they've lived in the same house, but pretend they don't even know each other."

Jake nodded, remembering their interaction with each other at the library. "So what does all of this have to do with me?"

Thomas shook his head and looked like he was ready to spit. "I thought all of this was over, but apparently Lamar still blames Isaac for the lost pudding mold. He's been threatening to sue so he can get enough money to dredge the river and find his silly mold."

Jake started laughing. "How long has this been going on?"

"The mold was lost ten years ago."

Jake shook his head. "What's so special about it?"

Thomas threw up his hands. "Apparently it's worth more than the rest of his collection combined. After the fire gutted his house, he started wearing the mold around his neck. It was supposed to be the last remaining mold of only six molds made for King Henry the IX. The legendary German Potter who made it was famous for his decoration and even his smallest pieces are now fetching thousands at the auction houses in London and New York."

"How much was it supposed to be worth?"

"Well, because it appeared in a portrait with the young prince, it's said to be worth ten thousand dollars or more."

"Why doesn't his sister just pay him off?"

"She's already tried that. He has this crazy idea that he could make that much money in a month if he could get the museum open and have the King's pudding mold as the crown jewel of the collection. He insists that the museum will be the beacon of hope for Niederbipp, bringing tourists from all over the world. Roberta believes that if the museum is ever built, the curse of the molds will turn on the city and burn it down."

Jake looked at Thomas and both men began to laugh.

"I'm relieved that you think this is funny. I'm sure you haven't heard the end of it."

Jake continued to laugh. "I was just beginning to think this town was a little dull, but I have to admit this is really funny."

"Oh, really? Try living with it for a decade. I don't think it was very funny for Isaac. And Albert is having a fit. He's afraid the Mancinis are going to chase you off. He's down at the bakery right now finishing up my work so I could come talk to you. You should know that half the town has probably heard about this by now. I wouldn't be surprised if you get a lot of visits in the next few days. People want to keep you here, Jake. They haven't even seen your work yet, but they know our town needs a potter. I know it puts a lot of pressure on you, but most of the older folks considered Isaac the resident guru. I wanted to tell you about this earlier, but the others didn't want to scare you away."

"So what am I supposed to do? I'm anything but a guru."

Thomas looked at Jake and shook his head. "I wish I had an easy answer for you. People are already impressed though. We've already heard that folks are happy with the decision we made. People come to the Pottery because they want to connect with another human. If they can see a magic show while they're here then it's even better. I'm not sure if it's the tea, the Pottery, or witnessing creation, but people open up. They start talking. They bare their souls. I was always amazed at the changes I saw in people after they visited Isaac. He had a pocketful of true wisdom that he shared, but he always insisted that giving folks a chance to talk helped them figure things out. I don't know if he was a guru, but he sure helped a lot of folks work through their issues. I don't know where I'd be without him.

"Jake, we know you're not Isaac, but I want you to know you have my trust and I've been praying for you since I met you. I need to get back to the bakery now, but I'll be back. Thanks for not flipping out about Roberta." He stood and hung his mug back on the nail.

"Father, don't worry about me," said Jake with a broad smile. "I feel better about Niederbipp today than I ever have. My mom always said that it's the quirks that make a person endearing. Maybe the same is true about a town."

"God bless you, Jake. If you're looking for quirks, we've got more than our share. I just hope we're not wearing you out."

"Forget it. I'm fine. But maybe you could drop by every few days. I'm sure I'll have more questions."

"I will," said Thomas, a smile returning to his face.

Jake spent the rest of the afternoon trying to glaze. As predicted, lots of folks dropped in for a visit, but most of them stayed only long enough to interrupt the work.

Albert stopped by shortly after Thomas left and invited Jake to dinner. Their collection of pottery was impressive, but it was Lin's cooking that most delighted Jake. A cordial conversation followed and Jake was on his way out when their daughter, Alice, dropped by for a "surprise visit." It quickly became apparent that she had heard about Jake and would have made it for dinner if it weren't for the traffic accident on her way out of State College. Alice was beautiful and Jake was charmed by her modest

and gentle nature. He learned that she was an English major at Penn State, with a minor in modern dance. By the time he left at midnight, Jake hoped he would see her again.

NOTE TO SELF - CLOSE SKETCH BOOK WHILE GLAZING!

21

THE APPLEMAN'S TALE

Jake warmed himself in front of the kiln on Wednesday morning, recording his thoughts of the previous day. It was still before opening time, so he was surprised when he heard the front door open. Reluctantly he stood, wishing he would have kept the door locked until he had at least finished his writing.

"Good morning," he hollered over the counter, not yet able to see whoever it was who had entered the showroom.

"Good morning," came the reply, a friendly male voice.

"I'm just finishing something," responded Jake. "Please let me know if I can help you."

A few seconds later, a familiar face appeared over the counter. Jake looked up to see the man watching him.

"Oh, hello."

"Good morning, Jake. Do you remember me?"

"Sure, you're the Apple Man."

He smiled, showing off his gleaming white teeth. "That's right, but most people just call me Josh."

He was dressed in a simple flannel shirt with wide elastic suspenders, but it was his face that intrigued Jake most. He was the picture of happiness, with plump healthy cheeks, rosy from sunburn that made his bright green eyes glow. His graying hair stuck out in tufts from the sides of his straw hat. His smile seemed to fill his whole face and Jake found it was contagious.

Josh lifted a brown sack from Sam's bakery. "My wife usually brings the kids to school," he said as he moved around the counter, "but I had a couple of errands to run so I told her I'd take them today. I didn't figure on most of the shops being closed until later. I'm glad you were open. I picked us up some pastries and hoped I could blow some time with you and take you up on that cup of tea."

"Sure," said Jake, closing his book and getting to his feet. He was tired from the late night and knew he ought to be getting some work done, but he set his agenda aside and made a pot of tea. He turned to see Josh standing on his tiptoes, straining to reach a dusty gray-blue mug hanging from the overhead beam.

As Jake rinsed the mug, Josh explained that he had been busy with the orchard and hadn't been in for a visit since Christmas. Josh opened the paper bag to reveal two miniature apple pies, offering one to Jake.

"I haven't tried these yet," Jake said as he took his first bite.

Josh waited until he had swallowed before he began to explain. "The pastry is Sam's, but the apples are mine. I just delivered some apple pie filling to Sam this morning. He's one of my best customers." With that, he took a big bite of his own miniature pie. They ate in silence, except for the sounds of chomping and slurping and licking of fingers.

"So, rumor has it you're getting to know some of the more colorful characters in Niederbipp," said Josh, once he had finished his treat. "We miss out on most of the gossip since we live outside of town, but my wife came home from picking up the kids from school yesterday and told me you've been having some trouble."

"What'd she say?" asked Jake, curious what was being spread.

"Just that Roberta Mancini pulled her nunchucks out of her purse and hit you over the noggin."

Jake broke into laughter. "Are you serious?"

"No," said Josh, laughing.

"But that's what I told the kids. I don't like them getting too close to the Mancinis. They're scary."

"Oh, they're probably more bark than bite," said Jake, playing it tough.

"You might be right, but some folks in town say that returning an overdue book to the library is more painful than a root canal. The kids talk about the torture devices she keeps behind her desk and uses to subdue anyone who is speaking too loudly in the library. I heard Father Thomas has to work there just to keep the peace. We only let the kids go to the library on Thursdays. That's Roberta's day off."

Jake wasn't sure what to think, but he knew there was truth to at least some of it.

"You seem to know a lot about this town. I'm guessing you grew up here?"

"Not even close. I'm from Chicago."

"That must have been a big change, coming from a city of millions to a small town."

"That's an understatement, but it's been a good change. I went from not even knowing the names of my neighbors to knowing what they're eating for breakfast. And our closest neighbor is more than a mile away."

Jake didn't doubt it, considering how fast word travels.

"Yeah, I'm not even sure why we have telephones in this town. Everybody has their own little bird telling 'em something," said Josh.

"So what brought you to Niederbipp?"

"The train," said Josh, laughing at his own dumb joke. "No, but seriously, it was the train. I needed a place to hide out for a while and when the train stopped here, I got off."

"Were you a bank robber?" asked Jake, playing off Josh's playful nature.

"I'm not sure you could get any closer than that. I used to be a stock broker, a hundred years ago. I made some foolish decisions because of greed and pride and lost everything: my home, my business, my health and nearly my life. It was Isaac who reached out and slapped some sense into me. I didn't come to tell you my story. I'm sure you're probably getting sick of hearing from so many people about the things Isaac did."

"No, not yet. I've actually kind of enjoyed hearing about him. Since I never knew him, it's helped me to figure out who he was. He must have been a pretty amazing guy."

"Yeah…, but you never would have known it just by looking at him. I think a lot of us have learned to look at other folks a bit differently. I know I always wonder if there's an Isaac inside the strangers I meet, especially those whose hands are always dirty and clothes are a little grubby. I might have been dead if my 'rock bottom' had been somewhere else. Fortunately, it happened to be the back porch right out there," he said, pointing to the back door. "I passed out, drunker than a skunk and would have died that night if Isaac hadn't found me and pulled me in, out of the cold.

"I wish I could say I had the sense to choose Niederbipp, but the truth is I was thrown off the train that night for being drunk and harassing the ladies. The next thing I remember is waking up the next day on this floor in so much pain I wished I was dead. That's when the butt kicking began."

"Isaac kicked you?"

"No, not exactly. He just put me on his old bike and sent me to work on Patrick Jacobs' farm, picking apples. It's unfortunate that most people have to be compelled to be humble before they want anything to do with God. For me, I had always believed that things of a spiritual nature were for the weak and poor. When I became both, my heart was finally soft enough to feel God's love. I'm not sure anyone can fully appreciate the grace of God until he knows he needs it.

"Over the next few months, Isaac taught me pure religion by example.

He fed me, clothed me, and let me use his second bedroom. He definitely taught me some great lessons, but more importantly, he helped me find the place where the universe could teach me."

"You're talking about Niederbipp?"

"Yes, but more specifically, the farm. I know I don't need to tell you, Jake, that there are things you can learn from hard work that you can't learn any other way. Shortly after I arrived, I traded in an expensive watch, the last clue of who I had been, for the down payment on my farm and got to work. From the beginning, I applied the principles Isaac taught me about tithing. During my frequent visits with Isaac, he helped me to recognize that God was shaping my life in the same way a potter shapes the clay.

"I often think about Patrick Jacobs, the old bachelor farmer. He'd been farming apples for close to seventy years when I bought his farm. He'd lived in the same house his whole life and was so stuck in the traditions he learned from his parents that he never tried doing anything new. Shortly after I bought the farm, I made a juice press. A freezer opened up more possibilities. I also became a bee keeper to increase my yield. My life and my work has not been easy, but I'm grateful to Isaac for teaching me to open my eyes, my mind, and my heart. I have learned over the years from my own experience and from watching others that God can make a heck of a lot more out of our lives if we're willing to be shaped."

Jake nodded thoughtfully. "I guess I've never really thought about it that way. There are probably lots of similarities to life and clay. I could probably come up with a few right now."

"And you're not even married yet," said Josh, with a wink. "Marriage shapes you up and throws you in the kiln. It's kind of a refiner's fire. It took me a long time to feel like I was worthy of a woman. Sometimes I still wonder if I'm worthy of the love of my wife. She picked up where Isaac left off in helping me become a better man."

The cell phone on Josh's belt rang and he asked Jake to excuse him while he took the call. Jake laughed as he extended the giant antenna and still had to speak loudly.

"Good morning, Beverly."

Jake's ears perked up.

"No, I'm here in town. Jeni is at home, but I know why she called. She's been trying to line her little brother up with your niece."

Jake could hear the excited voice blare from the speaker on Josh's phone. He recognized Beverly's voice and he knew what that meant. Josh was trying to line up his brother-in-law with Amy. He was surprised by the tension he felt as he continued to listen.

"Yes, I think Saturday night would be fine. I know he works until five, but I'm sure six-o-clock would work. I'll have him call tonight with the details...Sure...I will... Thank you."

Jake couldn't believe it.

"Sorry about that," said Josh, looking at the phone as he closed it. "I didn't realize it was so late. I need to get going, but I had another reason to stop by this morning. Isaac and I have traded honey for honey jars for many years now. I sell the jars in my farm store. Do you think you could whip up a couple dozen for us?"

"I think I can do that."

"Great! In exchange, I've been giving Isaac five gallons of honey in the fall. Do you think that's enough?"

Jake nodded in agreement.

"Very good," said Josh, getting to his feet. "If you don't mind, I'll stop by for some more tea from time to time and to check up on you."

"Sure," he said, extending his dusty hand to Josh.

Jake walked Josh to the door and said goodbye. He watched him walk back to Hauptstrasse, trying to figure out what he was feeling.

He went back to the studio to check on the kiln. It was already close to a thousand degrees. He sat back down on the stool near the kiln and picked up writing where he had left off. Jake had written only a couple of sentences when he leaned his head back and yelled. "Arghhhhh." He knew he had no claim to Amy. They had spent an afternoon together. Just one afternoon. He couldn't be jealous of someone else spending time with her, but he was. He was angry and he was jealous. He was angry at himself that he hadn't asked more questions and found out where Amy worked. He was angry at Josh for lining up his dumb brother-in-law. He was jealous of that dumb brother-in-law, whoever he was.

Jake wrote down what he was feeling and then read it to himself. It made him even angrier until he read what he had written before Josh arrived. He had written about his interest in Alice. He asked himself if he would feel the same way if Josh had lined Alice up with his brother-in-law. It took him less than a second to answer. No! He wouldn't. This was different.

He considered running up to the barber shop, learning where Amy worked, finding her and asking her for a date on Saturday night. He closed his eyes and shook his head, trying to be rational. One afternoon... one stinkin', glorious, wonderful, amazing afternoon. He was ruined. He closed his sketchbook, tying the leather thong around the pewter button much tighter than was necessary. He tossed the book on the table and grabbed a bag of clay.

ONE EYED GIRL

22
THE HEARTMAKER'S TALE

"Sam sends his greetings and bread," said Gloria, pulling a brown sack from her basket. "I just heard about yesterday. I thought I'd come and check on you."

The studio was filled with ware boards, covered with bowls, mugs, and vases in various stages of dampness. Gloria walked through the studio, leaving her basket on the counter. She turned and looked at Jake who seemed concentrated on his work at the wheel.

"It looks like you've had a busy morning," she said, looking at all the fresh pots.

Jake grunted, but didn't look up from his work.

"Are you alright?"

"No, I'm mad."

"Why? What's going on?"

Jake remained silent, looking for the right words. "It's nothing. I'm just stupid."

When he finally looked up at Gloria, she was smiling at him. She leaned against the table, her arms crossed, waiting.

"What?" he asked, smiling in spite of his frustration.

"She's really not worth it, you know."

"I know. I don't even know her. I'm just bugged that I'm such a social misfit. I don't have a clue about how I should respond to any of this."

"Jake, don't be so hard on yourself. If you don't think something is wrong with her, just talk to anyone. She's a really tough nut."

Jake looked up, his brow furrowed. "Who are you talking about?"

"Roberta Mancini," Gloria said, looking lost. "Who are you talking about?"

Jake started laughing. "I was talking about Amy. Beverly and Jerry's niece."

Gloria shook her head and started laughing too. "After hearing about what happened yesterday, I thought you must still be upset about Roberta."

"Are you kidding? I think she's crazy, but she really didn't bother me."

"So what's this about Amy?"

"Do you know her?"

"No, but I know *of* her. Joseph got his hair cut yesterday and said he heard that Jerry's niece is in town for the summer and that boys have been lining up to try to get a date with her. What does she have to do with you being upset?"

Jake felt his face flush. He wasn't sure if he was embarrassed or just angrier with himself for caring about Amy. "I just met her at church on Sunday. Beverly invited me to join them for a picnic that afternoon and...."

"And what?" asked Gloria, with a wink that caused Jake's face to flush again.

"And I'm an idiot. I had a really good time, but it seems pretty obvious that I'm the only one who did."

"Why do you say that?"

"Because I'm still thinking about her and she's running around with all the other guys in town."

Gloria shook her head and laughed out loud. "Jake, we've been out of the country for the last two weeks so I'm sure I missed some good gossip about you, but since we've been home I've heard that you've been lined up with a half a dozen girls."

"You can't be serious. I don't have anything in common with any of those girls except that we were born in the same decade. I just got lined up for dinner and probably never would have gone if the dinner wasn't included."

"That's not what I heard about Alice. I understand you two got along quite well."

Jake let out a long breath. "What is it about this town? I can't do anything without everyone knowing about it."

"Sounds like you're skirting the question, if you ask me."

Jake looked up at Gloria who was smiling broadly.

"Jake, I've been in this town long enough to know that anytime a new single person moves in, they get lined up with everyone available. I used to wonder if it was done in an effort to expand the gene pool, but you need to remember that this is a small, friendly town. Kids like to date here as much as they do anywhere. The problem is, when you grow up in a small town, everybody knows the dirt on everyone else. There aren't any surprises. When someone new comes to town, they stick out. Everyone wants to figure them out. Beverly's niece is probably going through the same frustrations you are. No one knows you, but you're single and have a pulse, therefore you qualify to date just about anyone."

Jake shook his head. "Maybe you're right."

"I know I am. You better knock this off before you pot yourself out of the studio. You're already going to be up 'til midnight trimming," she said looking around at all the pots he had made.

Jake followed her eyes over the pots, letting go of another long breath. "This is how I cope with things I can't handle. I go on a throwing binge. It's probably a good thing you stopped by."

Gloria smiled at Jake and let out a little laugh. "Isaac was the same way. Whenever he got stuck on a problem, he'd get busy making pots and soon they were spilling out the back door."

"Did that happen often?"

"Oh, probably once a month. He was always thinking about something and throwing on the wheel helped him work his way through it."

"It sounds like you spent a lot of time here."

"I did. I guess that's why he gave me my own mug," she said, looking up at the mugs. "While I'm here, I probably ought to dust it off so Albert knows I was here." She walked to the mugs and plucked hers from the nail.

Jake looked at the mug. It was cobalt blue. "Can I see it?" he asked, wiping his hands on his apron.

She handed it to him. He looked it over and was handing it back to her when he noticed a heart under the handle. "I haven't noticed that on any of the other mugs."

Gloria pursed her lips. "I think this is a one of a kind. I used to make the hearts Isaac used when he wrapped gifts."

"Are you talking about those bisque fired hearts in the jar on the counter?"

"Yeah.

"Why did you make them? Did you work here?"

"Kind of. I've probably made thousands of hearts over the years."

"Yeah, I just found four big bottles of them down in the cellar last week. I was wondering why he had so many."

Gloria laughed, shaking her head. "I knew there had to be more of them around here. I think he must have hid them away to keep me coming back."

Jake looked at her, wondering what she was talking about.

"Jake, like most of the folks that have visited you in the last two weeks, this was a special place for me. This was the place where my healing began..." Gloria smiled sadly ... "where I first felt the sun breaking through the clouds of sorrow. We told you the other night that we didn't have any children. The truth runs a little deeper than that. I was pregnant four times. Three of those ended in miscarriages. The fourth ended in our son being stillborn. I fell into a funk that lasted several years."

"It's hard to believe that you could have ever been depressed," Jake said, trying to lighten the sudden seriousness. "You seem to radiate happiness."

"Thank you. I hope I do. I *am* happy. I still get caught up in wondering sometimes what might have been. I can't think of anything more difficult than delivering a baby and coming home empty handed. Time has healed some wounds, but I think the pain will always be there. Isaac helped me understand that my life needs to go on."

"How did he do that? Thomas told me that a lot of folks believe Isaac was some sort of guru. I wouldn't have the slightest idea what to tell someone who was dealing with the same sorrow you were."

"A guru is something Isaac would never have considered himself to be. And maybe that's why his words had power....he was humble. He listened to people and, instead of putting a bandage on top of a sliver, he helped them remove the sliver and then applied the balm they needed."

"But how did he know how to do that? I could never just go up to a total stranger and say, 'Oh, you've got a big problem. I know how to fix you!' I'm just a kid with my own issues. I don't even know how to ask a girl out. I feel like folks expect me to know something, expect me to have some sort of magical powers, to be able to read their souls and know what they need."

"Jake, that is your greatest asset."

"What, my ignorance?"

"No, your humility. Isaac came to Niederbipp not much different than you. Time and experience teaches some lessons, but not all of them. The thing that gave Isaac's words power was his humility. He knew pain, loss, and sorrow and he wanted to help others through it. He wanted to love the way God loved. He looked beyond a person's problem and into their heart."

"How do you do that? I don't even know what's in my own heart sometimes. How am I supposed to see into others?"

Gloria smiled. "You listen, you watch, and you pray like crazy. People are complicated. Sometimes it requires all the stars to be in perfect alignment for someone to open up. You learn to recognize the signs and then you move, praying for help and understanding that something you say might be what that person needs to hear. In my case, my husband asked me to come here one day to pick up a pie plate for a gift for my mother-in-law. I hadn't been out of my apartment for over a year. I'm not sure what Isaac saw in me that day that started the conversation, but he opened his mouth.

"He told me that he knew it was none of his business, but asked if there was anything I needed to talk about. I didn't know Isaac at the time. I had seen him around town, but had never had reason to interact with him. When I didn't respond, he told me that he often saw sorrow in the world, but that only those who knew great loss had eyes like mine. I was angry and defensive. I didn't think he had any idea how I felt. When I finished telling him to mind his own business, there was a long silence. Without my asking him, he took the pie plate and wrapped it up, tying two tiny clay hearts to the ends of the ribbons.

"I was still angry, but when I looked up to thank him, I saw in his eyes the same pain he said he saw in mine. He seemed anxious to hear me and I found it easy to talk. He shared with me the sorrow and pain of losing his wife. I told him about my inability to deliver a live child and the anguish that came from that. Even though we were strangers, we cried together. By the time I left, I felt I had been able to share my burdens for the first time in many years."

Jake shook his head then spoke thoughtfully. "I know about loss and pain and sorrow, but I never would have guessed that you know the same sorrows. How did Isaac know who needed help?"

"Jake, when you're young, sometimes you think that you're the only one who knows about trials and heartache. When you get to be my age, you know that everyone knows those emotions to some degree or another. The details are as diverse as the individuals themselves, but suffering is part of the human condition. Isaac understood that. Everyone who walked through his door was human and therefore subject to the trials of life. Not many people who walk through the door are ready to share their burdens, but Isaac was ready for those who were. He felt a responsibility to lift up and strengthen those who needed his help."

"Maybe that's part of my problem. I don't know if I could ever feel that way. No offense, but why should I care about anyone else's issues? I'm not sure I can even handle my own. I committed to stay in this crazy town until the end of the summer, but to be honest, I've thought about leaving at least every other day."

"Then why did you come?"

Jake sat in silence for a long moment before responding. "Because I had this silly idea that I wanted to be a village potter."

"And now?"

"And now I'm wondering if I should have listened to my professors. They told me I was crazy to want this. I'd be better off in Greece where I don't have to deal with girls or the Mancinis or strangers wanting to tell me their life's stories."

"So you think you can run away from reality forever?"

"What is that supposed to mean?"

"It means welcome to reality, my friend. Life is weird. And this is life. It's unpredictable and sometimes crazy. You get hurt. Your girl falls in love with someone else. People you love die. There are wars, disasters, and bad things happening everywhere. This is reality, Jake. Sooner or later, you're going to have to deal with it. You can run away to Greece or Nineveh or wherever you want to run, but reality always catches up to you. You can't avoid it. You're human and everyone around you is also human.

We humans mess things up. We make life hard. A few of the lucky ones get to help people along the way."

Jake furrowed his brow and shook his head. "So what are you saying?"

"I'm saying open your eyes. You wanted to be a village potter. Here you are. Does that just happen? No, it doesn't. You've been preparing yourself for at least eight years to be here. The universe has been molding and shaping you to be here. Are there lots of other villages that need a potter? I don't doubt it. But the reality of it is that each of those villages is going to be at least as quirky as we are. People want you to be here. Are there going to be problems and challenges? Absolutely! And I hope for your sake that there are. Those same challenges that try to kill us make us who we are. They make us stronger if we let them. We can curse reality and try to hide, but it never works for long. I learned that after three years of being depressed. I hated my reality. I couldn't have kids so I locked myself up in our apartment. In the process, I cut myself off from life. I've learned that reality sucks sometimes, but it's better than locking yourself up and hoping that it goes away. Part of being human means that in order to see the good in life, we have to be exposed to the bad.

"The Garden of Eden was just a nice place to live before Adam and Eve were cast out of it. Then it became paradise. We rarely appreciate how good things are until they change. Take it from a florist, the reality of life is this: We have to bloom where we are planted, enjoy the sunlight while we can, and thank the heavens for the rain that not only beats us down, but feeds us and makes us stronger."

Jake let out a long breath. He looked up at Gloria and smiled weakly. "So that's it? Bloom where you're planted, huh?"

"I'm sorry. I didn't come here to lecture you. I'm sure Isaac would have said things quite differently. He taught me that even though life sucks sometimes, you don't have to open your eyes very wide before you realize how good you've got it. When you get busy helping others with their issues, you tend to forget your own. You may have heard it already, but Isaac was fond of saying that joy, in all its glory, comes only through unselfishness.

That's a tough lesson to learn, Jake, but it's true. Of all the things Isaac shared with me over the years, that's the thing that's been most valuable. It changed my perspective and it's changed my life."

She walked to the sink and washed her mug before hanging it back on the nail. "I've got to go. If you're still here the next time I drop by, I'll come for some tea and tell you the rest of my story."

Jake nodded.

Gloria walked  to the counter and picked up her basket before turning back to Jake. "I hope I haven't been too rough on you. I want you to know that the wind doesn't just blow people here without a reason. However long you decide to stay, I hope you'll make the most of it."

Jake didn't get up to walk her to the door. He was brooding. He looked over all the pots he had made. Gloria was right. He would be up 'til midnight. The first pots he had made that morning were ready to trim thanks to the warmth of the kiln and the dryness of the air. He got to work trimming his pots. As he did, Gloria's words began to sink in. This *was* his dream. The shop was smaller, the  kiln older, and the town quirkier than he ever could have imagined, but she was right. This was his dream and he knew if he was ever to give it a real chance, he needed to accept reality and stop thinking about what might have been. Still, he couldn't entirely give up the dream of Greece, reality or not.

He finished trimming his pots and putting handles on his mugs just after 10 PM. He stood up from his stool and stretched, sore from the work. He took off his apron and set it on the table. There lay the loaf of bread Gloria brought from Sam's bakery. Dinner. He turned off the light and climbed the stairs, humbled that his reality, regardless of its issues, included something as wonderful as Sam's fresh bread. He tried to remember if he had even thanked Sam for keeping him fed.

As he ate, Jake opened his sketchbook and began to write.

 GRATITUDE

Jake took a seat on the old stone steps, waiting for the bakery doors to open. He watched as Sam, Thomas, and several employees filled the shelves with the morning's offerings. The smell of fresh bread filled the air, sneaking through the cracks in the door and making Jake's belly growl.

The sun wasn't up yet, but it was light enough to see all the way up Hauptstrasse to the upper fountain. He thought about Amy. It had been four days since their picnic and Jake had been tormented ever since. His thoughts were interrupted when he heard the sounds of the glass doors being unlocked behind him. He turned to see Sam, his mustache dancing as he whistled a happy tune.

"Good morning Jake. You're up early. I can't imagine you went through that loaf of bread already."

"No, I haven't. I just wanted to say thanks for feeding me. I realized last night that I haven't thanked you enough for keeping me fed. Thank you. It's been awesome."

"You're welcome. I'm glad you like it, but you know why I gave it to you. I learned early in life that there's no such thing as a free loaf of bread and I've used it to get me what I want."

Jake laughed and shook his head. "I just finished my second glaze firing on Tuesday. I'm probably ready to get started on your mosaic."

"That's good news!" Sam said loudly, turning to Thomas and the others inside the bakery. "Hey everyone, Jake's going to get started on the floor!"

The others clapped and cheered. Jake smiled back at them, waving.

"We ought to talk about it so I can figure out exactly what you want," Jake said, looking down at the gray cement entryway. It seemed bigger than he remembered, but it was the first time he had seen the floor without people standing on it.

"Isaac made a big medallion for the center. I definitely want to use that," said Sam. "As for the rest of it, Isaac didn't leave any plans. I'd want to approve the plans before we move forward, but I think it's important for artists to be able to do what artists do best. I'm anxious, but I know you'll get it done as fast as you can."

Jake thanked Sam again for all the bread and walked back to the apartment to eat breakfast.

The kiln was ready to unload when he arrived at the studio. The planters turned out nicely and he set them aside so Mrs. Pfeiffer could choose the ones she wanted. His excitement rose as he unloaded the rest of the kiln. It was filled with some of his new bowls. The techniques he had played with during the last few months of school worked

even better using Isaac's glazes. One bowl really excited him. The pattern he had applied to the blue glaze with wax resist created sharp lines between the blue and green glazes, forming a really cool star pattern. When he pulled out the next bowl, he was even more excited. The technique he used to decorate this one was the same, but the color and design was different. This one was white with black spirals covering the entire surface. He was giddy.

He quickly pulled out the rest of the pots. Two of them were ruined where the layered glazes had become too thick and run off the bowls, sealing them to the kiln shelf. He cursed under his breath when he saw it, but his spirits were quickly restored when he remembered the good ones. Six large salad bowls had made it through the firing without blemish and they were incredible. Jake wanted to show someone—anyone—but no one was around to see.

He took the bowls to the showroom and fit them all onto the shelves in the front window, smiling as he did so. The new work excited him so much that he went back to the studio to see if he had enough bisqueware for another firing. He was disappointed when he discovered he only had half of what he needed. Instead, he loaded the pots he made the day before into the kiln, along with others he had made during the week, and got the kiln candling to dry the pots out slowly.

He went back to the showroom four times to look at the new bowls, his excitement growing each time he saw them. The two ruined bowls were a total loss and broke into pieces when Jake tried to remove them from the kiln shelves. The shelves themselves were heavily damaged and Jake spent the rest of the morning chipping away at the mess the glazes made when they had run.

By lunchtime, Jake needed to tell someone about his new work before he could do anything else. He jogged to the library to send an email to Dr. Lewis.

Jake's email was short. He told Dr. Lewis about his commitment to stay in Niederbipp for the summer and invited him to stop by anytime. He explained that he probably wouldn't be checking his email very often considering how long it took to do anything on the dial-up connection. Jake ended by telling him about the new bowls. It was very anticlimactic, considering that he had no picture of the new bowls to send as an attachment, but he sent it anyway.

Before the kitchen timer went off, Jake checked his inbox. Most of the emails were spam, but one piqued his interest. It was from Andreas Stephanopoulos. In broken English, Andreas said he was anxious to hear when Jake would be arriving and reported that he had a job for him as an apprentice for the summer. Jake looked at the email for a full minute before he remembered Gloria's hard words about reality. He responded with a quick reply, saying that he made other plans for the summer, but that he would like to be considered in the future.

Jake was surprised by the feelings he had as he left the library. Somehow, he felt resolved. He had made a commitment for the summer and he knew he needed to keep it. Having a back door to escape through had already made his time here difficult. He knew he needed to change.

24 GRANNY RUTH'S FAMOUS COOKIES

With change in mind, Jake decided to celebrate the new bowls by going out to lunch. The kabob shop he had seen on Monday was doing brisk business when Jake got in line to wait his turn.

By the time he was finally served, Jake had only a few minutes before the Pottery was supposed to be open again. He paid for his lunch and hurried around the corner. From the bottom of Zubergasse, Jake could see that a woman and a child were loitering outside his shop, looking through the window. When he remembered his new bowls, he kicked into high gear and picked up his pace.

"Hello," he said when he was still twenty feet away. The woman turned to face him. She clutched the hand of the child, a girl of about 5 years dressed in a brown velour sweat suit.

"Hello young man," said the woman. "I told you I'd come by if you decided to stay. I've heard from half the village already that you're working hard and I figured I'd better come and see what you were doing. I brought my granddaughter along to meet a real potter."

The little girl looked up at Jake and pulled a plastic bag full of cookies from behind her back. "We brought some cookies for the new potter," she said.

Jake recognized the woman from his first day in Niederbipp. It was she who had given him the tour of the  town and pointed him to the shop. "Wonderful," he said looking at the cookies. He took a deep breath. "Come on in."

He unlocked the front door and pushed it open, allowing the ladies to go in ahead of him. He followed, picking up a receipt lying on the mosaic entryway.

The woman and her granddaughter were already in the studio by the time Jake reached the top of the stairs. He put his uneaten kabob down on the front counter and watched the old woman raise her cane to the row of mugs.

"That one is mine," she said, pointing to one of the mugs.

Jake took another deep breath. He wanted to eat his kabob and relax, but he remembered Gloria's words. He put his desires on hold. "Would you like some tea?"

"Brilliant idea, my boy," she said.

Jake nodded, pulling the very dusty mug from the nail. He rinsed the mug in the sink before filling the old teapot and setting it aside to steep.

When he turned back to his guests, he saw that the old woman had already taken a seat on the stool in front of the wheel. Her young companion was leaning against her leg.

Jake unfolded one of the chairs against the wall and set it next to the old woman. "I'm sorry, but I've forgotten your name," said Jake.

"I wouldn't expect you to remember an old woman like me. My name is Ruth Stein and this is Eloise. I would have forgotten your name long ago if I hadn't heard it on the lips of a dozen old friends in the past few weeks. I'm glad you decided to stay, Jake. I made a bet about how long you would last. I lost and so here we are."

Jake smiled but wasn't sure if he wanted to know what the woman meant. He pulled two more mugs from the rack above the sink and set them on the small table in front of the wheel. He poured the tea and placed the sugar bowl in front of them.

"I understand you've had an eventful couple of weeks," she said. "I would have been here sooner, but I've been entertaining guests. Eloise is my oldest great-granddaughter and we've been baking a lot of cookies. A lot of my family has been in town for my birthday. When you're as old as I am and have as much posterity as I do, you can't really have a birthday party. Everyone can't fit in my house. So, I decided a couple of years ago that I might as well just open my home for visits from Mother's Day until Memorial Day. My grandson told me that I party like a rock star. I'm not sure what that means, but I love having family around."

"So when is your birthday?"

"Tomorrow."

"That's great. How old will you be?"

"Thirty-nine."

Jake smiled. "Great." He rolled his eyes, wondering if she was crazy, senile or both.

"Yup, Thirty-nine. The best part of that is that I'm younger than all my kids. I hoped to celebrate the milestone with Isaac, because he was the one who convinced me to restart the counting of the years." She took a sip of her tea and patted Eloise on her knee. "I came today to pick out a bowl for Eloise's trousseau."

Jake sat silently waiting for the punch line.

"I suppose you should have an explanation," Ruth offered. "In actuality, I'm not sure exactly how old I am. I stopped counting my true age many years ago and started again from the day I truly began to live.

"One day when I was about fifty, give or take five years," she sent Jake a quick wink and smile over the rim of her mug, "I went in to visit my doctor. I was tired and felt like I was running out of steam. I thought I might need some hormones or supplements or some of the other things my girlfriends were taking. The doctor ran some tests and then some more. They did blood work and more tests. They asked me to return in a couple of days and to bring my husband.

"When we arrived the doctor asked us both to sit down. He told me that I had inoperable cancer running throughout my whole body. I was told I had three to six months to live. He offered me morphine as my pain increased, but other than that, there was no treatment for me.

"The doctor's news stunned us. My husband and I had dreamed of growing old together. The work of raising our seven children was nearly over and the fun was just starting with the grandkids. I didn't feel like it was a very convenient time to die. Death seemed like such an abrupt end to a good life. As I contemplated the reality of it, my mind wandered to Isaac. He had more reason to understand death than anyone I knew, having lost his father-in-law and his wife in the same week. Yet he was always happy and cheerful. I decided he might be a good person to help me understand death and help me prepare my family for what lay ahead.

"The next day I came to town to visit him. I sat on this stool and opened my heart. I told him that I had only a few weeks or months to live. When I was done crying, he poured me some tea and asked if I knew how fortunate I was to know when and how I would die. I admitted I didn't.

"He told me that if everyone knew when and how they were going to die, they might be able to forget their fears and live a fuller life. By the time I left, I was excited about living whatever time I had left to the fullest. I went home determined to leave the best legacy I could.

"I decided to start by baking each of my children a batch of their favorite cookies and I put them all in the freezer to open on Christmas. On Thanksgiving, two of our children announced they would be having babies the next year. I was still feeling peachy, so I got busy and made quilts for each of my new grandbabies. Christmas came, and then New Years, and I was still alive and feeling quite vibrant. By the time my new grandbabies arrived, I was busy making plans for the next Christmas.

"My husband bought me the biggest deep freeze available and I made thousands of cookies to share with all of my kids, grandkids, in-laws, out-laws, and friends. I wanted to be remembered and associated with sweet things. On my one-year mark, I visited Isaac again. He laughed and cried with me as I reported what I had done with the last year of my life. He asked me to go to the showroom and pick my favorite mug and then we toasted the year with a cup of tea. His enthusiasm gave me courage and made me forget my sorrows.

"When I visited him a year later, Isaac had a cupcake waiting for me with two candles. I reported on my grandchildren, my cookies, and my violin lessons. My mug was hung again on the nail and I promised I would do my best to come again the next year.

"When I blew out five candles a few years later, Isaac told me he was running out of space on a cupcake and was going to have to upgrade if I kept refusing to die. I became known for my cookies and was approached by a specialty bakery in Pittsburgh that was interested in buying cookies from me on a daily basis. I had just upgraded to a professional oven that allowed me to bake five sheets of cookies at a time so I could keep up with the demands from the family. I figured I could make some money in my spare time. Before long, I was making hundreds of cookies every day. My oldest grandkids began helping me after school. My daughter-in-law developed a brand name for me, 'Granny Ruth's Famous Cookies.'

"At my ten-year birthday, I invited Isaac to a party at our home with many other friends and twenty-one grandchildren. I was so busy living that I hadn't thought about death for a long time. My doctor told me I was a walking time bomb and so I decided to announce the facts to my children for the first time.

"I stood in the middle of all the people I loved in the world, my heart overcome with gratitude to God for giving me those ten years. As I explained my prognosis, I told them that I had not said anything before because I wanted to make each day count; I wanted to enjoy my time with them without being treated like I was somehow fragile. I thanked them for the most rewarding ten years of my life and told them that if I died the next day, I would not be sad. I had lived every one of the last 3,650 days and experienced every happiness a person could ever dream of. I told them if I wasn't around for Christmas, they knew where to find the cookies.

"I didn't die that day or the next. I kept getting up every day, figuring it could be my last and the time bomb of life would finally catch up to me. But somehow I kept eluding it. My twentieth birthday party had to be held at the park because my posterity had outgrown our home and yard. I sold my cookie business the year before and presented a scholarship to each of my grandchildren. I continued making quilts for my babies and making cookies on a smaller scale for all the family. The grandkids decided to take advantage of the situation, suggesting that I might not be around for their birthdays. I gave into the temptation to spoil them and soon we were eating cookies whenever there were children around.

"Before my 30th birthday, my doctor died, swearing on his deathbed that I was cheating death and that I should expect to see him on the other side any day. I left him a plate of cookies and bid him farewell. A few months later, my husband died. He had lived a good life and brought me a lifetime of happiness. We always thought it would be me that went first, but by golly, I just kept on living."

Jake listened intently to Ruth's tale. He looked at her aged, withered face as she drank her tea from the old mug. Her great-granddaughter had the same blue eyes, but Eloise's smooth and creamy skin was in sharp contrast to the older woman's skin that seemed one size too big and hung from her neck and arms.

Ruth smiled at her granddaughter, and ran her hand over the top of her hair. "We'll pick out a bowl for you as soon as you're ready."

"What kind of bowl are we going to get?" Eloise asked.

"I was thinking maybe a mixing bowl. My first mixing bowl came from this shop. I must have mixed enough dough in that bowl to make a bazillion cookies."

Eloise laughed out loud, repeating "a bazillion cookies."

She pulled the old woman off the stool and the two of them made their way to the racks of pots. Jake was impressed with the apparent closeness that they shared, even though ninety years or more separated them.

"I've heard of all kinds of miracles, but forty years is truly amazing.

Are you cured of all your cancer?" he asked, feeling like a reporter for a tabloid.

Ruth turned from the stacks of pots.

"I don't know. When my doctor died, I never found another one. I knew he didn't know any more about my body than I did. I still have my bad days, but when I hear the patter of little feet on my front porch, I get myself out of bed to be with my grandkids. It's hard to feel sorry for yourself when there is so much love around you. There are lots of ways to kill cancer, but most of them focus on the disease. I just decided I was too busy to put up with it. I had too much loving to do. I've heard it said that you should live each day as if it were your last. I think that's a pretty silly notion that often leads to foolishness and selfishness. Isaac taught me the importance of living each day to spread happiness and love. He shared with me the secrets of joy and when I learned these things for myself, I was driven to keep living so I could share them with my ever-expanding family. I've found that if I spend my time cursing the clouds for blotting out the sun, I'll miss a great day with the grandkids, lying on a blanket and discovering pictures in those clouds."

Eloise smiled at this. "Granny always finds the funniest things in the clouds."

Ruth looked down at her and smiled. "Life is all about finding joy," she said. "I learned that one cookie at a time."

"This one is pretty, Granny," Eloise said, lifting a yellow and blue mixing bowl from the shelf.

"Thank you," Jake said. "I made that one. It just came out of the kiln on Monday."

"Very nice," said Ruth. "It looks like you have an eye for color." Eloise handed her the bowl. As she hefted it in her hands, she ran her gnarled fingers over the smooth glaze. "Well done," she said, shuffling towards the counter.

"Thank you. Nice choice," he said, shooting a grin towards the little girl. She smiled back, beaming with pride in the acquisition of her first mixing bowl, a prize few other young girls would appreciate.

"Can we get started on my cookies today?" she asked Ruth.

"I think your brothers would like that."

"And can we bring some to Jake too?"

"Of course we can."

Jake smiled at both of them as he wrapped the bowl in brown paper for the walk home. He thanked them and walked them out.

Jake returned to his kabob. It was no longer warm, but he enjoyed it anyway. He was leaning against the counter, eating, when he saw the receipt he had picked up off the floor when he came in. He was about to throw it away when he noticed something written on the backside. He flipped it over and began to read.

Jake set down his kabob and read it again. He had only been gone an hour. She must have come during her lunch break. He flipped the receipt over again, looking for any clue. The receipt was for a pair of Mary Jane shoes for thirty-two dollars and thirteen cents. It was dated May 11. She had made the purchase exactly a week before. He imagined that she might have had the receipt in her purse and used it to scribble a note when he wasn't there. He read the note a third time. She had come by twice trying to find him. He took a deep breath, wishing he had just stayed around.

Jake wedged Amy's note into the middle of the order book. He picked up his kabob and nearly swallowed it whole. He was considering if he should stop by Beverly and Jerry's home to visit Amy when he heard the bells jangle against the front door.

Jake looked up to see Mrs. Pfeiffer.

> Jake –
> Do you ever work?
> I dropped by Monday
> afternoon and again to-
> day to say hi. Where are
> you? I like the stuff in
> your window. I guess
> i'll have to stop by
> again and try to catch
> you. See you later.
>   – Amy

"Hello, Jake," she said as she entered.

"Hello, Mrs. Pfeiffer. Good timing. I just pulled your planters out of the kiln this morning." He pulled the planters from the shelf behind the counter and lined them up for her to examine.

"Ooh, they're beautiful!" she exclaimed, approaching the counter. "They're much prettier than my last ones. It seems a pity to put dirt in them. How am I ever going to decide which ones to take?"

Jake had glazed each of the planters differently, using a brush and wax resist in different patterns. This method allowed the buff-colored clay to be exposed, forming designs around the smoother glazes. Six different planters, six different designs and glazes.

Jake watched as Mrs. Pfeiffer examined each one. "It would be a pity to separate these; they all look so good together. If you don't mind, I'd like to take them all home."

Jake looked up, surprised. "No. Yes. That's fine!"

"The problem is I parked up at the parking lot by the library. I could go and get my car and bring it around to the back door."

"That's ok, I'll carry them." Jake said, scheming to use the errand as an excuse to look for Amy.

"Oh, I'd hate to have you do that. They must be heavy."

"No, they're not so bad. They all stack inside each other. It wouldn't be any trouble."

"Well, if you really don't mind, that would be great. I'm in a bit of a hurry."

Jake wrapped and stacked the planters. Mrs. Pfeiffer handed him three hundred and fifty dollars and told him to keep the change since they were much prettier than she had anticipated. He followed her out the door. They walked together down Zubergasse and then up Hauptstrasse.

Gloria was replanting the flower box under the front window of her shop when they passed. She turned to watch Jake and Mrs. Pfeiffer walking up the street. Jake smiled and nodded when he saw her. She returned the smile and winked at him before turning back to her work.

By the time they reached Mrs. Pfeiffer's car, Jake's fingers and arms were sore from the weight and strain of the planters. He laughed to himself when he saw the bumper sticker on the back of her old station wagon: "Save the Snails." He loaded the planters into the back seat and thanked her for her purchases.

As he walked past the barber shop, he considered dropping by to say hello to Jerry and seeing what he might find out about Amy. He stopped on the corner and looked at the barbershop, trying to decide what to do. After another thirty seconds, he stepped off the curb.

Screeeeech! Honk! A silver Jetta came to a stop just inches from Jake's knee. He jumped back as the man behind the wheel screamed and gestured with his hands. Everyone on the crowded street turned to watch the commotion as Jake flushed scarlet and adrenaline coursed through his veins. He waved to the man in the car and turned his back towards him, walking away.

Jake didn't take his eyes off the cobblestone until he reached Zubergasse, not wanting to meet the eyes of anyone still looking at him. He had nearly been hit by a car trying to learn more about Amy. He wondered if it was a sign.

Before the day was over, Jake had read Amy's note at least a dozen times. There was hope again where hope had been dashed. As he closed up for the day, he carried her note to his apartment, placing it in his sketchbook after he recorded his thoughts.

25 THE WANDERER'S TALE

"You must be the new potter," a clear voice rang out over the aisles of food. Jake, shuffling through the condiment shelves looking for a good mustard, looked up to see a tall man's face looking over the aisle at him.

"Yes, I am."

"Well, welcome to town, man. My name is Kai," he said, extending his hand to clasp Jake's. From his youthful face, Jake guessed he was only a few years older than himself, but his eyes were a curious blue gray color he had only seen in older people.

"Thank you. My name is Jake."

"Awesome to finally meet you. We've been hearing about you for weeks. Can I help you find anything?"

"Yeah, I'm looking for a good mustard."

"Right on. What are you looking for in your mustard?"

"Well, I guess I'm looking for one that is strong, but not so strong that it cleans out my sinuses."

"Dude, I totally know what you mean. This is the one we use. It's full bodied and tastes good on everything from sandwiches to chicken nuggets."

"Cool," said Jake. "I'll give it a try."

Jake was amused with this fellow. He looked and sounded like he'd be more at home in a surfer movie than a small town like Niederbipp. Yet there was something about him that told Jake he was happy here.

"Kai, can you help Mrs. Meier to her car with her groceries?" A woman's voice came from a couple of aisles over.

Kai looked up. "Sure Molly. I'm just helping Jake, the new potter, find some mustard."

Molly came around to where the two men were standing. She was a pretty girl with long brown hair that curled on the ends where it met her shoulders. She wore an apron, which was tied over her obviously pregnant belly. When she saw Jake, she smiled and stretched out her hand to shake his.

"Hello. It's a pleasure to finally meet you."

"Thank you. Nice to meet you too." She put her arm around Kai's back just in time to hear, "Uh hum," coming from the front of the store.

"That must be Mrs. Meier," she said. "Hurry and help her, honey, and I'll keep Jake company while you're gone."

Kai left to help like an obedient child.

She watched as the front door closed before turning to Jake. "So, how do you like it so far?"

"It's been good," he said, deciding to keep it brief and positive.

"I've been here all my life. I actually grew up right here in the produce section. I was the stock girl. My dad bought the store from my grandfather and now Kai and I are in the process of buying it from Dad."

"That's great. It must be a lot of hard work."

"Yeah, it is. Probably about like your work."

"I don't know about that. I get to make my inventory. It must be difficult keeping things stocked, organized and fresh."

"It used to be a real bear, but Kai is really good with computers and he has made things easier. I couldn't do it without him."

"How long have you guys been married?"

"Four years in July," she said with a smile.

"That's great. Congratulations."

The door opened and Kai came bounding back into the store with a smile on his face.

"I was just thinking, you ought to come to dinner tonight."

Jake grinned, genuinely amused at the tall man's childlike exuberance.

"That's a great idea," Molly interjected, "except for one thing."

"What's that?"

"Hello! Our kitchen is completely torn apart."

"Oh yeah. You're right. I totally forgot about that."

Molly shook her head and turned back to Jake.

"We decided to remodel our kitchen before the baby comes. We just started tearing it apart last night."

"Total bummer," said Kai, looking dejected.

"Hey, I'm not much of a cook, but you guys can come to my place," suggested Jake.

Kai's face lit up like he had just been invited to a birthday party.

"That hardly seems right," Molly said. "You're the new guy here."

"Nonsense. It would be nice to have someone over. It's a little quiet at night."

"Great," said Kai. "We'll be there."

"Let's say six. That will give me a chance to clean up a bit."

"Are you sure it's not too much trouble?" she asked.

"No, not at all."

They walked to the register and Molly rang him up as Kai helped other customers.

"See you later then," Jake said, picking up his bags.

"Thank you," she said, with a smile. "We'll look forward to it."

As he unloaded his groceries, Jake began thinking about what to cook for dinner. He checked the cupboard. He had pasta sauce, but only enough

noodles for one person. He considered going back to the grocery
store, but didn't want Kai and Molly to think he was going to a
lot of trouble. He made himself a sandwich and took it back to
the shop so he could work and eat while continuing to think about
the menu for the dinner party.

At 5:00, he locked the front door and went upstairs to clean up
the apartment. He took out the garbage and swept the floor, but still
no ideas came to him. Finally, at 5:30, he went back to the pantry. He
stood in front of the open doors. There was half of one meal and half
of another, but nothing appealed to him until he saw the big cloth sack
of flour.

Since Jake was a child, he had always loved pancakes for dinner.
His mom had called it comfort food. At breakfast, it was just pancakes,
but for dinner, they had a way of comforting the soul. Plus they were
easy to make. He had the recipe memorized. Soon, the kitchen counter
was crowded with the bag of flour, baking soda, eggs and oil. By the time
his guests knocked at the door, Jake had a respectable pile of pancakes
ready to eat.

"Come in," he yelled at the door when the knock came.

Kai was the first one in. "Whoa, it smells like breakfast."

"Half way there," said Jake. "I hope you guys aren't allergic to
pancakes."

"Are you kidding?" said Molly. "I love pancakes."

"Me too," added Kai.

"Good, cause that's all I got, but I have a bunch of 'em." Jake nodded
to the plate heaping with light brown pancakes.

"How can I help?" asked Molly.

"I haven't had a chance to set the table yet. Do you mind?"

"Not at all," she said with a smile and a nod. "Come on," she said,
grabbing Kai's elbow and pushing him towards the shelves. "Hand me
those plates up there."

Jake watched as Molly pulled out the drawer under the table where the
silver was kept.

"I love this old set," she said

"So do I," said Jake. "It must have a lot of history."

"It sure does. Isaac told us about it shortly after we were married, didn't he, Kai?"

"That's right. I remember that now. It was the only time I ever saw the old man cry."

"Sounds like a good story," said Jake, as he flipped the last pancake.

"Yeah, it is," said Molly. "The set actually belonged to Isaac's parents. His uncle sent it to him and Lily just after they were married. Isaac said it was badly tarnished from the house fire that killed his parents. He cleaned it up and Lily insisted they use it all the time. I guess it was one of the few things that wasn't destroyed in the fire."

"I asked him about the silver many times, but he rarely ever wanted to talk about it. From piecing things together over the years, I think Isaac was out of the country on business when the fire happened. It took them a whole month to track him down and by that time his parents had long been buried."

"Wow. The more I learn about this man, the more fascinating his story is. Do you know where he came from?"

"Somewhere in Ohio." said Molly. "He never talked about it, but I figure it must have been a place a lot like this. One time he told us about how he always wanted to go to the big city when he was a kid, but after he had been there for several years, he wanted nothing more than to return to a small place with friendly people."

Jake nodded his head thoughtfully. He put the batter bowl in the sink and filled it with water before hefting the overflowing plate of pancakes.

"Let's eat," he said, walking to the table.

Kai and Molly took the bench seat under the window and left the chair for Jake.

Kai said grace, thanking the heavens for pancakes and new friends.

"Help yourselves," said Jake, scooting the plate towards the couple.

Kai pulled four pancakes from the top of the stack and piled them on his plate. "What mix do you use?" he asked.

"Hey, hey. No mixes here. This is an old family recipe. I wish I had some buttermilk, and I would have made you my secret ancestral buttermilk syrup."

"I've heard of buttermilk pancakes," said Molly, "but buttermilk syrup?"

"That's right. We'll have to do this again. After you have buttermilk syrup, you'll have trouble eating anything else."

"Anytime," said Kai, "as long as we can have your pancakes too."

"So tell me, how did you guys meet?" Jake asked.

Molly looked up. "Well, that's kind of a funny story," she said.

"Yeah," said Kai, "but it's a good one."

Molly continued, "I used to date the mandolin player for the Bluegrass Darlings."

Jake almost choked on his pancake. "The Bluegrass Darlings?!"

Molly looked surprised. "Have you heard of them?"

"Sure. I love their music. I have all their albums on my iPod. I was surprised to see that Isaac has all the albums in the studio. That's amazing. You used to date John Daniels?"

"Yeah. Do you know him?"

"No. I mean, I know of him. I've loved their music since I discovered them in college."

Molly smiled. "Then you'll know the song, "Molly's Folly" from the Blue Mountain album."

"Sure. Is that you?" he asked, not believing his ears.

"Yes sir," said Kai. "That's my Molly."

"That's amazing," said Jake. "How did you get to know John Daniels?"

"We went to school together. He was my first boyfriend. He and Paul Darling started making music back in high school."

"Whoa! You know Paul Darling too?"

"Sure. And Jim and Adam too. I grew up with those boys, long before they became famous."

"That's incredible. It was because of John that I bought a mandolin."

"You play?" she asked.

"Owning an instrument does not make you a musician. I picked one up at a pawn shop a few years ago and I sold it back to the pawn shop just before I left Albany. I was terrible. I've never been able to figure music out."

"Funny," she said, "Isaac was the same way. That's one of the reasons he invited the boys to play in the studio."

"What? The Bluegrass Darlings played in the studio?"

"Every week for many years," she said.

"This is incredible. Those guys are the most talented musicians I've ever heard. I had no idea they came from Niederbipp."

"Haven't you ever heard the Allegheny River Blues?" asked Kai.

"Of course."

"Well, that song was about John losing Molly to me," he said proudly.

Jake shook his head. "I can't believe it. Those guys are my heroes. I can't believe you know them."

"Anyway," Molly said, rolling her eyes and continuing her story, "I met Kai one night in the studio during band practice. It was near the end of our senior year in high school and John and I had been an item for about a year. The band had already released a couple of low budget albums and was just beginning to get some attention from the major record labels. I came early one night with John to help get the studio ready and when we came in through the back door, I saw this tall bearded guy sweeping the floor. He was really friendly and helped John move some stuff out of the way so the band could set up."

"Was that you?" Jake asked turning to Kai.

"Yeah. Isaac had just given me a job that afternoon. I had only been in town a couple of days. I was on a trip around the world but only made it this far before I ran out of money. I was down by the fountain that afternoon, playing my harmonica, bumming change, when I met Isaac. He invited me to come here for lunch.

After lunch, he wished me well on my journey and gave me a mug. As I was leaving, he offered to put me up if I ever needed a place to stay. I thanked him and went back to work at the fountain.

"About an hour later, as I was minding my own business, playing my music, this cranky old guy came up to me and told me I was gonna have to leave.

"I got pretty upset, and told him it was a free country and that a man could make music wherever he wanted. When I continued to protest, he told me he was the Mayor and he wouldn't allow riff-raff like me into his town.

"I picked up the mug I had been using to collect funds and started walking away, but he stopped me and accused me of stealing the mug. When I told him that Isaac had given it to me, he looked like he was about to blow up. He turned and stomped off.

"The next morning, I stopped by to warn Isaac about the Mayor. He blew it off and told me that he was surprised to see me, figuring I had hitchhiked out of town the evening before. When I told him I needed to earn some more money before moving on, he called a couple of his friends to see if they needed any help.

"The miller hired me for a couple of hours carrying sacks of wheat from the shed to the mill. I washed the windows at the barber shop and then took Sam's wagon to the miller to fill it with sacks of flour.

"At lunch time, I wandered back to see if Isaac had any more leads. He fed me lunch and told me about another friend who needed some help too. I spent the afternoon working at Brian's computer store, unloading boxes and stocking shelves.

"Just before closing time, a middle-aged man came in and asked for some help with the computer program he had just purchased. The manager wasn't very helpful and told the old guy that he was swamped until the weekend. I could see the wind go out of the old guy's sails as he expressed the need to find an employee to help with all his work.

"When the man was gone, I found out the man was Bob Braun, the town grocer. I found out the program he was having trouble with was one I learned in high school. I felt bad for him, but I was a wanderer. I had left California six months earlier on my world tour and hadn't even made it out of North America. The plan had always been to wash windows on every continent. I figured by then I would know where I wanted to put down roots."

Jake nodded, understanding the wanderlust that Kai was talking about. Again, he decided he would keep things positive. He encouraged Kai to continue his story.

"Isaac set me up in his second bedroom and kept me busy with odd jobs around town. I met Molly later that week when the band came to the studio. They even let me jam with them on my harmonica. I thought about staying a little longer, so I stopped by the grocery store to apply for a job. Bob informed me that he was looking for someone who bathed on a regular basis. It's not that I was opposed to bathing, I just didn't have a lot of opportunities.

"I hitchhiked out of town that weekend and ended up in Quebec a few days later. After washing dishes at a restaurant for a week, it was time to move on. I didn't have the money to buy an airplane ticket across the Atlantic, so I hung out at the port, trying to get hired onto a ship. After a couple days, I was warned that I should leave. I didn't think I looked like a terrorist, but after 9-11, anyone with a dark beard probably did. I got a haircut and shaved my beard and got out of Canada as soon as I could.

"So why did you come back here?" asked Jake.

"Sitting around at the port gave me some time to think. I'd been traveling for more than six months and the only place I'd ever felt welcome was here. When I finally made it back, I felt like I was coming home."

Jake looked at Kai, not really understanding him. "No offense, but it seems kind of crazy to think about giving up your dreams of seeing the world in exchange for life as a small town grocer. How did you make that decision?"

"It was a lot easier than I ever thought it would be. I'll admit that there were many days that I wanted to put on my traveling shoes and head off for the unknown, but I spent a lot of time talking to Isaac and Albert about it. After a year, I realized this was the life I'd gone looking for."

"Is that when you started dating Molly?" asked Jake.

"No, I had to wait for her to grow up."

Molly slugged Kai in the arm. "I'll pick up the story here."

Kai leaned back in his chair and put his hands behind his head.

"I came to the store after school like I always did," she began, "and Daddy introduced me to the new stock boy, Kai. I didn't recognize him because he had shaved. I was just glad to have someone to help out around the store.

"When he showed up to band practice that week, my girlfriends thought he was cute, but I wasn't interested. I had John. As time passed, Kai was soon running the store better than my father ever had. He was a natural with the computer program and my father gave him a big raise.

"After graduation, I spent more time in the store. Kai and I became good friends. Daddy always liked Kai and treated him like he was part of the family. He had a standing invitation to Sunday dinner and was always such a gentleman.

"In the fall, my girlfriends and I all scattered to our different colleges. I came home often to help Daddy, and Kai was always there. I still remember the visit when I realized how cute he was. I was still young, though, and felt guilty because I thought I was in love with John.

"After I got my Associates, I decided to come home and work for six months before I continued my studies. Coming home for more than just a visit felt better than anything I had done in two years.

"One night after dinner, I asked Kai if he wanted to join me for a walk around town. He invited me to get some ice cream and as we sat under the patio lights at Mancini's, I realized I had never asked him about his dreams. We had spent a lot of time talking about my school and my plans for the future, but I knew nothing about his.

"He told me about growing up on the beaches of Southern California and how his mother's messy marriages left him hungry for a better life.

After high school, his mom kicked him out, so he decided to become a tumbleweed and go wherever the wind blew him. He told me that after the wind blew him here, it stopped blowing. He told me that he liked helping people, that it had made him happier than he had ever been before. He told me that he hoped to buy the store over time and become the grocer for the next generation.

"His dream seemed so simple, yet I began to feel jealous of him for knowing what he wanted out of life and already being on the path to get there. I remember being quiet the rest of the evening as I realized that my two years at college had left me with more questions than answers. I began thinking that six months at home might not be long enough to find myself and decided to give myself as long as I needed.

"As I worked with Kai each day, I saw how much happiness he derived from his work. In hindsight, I realize it was during those weeks that I began to fall in love with him. We spent more and more of our evenings on walks around town. I remember the first night he held my hand," she said, reaching for Kai's hand. "I don't know exactly when it was, but one day I realized that Kai loved me too. Working beside him became something exciting to me and I woke each morning looking forward to seeing him.

"One Friday afternoon, we were working together stocking produce, when John walked in. It had been a few months since I had seen him because he had been on tour with the band. He asked me out for that evening. We went to dinner at Robintino's and then for a walk down by the river. We talked about old times and his concert tour and the events of my summer. He held me close and told me how much he had missed me, but for the first time since we'd been dating, I wasn't sure I felt the same way. I was shocked when he got down on his knee and opened a small box to reveal a diamond ring. I felt sick inside.

"He told me that being away on tour had made him realize how much he loved me and wanted to be with me. I was touched, but at the same time, I was torn. He was the only guy I had ever dated. But being away from him had allowed me to open my heart to other possibilities. John left town the next morning.

"Kai finally kissed me around Christmas. We were engaged by the time the snow melted and were married that summer. Kai asked Isaac to be his best man and the band came back to play at our wedding party, including John who was still sore and wouldn't talk to me. I think it was on that visit that he wrote the Allegheny River Blues."

"I always knew there was a lot of passion behind that song," said Jake. "It makes sense now that I know the story behind it."

"Yeah," responded Molly. "It took John a while before he was able to talk to me, but with time, he came around and realized how happy I am with Kai."

"That's a great story," said Jake.

"I like it," said Kai, smiling back at Molly. "Sometimes I wonder what would have happened if I had not come back to Niederbipp. I wonder where I'd be now. I wonder what would have happened if Isaac had not found me by the fountain and invited me to share his lunch. I have a hard time imagining that I would have found a more fulfilling life. He gave me a chance to find myself, and to find the love I was looking for."

"So what are your plans now?" asked Jake.

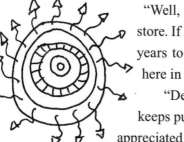

"Well, we've been paying Molly's dad off for the store. If all goes as planned, that will take another ter years to finish, then we plan to raise our kids right here in Niederbipp."

"Despite all my efforts to leave this place, it keeps pulling me back," added Molly. "I never really appreciated it when I was a kid, but now as I think about raising my own children, there is no place I'd rather be."

Jake nodded thoughtfully. Niederbipp, he thought, might be a good place to raise kids, but the thought of living here for the rest of his life still seemed… suffocating … claustrophobic…crazy.

Molly stood up and began clearing the table. "I'll wash if you boys dry," she said and the three of them stood around the sink, washing and drying dishes like family.

"You'll have to excuse us," said Molly. "We have a kitchen to tackle and only a month before the baby arrives."

"Do you need any help?"

"Yes, but not tonight," said Kai. "We're just ripping stuff out right now. I'll ask for your help when we get ready to hang the new cabinets, if you don't mind."

"Not at all. I'd be happy to help."

"You got it. Give us a week or two and we'll be ready."

Jake shook Kai's hand and Molly surprised Jake by giving him a hug the best she could with her bulging belly between them. "Thanks for the pancakes," she said.

"Yeah," added Kai, "they were awesome."

"We'll see you soon," said Molly, as they closed the door behind them.

26

THE FIRST DATE

Jake lay silently in his bed and watched as the sunlight filtered through the shutters, painting stripes on his bedroom wall. The song of the church bells rang out through the town. His hopes of seeing Amy drew him from his bed and rushed him through his morning routine.

As he walked through the courtyard outside the chapel, he smiled at the patterns of sunlight that danced on the cobblestone through the greening canopy. When he reached the chapel steps, he was met by the other faithful whom the bells had summoned. He held the giant doors open for a group of older women dressed in black. They were so engrossed with their own conversation that few of them noticed the gentleman potter who had opened the door for them, greeting them with a smile. The last of these women, whose appearance matched the others, but seemed to be flying solo from the gaggle, looked up into Jake's eyes with kindness.

She nodded and simply said, "Thank you."

"You're welcome."

"Kind boy, are you the young potter?" she asked quietly, with a hint of an accent, looking down to the floor.

"Yes I am. How did you know?"

"You can tell a lot about a person by looking at his shoes," she said smiling. Jake's attention was immediately drawn to his shoes and he realized he had absent-mindedly slipped on his studio shoes that were covered with splatters of glaze and clay. He was dumbstruck, feeling himself blush.

"Welcome to Niederbipp. My name is Hildegard. Isaac and I were good friends. I'd like to drop by for a cup of tea sometime." She smiled again and quickly rejoined her friends without giving Jake a chance to respond.

He followed her through the tall doors and found his way to an empty pew in the middle of the chapel, folding his feet underneath him so no one else would recognize his faux pas. Jake closed his eyes and listened to the organ play a familiar melody, trying to think happier thoughts.

The chapel filled with congregants and Jake soon forgot his shoes as he watched the people. It had occurred to him several times since his arrival in Niederbipp that there weren't very many young people here. He was scanning the congregation, looking for others who looked like they were close to his age when he saw her. Amy and Beverly came through the big doors and took a seat on the third to last pew, just in front of the women in black. Jake felt his hands begin to sweat, but he smiled to himself.

The congregation stood to sing. Jake had a hard time concentrating on the words and misread them four times. The skinny, bald man at Jake's right who was sharing his hymnbook removed his glasses and offered them to Jake. Jake shook his head and tried to concentrate more, but he messed up again on the second hymn and three more times on the closing hymn. The sermon was completely lost on him. He had been looking forward to seeing Amy all week, and now he wished he had used some of that time thinking about what he might say to her.

When the benediction was finished, Jake stood quickly, hoping to catch Amy. The aisle filled with congregants in front of him, impeding his way. They moved slowly and collectively towards the door. Jake panicked when he lost sight of her.

The courtyard was crowded by the time he made it to the door. Jake stood on his tiptoes trying to find Amy. After a moment, he spotted them near the edge of the courtyard. It looked like Beverly was talking to another woman. Amy stood by her side. He prayed she wouldn't leave before he could reach her, imagining how foolish he would feel trying to chase them down.

Jake moved quickly towards her in a zigzag pattern, avoiding the older women who had tried to line him up with their granddaughters. The crowd was thick, making his progress slow, but finally he broke through.

"Hey," she said with a smile that made Jake's heart rate multiply and his face flush.

"Hi."

"I was looking for you," she said.

"You were?"

"Yeah, I didn't see you during church. I was hoping I'd run into you."

"Me too. I've been into half the shops in town this week, trying to find out where you work. I've cursed myself all week for not asking more questions last Sunday."

"You could have just stopped by the apartment. You know where the barber shop is, right?"

"Yeah, I just didn't want you to think I was stalking you." He decided not to talk about the fact that he had nearly been killed crossing the street. "It's a small town and I didn't want you to feel like you couldn't get rid of me if you didn't want to see me."

She smiled and shook her head. "You think too much, Jake. I spent the week wondering if I'd see you again. Didn't you get my note? I stuffed it under the door at your shop."

"Yeah, I did. Thanks a lot."

"And even after that you didn't call me or anything? What are you trying to do, play hard to get?"

"No, I really wanted to, it's just that I don't..."

She looked at him, waiting for him to finish, but when she saw his face turn red, she changed the subject. "My aunt keeps trying to line me up with every eligible bachelor this side of the Allegheny. It's been a nightmare."

"I'm glad I'm not the only one who's getting lined up. I spent my first couple of weeks here trying to come up with creative ways to nicely say 'no' to the ladies from church who want me to meet their granddaughters. I've enjoyed some good home-cooked meals, but it's been pretty painful."

"So you haven't been trying to avoid me then?"

"Are you kidding? I've wanted to see you, but I was afraid I'd botch things up."

"Sounds like we've wasted a whole week," she said.

Jake smiled and felt his face flush, hardly believing his ears.

"It's been a crazy week," he said. "I'll tell you about it sometime if we get a chance to talk."

"What are you suggesting?"

"Well, maybe, if you're not doing anything later... maybe we could go for a walk or something."

"Are you asking me out?"

"I guess that depends."

"On what?"

"On whether you'd say yes."

"Why don't you try me?" she teased.

"Do you want to go for a walk with me tonight?" he asked, hardly believing the words he was saying.

"I do. But I have a lunch date and another one at three. What time would you like to pick me up?"

He wasn't sure if she was joking. It had been years since he had gotten this far with a girl, yet she seemed willing.

"Uhhhhhhhh," he moaned. "Umm, how about six?"

"I think I can fit that in."

"Good," he said with a nervous grin, his palms beginning to sweat again. He was saved from the discomfort of the situation when Beverly ended her conversation and turned around.

"Hello there, Jake."

He turned to face Beverly. "Hi. I was just asking your niece for a date."

"Well I hope she said yes. She's been waiting for you to call on her all week." He stole a glance at Amy who smiled boldly and raised one eyebrow.

"I'll see you later then," he said, taking a few steps back, trying to avoid the already awkward situation.

"Don't forget," said Amy, and Jake turned to see her smiling.

The afternoon passed slowly for Jake. He wondered how Amy was passing her time. He wondered why he had delayed the date until six. He spent the rest of the afternoon wondering what they would talk about. 6:00 was usually the dinner hour. Would she be expecting dinner? He wondered if any of the restaurants would be open on a Sunday evening. His mother had tried her best to teach him simple table manners, but he was sure his manners were rusty after four years of living with roommates.

By 5:00, he had developed a sizeable ulcer in his stomach and could feel his guts disintegrating from contact with his stomach acids. He knew he needed to get out of the apartment. He decided to walk past the restaurants to see if they were open. Robintino's was open and their sidewalk menu posted the specials of the day, all of which made Jake's unusually sensitive stomach growl in pain. The kabob stand was closing up for the day, but the Ice Café would be open until eight.

He wanted this date more than anything, and yet as he walked the quiet Hauptstrasse, he wished he could put it off until he felt better. He sat on a stone bench, wanting to vomit. Knowing that would only give him bad breath for his date, he sucked it up, closed his eyes and tried to breathe his way through it. It would be better after he got there, he told himself. In his twenty-two years, he had been on less than a handful of dates and each of them left him feeling socially upside down and backward.

Before he was ready, the clock tolled six times. Jake stood and walked quickly to the barbershop on the corner then climbed the back stairs to the apartment. Jerry answered the door and welcomed him in. The apartment was neatly furnished and smelled of meatloaf or steak. His stomach immediately reminded him that he hadn't eaten anything since breakfast.

"How ya doin'?" asked Jerry, as he invited him to sit in the front room.

"I'm ok, I guess."

"Ya nervous?"

Jake tried to play it cool, but he nodded.

"If it's any consolation, so is Amy."

Jake raised his eyebrows in disbelief.

"She's a beautiful girl, but I'm afraid she doesn't have much confidence in dating. She's excited to go, but she's been pretty quiet since they got home from church. Just have fun. You two probably have a lot in common. She was disappointed all week that you didn't call on her again. I can't say Bev made it any easier on her, telling her she was sure you would drop by, and then when you didn't, she tried to console her by lining her up with some of the guys who grew up here. I can't figure out what she was thinking. The only thing Amy has in common with any of them is her age. I'm afraid it went about as well as I knew it would and she came home even more disappointed than she was before."

Jake shook his head. "I'm an idiot with this kind of stuff. I wasn't sure how she felt so I figured I'd give it some time, but I really wanted to see her."

Jerry sat back and smiled.

"You two remind me so much of Bev and me. It took me months to ask her out and even then I brought her little brother along with us to keep things comfortable. She still teases me about that, but it all worked out and we've been together more than fifty years."

Beverly entered the living room followed by Amy. Jake stood to meet them.

"Sorry to keep you waiting," said Beverly. "So, where are you two off to?"

"I thought we'd just walk around town. There's a lot of the old town I still haven't discovered. I thought Amy might be able to show me around a bit."

"Oh, you really ought to take Jerry along. He knows more about this town than just about anyone."

Jerry looked up at Amy who was mouthing words to him. "Woman, can't you see these kids want to be alone? I'll give them a history lesson if they ask for it, but I'm not gonna be a buttinski on their first date."

"We'll be back after dark," said Amy to her aunt as she made her way towards the front door. Jake followed, anxious to get out.

"You two just take your time. It's a lovely evening. Come back when you get tired." Amy turned back and gave her aunt and uncle a little hug before setting off.

"I'm sorry I kept you waiting. Aunt Bev said it was important so Jerry would have a chance to interview you."

"Is that what that was?"

Amy turned to face him and they both laughed out loud.

"I'm sorry I'm so awkward. I haven't had any experience with this stuff."

"I'm glad to hear it," she responded. "Dating has been a series of fiascos for me. I hoped coming to Niederbipp would give me a chance to get away from dating altogether."

"I'm sorry," he said, slowing his pace. "If you'd rather not do this, maybe we should call it quits now so I can go home and vomit."

She stopped and looked at him, her face not more than six inches from his. "Last Sunday was the most enjoyable day I've ever had with a guy. That's why I was hoping to see you again."

"I'm really glad to hear that. I've been thinking about it all week, wondering what you were thinking. I don't remember ever having a better time."

"When I didn't hear from you all week, I wondered if I had just imagined the whole thing. By Saturday, I figured you must have a girlfriend."

"Wow," said Jake. "We really have wasted a whole week." She smiled and nodded.

"So where are we going?" she asked as they sallied down Hauptstrasse.

"First thing I want to do is find out where you work. I don't want to waste any more time wondering if I'll run into you. I visited most of the stores, and couldn't find any place I could imagine you working."

"We just passed my work."

"I guess I didn't make it up the street this far," he admitted. "Where is it?"

She turned around and headed back up the street. "I work at May's, the department store right across the street from the barber shop."

"You're kidding! What do you do there?"

"I sell makeup," she said, looking embarrassed.

"That doesn't sound like you."

"Thanks. It's not me at all. I never wear makeup, but I got the job because I'm good with colors. I've only been working there for a week and a half, but I learned more about cosmetics on the first day than I ever knew before. I was never much of a girly girl. I tell the ladies who come in that the trick with makeup is to make it look like you're not wearing any at all. Most women just have a problem with colors. Once we figure out the right color, it's pretty easy to sell them what they need."

They stood at the glass doors of the department store and looked through the darkened space. The window displays hosted mannequins dressed in the latest styles.

"Do you like it?" asked Jake.

"It's a job. There are hundreds of things I'd rather be doing, but I need the money. Aunt Bev and Uncle Jerry have been generous, but I want to carry my own weight, and being sick for the first two weeks was a real drag."

"Is that what caused your sneezing fit last Sunday?"

"Can you believe that?" she said, with a little laugh. "That was crazy.

I think it was caused by the corsages the women were wearing. I was mortified."

"You got my attention," he said, with a wink.

"Yeah, and the rest of the congregation's too."

They laughed together as they started back down the street, taking more time to look at the window displays. She lingered at the shoe store, eyeing the different shoes in the window. Jake was amused at the shoes she was interested in. She skipped over the high heels and pumps, focusing on the colorful leather Mary Janes and a pair of black and white leather wingtips that she said reminded her of Shamu, the killer whale.

"So how are those new Mary Janes you bought last week?"

She looked at him incredulously. "How do you know about those?"

Jake raised his eyebrows and left her wondering.

"So you have been stalking me then?"

"No! You wrote your note on the receipt. I was wondering what they look like."

"If I told you, you might not have a reason to ask me out again."

"And you'd like that?"

"Sure, if you're not too busy with your girlfriends."

By the time they reached the end of Hauptstrasse, darkness had fallen. They had seen other window shoppers when they began, but as time passed, they found themselves alone. Their conversation had been friendly and much easier than Jake had imagined.

"I want to see your shop," she said when they reached the intersection of Hauptstrasse and Zubergasse.

"Really?"

"Yeah, when I was there on Wednesday, you had some really cool bowls in the window."

"Which ones?"

"Oh, those ones with all the color and the geometric patterns painted on them."

"Those are my newest designs, but some of them sold yesterday."

"That's great."

"Yeah, I was pretty happy about it. Most of the work I've sold so far has been the stuff Isaac left. Those bowls were really the first things I've made that sold."

They walked past the lingerie store. Amy smiled as Jake diverted his eyes from the posters in the windows, but she didn't say anything. She liked that he was easily embarrassed.

"This is kind of a lonely street," said Amy.

"No kidding. I've been wondering how to get more people to come up from Hauptstrasse. There have been a couple of days that not even one person has come into the shop."

"That has to be frustrating."

Jake nodded. "I guess I shouldn't complain too much. It allows me to get more work done. Yesterday was really busy and I hardly got anything done at all."

They came to the display window for the Pottery and Amy stopped short. "It might be good to plant some flowers in the window box. That might bring more people up."

"Not a bad suggestion," he admitted. "Someone told me that Isaac usually had them planted in the springtime. I just don't know anything about flowers or any of that stuff girls are usually good at. You should have seen me try to gift wrap something yesterday for a customer. She finally asked if I wanted some help and when I admitted I did, she unwrapped it all and started over."

"I could help you with the flowers. I helped Aunt Bev plant geraniums in her flower boxes the first day I was here."

"I'd like that."

She looked in through the window. "You have sold some stuff. It looks like my favorite one is gone."

"Which one was that?"

"The blue one with the  green star in the middle."

Jake laughed. "That was the one I couldn't wrap. I sold it yesterday."

"Don't you hate it when you sell the really good stuff?"

"It's hard to see some things go, but I love to see the smiles on the faces of the people who buy my work. Plus, if I didn't sell it, it would be hard for me to keep making it. I used to hoard my pottery in college, but my room got so full that my roommates were breaking stuff just getting out of bed."

"I have a hard time parting with my paintings. I've never really needed to sell them. My dad took care of me in college and I haven't thought much about the business end of it. I think that's part of the reason he's not happy that I'm here, 'putting off reality', as he calls it."

Jake gave her an inquisitive look, remembering Gloria's lecture about reality.

Amy continued. "He's a successful businessman. All my brothers have followed him and are successful too. He wonders where he went wrong with me. When I chose to study art, I waited a whole semester to tell him. He probably would have stopped paying my tuition, had it not been for my mom. She's the only one who likes the idea of having an artist in the family."

"So what do you do with all of your paintings?"

Amy took a deep breath. "I've given away a few of them, but most of them are in boxes at home. My mom has a couple hanging in the house, but most of my favorites are collecting dust in my parent's basement."

"Sounds like you need to find a gallery."

"I don't know. It seems like such a dream to be an artist. I love to paint, but I feel like the whole world is telling me to do something more practical."

"I like the idea of you being a painter. I really enjoyed watching you work on those sketches last Sunday."

"Agh, those were just doodles."

"If I could doodle like that, you wouldn't find me working at a makeup counter."

"What would you do?"

"I think I'd at least try to make it as an artist before I let the world tell me to be practical. You have to have passion to be able to develop the talent you have. There are lots of ways to make money, but I don't know too many of those ways that make you happy at the same time."

"You're probably right. My dad would hate you," she said with a smile.

Jake laughed. "Sometimes you have to do things that don't make any sense. If you're heart's telling you to do something, it seems like that's the only way you'll ever be happy."

"Where did you learn that?"

"My mom told me that," he admitted. "That was some of the best advice I ever received."

"It's a lot to think about."

"Do you want to see inside the shop?"

"Sure."

Jake reached into his pocket, pulled out a key ring and unlocked the front door. He swung it in and stood aside for Amy to enter.

"This is a great space."

"Thanks. It's smaller than I'd like, but I'm trying not to complain, all things considered."

"That's right. Aunt Bev said something about you winning some sort of contest and inheriting the whole thing."

"Something like that, I guess. To be honest, I'm not really sure how it all happened. I just answered an ad in a magazine and the next thing I knew—they wanted to give me the whole thing."

"That's pretty amazing."

"Yeah," he said with a nod. "It's been crazy."

"What's over here?" she asked, finding her way past the front counter to the studio.

"This is where it all starts," said Jake as he walked past her on his way to the kiln. "I started glazing yesterday and I plan to fire again on Tuesday."

"Will you have any more of the blue bowls in there?"

"Yeah, I just glazed a few more yesterday," he said, pointing to four bowls on the ware board.

She walked toward them and was about to touch them when he spoke.

"They're really fragile right now. I try to touch them as little as possible until they're fired so the glaze doesn't rub off."

"Which ones are going to be blue and green?"

"All of them." The bowls were dull grey and a pukey shade of green, nothing like the shiny cobalt blue and emerald green that the other bowl had been. "The colors change a lot in the firing."

"That must make it tough to glaze them."

"Yeah, it takes some getting used to. The black glaze is red until it's fired. The copper red glaze actually goes on pale green."

"So how do you know which is which?"

"You have to trust the writing on the bucket. It takes a while, but you get the feel of it."

Amy shook her head. "Sounds pretty complicated to me. If I opened up a tube of black oil paint and it was red, I'd probably think it was mislabeled and take it back to the store."

"Yeah, glaze doesn't really work that way. All of these glazes were already mixed when I got here, but you couldn't buy any of them at the store. They're all made with a recipe, a pinch of this and a dash of that. It's pretty complicated."

"I had no idea."

She turned around and looked at the rest of the studio. "I remember visiting some of my friends in the ceramics studio at school. It looked like a lot of fun."

"You mean you graduated from college as an art major and you never worked with clay?"

"Not this kind. We had to choose between pottery and sculpture and I chose the cleaner of the two."

Jake shook his head. "Well, if you're not afraid of getting a little mud on your hands, I'll have to show you what you missed out on sometime."

"That's a deal," she said with a smile. She looked up at the mugs hanging from the old wooden beam overhead. "Why are those there?"

"I just started learning about those. So far, I only know a few of the folks who own them. I suppose own really isn't the best word, because as part of the deal, the mugs have to stay here."

"So what's the deal?" she asked, genuinely intrigued.

"As I understand it, it was part of Isaac's way of checking up on his friends. They would stop by and bring a pastry and in exchange, they would share some tea and talk about life."

"Some of them are really dusty."

"Yeah, I noticed that too, but the clean ones are the people I've already met."

"It sounds like he had some good friends."

"Oh, you wouldn't believe it. Everyone who has come into the shop gets teary eyed when they talk about him. I don't know anyone who has as many friends as he did. Every time I turn around, I meet someone who he helped or loved or taught them something incredible. At first I was annoyed with all the visitors, but I'm starting to enjoy meeting his friends. It has given me a different appreciation for the town and especially this studio. I never knew the old potter, but I have a great respect for him."

Amy took a seat on the stool and crossed her legs as she continued to look around. "I'm a little jealous," she admitted.

"Why?"

She thought for a moment before continuing. "You and I are the same age and you're living the dream while I'm selling lipstick and eye shadow."

Jake sat down on the other stool. "I guess I haven't thought much about it. I don't know if your Aunt told you, but I was supposed to be in Greece right now."

"No, she didn't say anything about that."

"Yeah, I was planning on spending the summer working for a Greek potter. I had my ticket and everything when I answered an ad in a magazine. I decided to stop here on my way out of the country and the Mayor talked me into staying for the summer. It wasn't until just a few days ago that I thought I had made a terrible mistake. I wanted to see the whole world before I settled down. This kind of cramped my style."

"So what is your style?"

"I don't know yet, and maybe that's what my trouble is. I still feel like I'm just a kid. I know I want to be a potter when I grow up, but it just feels too soon, like my dream has taken some crazy tangent that I didn't plan."

"Yeah, but isn't this awesome? I mean, I don't know any artist who wouldn't kill for a studio of their own. You've got it made. You're living the dream most of us only hope for. I don't get what's wrong with it."

Jake took a deep breath. "This is someone else's dream. It's different from what I wanted and it would take a lot of work to turn it into what I really want."

"How would your dream be different?"

Jake looked around at the studio. "Where do you want me to start? The kiln is at least fifty years old. The paint is chipping off the walls. The building itself is almost three hundred years old. The tradition is charming, but it's also suffocating and inhibiting."

"Jake, I don't think you realize how lucky you are. I understand that it's not your dream studio, but does any artist ever get that before they're rich and famous?"

"I don't know." He shook his head and looked away. He knew she was right, but he didn't really want to talk about it.

"Do you want a cup of tea?" he asked, trying to change the subject.

She nodded.

He pulled two cups from the rack above the sink and readied the tea. When he turned around, she was smiling at him.

"I'm impressed," she said.

"By what?"

"You followed your heart, like you told me to do, and it looks like it's worked out for you. I probably spend too much time being afraid, worrying about what could happen. You've opened my eyes to what can happen if I ever overcome my fear."

Jake poured the tea and handed Amy a mug.

"I appreciate your admiration, but I'm hardly a shining example of overcoming fear. This is the first date I've had in three years. Dating horrifies me."

"I don't know. You seem to be doing ok."

"The night is still young. There are still a million things that could go dreadfully wrong."

Amy laughed. "Ok, dating may be one thing, but you were planning on going to Greece for the summer. Now you're here in Niederbipp. I'm guessing that you have never been to Greece and probably had never heard of Niederbipp before you came here."

Jake nodded.

"I never would have done either of those things, at least not by myself. I'm a pretty adventurous person, but I've never jumped into anything with both feet."

"I didn't have anything to lose. I wish I could claim it was courage, but this just happened to me on my way to plan A. I still find myself wondering if the bus I came in on was involved in an accident and I'm in a coma in a hospital somewhere, dreaming all of this."

"Ok, but you're doing it. You're following your passion. You've spent the last three weeks doing what I hoped to do when I came here. You're making art. I panicked and applied for a job and all the time I'd planned to spend painting evaporated."

"So why'd you get the job?"

She shook her head. "It's fear. I'm so afraid of failing at this. I know it doesn't make any sense, but I figure if I don't try, I won't prove my dad right by becoming a big fat failure. I've spent the last several years being told that being an artist is a silly dream, a waste of time."

Jake bumped her hand with the back of his. "Do you mean to tell me you bought that?"

She looked at him, confused.

"When was the first time you believed you were an artist?"

She thought for a moment. "Probably in kindergarten."

"Me too. Everybody starts out believing they're an artist. The problem is, we start listening to the crap adults and other kids say about our art. Maybe we colored outside the lines. Maybe our dogs looked like monkeys. One by one, kids give up. They start believing they're not really artists. Pretty soon, there are only a few of us left."

"So what are you saying?"

"I'm saying that you've made it this far wanting to be an artist. You have run the gauntlet of criticism and made it through and now you're just gonna give up?"

"I just don't have the confidence you have," she said in her defense.

"But you've got the talent! What is confidence? I'm not sure it's anything more than stubborn ignorance. Amy, if you don't try now, you're never going to and you know it. It's a sad thing to try and fail, but it's even sadder to fail because you never tried."

She took a deep breath and exhaled. "I know you're right. I need to hear this more often. It's going to take a lot for me to overcome my fears. I know I want to be an artist, but I feel like I'm standing on the edge of a big cliff, and way off in the distance is the person I want to be someday, but there's no bridge between here and there."

Jake took a deep breath and exhaled. "I know what you mean. You seem to think I have this figured out, but I'm as confused as you are."

"Why does this have to be so difficult?"

Jake looked thoughtful for a moment and then replied. "If all the kids in our kindergarten class became artists, we wouldn't have firemen, dog catchers and doctors. It might be a pretty messed up world if it was easy to be an artist. I guess I've never really thought much about it, but maybe Darwin's Theory of Natural Selection also works with choosing a profession. We should probably thank God we're not all artists. The world would be more colorful if we were, but I'm pretty sure it wouldn't function very well."

"Oh, I don't know about that. I think it might be a gentler world."

"How so?"

"I don't think I know any artists who aren't pacifists. If you're involved in the creation process, it's difficult to also be involved in destruction. I've often wondered if that's not the reason God gave us art and artists, so we can help rebuild the world every time it's destroyed."

"So when are you going to start painting?"

"Tomorrow," she said firmly. "I've put it off long enough. You're right. If I don't do it now, I may never do it. I came here to paint on canvas, not on ladies' faces." They laughed together.

"I need to figure out a way to quit my job."

"It seems pretty easy to me. You give them your notice. Tell them it's not working out."

"But what do I do about money? I need some cash flow and I don't want to ask my dad. I don't think I can handle another one of his lectures."

"How much do you really need? You live with your aunt and uncle. They don't expect you to pay for food, so rent and food are taken care of. We've already established you don't wear makeup, and I don't think you smoke or drink or have any drug habits. How much cash do you have?"

"Almost a thousand dollars."

"And you're worried?" he mocked. "The way you're living, that could last you 'til Christmas unless your closet spontaneously combusts and you have to buy a new wardrobe. Even then a thousand dollars would last you till fall." Jake leaned back against the table and smiled. "What other lame excuses do you have?"

She turned to him and punched him softly in the stomach.

"Tell me I'm wrong," he challenged.

She recoiled and leaned over, putting her elbows on her knees.

"You're right," she said, after a moment of thought. "I have to try. I've got a lot to think about."

Jake was smiling when she turned again to look at him. "What?" she asked, slugging him again.

"Ouch! Why do you have to be so brutal? What kind of pacifist are you?"

"One who has five older brothers and doesn't like to admit she's wrong."

"Well, you need to know I am an only child and I am a true pacifist." They laughed together.

"I have to be to work tomorrow at eight," she said. "I better get home. I still don't have the energy I had before I got sick, and besides, I need my beauty sleep."

If there was one thing she didn't need, it was beauty sleep. As much as he wanted to tell her how beautiful she was, he couldn't. "Can I walk you home?" he asked.

She looked at him and raised one eyebrow. "You better. This was a date, and if you don't, Aunt Bev probably wouldn't let me go out with you again."

"Is that something you want to do?"

"What?"

"Go out with me again?"

"Are you asking me out again?"

Jake fought off a blush. "Yeah, I guess I am."

"Well don't act so sure," she responded in a sassy way that made them both smile.

"Come on," he said. "I'll walk you home."

They walked out the front door and along the same route they had come, stopping a few times to look at the window displays and taking their time. The evening was beautiful, warm and magical. When they reached the steps that led to her aunt and uncle's apartment, Amy turned to Jake with a broad grin.

"I had a really good time tonight."

"Me too. I was just thinking the last time I had so much fun was…. last Sunday."

Amy smiled even brighter. "I hope I don't have to wait another week to see you again."

"Well, you know, I just remembered I'm out of eye shadow."

She laughed and slugged him again. "Oh sorry," she teased, "I forgot you're an only child."

"Unbelievable," he muttered, shaking his head.

"So when are you going to ask me out again?"

"I thought I'd wait until the bruises fade. I can only handle so many slugs in a week and I'm pretty close to my limit."

"You're such a liar. You know you like it."

"I think I'd like a hug better," he said, not believing his own ears.

She looked at him with eyebrows raised.

"Did I say that out loud?"

"Yep. Sounded pretty smooth to me. Like you've used it on a lot of girls before."

Jake just shook his head and smiled. "I've learned a lot tonight," he said.

"Oh yeah, like what?"

"Like not dating anyone who grew up with five older brothers."

"Is it that bad?"

"No," he admitted. "You're right, I do like it."

"I learned how to throw punches from my brothers, but they also taught me how to give a bear hug." And before Jake could respond, she had wrapped her arms around his ribs and was squeezing the wind out of him. He started laughing and hugged her back. It was a nice hug after she loosened her grip a bit—the first real hug he had ever had from a girl. Sure, there had been friends in high school and college that had given him a friendly hug, or put their arm around him in a half hug, but this was different. It felt ….wonderful.

"I had a really good time tonight," she said.

"You already said that."

"I guess I did," she said, biting her lip.

"I'll see you this week," he said, as he took a step back.

"I hope so. I look forward to it."

Jake smiled brightly as she took a step backwards and began climbing the stairs.

"If I don't see you, I'll come and find you. I know where you work."

"You'll see me," he said, turning to walk away.

As he made his way back down Hauptstrasse, he smiled. It had been without a doubt the most glorious evening he had ever spent with a girl. He was overwhelmed by her charm. She made it clear that she wanted to spend more time with him, but they both had work to do and despite the good time they had together, he was still feeling very unsure of himself. The good news was that he hadn't vomited. The inner turmoil he'd experienced that afternoon was now behind him and confidence had taken its place.

Amy had also given him a lot to think about. She was jealous of his circumstances. He hadn't considered his situation enviable, but maybe he had been blinded by his dreams and his ego. As he climbed the stairs to his apartment, he considered the first time he sat there, cursing himself for coming to Niederbipp before he had even given it a chance. He had been impetuous and impatient. It wasn't his dream studio, but it wasn't all bad either. Amy had opened his eyes.

As he recorded his thought in his sketchbook, he was filled with happiness and gratitude for his friendship with Amy. He went to bed, looking forward to the next time he would see her.

27

The Mayor's Tale

Jake woke the next morning before the sun was up and couldn't get back to sleep. He lay in his bed thinking about how life had changed in the weeks since his arrival in Niederbipp. Amy was right; he had jumped in with both feet, or at least with one and a half. He was doing what he always dreamed of doing—making pots. He realized that he was even enjoying it and Gloria's straight talk had instigated a change in his attitude. She had called it as it truly was: reality, with a healthy dose of quirks sprinkled on top.

He got out of bed and started a load of laundry when he remembered the kiln. It had been too hot to open the night before and he wondered if it would be ready now. It was still dark outside so he descended the staircase in a t-shirt and boxer shorts and a pair of old sandals he kept by the door.

He swung the back door open and switched on the light, illuminating the studio and blinding himself. He shuffled to the shelf next to the kiln and retrieved a pair of long leather gloves with blackened fingertips.

He opened the kiln slowly. It was still hot inside and he was grateful for the gloves as he began unloading white bisqueware, stacking it on every flat surface. As he reached further into the kiln, he began to sweat.

He was excited for the new possibilities these pots represented. They were like blank canvases, but Jake could already imagine what they would look like when he was done with them. Patience had always been difficult for Jake. These pots had been made up to seven days before and it would be another five days before he could take them out of the final firing...two weeks to see the fruits of his labor.

It was not until all of the horizontal surfaces within a few steps of the kiln were covered with cooling pots that Jake decided to stop until the kiln was completely cool. He sat down on the stool, his sweat cooling and causing a chill. As he looked down at the goose bumps on his legs, he realized he was not wearing any clothes. He felt silly, sitting there in his underwear, looking at pots like a child in his pajamas on Christmas morning.

He had his back turned toward the door when the knock came. He turned to the door and saw a tall, dark figure silhouetted in front of the dawn skies. His first thought was to hide. Maybe the stranger would go away. The stranger knocked again and this time the knock was followed by an announcement.

"Jake, good morning. It's me, Mayor Jim." Jake was mortified. He knew he needed to do something so he did the only thing he could do; he stood and walked to the door in nothing but his underwear.

"Good morning Mayor," he said nervously as he opened the door.

The Mayor looked him over from head to toe before responding. "Good morning Jake," he finally said, failing to hold back a smile. "I was out for my morning stroll and saw your light on. Is everything alright?"

Jake bumbled for words for a moment, not knowing where to begin. "I must look pretty silly," he said, trying hard to stretch his undershirt over his polka dot boxer shorts.

"Indeed," the Mayor responded with a nod.

"I couldn't sleep, so I came down to unload the kiln. I must have lost track of time."

"Indeed," the mayor repeated, smiling.

"I'd invite you in, but I'm not wearing any clothes." At this, they both burst into laughter, putting Jake's nerves at ease.

"I'm glad it was me and not my wife," the Mayor said between chuckles. "You'd never hear the end of it, had it been her at the door. Tell you what—I'll run over to Sam's and get us some breakfast if you agree to put some clothes on."

Jake grinned broadly. "Deal," he exclaimed.

The Mayor left for the bakery as Jake slinked his way up the stairs to his apartment, looking around to see if anyone else had seen him. He washed his face with cold water and slipped into his work clothes. After dressing, he went back to the studio to brew some tea. The Mayor returned a few minutes later.

"The old timers in town know that Sam makes his famous apple streusel only on Monday mornings. It's a little secret you ought to be aware of," he said, handing the brown package to Jake while he removed his hat and hung it on the nail near the door.

"Would you like some tea?"

"Don't mind if I do," said the Mayor.

He watched as the Mayor looked skyward until he located his mug hanging on a nail. He reached up and plucked it from its resting spot. Unlike many of the others, the Mayor's mug was relatively dust free. It was a tall mug that bellied out toward the bottom and had a bold handle. Jake grinned as he compared the mug to its owner.

"Do you make it a habit of joining the little people for breakfast?" Jake asked as he poured the Mayor's tea.

"No," he said out of the corner of his mouth, which was already full of apple streusel. "I thought it was time to pay you a visit to see how you're doing. I just returned from a mayor's convention in Atlanta. When I saw your light on this morning, I thought it might give me a good excuse to stop in and say hello."

"I'm glad you did. I'll try to be more presentable next time."

With that, the two men laughed again–Jake, a nervous laugh and the Mayor, a rather loud and hearty laugh.

"I've been curious how you're getting along."

"I think I'm doing ok. It took a couple of weeks to figure a few things out, but I am grateful to be here and I am enjoying the town." The words had escaped spontaneously from Jake's lips and he hesitated, wondering what had changed overnight.

"That's good to hear, son," the Mayor responded, with the power and authority of a reigning patriarch. "I'd like to see what you are making," he said, apparently oblivious to the bisqueware stacked all around him.

"You came at a good time," Jake said, choosing to give the seemingly unobservant Mayor the benefit of the doubt. "I just unloaded these this morning." He stood and walked to the showroom, retrieving two of the new bowls. "These came out of the last firing," he said, handing the Mayor one of the bowls.

"I've never seen anything like these come out of this shop. Do you think you can sell them?"

Jake wasn't sure whether to laugh or cry. "I think so. I already sold a couple on Saturday."

"Well, they certainly are different," the Mayor said, offering Jake neither praise nor criticism.

"Well, they're new," Jake said, not sure what direction the Mayor was going. He picked up the streusel and bit into it, filling his mouth in hopes that the sweetness would take the place of anything he might later regret. He assumed the Mayor knew very little about pottery or art and he hoped that the rest of the town might be more accepting and excited about the new direction.

After enjoying a few bites of streusel, Jake decided to try and sway the conversation in a more positive direction. He knew the Mayor had been in town for many years and guessed that he had been well acquainted with Isaac. He hoped the Mayor would have a good story. "Tell me about your mug, Mayor," he said.

"Mine was one of the early ones," the Mayor said, in a way that almost sounded like a school boy boasting that he was the first to be chosen for the baseball team.

Jake looked at the Mayor's mug. Its handle was much thicker than some of the others. It was the largest, but far from the prettiest. It was glazed black on the inside and top half and had a nice rusty red glaze on the bottom half.

"I still remember the day I picked this mug...must have been more than fifty years ago. I was just a kid back then, probably only fifteen and I really thought I was a big shot."

Jake wondered if much had really changed from that notion.

"My father was the editor of the paper and my mother was the heiress of the Franklin family estate."

The Franklin name meant nothing to Jake, but he went along with it as if it should.

"My Mom often talked about moving away from Niederbipp and raising me among a higher class of people, but Dad's job at the paper kept us here. My grandfather's money, on the other hand, gave us all sorts of elaborate vacations to ancestral homes near and far. I had my own maid, a nanny, and a chauffeur who dropped me off at school every morning in a polished black Bentley.

"I didn't have many friends when I was younger and my grades were never very good. My mother had all sorts of excuses for me, convincing me that I was better than the kids at school and smarter too. I began to believe her. If I ever had any friends, they were mostly gone by the time I was fifteen, and the few kids who still chummed around, did so only for the perks. After a while, even my bribes stopped working and I found myself alone in the world, a creature of my mother's making. I was the richest kid at school, and yet I was the poorest one among them."

The mayor took another drink from his mug, his brow down now. Jake listened to the silence that grew awkward after the first minute had passed.

"So tell me, how did you get to know Isaac?"

The Mayor looked up, startled away from the distant memory that obviously still plagued him. "He invited me into his shop one day when I was feeling particularly lonely. It's been a long time, but I seem to remember him planting flowers in his flower box when I walked by. I had just been in a scuffle with some of the kids from school and I was angry at the world. Somehow, he had time for me. He knew who I was. No one had ever called me Jimmy. My mother had always insisted I be called James or at least Jim, but Isaac got away with Jimmy from that first day.

"He made me feel welcome in a way I had never felt before. We talked about school and life and dreams. My parents had always told me that I was good at arguing and I decided early on that I wanted to become a lawyer. I remember him telling me that the world needs kind people to practice the law.

"I returned often over the next several months. Isaac was nearly twenty years older than me, but he understood me. I confided in him about my lack of friends, and he surprised me by telling me that he couldn't imagine anyone not wanting to be around such a nice kid. His words caused me to think about how I treated others. I rarely showed the same face to others that Isaac drew out of me. His kindness rubbed off, and before long, I found myself approaching others with the same kindness he had shown me. I was surprised at the reaction I received. The kids I once alienated and treated with snobbery became friendly.

"After my junior year of high school, I visited Isaac one summer afternoon. I happily reported to him how things had changed. I was no longer a loner and I was spending more of my time surrounded by friends.

"I remember he told me he believed my Grandfather would be proud of me. We had never mentioned my grandfather before in conversation. I wasn't aware that Isaac even knew him. Isaac explained that he had spent time with my grandfather after Lily died, hoping to glean some of his wisdom. They used to walk together in the evenings and became good friends, even though my grandfather was several decades older than him.

"Isaac told me that my Grandfather lived by a creed from the Bible:

'Where much is given, much is expected.' [3] He said he spent the last days of his life trying to make up for the time he had lost while he accumulated his wealth. He was determined to spend the remainder of his time serving others. He hoped his wealth would make it possible for his posterity to serve the community.

"Isaac told me that my grandfather often spoke of me being his hope, the one to continue with his dreams of serving the people of Niederbipp. My parents had never mentioned any of this and I felt slighted, like my destiny had been covered up. I knew my grandfather was a very wealthy man, but I had never known the hope he had for how that wealth would be used.

"During the rest of that summer, I began to devise a plan to make my grandfather's dream a reality. When fall came and school started, I was elected student body president. I spent the year making friends and learning how to serve. I adopted for myself my grandfather's creed and tried to be a friend wherever I could.

"By the time I graduated from high school, I was named 'the person most likely to succeed.' I went away to college and then law school and got a job at a Manhattan law firm. A year later, I married and made partner and my wealth and prestige began to grow.

"My father passed away just a week before my fifteen year reunion and I returned to Niederbipp, a hotshot.

"After burying my father, I visited Isaac. My mug still hung where I had left it, but it was hard to recognize under a thick layer of dust. I remember very little of our conversation, except for a question he asked me. He reminded me that I had adopted my grandfather's creed and asked if I was still trying to live by it.

"I don't remember how I responded or even if I did, but I remember how his question made be feel. It had been years since I had even thought about it. I was busy making a life for myself, getting my education, becoming partner, and getting married. We returned to the city, but thoughts of my visit with Isaac stayed with me. I asked myself the same question every day for several weeks. I recognized that between my quest for success and my other pursuits, I had largely forgotten the creed that had once served to make my life better.

"One day while I was preparing for a court case, the senior partner of the law firm came into my office. After stressing the importance of my case to the reputation of the firm, he told me he wanted me to pull out all the stops and destroy our opponent's council. He said it was time the city knew that we were strong and ruthless. I agreed, but felt uncomfortable.

"That night as I lay awake thinking about the case, I remembered my first visit with Isaac. 'The world needs kind people to practice the law,' he had told me. I knew my case was strong. There was little chance I would lose, but I didn't feel comfortable with my boss's request to destroy our opponents.

"Instead, the next day when I went to court, I presented my case clearly, laying out the facts and presenting the evidence. We won the case without a hitch but when I returned to the office the next day, my boss was furious. He suggested that I take some time off and think about what I wanted in life. If I was willing to do as I was told, I would be welcomed back. If not, I would need to find a new place to work. I think he expected I would return the next day, but my decision had already been made.

"My wife was happy to move to Niederbipp, having fallen in love with the town when we were home for the funeral and reunion. We moved into the old family mansion to help mom and I set up a small office in town, determined to practice law with kindness, or not at all. A couple of years later when the Mayor retired, I decided to run. In the years since that time, I have made hundreds of visits to this shop to visit with Isaac. It seems I have to be reminded from time to time about the power of kindness and my grandfather's creed. There are still moments when my old self comes out and I forget that the root of public service is service.

"It wasn't much more than a couple of years ago that Isaac helped me to remember the value of kindness once again. I tried to scare a bum out of town who was panhandling down at the fountain when I saw he had one of Isaac's mugs."

Jake smiled, knowing he was talking about Kai, but he said nothing, wanting hear the story from the Mayor's point of view.

"I accused him of stealing the mug but when he told me Isaac had given it to him, I dropped in to give Isaac a lecture about encouraging riffraff to hang out in our town.

"I was pretty angry for some reason and let it out with fury, suggesting that I was working hard to keep the town free of hoodlums and would appreciate his help. When I finished my little tirade, Isaac looked from the wheel and kindly said, 'Jimmy, aren't we all beggars?'

"It had been several decades since he called me Jimmy, and hearing it caught me off guard. I sat in silence for a long time, recognizing the kind reprimand he had just given me. I too had come to his shop, a beggar. He had filled my cup not only with tea, but with love and kindness and friendship when I had none.

"I now buy my groceries from that beggar. He is one of the hardest working young men I know. You may have met him already?"

"Yeah, I had dinner with Kai and Molly last Friday."

The Mayor nodded. "Jake, wealth nearly ruined me as it has so many generations of young people who know privilege without knowing the work it took to get there. It made me slothful and I lost touch with the world around me.

"Because of my change of heart that began here in this shop, I raised my children in a different way. My wife is a practical woman who believes spoiling children only makes them irresponsible, so our children learned how to work. We never had a maid or a chauffeur and our children learned the realities of life. We paid for each of them to attend college, but I wanted them to learn to make it on their own. Their trust funds will be available to them when they reach the age of fifty-five. The rest of the family fortune was put into a trust to fund local charities. I know my grandfather would have wanted it that way. I only wish I would have had the chance to learn in my youth the things I taught my children.

"Jake, you may not know that we interviewed five individuals to fill your position. I think you should know why I chose you." Jake sat up, eager to hear.

"When you first shook my hand, I knew what kind of a young man you were."

Jake looked surprised.

"I knew by your firm grip and your rough and calloused hands that you're not afraid of work. Your talent and your education were also impressive, but it was your hands that impressed me most. I told myself at that point that anyone with hands like that would be able to succeed here."

Jake smiled. "Thanks for the confidence."

"We're glad you're here," said the Mayor. "Have you heard from the others yet, Sam, Thomas and Beverly?"

Jake shook his head. "Sam has dropped by with bread and Thomas stopped by last week for a couple of minutes, but I haven't had much of an opportunity to speak to them yet."

"They're good men," said the Mayor. "You'll enjoy their stories. Beverly tells me you've become friendly with her niece." Jake immediately blushed.

"We're really just getting to know each other."

"She's a beautiful young woman. I might warn you that word tends to travel fast around town."

He glanced down at his watch and straightened his back before setting his mug down. "I better get going. My secretary set up a meeting for me with a man who wants to open a museum on Hauptstrasse. If you haven't noticed by now, we have some pretty colorful folks in town."

"That's what I hear," said Jake, grinning.

The Mayor stood and reached out his hand to shake Jake's. "If I can be of any service to you, please let me know."

Jake thanked him and took his mug, hanging it back on the nail. With bisqueware spread all over the studio, Jake decided to do some glazing. He first loaded the bowls he had glazed on Saturday into the kiln, making room in the studio. He worked for a couple of hours, but the bright day and the gentle breeze blowing through the open back door distracted him. At noon, he turned his back on his work and left to explore his new world.

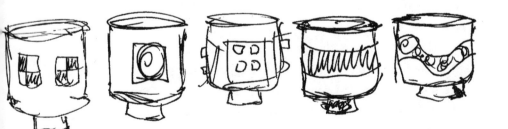

28
THE ESCAPE

Jake packed his backpack with his sketchbook, some bread, and an apple, then filled his water bottle before descending the stairs with his keys in hand. He had seen the motorcycle during his first week in Niederbipp when he was cleaning and organizing, but had yet to ride it. He opened the door of the rickety shed and struggled to roll the motorcycle out without tipping over the ancient pedal bike parked next to it. It was an old red Honda with big fenders and chrome mufflers. Jake guessed it was probably forty years old, but it was still in great shape.

He brushed off the seat, scattering the dust that had accumulated over the winter months. He found a helmet and pair of goggles perched on the rearview mirrors. After sitting on the saddle and adjusting the mirrors, he caught a glimpse of himself and smiled at his reflection. He looked silly with the old goggles and the bubblehead helmet, but decided to keep them on.

He put the key in the ignition before folding out the arm on the kick start, then stood on the kick start and quickly stepped down. He repeated the motion again and again. After a dozen kicks, the motor started up slowly, coughing and rumbling. He twisted the handle in his right hand to give the motor a little gas and it began to purr lightly. He was excited as he settled onto the saddle.

He rolled slowly across the cobblestone parking area and onto the lane, winding his way through the narrow passages between the old buildings.

Soon he was on the pavement. He drove out of town toward the hills. The road was smooth and quick and, though the day was warm, he was soon chilled as he cut through the air. Within a couple of minutes, he was surrounded by pastures and farmland. As he came to the top of a hill, he was overwhelmed by the beauty of the vista before him: a patchwork of fields on the low lands, surrounded by woods of maple and elm that covered the highlands of the rolling hills. The road cut through the patchwork and summoned him onward.

Down the gentle slope he flew, as fast as the old Honda could carry him. He passed by pastures of horses and large, lazy cattle prostrating themselves under the noon sun. He waved to a farmer perched on a tractor, tumbling the drying grass. The landscape was dotted with charming old farmhouses and barns. He drove through the valley and up into the hills where the shadows of the tall trees stretched across the road and chilled the air, causing goose bumps to rise over his bare arms and neck.

Then down, down again, he rode into the next valley. Another small town, much smaller than Niederbipp, rose from the hills and he slowed to observe the beautiful stone and clapboard homes and buildings. He waved to a large old woman wearing a flowered dress and knee-high rubber boots, hanging underwear out to dry on a clothesline. An old man waved his cane and smiled a toothless grin as Jake rode by. He quickly regained his speed when he awoke an angry bulldog from his nap that chased Jake as he drove out of town.

He came to a stop on the top of a hill crowned by a tall tree whose flowered branches reached out like hands, trying to steal the billowy clouds from the bright blue sky. He parked the bike and took a seat on the hand-hewn bench that stood at the trunk of the tree.

His skin was chilled and he rubbed his bare arms with his hands. From here, he could see parts of three valleys and the hilltops that separated them. He watched as a bumblebee buzzed and hovered over a patch of dandelions near his feet. Even the weeds were beautiful. The dandelions spread out in every direction, complimented by the tall grass that danced in the gentle breeze. He took a deep breath, taking in the scents of the late spring afternoon.

Jake walked to the Honda and lifted his backpack from the milk crate strapped to the rack. He returned to the bench before pulling out his sandwich and water bottle. He no longer felt confined as he had from time to time in Niederbipp. The beauty of the day and freedom he felt was comforting. He finished his sandwich and nearly emptied his water bottle before he stood and returned to the scooter, excited to continue exploring.

He rode into the next valley that was much less populated. The forests were thicker and darker. When the forest showed no signs of clearing or opening wider than the width of the road, he decided to turn around. He figured he was at least twenty miles from Niederbipp and guessed it was 3:00. He knew Amy would be getting off work in a couple of hours and he thought about surprising her by taking her to dinner.

When he saw a green field of freshly mown hay, he stopped. He was tired and his shoulders ached, so he parked the scooter on the side of the road and walked to the field to rest. He removed his helmet and lay down. Jake smiled to himself as he watched the billowy clouds float by. As a child, he had spent time with his mother in the park, laying on their backs, naming the images they discovered in the ever-changing clouds. She would like it here, he thought.

He tried to imagine Amy lying on the grass next to him, watching the clouds. They hadn't made any plans for the week. The door had simply been left open and as he lay on the soft grass, Jake began wondering what this week would bring. As he considered his options, he drifted off to sleep in the warmth of the afternoon sun.

When he awoke, he was disoriented. The afternoon was gone and he guessed it was probably after 6:00. He figured that if he left right then, he might have time to visit Amy before dark. It would be too late for dinner, but he thought it would be nice to check out the Ice Café. Gathering up his things, he returned to his scooter and zoomed off down the road. As he climbed the next hill, the scooter began to shake and sputter. Then, once he reached the top, it quit completely. He looked down at the gas gauge and shook his head when he saw that it registered full. He got off the bike and released the saddle to expose the gas tank. It was completely empty. He would have to remember that the gas gauge was broken, but that was of little consolation now. It would be dark in an hour and he was quite sure he was still five miles away from home. He remembered the story Brian had told him about Isaac running out of gas and returning to find his car stripped. He decided it would be better to push the scooter home than lose the only motorized vehicle he owned.

He coasted down the hill as far as he could and then got off and began pushing the scooter. Darkness was falling and the colors of the countryside began to fade to gray as he pushed his scooter through the valley, jumping on and coasting whenever the grade allowed it. Two tractors passed him on their way home after a day in the fields and the farmers waved and smiled as they passed him.

Finally darkness fell and still he pushed on, encouraged by the soft glow of the town lights in the distance. The sweat from his exertion turned cold and his hopes of seeing Amy vanished when he saw the last hill he had to climb. His whole body was tired. Of the last five miles, he had been able to coast only half a mile and his shoulders ached from both the pushing and the awkward stretching he had to do while he pushed.

Finally, he reached the top of the hill and looked down into Niederbipp with awe. The lights of the town illuminated the streets and Jake was reminded of the charm he discovered here after the May Day celebration. He coasted down the hill to the streets of town and pushed the scooter along quietly until he returned to the shed.

It had been a wonderful day, despite the unexpected turn of events. He climbed the stairs to the apartment, grateful that he had gotten as far as he had before he ran out of gas.

He washed his face and lay down on his bed to eat the apple he had forgotten about. He was too tired to cook. Too tired to move. Too tired to do anything but fall asleep in his clothes, dreaming he was a bird flying over the countryside.

"ART IS THE HEALING OINTMENT THAT OOZES FROM OUR HEARTS AND MINDS & HEALS OUR ACHING WORLD." — FRED BABB

A PICNIC IN THE GRAVEYARD

Jake was busy loading the kiln the next morning when the bells on the front door jingled and two men entered the shop. He put down a big bowl and rounded the corner to greet his customers.

"Good morning," he said cheerfully.

"Good morning," came the response from the younger man. The older, taller man's eyes shifted around the showroom at all of the pots. The men didn't fit any stereotype of pottery buyer and their denim clothes suggested they too were men who made their living by hand. Jake wondered if they were lost.

"What can I help you with?"

The younger man looked at the older man whose eyes had rested on one of the new bowls from the last firing. When the younger man saw that his companion was not listening, he swatted him on the arm, putting an abrupt end to his stare. "What?" he whined, rubbing his arm.

"The invoice," said the younger man.

"Oh yeah." The older man pulled a clipboard from behind his back where it had been tucked into his belt. He handed it to the younger man who got straight to the point.

"We just delivered a tombstone to the cemetery. The priest told us that we should deliver the invoice to you." Jake was stumped as he took the clipboard in his hand.

"I never ordered a tombstone," he said as he looked over the invoice.

"No, you didn't order it. It says on top there it was ordered by Isaac Bingham. Do you know him?"

"No. I mean, not really... He's dead, you know," he said, still confused.

"Of course he's dead. No living man ever needed a tombstone, did he?"

"I guess not. When was this ordered? He's been dead for almost two months now."

"Well, if you look up in the right corner there, you'll see the order date."

Jake looked at the corner that had been smudged with what looked like strawberry jam. "It looks like you guys had breakfast on your invoice."

The younger man raised his head to the other man, whose eyes were still wandering around the room.

"You make all this yourself?" he asked, breaking his silence.

"No, not all of it; actually, not much of it. It was made by Isaac, the potter I replaced."

"Nice stuff."

"Judd likes coming to Niederbipp because of the baker's pastries. I'm guessing that's his jelly on the corner there," said the younger man.

"Best jelly-filled pastries in the county," said the man, now known as Judd.

"Right," said Jake, turning his attention back to the invoice. Through the jelly in the corner he was able to read the date. 9/22/2004. "This was ordered a few years ago. I'm sorry, but I really don't know anything about this. Did Father Thomas say anything else?"

"Only that you would probably want to know about it so you could get started on the tiles, or something like that."

"Tiles?"

"That's all he said."

"Well what does the tombstone look like?"

"I'm not sure how it qualifies as a tombstone at all, but I guess that's what was ordered. It looks like a bench."

Suddenly Jake knew what the man was talking about.

"We had to make it up special, and out of cement instead (stone we usually use. The funny thing is that it doesn't even any writing on it, no dates or names or anything. We don't mak stuff, we just deliver it, and we got a lot of work to do so if you mind signing on the X, we can be on our way before Judd gets hu again."

"But how much do I owe you?" he asked, quickly figuring in mind how much money was in the till and knowing it would no nearly enough for a tombstone.

"It's been paid for," said the man, impatiently. "I just need a signature that you received it." Jake signed the invoice and handed the clipboard back to the man.

"C'mon," said the younger man, handing Jake a copy of the invoice. "We better get going if were gonna make it back by lunch." Judd reluctantly turned to go.

"Wait," Jake called out, as the two men were walking out the door. He reached into a wicker basket and pulled out two mugs, taking them to the men standing in the doorway. "Thanks for bringing that by," he said, handing them the mugs. The older man took the mug he was handed and cradled it in his giant callused hands like he was holding a tiny bird. His whole face smiled as he looked up at Jake.

"Wow! I can't believe it. Thank you."

"You're welcome," he said, as the two men walked away. He knew it was not a good business practice to give away the things he was supposed to be selling, but something told him that Isaac would have done the same thing.

At noon, Jake heard the church bells ring just as he was loading the last of the pots into the kiln. He swung the old door shut and latched it before opening the gas valve and striking a match to light the flame.

He locked the doors and climbed the stairs to his apartment where he hastily made himself a sandwich with two thick slabs of Sam's bread and more peanut butter and honey than was needed for three sandwiches.

He wrapped his sandwich in wax paper and grabbed the bottle of apple juice Josh had given him then headed for the cemetery. He was nearly there when he decided to stop by the department store to see if Amy might be interested in joining him for a picnic. As he approached the store, he saw his reflection in the glass door and hesitated. In his grubby work clothes, splattered with clay and glaze, he knew he wasn't dressed to impress.

He opened the door and walked inside, looking for a sign to announce where the cosmetics counter might be. When he didn't find any such sign, he began walking past the rows of shoes, searching over the shelves for anything that looked like a makeup counter. A woman dressed in a black leather skirt and a white silk blouse approached him.

"Can I help you?" she asked, looking down her nose at him.

He turned to look at her, flustered. "I'm looking for the makeup counter."

She gave him a funny look and pointed over her head. "It's in the back corner."

He made his way there, not realizing that he drew the attention of all the sales people on the floor. His eyes were fixed on the back corner of the room, hoping to catch a glimpse of Amy's ginger hair.

He relaxed when he spotted her, dressed in a white lab coat that she wore over her summer dress. She had her back to Jake, talking to her co-worker, who was similarly dressed. Her co-worker, glancing over Amy's shoulder, saw him first. Her smile caused Amy to turn around where she met Jake's eyes.

"Hello."

"Hi, there," responded Jake.

"What brings you to the cosmetic counter?" she said with a teasing smile. "Are you already out of the eye shadow I sold you last week?"

"No," he said seriously. "I'm afraid the color was all wrong."

"Really?" asked Amy, feigning surprise.

"Yeah, it looks absolutely dreadful with my overalls. I was hoping you had something, perhaps a little more denim-like."

Amy smiled. Jake was glad he had come.

"Hey," he began again, leaning now against the counter, "I was just heading up to the cemetery to have my lunch and wondered if you might want to come."

"The cemetery, huh?"

"Yeah, some guys delivered Isaac's tombstone today and I thought I better go take a look. Is it your lunch break yet?"

Amy turned to her co-worker. "Do you care if I take the first lunch today?"

"No, that's ok," the girl responded.

"But I don't have a lunch," Amy said as she walked around the counter. "I was planning on going back to my aunt's for lunch."

"I don't mind sharing, but it's only peanut butter and honey."

She looked down at his sandwich wrapped in wax paper. "Sounds good to me." She grabbed his arm and began walking toward the door. They didn't notice the look of bewilderment on the face of the girl who remained behind the counter.

Jake felt his face flush. This was the first time that Amy had really touched him on her own accord besides the slugs and jabs she had given him, and though he welcomed her touch, he was still shocked by it.

Out in the bright sun, Amy looked at Jake. "What a great idea. I'm glad you came. It's been a slow day."

"Yeah, I'm glad you could come. I'm sorry I'm dressed so poorly for a picnic. I didn't think about it until I was already here."

"Are you kidding? You don't need to impress me. I'm an artist too, remember?" She looked down at her clothes. "Oh brother, I forgot to take off my jacket."

"We can go back if you need to."

"No. I only get an hour for lunch and on a day like today I don't want to waste a minute of it." She took the bottle from Jake's hand as they climbed the stairs to the churchyard.

"So what's the story with this tombstone?" she asked as they approached the gates of the cemetery.

"The way I understand it, it's my job to finish the grave marker for Isaac. I guess that's the way it has been done for six generations; the new potter creates a bench to memorialize the one who has gone before him." He unlatched the gate and opened it for Amy to step through.

"What exactly do you have to do?"

"I'm not entirely sure."

Amy turned to look at the graveyard. "It's beautiful here."

"Yeah, graveyards always creeped me out before I saw this one. There's so much life here."

"No, you're right. This is different than any graveyard I have ever seen too."

Jake turned to look where the new cement bench stood and walked toward it.

"This must be it," he said, taking a seat on its sun-warmed surface. Amy sat down next to him and began unwrapping the sandwich. She mopped up the globs of crystallized honey that were stuck to the paper and licked her fingers.

"Wow, how much honey did you use?"

"Just enough," he said smiling. Amy ripped the honey-laden sandwich in two and handed Jake the larger of the two halves.

"I love it when the bread gets kind of crunchy from the honey," she said, breaking the silence. She pulled off a piece of the honey-saturated bread and lifted it to the sky, blocking out the sun with it. In the light, the bread glowed like pure gold. Jake watched her, smiling.

"What?"

"Nothing, I've just never met anyone who likes peanut butter and honey as much as I do."

"Are you kidding? I lived on this in college. Some of my earliest still life paintings were of peanut butter jars and honey bears and sandwiches glowing in the sunlight. My first show was titled "Simple Pleasures." It was all pictures of food. Cupcakes, ice cream, chocolate bars, but my favorites were the ones of the sandwiches."

"Do you do commission work?"

"Sometimes, why do you ask?"

"I'd like to commission you to paint me a sandwich. What would it cost?"

"I don't know if you can afford it. Paintings like that aren't cheap."

"Do you have installment plans or do trade?"

"We might be able to work something out."

"Just name your price."

"Ok, it will cost you place settings for four and at least one sandwich a week for the rest of the summer, payable only in picnic style, at a place and time of my choosing. Oh, and next time I'd like some milk if you don't mind. Apple juice is nice, but it doesn't go well with peanut butter and honey."

"That better be a pretty big painting. For that price, it better be big enough to cover the dome of the Sistine Chapel."

"Oh, are your place settings that expensive?" she mused.

"No, but my sandwiches are." They laughed together as they both thought of the great deal they were getting.

"Cheers to the simple pleasures of life," Jake said, raising the bottle of apple juice to the sky.

"Cheers," she said, smiling back. Not having cups made the toast a bit awkward. He handed the bottle to Amy, who took it and drank. They ate their sandwiches and talked about their jobs, laughing and enjoying each other's company until Amy remembered the reason why they had come to the cemetery.

"So what do you think you'll do with this bench?"

"I'm not really sure." He glanced at the nearest bench, not more than ten feet away. They stood together and walked closer to inspect it. The colorful bench memorialized Henry Engelhart, Isaac's father-in-law. Jake pointed to the benches under the old crabapple tree and explained what he had learned from them. The other benches were by themselves, standing either against the wall or the iron fence that surrounded the graveyard.

Grass had already begun to grow on the mound of dirt that lay over the still-new grave. Looking to the right, Jake saw a small grave marker embedded with pieces of colorful pottery.

He pulled away some of the grass that had begun to creep its way over the marker and read the inscription:

Lily Engelhart Bingham
January 22, 1929- March 14, 1954
Loyal Daughter, Beloved Wife

Jake, who had been kneeling as he pulled away the grass, leaned back and sat on his heels, staring at the grave marker.

"What is it?" asked Amy, who had taken a seat again on the new bench.

"I've heard a lot about this woman and the love Isaac had for her. It almost feels like I know her. She wasn't much older than us when she died."

"It sounds like this must have been a place for a lot of tears," Amy suggested.

"Yes, but from all I've learned about Isaac, I know it must have been a place of hope too."

The gate of the graveyard whined as it was opened, drawing their attention. Jake stood to see Father Thomas climbing the stairs.

"Ahh, Jake, I was hoping I'd catch you."

"Hello, Father," said Amy as he approached.

"Why, hello Amy. What a surprise to see you."

"We thought it was a nice day for a picnic," she said smiling.

"I'm glad to see that the two of you have gotten acquainted. Your aunt was worried you wouldn't have anyone to chum around with while you were here. It seems she was wrong about that." Thomas turned his attention to Jake. "So what do you think?"

"Well, it looks like I have my work cut out for me. I've made tiles before, but this is a little more complicated."

"Have you looked at the other benches then?" asked Thomas.

"Just a little bit. I probably have a lot of thinking to do before I get started. Do you have any suggestions?"

Thomas moved forward and sat on the older bench, across from where Amy still sat.

"Isaac is of course the first of the potters to die since I came to town, and the tradition of the benches is still somewhat unfamiliar to me. I had occasion to talk to Isaac about it a few times over the years. You may have heard that he spent a lot of time here."

"Yeah, I've heard that from a few people. What can you tell me?"

"Only that the potters used a lot of symbols in their work. Isaac often lamented that he didn't know the meaning behind some of the older benches, but other things remain clear, even to me. For example," he said, pointing to a tile on the bench on which he sat, "this tile here is an example of some of the symbols they used."

Jake looked at the tile. "A beehive?"

"That's right. The beehive is an ancient symbol used in many cultures to signify community, work, and industry. You might know that Henry Engelhart was also a bee keeper."

"No. I've never heard that."

"It's true. Isaac also kept bees for many years, until he decided it was time to give it up to a younger generation. He gave the bees to Josh Adams, who owns an apple orchard on the edge of town. He claims the bees make the sweetest honey in the world, and his apples aren't bad either."

Jake smiled and lifted the bottle of apple juice. "I met Josh at the May Day celebration. He dropped by the shop last week to tell me some of the things he learned from Isaac."

"Yes, Josh and Isaac were good friends."

"Do you have any thoughts about what sort of symbols I should use on the tiles for Isaac's bench?" asked Jake.

"I'm not saying you need to use symbols at all. I just thought it might be a good idea; that is if you are looking for ideas. I suppose I could imagine a bench that is much like Isaac was."

"How's that?"

"Well, Jake, you've been around the town long enough to know that Isaac had a lot of friends."

Jake smiled and nodded.

"But I don't know if you've been around long enough to know that Isaac changed the lives of many people, including mine. He was a man of incredible faith, love, and understanding. He was the most unselfish person I've ever met. He had a knowledge of the Bible and other good books,

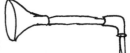

but his goodness didn't end with his knowledge. His knowledge led him to action. He strongly believed that faith without works is dead. 4 There were more small acts of kindness done by that one man than the rest of the town combined. And all that he did, he did in silence. He was never one to toot his own horn. People would wander into his shop and come out better people for knowing him. He inspired us all to be better people. I think that Isaac was a fine potter, but his work with people far exceeded the beauty of his finest vessels."

"So how do you embody that in a bench to his memory?" Jake asked, feeling overwhelmed.

"You're the artist, but I will give you this advice: If you will study the New Testament and learn to understand the parables of Jesus, you will begin to understand Isaac. His life and his work were full of parables. It was not until I became friends with him that I began to understand Christ. I learned more in a week with Isaac than I had in the four years I spent in seminary."

Amy touched Jake on the arm. "I would love to stay and hear more about this, but I need to get back to work."

Jake looked up at the clock on the church steeple. "Yeah, me too," he said. "Father, can we continue this discussion later?"

Thomas nodded. "If you don't mind, I'll stop by for another cup of tea. Word on the street is that you're making some really nice new work. I'd like to see it."

"You're always welcome."

Amy and Jake gathered their things and hurried off.

"It sounds like this project is going to be tougher than you thought," she said once they were out of earshot.

"How do you figure?"

"Well, its one thing to make something pretty, but it's an entirely different thing to make something that is pretty and has deep meaning. Not only that, but it will be scrutinized by everyone who ever knew Isaac. I'm sure you won't be able to make everyone happy."

"Oh, I gave up that notion years ago."

"I think that's one of the things I like best about you," she said as they descended the stairs to Hauptstrasse.

"What's that?"

"You have a strong inner compass. That sounds cheesy, but you seem to know what you want and are willing to work hard for it, regardless of what others think. Take your clothes for example."

"Hey, I like my clothes," said Jake, feigning defensiveness.

"But there aren't many guys who can walk into a department store with everyone looking at him and not care what they think. I wish I had the guts to not care what others think."

"Excuse me, but you walked out of that department store holding the arm of that mad man you just described and you didn't seem to care a bit about what people were thinking."

"I guess I did. You see how good you are for me?" she said, flashing a smile that sent electricity through his whole body.

The bell chimed before anything more could be said and Amy ran to the door, but turned and yelled back before she opened it. "So when are you bringing me my next sandwich?"

"Come by the Pottery when you get off and we'll talk about it," he yelled back. She waved and ran inside.

Jake took his time walking back to work. He didn't have a boss who kept a time card for him, but he still felt a responsibility to be there when the sign said he would be.

As he approached the fountain that marked the intersection of Zubergasse and Hauptstrasse, Jake watched as a couple stood, kissed each other, and went off their separate ways. Within a few steps, he was standing in the same space the couple had just been occupying. He wondered what it was like to hold someone like that. He sat down to contemplate the imaginings of his heart. The fountain was running and the sound drew his attention. He turned to look up at the statue on the fountain, surprised that he had never noticed it before. It was a woman of heroic proportion, dressed in a long robe. He didn't know many of

the Catholic saints, but he guessed it was a saint because of the gilded halo that encircled her angelic face. In her hand was a staff and at the end of the staff, there was a hook. He thought at first it was a shepherd's hook, but as he stood to take a closer look, he saw that it was a pruning hook.

Jake thought of the significance of the pruning hook. Somewhere in his memory from church he remembered a scripture about beating spears into pruning hooks as a sign of peace.[5] He took a closer look at the statue's face and saw it wasn't a halo, but a crown of gilded olive leaves, again a symbol of peace. He didn't know who she was, but he liked the idea of a symbol of peace being front and center in the middle of the town fountain. If there was this symbol, surely there were others. The church would likely be full of them.

Jake remembered the trip he had taken to Italy on one of his summer adventures. He was intrigued by the use of symbols he found in art and architecture, but most of all in the cathedrals. He learned that the use of symbols enabled common folk to understand the gospel without knowing how to read or write. The stained glass windows told  stories that anyone could understand, even if they didn't understand Latin. As he made his way back to the shop, he admitted his work on Isaac's bench would require far more than he had originally suspected. He knew he would need to spend more time with Father Thomas, going over ideas on symbols and learning more about the parables Christ taught.

His thoughts ran deep that afternoon. Glazing had always been a meditation for Jake. There had been many years that he hated the glazing process, after having ruined too many decent pots with a bad glaze job. After one particularly bad firing, where most of his pots came out ruined, he decided he was going to learn to glaze. He practiced on pottery other students had abandoned. Decorating pots he had no hand in creating was a liberating exercise.

The task that had started out as a necessary evil slowly became fun and Jake became passionate about glazing. He began to design his pieces for their ability to showcase a glaze rather than his previous method of making the piece and then wondering how in the world he might glaze it. Overcoming the weakness he had in glazing gave him great confidence.

Jake's thoughts drifted to his conversation with Father Thomas in the graveyard, specifically Thomas's suggestion to study the parables of the Bible in order to understand Isaac better. Jake had found a yellowing paperback Bible in the studio just a few days earlier. He was curious. He washed his hands and sat down to read.

He flipped the book open to Matthew. Many of the verses had been underlined with pencil and small notes were written in the margins of a few pages. As Jake read, he remembered the lessons he learned as a boy, but was also surprised by new insights. His own faith had gone through a series of hills and valleys. He felt better as he read about Christ's apostles, those who had been witnesses of His teachings and miracles, yet still had questions of faith and misunderstanding of gospel principles. Even Peter, the senior apostle, had his moments of doubt and weakness. Jake felt that if Jesus' closest companions experienced lapses of faith, then it must be part of the human condition.

Within just the first few chapters of Matthew, Jake found several symbols and metaphors that Christ used to teach the people, but when he read chapter 5 verses 14-16, he knew he had found one of the symbols that Father Thomas had referred to. Isaac was like a candlestick, giving light to everyone around him. His good works and lessons gave people hope and helped them to become stronger. Jake opened his sketchbook and drew a candle. Then he copied down the verses. There was something about the image of a candle that felt right to Jake.

14. YE ARE THE LIGHT OF THE WORLD. A CITY THAT IS SET ON A HILL CANNOT BE HID

15. NIETHER DO MEN LIGHT A CANDLE, AND PUT IT UNDER A BUSHEL, BUT ON A CANDLE STICK., AND IT GIVETH LIGHT UNTO ALL THAT ARE IN THE HOUSE.

16. LET YOUR LIGHT SO SHINE BEFORE MEN, THAT THEY MAY SEE YOUR GOOD WORKS, AND GLORIFY YOUR FATHER WHICH IS IN HEAVEN.

By closing time, Jake had made it through Matthew and was starting on Mark, his mind and sketchbook filling with ideas, symbols, and metaphors.

Amy walked through the open back door, waking Jake from his thoughts. He smiled when he saw it was her.

"Is it that time already?"

"Don't sound so excited to see me."

"Sorry, this afternoon has just really gone by fast."

"What have you been doing all day?"

"Well, I glazed some pots and I've been firing the kiln and reading."

"Anything good?" she asked as she took a seat on the stool next to him.

"Just the Bible," he said with a crooked grin. She looked surprised, but said nothing.

"Hey, I was talking to my aunt about some places to go painting. She said Taufer's Pond is really beautiful and only takes fifteen minutes by bike to get there. I was hoping we might go there tonight, if you're not busy."

Jake glanced at the kiln. The needle on the pyrometer indicated it was 1800° F. "I think the kiln will probably be ok without me. I picked up some sunflower bread this morning from the bakery. I don't have any meat for sandwiches, but I do have some yogurt."

"What are you going to make with yogurt and bread?" she asked.

He looked at her intently, wondering if she was joking.

"What?" she asked, feeling the stare.

"Haven't you ever had yogurt and bread?"

"You mean together?"

"Yeah, of course."

"No," she said turning up her nose.

"Hey, outside of peanut butter and honey sandwiches, this is all I lived on in college."

"We're not in college anymore," she said with a smile.

"It's true, but old habits are hard to break, especially when the cash flow situation hasn't changed dramatically. But even if I ever did have a bunch of money, I don't think I'd ever give up bread and yogurt."

"If it's that good, I guess I could give it a try."

"Done," he said, getting to his feet.

Amy followed. "I've got to get my bike and paints and change into some shorts. I'll be right back," she said as she left the shop. Twenty paces ahead, she turned to holler back at Jake who was climbing the stairs to his apartment, "Are you sure you don't want me to get some sandwich meat from my aunt?" Jake threw his hands at her and laughed as he opened the door and walked in without responding verbally.

30
TAUFER'S POND

Ten minutes later, Amy returned with her French easel strapped to her back. She had borrowed her aunt's old bike and carried a hand drawn map her uncle had given her. Jake had packed dinner in his old school backpack and dusted off the seat on Isaac's old bike.

"Sure you don't want to take the scooter?" Jake asked as Amy rolled to a squeaky stop at the back door. "It needs gas, but it would be faster going."

"No thanks, on a night like tonight, I'd rather ride a bike. That is, unless you don't think you can keep up?"

Jake smiled a broad grin. "Is it a race then?"

"No, we only have one map. If you got lost, I'd go hungry and if I got lost, you'd have no one to talk to. We better stick together," she said with a wink.

Jake mounted the old bike which looked like it had been built to withstand being run over by a tank in the Second World War. Before they got to the end of the street, Jake knew he would not be winning any races tonight, even with Amy's bike having the aerodynamic disadvantage of a large basket on the front end. Soon they were out of town, climbing slowly up the rolling hills covered with sunflowers and alfalfa. It was a different way than Jake had gone the day before on the scooter, but the scenery was much the same.

"I can't believe I've been here almost month and never been out this way," he said as he pedaled up alongside Amy.

"It seems like we've wasted a lot of time. I came here to paint this summer. I can count on two fingers the number of paintings I've begun and I don't even need fingers to count the paintings I've finished."

"What do you want to do about that?"

"It seems I have two choices. I can stop hanging out with you, or you can join me more often when I paint."

"Is that an invitation?"

"Only if you think you can pull yourself away from your work," she said, pretending to be really interested in the road.

"I've never really been a model before, but I hear they make pretty good money."

She grinned broadly. "Does that mean you'll come with me then?"

"Who else will make your sandwiches? And besides, it's not safe out here in the wilderness for a female painter."

"Oh, am I going to be attacked by the sunflowers?"

"You never know."

"Then it's a date," she said, as she pulled a hard right onto a forest path. "That is if you can keep up." She pedaled away into the trees. Jake tried his best to slow the old bicycle, but his momentum kept him going far past the turn off. By the time he had turned around and was on the same path, Amy had disappeared in the dense trees.

She was unpacking her easel on the bank of the pond when Jake finally caught up.

"I'm glad you came," she said, as he parked his bike next to hers. "I was getting hungry."

"I've never dated a girl like you," he said, walking towards her.

"Is that what we're doing then? Dating?"

Jake felt foolish. He walked up alongside her, but didn't look at her, not knowing what to say in response. She looked over at him and when he didn't look at her, she turned and slugged him in the shoulder.

"Ow!" he feigned. "What was that for?" He rubbed his arm, pretending to be hurt. "I already told you that I was an only child. I'm not sure if I told you that I was raised by a mother who taught me that hitting people was bad manners."

She laughed out loud and looked at him incredulously.

"I grew up shy and reserved and never really talked to girls until college," he continued. "I just don't know how to respond to you sometimes. Part of me wants to slug you back and part of me wants to hug you."

"You're a sweet boy," she said, pulling out her palette before securing her canvas to the easel.

"What is that supposed to mean?"

"Oh Jake, you have no idea how long I've wished for a friend like you."

"Go on," he said, kneeling down to unpack his backpack.

"I don't know how to say this without sounding conceited, so I'll just say it and hope you'll know what I mean."

Jake looked up and nodded.

She hesitated for a minute. "I've had a lot of boys pursue me over the years, but I always felt they were more interested in romancing me than getting to know who I am. I fell for a couple of them until I realized their interest in me was solely to satisfy themselves. I once dated a guy for six months and every time I invited him to go painting with me, he tried to talk me into going to a sporting event or hanging out with him and his buddies. I felt like his interest in me was only skin deep. He never once saw my paintings. He never even asked. He always told me that he planned to make more money than God so he could buy me a big house and keep me busy raising our own football team."

Jake looked up, surprised.

"Oh, I'm sure he made it sound more romantic than that, but that's what I heard. He was a charmer, but he never saw me for who I am. One night he took me to a fancy restaurant and then to a symphony. I thought he was finally coming around, getting away from the sports and his buddies and truly trying to impress me. But when he dropped me off that night, he walked me to the door and got down on his knee and asked me to marry him. Just then, the lights of a dozen parked cars turned on, lighting up the porch. He pulled a jewelry box from his pocket and opened it to reveal the biggest diamond I had ever seen. I was in a state of confusion...the lights, the question, the diamond.... I looked down at the diamond sparkling in the headlight and pulled it from the box. I held the ring closer to my face, not believing my eyes.

"It was a diamond in the shape of a football. I put the ring back in the box and handed it back to him. His friends began to cheer, not realizing what I was doing. I turned away and went inside without saying a word, leaving him kneeling on the porch and his friends cheering in the background like he had just scored a touchdown.

"I was disgusted to realize I had wasted six months with a guy who thought I would be excited about a football-shaped diamond. That night I swore off guys forever, promising myself to be a spinster artist 'til the day I died."

Jake laughed out loud.

"What's so funny?" she asked, looking down from her easel. He stopped laughing when he realized she wasn't.

"I'm sorry. I guess it's just that we all have stories from our past that are painfully funny. I don't mean to laugh at you. I'm sure he was a nice guy," he said, laughing again.

"So what about you?" she asked, looking over her easel as he spread the blanket over the long grass.

"What do you want to know?" he asked, feeling unusually calm and eager to talk.

"What has your dating experience been like?"

"Oh, far less interesting than yours I'm sure. My mom called me a late bloomer. I was so incredibly shy that I didn't have much to do with girls. I've never really had a girlfriend."

"Oh come on," she chided. "I'm sure there were lots of girls who liked you."

"Nope. If there were, they never told me. I've been haunted most of my life by a girl I fell in love with when I was very young, and I've never really gotten past the fear of making a fool of myself again."

"Oooh, that one sounds interesting." Jake walked over next to her. She had just finished painting the canvas with a yellow ochre wash and began to sketch in the rough shapes of the landscape with a fine brush, trailing burnt sienna. "Go on," she said.

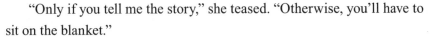

"With what?"

"I want to hear your story."

"Can I watch you paint?"

"Only if you tell me the story," she teased. "Otherwise, you'll have to sit on the blanket."

"I've never talked to anyone about this. I'm afraid you'll think I am a real loser if I share it." She raised her eyebrow, but said nothing.

"Her name was Rebecca," he began. "She lived in my neighborhood and we grew up together. I used to think she was the prettiest girl in the whole world and I loved her from the day she moved in. We were in the second grade. I remember hoping our teacher would choose me to be Joseph when she was chosen to be Mary in our nativity play we did one Christmas. I wanted so badly to be near her, but instead I was chosen to be one of the sheep and Marty Spencer got to be Joseph."

"A sheep?" She said through her giggles.

"Easy. Do you want to hear this story or not?"

"Go on," she said, biting her tongue.

"Rebecca had more friends than anyone and though my admiration for her continued to grow, so did the social distance between us. I became more reclusive as she blossomed. By high school, she was the most popular girl in school, but she was still nice enough to say hello to me at the bus stop every morning. I loved her for that.

"When she got her driver's license, she would occasionally offer me a ride home. We ended up in the same English class our junior year and our seating assignments put us right next to each other. She would often engage me in conversation before and after class. I look back on that now and realize how starved I was for attention.

"Over the course of that year, I fell in love with her, but I said nothing to her about it. It was during that year that I also began getting serious about pottery. I still remember giving her my first good vase. Her response was more than I could have ever hoped for. She threw her arms around me and hugged me tight.

"That summer, I started mowing some lawns to earn money for college. Rebecca's dad hired me to take care of their yard. Each week, as I went to mow her lawn, I hoped that I would catch of glimpse of her. One morning as I was mowing, I saw her taking out the garbage. She waved and said something over the roar of the mower, but I couldn't hear her. It wasn't until the summer was over that I found out she was telling me to call her sometime. I'm not sure I could have called her even if I had heard her. I was so painfully shy.

"When school started again that fall, I figured out a way to get into a couple of her classes. In my efforts to be near her, I even signed up for sewing class. I made such a fool of myself . I think that was one of the reasons I decided to stick with pottery."

"Why?"

"With clay, if you make a mistake, you can fix it rather than having to start over. If you cut too much off, you just have to add a bit more onto it. You can't really do that with wood or cloth or metal without it showing up. I needed to work in a medium that allowed for a lot of mistakes. While Rebecca and her girlfriends were making dresses and skirts and stuff, it took me almost a whole semester to sew a pair of boxer shorts and even then one leg was twice as big as the other. My teacher passed me just because I tried so hard."

Amy laughed, but bit her lip and hid her face behind the canvas.

"Before the end of our senior year, I mustered all my courage and asked her to the last dance, our senior prom. I rented a tux and arranged to double with the guys that asked her friends. My mom helped me pick out a huge corsage.

"It was a nightmare from the beginning. When I picked her up, I tried to pin the corsage on her dress and poked her in the chest with the pin. She was very understanding, even when we got to the restaurant and I noticed none of her friends were wearing corsages. The girls laughed at it and I felt even dumber when the guys told me that girls hate corsages and that they had all given their dates bouquets of cut flowers instead. Then I made the mistake of ordering spaghetti at dinner which I ended up wearing on my nice white shirt. I tried to wash it off, but only spread it further and got my shirt all wet. She was very gentle, but I began to withdraw.

"I stepped on her feet at least a dozen times during our first dance, and still her patience continued as mine wore thin. I was so embarrassed. I sat out the next several dances, deciding I'd be better off sipping punch. She kept dancing with her friends and the other guys. After eight or nine cups of punch, I needed to visit the bathroom. I slipped out and walked to the men's room, just as I heard the principal take the mic and announce that the crowning of the Prom Queen would take place after the next dance.

"A rush of excitement went through me, wondering if it might be Rebecca. I quickly relieved myself, but when I tried to do up my zipper, it was stuck. I fought with it for a couple of minutes, but I couldn't get it to budge, so I took off my jacket and tied it around my waist so the arms of the jacket would conceal my fly. Then I went to wash my hands and water sprayed all over my front side. I was mortified. I stood in front of the mirror, full of self-loathing. I felt like I was worse than naked. I made a choice that night that I have regretted ever since. I've relived it over and over again in my nightmares. I walked out of the bathroom and kept on walking, all the way home.

"Rebecca was crowned Prom Queen that night, and I was nowhere to be found. I tried to tell her what happened for the next two weeks at school, but she avoided me. Her friends talked only in whispers around me and the guys we doubled with treated me like I was a freak."

Jake looked up at Amy. She had stopped painting and was looking at him carefully.

"I am so sorry," she said, in the kindest voice he'd heard in a long time.

"It's not your fault. I was such a loser. I never even found a way to explain what happened. Because of that event, I avoided girls in college."

"Ok, you win," she said, trying to put an end to Jake's sad story. "There are few who make it through high school undamaged," she said cheerfully. "I remember a lot of painful moments, but that, my friend, is one of the best I've ever heard."

"You're the first person I've ever told."

"You're kidding. Not even your parents?"

"Are you crazy? I have no idea how my mother would have handled the news that her son was a loser. I told her I had a good time to keep her off my back and avoided the topic all together."

"What about your dad?" she asked. "Didn't he ask a bunch of questions?"

Jake paused. "He probably would have, but…" and he paused again.

"But what?"

"Well, I really don't know my dad. He left us when I was only three."

"Boy, I'm really bringing up some hot topics tonight. I'm sorry."

"Don't worry about it. My mom and I were really close until she passed away about eighteen months ago. She was my best friend. If it hadn't been for her, my life might have been sad, but she was an angel."

"Jake," she said, touching his shoulder, "I had no idea. I'm sorry."

"Don't be. Life hasn't been easy, but I'm not sure anybody's is. I found my passion in art and that saved me."

She sat down next to him on the blanket and put her hand on top of his. "How did she die, Jake?"

"Cancer. She was diagnosed the first time when I was fifteen. After chemo and radiation treatments, it went into remission and we thought she was going to be alright. Five years later, she went in for a checkup and they found it had returned. She passed away two months later when I was home for Christmas."

"Wow. I can't imagine losing a parent, let alone two of 'em. Do you know anything about your dad?"

"Only that he was a drunk and beat my mother. He has never made any contact with me over the years. For all I know, he's probably dead too."

They sat in silence together for a long moment.

"So are you ready to try yogurt bread?" he asked, ending the silence.

"Yeah, I'm starving."

He had already laid out the bread on a round cutting board he carried in his back pack from home. He quickly cut several large slices of the sunflower bread and took off the top of the yogurt.

"Do you want to try it the clean way or the best way?"

"What's the difference?"

"Well, I only really know the best way, since that's the only way I've ever had it. It's not very refined and tends to get you a little sticky. I'm sure there is some clean way that is more sophisticated, but I'd have to make that up as I go."

"Bring it on," she said.

Jake handed her a slab of bread. Taking one in his own hand, he dipped the bread into the widest part of the plastic yogurt cup and handed the cup to Amy. She did the same.

"Now the rest of it is pretty straightforward," he said. "You just eat the bread and when you run out of bread that's covered with yogurt, you dip it again."

"Double dipping?" she asked with wide eyes.

"That's right, unless you've got a problem with that."

"I don't, but my mom would kill me. That was always a major taboo at my house."

"Me too," he said with his mouth full of yogurt bread. "But so was talking with your mouth full." She laughed and took a bite.

"This is surprisingly good," she said after she had swallowed. They sat and ate in near silence, passing the yogurt back and forth until the yogurt cup was empty. Amy used her bread to swab the inside of the container clean.

She lay down on the blanket and looked up at the sky. "I feel like I need to play fat dog."

"What's that?"

"When you grow up with five brothers, you learn a lot of crazy games. I think they might have invented it to get out of doing the dishes after Sunday dinners. The rules are pretty easy and they always said everybody who plays wins. You basically just stuff yourself with good food and then lie on the ground like a fat dog for a couple of hours."

Jake started laughing and lay back on the blanket.

"Unfortunately, I rarely got to play. My mom always made me help clean up the dishes. I didn't get much practice until I went away for college, but I'm pretty good at it now."

"It must have been fun growing up with older brothers."

"It was wild! My parents didn't really know what to do with me after having five boys so I was a tomboy growing up. My brothers looked after me, but nearly teased me to death. I didn't realize how different I was until I went away to college and had roommates. I couldn't believe how prissy some of the girls were. They spent all morning getting ready to go to class. I'd get out of the shower, run a comb through my hair and be out the door in ten minutes flat, including breakfast. They would laugh if they knew I had a job at a cosmetics counter. It's the last place I thought I would ever be working."

"So you're not planning on making a career out of it then?" Jake asked with a smile.

"No way, not for a million bucks!"

"Come on, a million bucks?"

"Would you spend your life at a cosmetics counter for a million bucks?"

Jake thought for a minute. "I guess you're right."

"No, I've had to fight with my parents for too many years to think of trading the life I dreamed of for a life where I'd dread getting up in the morning. I forgot to tell you that after our discussion on Sunday, I gave my two week's notice yesterday."

"Congratulations! That ought to free up a lot of time for you to paint."

"Yeah, I hope so, but Daddy has already responded by cutting off all funds. I'm just glad I don't have to pay rent."

"How did he find out?"

"I sometimes forget that he grew up here. My boss is one of his old friends and Daddy just happened to drop him a line yesterday afternoon to check on his little girl, just an hour after I gave my notice. He called me last night to scream at me."

"That must have been pretty tough,"

"I'm used to it. It's been the same old story every couple of weeks for the last few years. I think I have the lecture memorized."

Jake shook his head in amazement. "What about your aunt and uncle?"

"Aunt Bev has always encouraged me to paint. That's why I figured this would be a safe haven."

"Has it been?"

"There is something strange about this town. I've never spent more than a few days here at any one time, but this feels more like home to me than my home town ever did. I can think here. I can dream here. I'd love to find a way to stay, but if I can't find the time to paint and then find a place to sell my paintings, there is no way I can stay here very long. I've been curious since our talk on Sunday why you chose pottery."

Jake rolled on his side and looked at her. "The simple answer is that I've met a lot of potters in my travels. I've never met a rich one, but I've never met one who was unhappy."

Amy smiled broadly. "You get it. You get it! I've tried to explain the same thing to my family and friends, but I never boiled it down to the simplicity of how you just explained it. My dad has worked hard to provide us with a big home on the right side of town. We had all the necessities of life and many of the luxuries too. But there has to be more than making money and coming home at the end of the day frustrated and angry, unable or unwilling to do anything but hang out in front of the TV all evening. Mom didn't even like to be around my dad and kept herself busy with tennis and service clubs and shopping. How do you tell your parents that you don't want the same life they had without sounding ungrateful?"

"Have you come up with any answers?"

"Yes, but I don't think they're going to like it. After the lecture you gave me Sunday night, I decided you're right; I need to be painting."

"How do you know I wasn't just trying to fill your head with false hope?"

"Because it spoke truth to my soul! With all the negativity coming from my family, it was and is refreshing to hear your take. Your encouragement and friendship have come at a really crucial time. I know this is the path I need to travel and I'm glad I have someone to share the journey with."

Jake nodded.

"Is living the life of a potter as attractive as you thought it would be?"

"I don't know. Is anything ever as attractive as you think it will be?"

"You're right," she said with another broad grin. "What are you going to do?"

"I don't know. I promised the Mayor I'd stay until the end of August at least, but after that, who knows. I've basically been given the shop and the apartment for as long as I want to stay in Niederbipp; all this from a man I am not related to and have never met."

"And that's a bad thing?" she asked, raising her eyebrows.

"It's complicated. I am the eighth potter to work in this shop over the past two hundred and ninety years. People don't come to just buy pots; this is part of their life. It's almost like salmon returning to the waters where they hatched. They come in, take a deep breath, drink a cup of tea, and settle down to share stories of how Isaac changed their lives. I'm no life changer. I'm just a kid who wants to make pots.

"I've wanted to be a potter since I was in high school. I admit that some parts of this arrangement are awesome. Maybe there are even a lot of things I like, but I don't know if I'm ready to settle down. I feel like I'm too young to have my life figured out. I feel like a groom in an arranged marriage and I'm waking up next to the stranger I'll spend the rest of my life with. The world is big and there's still so much of it I want to discover."

"So what are you going to do?"

"I guess I have to get used to it, change it, or move on. So much of my life has been about the journey, choosing the less-traveled roads, traveling to places all over the world. Now I'm here, doing exactly what I hoped to be doing for the rest of my life. That sounds really comforting, like I've arrived, like I have it all figured out. The problem is I was anticipating it taking a lot longer to get here. If I decide to make this work for me I'm afraid I'll always wonder what I missed out on by skipping those ten years of struggle and experience."

"Sounds like a gift to me."

Jake nodded. "I've tried to look at it that way too, but I wonder if it's not like trying to help a chick out of its shell, if I need all those crazy experiences ten years of living can give me. When my mom was being treated for cancer the first time, she often told me that struggle is necessary to make us stronger. I always hated it when she told me that, but it seems there are some things that can't be learned any other way."

"You're telling me you haven't seen challenges in the last few weeks?"

Jake laughed. "No, I have. They're just not the challenges I expected."

"Do we ever get the challenges we expect? I know I didn't pick mine.

It seems to me that no matter what we plan for, we always have something smack us upside the head."

Jake nodded thoughtfully. "Maybe that's what reality is: the smacks we get on our way to living our dreams."

"I like you, Jake. You make sense to me."

"That makes one of us," he said, laughing.

"Can we do this again tomorrow and the day after that too?"

"I'd like that, but you have to paint."

"I guess I am going to have to learn to paint while I listen and talk."

"Then sign me up. I'm grateful to have someone who can help me verbalize my thoughts and listen to my incoherent rants."

"As long as you feed me, I'll listen to anything," she said with a wink. "I think we have about an hour before it's too dark to paint. Do you mind if I try to finish my painting before we leave?"

"Not at all," said Jake, standing up and offering Amy a hand. She took it and stood. "I'll clean up, and then, if you don't mind, I'll go sit over there on the rocks and work on some sketches."

"Sure. What are you working on?"

"Oh, just some thoughts for Isaac's bench. I got some ideas this afternoon while looking at the Bible."

"I was going to ask you about that."

"About what?"

"I guess the real question is about faith."

"What about it?" He asked as he folded the blanket and stuffed it into his back pack.

"I wonder what you believe?"

"You mean as far as church goes?"

"Well, kind of I guess, but really I was wondering what you believe."

"What do you mean?" he asked, wanting to make sure he understood before he answered such a delicate question.

"Well, you know how some people go to church, but when you ask them what they believe, a lot of them really don't believe what they hear on Sunday. For lots of people, church just seems to be a social thing. I guess

I'm just wondering what you believe?"

"That's a big question."

"Ok, you're right. Let's narrow it down. Your mom passed away over a year ago; how has that affected your faith?"

Jake thought for a moment before he responded. "I've never really talked about this. I don't think anyone can lose someone they love without hoping they might see them again. When my mom was first diagnosed with cancer, we both had a lot of questions about mortality. When you're fifteen, death isn't something you ever think about.

"We began attending many different churches, looking for answers. My mom was a biochemist and worked in a lab and had never needed faith. She found her answers in science. The threat of death opened up a new set of questions. She began having conversations with a co-worker, Mr. Williams, and his insights on faith and the purpose of life gave us both reasons to hope.

"He invited us to his home one evening to have dinner with his family. He and his wife had five children. When we sat down for dinner, he asked the youngest one, a boy about five years old, to ask a blessing on the food. I don't remember what he said, but I remember how it made me feel. I was envious of the faith that little kid had. Over the next few years, my simple faith became stronger as I sought and received answers.

"When I got to college, I had a new set of questions. Because of my father's habits, alcohol had never been a part of my life, and suddenly it was all around me. You might laugh when I tell you this, but I never once went down that road. There were times when I got close to taking a drink, but then I'd remember the pain my father's habits caused me and my mother. If it had not been for the love of my mom and the answers I found, I think my life might have been very different. There are lots of things I still question, but I believe there is a God. It's hard sometimes to keep the faith when I see so many bad things happening around the world, but I want to believe that God loves us. I'm not sure how Jesus' sacrifice works, but I have hope that it does. There have been times in my life when I have doubted all of this, but those doubts have always been overshadowed by hope."

Amy stopped painting and was listening intently. "That was beautiful," she said, when he finished. "I appreciate your candidness."

"So what about you?"

"I rarely have occasion to talk about faith with anyone, but when I saw you reading the Bible today, I knew I could ask you. I didn't discover my faith until just a couple of years ago and it's still very young.

"We went to church when I was a kid. Dad would drop Mom and us kids off on Sunday morning while he went golfing with his buddies. By the time I was ten, my mom and I were the only ones going. My brothers followed the example of my father and took up golfing or other activities on Sunday mornings. I stopped going about a year after my mom stopped. She didn't like the new preacher and I was on a witch hunt for hypocrisy, which is easy to find if you look for it. I think I was sixteen and I decided my Sunday mornings could be better spent in bed.

"There was no protest from anyone and no one from the church came around to look for me, so it was easy to forget the whole thing. At least I thought it would be. But I always had questions in my mind, wondering about the purpose of life. I looked at my dad, a workaholic who was never happy. I saw my brothers excelling in school and getting great jobs, but they didn't strike me as any happier. My mom, I think, still has faith in her heart, but I'm not sure it has seen the light of day in a long time. I don't ever remember there being a Bible in our home, and we rarely prayed, unless you count  my dad's cries to God to let his team win."

Jake smiled.

"And then I left home for college. I didn't have many rules at home. My brothers had worn my parents down. I was never interested in drinking before college, but most of my roommates were binge drinkers and spent their weekends either partying or recovering from partying. Unfortunately, I went with them a few times.

"One Sunday afternoon, I woke up with a splitting headache. I was lying on my bed with my clothes on and I couldn't remember how I got there or where I had been the night before. I was sick and lost. I decided I never wanted to do that again. The next weekend, I told my friends I was sick and went to the painting studio on campus instead. I had a lot to catch up on, but more than anything, I needed to think about my life. That night, I had my first spiritual experience."

Jake looked up.

"I've never told anyone this." She took a deep breath. "I'll tell you, but you have to promise not to laugh."

"Ok...I promise."

"It was something I can't describe and can't explain, but I felt the love of God as I painted into the night. The next night, when my friends went to another party, I went back to the studio and painted again. I continued to feel the same peace. It sounds silly, but I don't know how else to explain it."

Jake was smiling.

"What are you smiling at?"

"You don't need to explain it. I've felt it too as I've been alone working on the wheel. I've never talked to anyone about it either, but it's happened more times than I can count. Does it feel like there is someone helping you create what you're painting?"

"Yeah, almost like my hands are someone else's."

"I can't believe it," he said, a rush of tingles racing up his spine. "I've felt that same feeling."

"What is it?" she asked.

"I don't know for sure. I've thought that it might be a sign that I am doing what I was made to do, almost like the creation of the world is continuing on a small scale, through my hands."

"That's a beautiful way to put it."

"Do you still feel it often?"

She looked down at her palette. "Every time I paint," she said quietly, tears forming in her eyes. "I know I have to do this. I started going back to church a couple of years ago. I went searching for the feelings I feel when I paint. I found it every once in a while, but there's something different about the church in Niederbipp."

"You feel it too?" he asked.

"Yeah, I do. There is something about that building. Do you know much about it?"

"Only that it was built by the first settlers of the town. The first potter made the tiles for the roof and the floors. I think it was the first building to be completed in Niederbipp. From everything I've learned, faith was a driving force for the people who founded this town."

"My ancestors were among those founders. I've only picked up bits and pieces over the years from stuff Beverly has said, but my ancestors were all Quakers, or at least a branch of Quakers."

"You mean like that guy on the oatmeal box?"

"I'm not really sure. I've wanted to ask my aunt more about the religion. I figure I ought to know something about the people I come from."

"So if it's a Quaker church, what's up with Father Thomas? He looks like a priest, but he never wears all the garb that the priests did at the Albany Cathedral. He just has his black clothes and the white collar. I suppose I could ask him. I'll probably be seeing a lot more of him in the next little bit as I work on Isaac's grave marker."

"Let me know what he says."

"Maybe you'll be there. I want to start working off that painting you're doing for me and the graveyard seems like a fine place for a picnic."

Amy nodded and grinned.

"I better let you paint," he said, picking up his sketchbook and walking to the rocks on the right side of the pond. Out of the corner of his eye, he watched as Amy worked. She looked up at the landscape in front of her and painted a stroke, moving quickly as the light was fading. As he sat on the rocks and tried to sketch, his mind was full of thoughts about her and the conversation they had just had. He wondered why she was so easy to talk to, unlike any girl he had ever known. Time passed and the long shadows faded into the darkness.

"We better get home; Aunt Bev will start to worry."

Jake stood and stumbled over the rocks before he found his footing on the small path that circled the pond. In a minute, he was standing next to her.

"Nice painting. You captured the darkness so well."

She laughed. It was too dark to see a thing.

"I'm sorry I distracted you. At this rate, it might be better for you to keep your day job."

"No! We'll figure it out."

By the starlight,  Jake held the wet canvas by its edges as Amy carefully put her palette into its place and folded up the french easel.

They walked to their bikes. It was near pitch dark now and the path through the trees was even darker. They waded through the darkness, pushing their bikes, their eyes straining to make out rocks and stumps.

In a few minutes, they found their way back to the road and decided to ride slowly, side by side, so they wouldn't run over each other.

"Have you ever seen stars like this?" she asked.

"Not enough. Maybe that's the problem with the world today, that we're too busy to take time to look up at the stars."

"Do you think it would help?"

"It couldn't hurt," he said as they rolled over the hill, the lights of the town illuminating the road before them.

"It's been a great evening," she said, when they had pulled up behind the barber shop.

"Hey, it's been a great day. I'm sorry again that it was such a bad night for painting."

"Jake," she said softly, "if I had come home with a finished painting, I would have been happy, but instead, I've come home with a new friend and that's worth a thousand paintings."

"Thank you," he said. He leaned over to give her a hug. Despite the back pack and French easel strapped to their backs, and two bikes between them, it was one of the best hugs Jake could remember.

"Can I see you tomorrow?" he asked.

"I'm expecting it. You've got a painting to work off."

Jake laughed.

"I've been meaning to ask where you were last night. I stopped by after work but everything was dark."

"I went for a ride yesterday on the scooter and ran out of gas. I wanted to stop by but I didn't get back until almost ten and I was tired from pushing the scooter for the last five miles."

She shook her head. "Thanks for taking me."

"You were working when I left. I would have waited if I had known you wanted to go, but then we would have both been walking home. We can go sometime if you want. I just have to get some gas first."

"Would the scooter carry both of us?"

"Yeah, no problem. It would go a little slower, but I think we could make it. There's even a basket on the back for your easel."

"So when are we going?"

"We could go Sunday afternoon."

Her face lit up. "I'd like that. I don't want to waste any more time."

Jake's hands were tingling from rolling over the cobblestone when he coasted to a stop outside the back door of the studio. He parked his bike under the stairs and went up to bed, happier than he could ever remember.

31
THE PRIEST'S TALE

At 3:00 in the morning, Jake sat straight up in bed. He had forgotten the kiln. He ran down the stairs in his boxer shorts, praying the kiln hadn't turned into a fiery inferno. He looked at the clock on the wall and ran his hands through his hair. It had been fifteen hours! He turned off the gas and closed the damper before recording the time in the log book. He was angry with himself for forgetting. He flipped through the book, hoping to be comforted by finding another record of a long firing. The more he looked, the more concerned he became. None of the firings for the past few years had lasted longer than thirteen hours.

He walked to the kiln, put on a leather glove and pulled the plug from the peep hole. The pyrometric cones that indicated the temperature inside were completely melted. He took a deep breath and stepped back from the heat radiating from the kiln. He wanted to scream, or at least cry. He knew his work was probably ruined, but he was even more upset about the kiln and the shelves. Would they be ruined as well? He turned off the lights and went back to his bed.

Jake tossed and turned for the next three hours, dreaming about pots that looked like they had been attacked by Salvador Dali: warped and melting. Finally at six, he got up and went down to the studio to get to work. He knew that if the kiln was damaged, he wouldn't be able to fire anything until he repaired it. That would take days or even weeks, depending on how soon he could get new bricks and shelves. There was nothing he could do about that now, but he could make pots. He needed to make pots. He needed to sit at the wheel and let his frustration go, turning his emotion and fury into something positive.

He was already sweating before he finished wedging the clay. When he sat down at the wheel with his back toward the kiln door, he broke into a heavy sweat. He stayed there, sweating, punishing himself for not being more attentive, for not remembering the kiln. This had happened once before at school. That firing had only gone two hours beyond what it should have, but the door had been damaged and had to be replaced. He tried not to think about it.

By 8:00, Jake had already worked his way through two hundred pounds of clay. New bowls and vases filled the shelves and covered most of the flat surfaces in the studio.

Dripping with sweat, Jake stood and walked out the back door, looking at the golden sky. He took a deep breath before collapsing on the stairs,

exhausted. A pot filled with young peppermint stalks sat next to him, sharing its fragrance. At least he hadn't killed the plants yet.

As he sat on the steps, Jake prayed that things would be all right. Away from the radiating heat of the kiln, he began to cool down quickly as the morning breeze blew against his sweaty shirt. His prayer ended when the shivers set in. He was hungry and thirsty so he pulled himself off the stairs and made a pot of tea.

A minute later, a knock came at the front door and Jake went to answer it. He nearly hugged Father Thomas when he saw him. Jake needed to talk to someone. He hoped Thomas might have some good news or at least something that would distract him from the disaster.

"I was just on my way home and saw your light on. Is everything ok?"

Jake pursed his lips. Thomas looked at Jake. His apron was smeared with clay. Slip was dried on his arms and hands. Thomas walked past Jake, eager to have an answer. He looked into the studio and immediately turned to Jake.

"What happened?"

"It's the kiln. I forgot about it   last night and over-fired it."

Thomas nodded. "I'll be right back."

He rushed out the front door. Jake wondered if he was going to get the Mayor. Would he be looking for a new place to live by the end of the day?

A few minutes later, however, Thomas returned—with a brown bag.

"I've seen this before," he said with a smile. "I'm no doctor, but I've been told that the cure for this particular malady is a good, stiff cup of peppermint tea and a big ol' helping of Sam's marzipan slice."

Jake started laughing, relieved. "So you didn't rally the posse to chase me out of town?"

"No Jake. You're ok. Like I said, I've seen this before. I knew something was wrong when I saw all the pots you made this morning. This happened a couple of times to Isaac too and he responded the same way you did. Of course, he responded this way to a lot of things that frustrated him. You potters are lucky. You can turn your pent up frustrations into pots. The rest of us have to cuss and drink and kick things."

Jake smiled and shook his head. "But it went three hours longer than it was supposed to. Everything is probably ruined."

"Those bricks are old, Jake. If they're broken, they can be replaced. But I doubt they are. This shop is old, but everything in it was built to last. Isaac rebricked that kiln fifteen years ago when the old bricks finally gave out after a hundred years. I helped him do it. There was a new kind of brick that was out on the market that was lighter and easier to cut and work with, but Isaac chose the old brick because it was more durable. He wasn't just planning for his future, he was planning for yours.

"The shelves are old too. If they're broken, it won't be hard to buy some more. As for the pots, well, they're probably ruined, but as Isaac used to say when tearful people brought their broken pots to him, 'it's only dirt!' It'll take time, but they can be replaced. It looks like you've already made enough pots to fill the kiln again."

Jake nodded, relieved.

"Now, let's make some of that tea."

"I just made some before you knocked."

"Is it strong enough?"

Jake smiled. "I'm not sure."

"In a case like this, it needs to be really strong if you want it to work. You need that menthol to get into your lungs when you drink it. If it doesn't clear your sinuses, and make you a little dizzy, you know it's too weak. I better pep it up." Thomas stood and walked to the canister. He pulled off the lid and looked up at Jake. "You've been going through this tea pretty quick. Do you have any more?"

"There's a little bit more in the apartment. I've developed a small addiction to it."

"Yeah, Isaac always had the best tea. I used to help him gather the mint throughout the summer months and dry it for the winter."

"I've been wondering about that. I don't know anything about growing or harvesting peppermint, or how one makes it into tea."

Father Thomas smiled. "City boy, are ya?"

"Yes, I am. My mom raised a small garden, but we never had peppermint, and I'm ashamed to admit I never helped her in the garden."

"You know it grows like a weed, don't you?"

"Yeah, I've seen it growing wild in patches here and there around town. It's growing nicely in the planters on the back stairs without much effort."

"The trick to growing peppermint is to confine it. It'll spread like weeds, and if left unchecked will choke out anything else. A flowerpot is a great place for it. Isaac used to transplant it to unused or neglected patches of dirt around town. It was his way of beautifying the town. He used to cut stalks of peppermint and tie them together before washing them and hanging them to dry over his kitchen sink. When the leaves were dry, he would pull them from the stalks and crumble them in his hands."

"That sounds too easy. There has to be more to it than that."

"Unfortunately, I think you're right. A lot of people try, but they can't make it taste exactly like Isaac's. He was known for his tea and folks came to visit from far and wide so they could enjoy a cup of it. People regularly tried to talk him into selling the loose tea. One guy even suggested he could make Isaac rich if he would sell him the recipe, but he kept the secret to himself."

"Someone told me that it's made from the peppermint of a hundred gardens."

"That's probably true. He had it planted everywhere and would use the peppermint harvest as an excuse to stop and see old friends, and make new ones. He had a way with people that could get him in any door and folks were always happy to see him.

"I've done a lot of experiments over the years, trying to duplicate his tea, but it's never been the same. There has to be some secret ingredient that I don't know about."

Jake raised his eyebrows at this news. "A secret ingredient?"

"Yeah, one night, a couple of years ago, I saw Isaac sneaking out of my backyard with a pail full of gooseberry leaves. It was the same pail he used to collect peppermint and I wondered if there wasn't a connection. The next time he shared his tea with me, I suggested that it tasted strange, like gooseberries. He came up with a couple of lame reasons why that could be, but when he saw me smiling, he knew that I knew his secret. He told me if I ever let the secret out, I'd have to find a new place to drink tea and shoot the bull."

"So, how many gooseberry leaves did he add to the mix?"

"That's the secret. I wish I knew."

"He never told you?"

"No. Once I knew the secret ingredient, I tried some more experiments. Mine was always more bitter than Isaac's. There has to be some other ingredient that I missed, something to help get rid of the bitterness, while adding that extra spark of sweetness that not even several cubes of sugar can achieve. We may never know."

Jake sighed. "I'll be out of it within a week."

"Then it's important to savor it. You never know how long a good thing will last." Thomas stared away to a distant place and Jake knew he wasn't speaking of the tea alone.

"Tell me about your mug," Jake said, stirring him from his thoughts.

[handwritten margin note: PEPPERMINT + GOOSEBERRY LEAVES + ?]

"I picked this mug thirty-five years ago. It reminded me of the color of my mother's hair: Irish red."

"It's a beautiful color. The glaze is called Ohata Kahti; it's an old Japanese glaze that is rich in iron. That's what makes the glaze red."

Father Thomas raised an eyebrow as he stirred his tea. "It sounds like you know your stuff. Isaac told me he got the recipe out of an old book from an English potter who studied in Japan."

"That's right. Bernard Leach. He died back in the seventies, but potters from around the world still make pilgrimages to his studio in St. Ives. I stopped by a couple of years ago while I was visiting England. I can't say that I love his work, but he changed the way people think about pottery, making it an art rather than just for utilitarian uses."

"Judging from your new work in the window and the way the town is talking about your pottery, I think your philosophies must be much the same."

"I've never really thought about it that way. I've always considered my work functional first, but I have a good time decorating it too. I want to make stuff that makes people happy."

"Well, your work is certainly impressive."

"Thanks. I was hoping to get some nice pieces out of this firing, but I guess I'll have to wait a week or two." Jake shook his head.

"You need some more tea and that marzipan slice." Thomas stood and filled Jake's mug before unwrapping the cake. It was beautiful. Two layers of white cake alternated with two layers of raspberry cream, topped with a fine sheet of cream colored marzipan. "There are very few ailments that marzipan can't cure. Come to think of it, I haven't found one yet." He winked at Jake and took a big bite of his cake, purring as he chewed.

Jake joined him. The two men ate in silence, other than the noises that are created when consuming particularly delectable treats. Jake had to admit that he did feel better. He knew he faced disappointments, but for now, there was tea, good company, and marzipan to dull the pain.

"So how was your date last night?" Thomas asked.

"It was great. We went out to Taufer's Pond. Amy wanted to work on…..hey, wait a minute. How did you know about my date?"

Thomas started laughing. "We all have our little birds."

"Well I'm sick of this," Jake said, smiling. "Am I ever going to be able to do anything without the whole town knowing about it?"

"No. We're just looking out for you. If it's any consolation, it was the same way when I used to date."

"Actually, no. It's of no consolation at all. I think…… What did you say?"

"It was the same way when I used to date."

"Wait, what?" asked Jake, doing a double take.

"Things aren't always the way they seem, Jake. I used to date. I was even engaged once."

"To be married?"

"Yes, to be married."

"What happened?"

"She was killed in an accident, twenty-five years ago."

Jake furrowed his brow, surprised and also saddened. "Is that why you entered the priesthood?"

"No. I entered the priesthood right out of high school."

While Jake did the math, Thomas emptied the last of the tea into his mug.

Jake looked confused.

Thomas took one look at him and started to laugh. "Jake, you'd never be able to guess my past, so I'll tell you."

Jake looked at him intently.

"It was a dark and stormy night….." Thomas busted up.

Jake smiled a nervous smile. He had underestimated Thomas and Thomas knew it.

When he stopped laughing, he spoke again. "Jake, I was your age when I came to Niederbipp. I have the proud distinction of being the only citizen of Niederbipp who arrived by boat."

Jake raised an eyebrow.

"The word 'boat' fosters all sorts of images in most people's minds. Mine was a row boat—a sinking row boat without any oars. I wasn't always the pillar of faith and piety that I am today. When I was a kid, I was a bit of a buffoon and generally leaned toward the irreverent. I was the bonus child in a large Catholic family, which meant that my closest of nine siblings was ten years older. My mother gave my soul to God before I was even born, so I didn't really have a choice—I joined the priesthood. My father died when I was twelve and our parish priest took me under his wing to help my mother. Father Matthew was a rather sober fellow, on occasion. The rest of the time, he indulged himself with the sacramental wine. Before I was fifteen, I became his drinking buddy. My Irish blood gave me a natural propensity to drink, but it also enabled me to hold my liquor.

"I took my habit with me when I entered the seminary after high school. Father Matthew arranged for me to attend Saint Vincent Seminary in Latrobe, about an hour southeast of Pittsburgh. In addition to my studies, prayers, and meditations, I was also assigned to work in the kitchen. I developed a knack for baking bread which also gave me access to yeast—one of the most important ingredients in good beer.

"It was a wonderful time to be removed from the world and focus on the things of God. And then, my time was up. I was assigned to work in Codham, a small town fifteen miles upriver.

"To make a long story short, it didn't go well. Within a couple of months, I managed to offend the whole congregation. As my flock got smaller, my drinking increased. One Sunday, when I was particularly soused, I attracted the attention of all the villagers by ringing the bell at 5 am. To make sure the people didn't fall back to sleep, I rang it again every fifteen minutes."

Father Thomas shook his head before continuing.

"Before church was even supposed to start, there was a nice line of folks out in front, armed with pitchforks and shotguns. I was tied up hand and foot, thrown in the bottom of a leaky rowboat, and sent down river."

"Really?!" Jake was stunned. He had never heard of a priest being thrown out of town. And Father Thomas seemed like the last man in the world to cause that much trouble.

Father Thomas chuckled then shook his head, his smile fading to a frown. It struck Jake that this was a difficult subject for Thomas to talk about. "I struggled against the ropes for a long time, but was tired from getting up so early. I finally drifted off to sleep after a couple of hours. That's when I had the dream."

"A dream?" Jake asked, leaning forward, eager to hear. "My dream wasn't much different than my circumstances. I was sitting on the seat of the rowboat, stuck in the middle of the river without oars to steer or propel me. Darkness fell as I continued to float along without direction. In desperation, I prayed for help. A light appeared on the far shore and came toward me on the water. I squinted and saw that it was a man, dressed in a white robe. Soon he was standing next to the boat and

I saw that it was Jesus Christ, standing on the water. When He asked me what I wanted, I told him I was stuck in the current and wanted to get to solid ground. He nodded, held onto the bow, and began pulling me to shore. He turned and smiled at me. I had never felt that much love before. It was like a physical sensation. He turned to me and said, 'Thomas, do you believe?'"

Thomas spoke slowly and deliberately. Jake set down his tea giving his undivided attention to what Thomas was telling him.

"And I said, 'Yes Lord, I believe.' He smiled brilliantly and again I felt consumed by his love. As I looked at his face, his lips didn't move, but I either heard or felt a voice in my heart say, 'then remember.'"

Thomas paused, thoughtfully, then cleared his throat before he went on.

"Soon after that, I woke up. The sun was much lower in the sky. I could tell that my face was badly sunburned and my hands throbbed from being tied behind my back. My robes were wet and I was quite uncomfortable, but I couldn't move. I lay in the boat wondering if my bones would be picked clean by magpies. My future that had once looked so clear and simple had, in a matter of a few hours, become very complicated and uncertain. I had no money, no job, no friends, no skills outside of my gospel knowledge, no clothes other than what I had on my back, and I was lying wet in the bottom of a sinking rowboat somewhere on the river."

"With your hands tied behind your back," Jake added. They both laughed. "So what happened? How did you get out?"

Father Thomas smiled, knowing he still had Jake's full attention. "I just lay there, helpless, until I heard someone whistling. At first, I thought I had died and floated right in to heaven, but then I recognized the whistling as the theme song from Mr. Ed.

Jake started laughing. "Mr. Ed?"

"Yeah, that was my first clue I wasn't in heaven. Then I wondered if I was in hell.

A man reached into the boat and untied me. He told me his name was Isaac and he built a fire to dry my robes. I told him my story before we walked to town. He fed me and offered me his second bedroom.

"The next morning, over breakfast, he told me that he too had washed up on the banks of Niederbipp and had chosen to stay because of the love he found here. He asked what I wanted to do with my life. After some contemplation, I inquired if the church in Niederbipp might be in need of a priest.

"Isaac explained that the founding fathers of the town were mostly Quakers from Germany and Switzerland, but that over time, others had come to town and had been invited into the fold, bringing with them parts of their traditions. As the Quakers were known as 'Seekers of Truth,' the church had become a melting pot. They were Christian in tradition and practice, but could no longer be strictly distinguished by any definition laid out by familiar denominations. They studied their Bibles and learned from each other and the spirit of God, but had no paid ministry. Instead, they gave their tithes and offerings to care for the poor and needy among them.

"He asked about my family. By then, both of my parents were gone and my brothers had cut off contact with me when I entered the seminary. As I explained my situation, I felt my despair becoming deeper. To my surprise, he looked at me and suggested that I was in an enviable position. I could choose any path I wanted without pressure from family or friends; I could reinvent myself without anyone reminding me of where I had been or who I was supposed to be.

"I had made a holy mess of the previous six months, but it was difficult to imagine doing anything else. When I explained my feelings to Isaac, he told me that if my heart was telling me to be a priest, I probably needed to listen. He gave me a pair of overalls and a t-shirt to wear until I could clean my clothes. He invited me to take the scooter and visit the surrounding towns to see if they might be in need of a priest. By noon, I had visited all of the towns within ten miles and learned that all of the churches were fully staffed. I returned feeling like God had forsaken me, but as I neared Niederbipp, I had the strange feeling I was coming home. I decided to visit the church and do some thinking about what I wanted to do with the rest of my life. Isaac's words to me about my rare opportunity to choose a new path had given me pause and I decided that such an opportunity deserved more thought.

"The chapel was unlike any church I had ever seen, yet it was warm and inviting. I was impressed by its unadorned simplicity. As I walked down the center aisle, I looked up at the figure of Christ standing on a small shelf, surrounded by the organ pipes

"I took a seat on a pew toward the front and leaned back to reflect on the simple beauty of the chapel. My heart was filled with peace and reverence as I recognized I was in a sacred place. For the first time in a long time, I began to cry. Through my tears, I looked into the face of the Christus and was overcome by the beauty of his smile. At that moment, I also saw Christ as he had appeared in my dreams, juxtaposed with the Christus standing above me. It was the same face, the same smile. And then in my mind, I heard again the words, 'Thomas, do you believe?... then remember.'

"I had never had dreams or visions and it was weird to have God talking to me. I sat there, not knowing what it all meant and yet my mind and my heart both told me there were meaning and answers to be found in this.

"Without a job or any money, it was impractical to stay in Niederbipp, but something was telling me I needed to be here. When I told Isaac about my feelings, he told me that it didn't seem likely that God would wash me up on the banks of Niederbipp if He didn't have something for me to do here. He told me about the waterfall just a mile down river and said that it would be unlikely for me to have survived if I had continued with the current. He told me that it might take me a lifetime to figure out, but that someone greater than me and the town of Codham would rather have me here, wondering what my purpose was, than dead in the river. And so began my life in Niederbipp."

"But I thought you said there is no paid ministry here. How did you become the town priest?"

"Who said anything about becoming the town priest?"

"But your clothes. I guess I just thought that…."

"Jake, not everything is as it appears. Remember how I told you I learned to bake at the Seminary?"

"Yes."

"Well, I knew if I was going to stay in town, I would need a job. I learned pretty quick that starting my own brewery wasn't an option since this is a dry town. Isaac was the only one who knew I was a priest so I decided to keep that a secret from the rest of the town and I got a job baking bread in the mornings for Sam. I just came from there. Thirty-five years later, and I'm still working for the old curmudgeon. He's one of my closest friends. I work in the morning for him and spend the afternoon doing odd jobs around town. I'm a part time plumber, tutor and, as you know, I help at the library."

"So why do you dress like a priest?" he asked, still not sure if this was fact or fiction.

"That started about twenty-five years ago. I heard the call to return to the ministry and, though I had never renounced my vows, I felt that I needed to do something to help me remember that I'm not just a baker or a plumber or a part-time librarian." He looked at Jake who was clearly confused. "I

know that sounds strange, but wearing the clothes of the clergyman helps me to remember where I've been and where my heart needs to stay. I do it for my mother whose dying wish was for me to be a priest and I do it for Emily, my fiancée."

Jake raised his eyebrows, confused, wondering if he would ever get a clear answer.

"After I had been here about ten years, I fell in love with a young woman. I was thirty-two and she was twenty-four. She was actually one of the students I had tutored when I first arrived in town, and we had always been friends. She went away for college and we lost touch, but the girl returned one summer a woman. I first saw her at church, and when she walked in, it was as if the sun itself had entered the little chapel. I didn't know who she was at first, she had changed so much, but she remembered me and invited me for a walk after church to catch up. Within a week, we were spending all of our free time together. She was more beautiful than a summer's morning and I was intoxicated by her presence. I worried at first about our difference in age, but she admitted that she had loved me since she was a teen. By the fall, we were dating and by Christmas I had collected all my money to buy her an engagement ring. We planned to marry the following spring, but that was never to be. On her way home from a New Year's Eve party she attended with some of her college friends, the driver fell asleep and the car rolled down an embankment and into the frozen river. No one survived."

Jake looked up, his brow furrowed. This was not the story he had expected. For a moment, there was an awkward silence in the studio, and then Thomas spoke again.

"To say I was devastated would be a most cruel understatement. I felt like my life was shattered. Every feeling I had ever had of being forsaken by God returned and was compounded by the dark clouds of depression. I closed myself inside my little apartment and cried for a week."

"Wow!" said Jake, not knowing what else to say.

"Wow is right! Joining the ministry early in my life had sheltered me from the heartache of love. For weeks I wished I had died with her. I ran through a million scenarios in my mind that might have produced a different outcome, but nothing could change the fact that she was dead and that I would never have her. I became really angry with God and stopped attending church, stopped praying, stopped caring. I refused visitors, refused to be comforted, and became negative and cynical. I asked myself questions like, 'How could a loving God let things like this happen?' I was determined to be miserable for the rest of my life."

"So what happened?"

"Isaac happened," he said, with his first smile since he had begun sharing his tragic love story. "Isaac made me recognize my own pitiful state and gave me the desire to change."

"How?" asked Jake.

Thomas shook his head, unable at first to explain. "I remember it was spring and the trees were budding when I saw Isaac crossing the courtyard that day, on his way to visit his wife's grave. I don't remember why I was there, probably just passing through, but I saw something I had never seen before and it intrigued me. I had been with Isaac to visit the graveyard many times over the years, but for some reason I had missed it before. Isaac had hope in his eyes that day, so real that it seemed he would be eating lunch with Lily. I followed him and stood at the gate as he dropped his basket on the bench and pulled from it a bundle of pussy willows, placing them in the vase on her gravestone. He smiled and whistled and the sun seemed to be shining on him brighter than the rest of the world.

"After a moment, he looked up and invited me to come and sit for a while. He smiled with sad eyes when he told me that it would have been his twenty-fifth wedding anniversary. I looked at him and when I saw his pain, I was filled with emotion. I explained that I was supposed to be getting married the next week.

"He put his arm on my shoulder and told me that he was sorry and that he knew my pain. I felt my hackles rise, but then I realized he was right. He did know my pain and he had carried it with him far longer than I had, and yet he was able to find joy in life and care for others.

"When I could speak again, I asked how he had gotten over losing his wife. He shook his head and with a little laugh admitted that he had never gotten over her. He told me she was the only woman who captured his whole heart and that the memories of their time together kept him going. He said that though she had passed through the veil, he often caught glimpses of her in his moments of silence.

"I asked him if he really still believed that stuff. He turned to me look me in the eyes before speaking and I'll never forget his words. 'I believe it with all my heart,' he said. 'There are few things I know for certain. The reality of God is one I have learned to never question, for it is the basis of all that is good in my life. Upon this one truth hangs all the truth I know. God lives. And he loves us.'

"It was easier for me to believe there was no God than to think He would allow things to happen that cause us so much pain. Isaac told me he knew I was hurting, but that God and time could help me remember the truth I once believed.

"In an effort to argue, I shook my head and told him that I wasn't sure if I ever really believed. Instead of engaging me in an argument, he spoke softly but confidently of the truths he had learned from the whisperings of a gentle voice as he sat in quiet places and prayed for direction. The ideas were new to me, and yet they were so full of peace that I knew he spoke the truth. He told me that before we were born on this earth, we were born in the spirit as children of God and that this period of time we call life is but a twinkling of an eye when compared to the eternities we came from and the eternities we face when we leave this world. He taught me that God and His angels gave us all the truth we needed to know to return to His presence and our job on this earth was to remember those truths.

"As I listened to him speak, I began to feel something burn within me, as if he had lit a candle in the cellar of my soul. From memory, he recited a poem from William Wordsworth. It too spoke truth to me and I've since committed it to memory.

'Our birth is but a sleep and a forgetting:
The soul that rises with us, our life's Star,
Hath had elsewhere its setting,
And cometh from afar:
Not in entire forgetfulness,
And not in utter nakedness,
But trailing clouds of glory do we come
From God who is our home...
...At length the Man perceives it die away
And fade into the light of common day.'

"After reciting this poem, he turned and gently reminded me that I once believed in the truth of which he spoke. It was up to me if I would choose to remember.

"Love and family, Isaac taught me, are two of the most sacred eternal truths. He believed that God knew of the love he shared with Lily and would grant them their desire of being together in the eternities. He told me he didn't believe God is vengeful or spiteful nor has any desire to make our life difficult or painful.

"He taught me that hope, coupled with the grace of God, can be our wings and lift us from the dust of despair, giving us dreams for a brighter day. He taught me that sorrow is part of this life, but only a small part and that joy can overcome sorrow when we forget ourselves and seek to love as God loves. He told me that if the Bible was true, that we would be judged according to our works, then we didn't have time to be angry and spiteful. His words were cutting, but they were filled with love and I needed to hear them."

"So that was it? That's when you decided to become a priest again?"

"Not exactly, but it was the catalyst for change. I returned to the Bible and began to remember. I found myself searching for God in all that I read and did. I no longer had time to be angry because I was focused on finding answers. And then one day, I found that gratitude had replaced anger in my heart. I was grateful to be alive, grateful to have been preserved and sent to Niederbipp,  grateful to have known true love. I learned that life, even with all of its inherent pains and problems, is good.

"I spent many more hours talking to Isaac about life, love, God, and eternity until my soul was healed. Then I awoke one morning to the same dream I had so many years before, but this time, the ending was different. After looking me in my eyes and telling me to remember, Jesus told me I needed to help others remember too.

"I did little but think about the dream for several days and the more I thought about it, the more I felt that it was calling me to the ministry. But I had been there before and I knew I couldn't do it in the same way. After a few more days with no answers, I came to visit Isaac. Though we had spoken many times since our visit in the graveyard, I was not sure how he would take my interest in the ministry so I approached it cautiously.

"When I asked him if he believed in dreams, his eyebrows rose. He told me from his studies, he learned that God had used dreams to communicate with his children from the beginning of time. I admitted that I knew dreams were used in Biblical times, but wasn't sure if the pattern continued 'til today. His reaction was thoughtful. He explained that the Quakers believed in the principle of continuous revelation, that the heavens were not sealed and that God spoke to people in many forms, including dreams and visions. He added that he could think of no time in the history of mankind when personal revelation would be more important. My heart leapt within me when he told me that he welcomed dreams as a sign of God's love.

"I shared with him my dream and when I was done, I saw he was nodding thoughtfully. I told him of my feelings about returning to the ministry and admitted I was completely unsure of the hows and whys, but that I felt I needed to do more than I was doing. With kindness in his eyes, he told me that if I chose to return to the ministry, I would be much better prepared than the boy who arrived, bound hand and foot so long before.

"He told me that because I had learned to love, I would be able to serve in ways I never could have without that knowledge. 'You cannot learn love from a book or a lecture,' he told me. 'Only by conquering our selfishness can we know the pure love of God.'

"So I began volunteering to teach more on Sundays. I volunteered to help others with their lessons and I began teaching the Wednesday night Bible study group that is still going on. One night, someone broke into the church and vandalized some of the pews. The town council met and decided it was time to have someone live closer to the church. I volunteered, being the only single man without a shop to run or a home of my own and I spent the next several weeks cleaning out the tiny apartment next to the church that had served as a storage room for over two hundred years. I have lived there ever since, paying rent to the town council."

"And the black clothes?" Jake asked.

"Well, among the books I found in the apartment was an old worn out copy of William Penn's, No Cross, No Crown. As I read, I learned about

the beauty of simplicity as outlined by the Quakers, and Isaac's clothes finally made sense to me. He kept his life simple so he could share with the poor. I was not a potter, but the simple clothes of a priest that I once wore made more sense to me and reminded me of the vows I took so many years before. The black clothes now serve to remind me of my new vows to serve the Lord and help others to remember."

"But what about Sundays? You've given the sermon every week since I arrived."

Father Thomas smiled. "That's just a fluke really. I was asked to substitute for someone who was away on vacation and last week was my regularly scheduled week. Oh, and then there was the week that Martina Schmidt got nervous and threw up just before the meeting started. I just happened to be prepared so I volunteered to step up. Susan Rosenthal will be teaching this Sunday, if all goes as planned. Maybe you'd like to take a turn to teach sometime?"

"Not anytime soon. I'm afraid it would probably turn out like Martina Schmidt's lesson did. I'm dreadfully afraid of public speaking."

Thomas nodded. "Let us know when you're ready."

Jake grinned, but hoped that day would never come.

"I'm afraid I've wasted your whole morning," said Thomas looking at his watch and getting to his feet.

"No, no. I've enjoyed the visit. You're not at all what I expected."

"Thank you," he said with a wink. "I better be off."

Jake stood and extended his hand to Thomas. "Thanks for taking my mind off my disaster."

"Don't look at me. You have witnessed the power of marzipan." Thomas grinned at Jake. "If you need any pointers on the tea, I'll be happy to stop by and do some taste testing. I'm anxious to see what you come up with. Help yourself to all the gooseberry leaves you want."

32
JAKE'S SKETCHBOOK

After turning over all the pots he threw that morning so they would be ready to trim after lunch, Jake rushed to the bakery to get some bread. Standing in line, he began to wonder how many other people he had misjudged. He watched as Sam cheerfully helped his customers. He had spoken to Sam nearly every day since he had arrived in Niederbipp, but he hadn't had the chance to really talk to him. He wondered what new insights he might get from such a discussion.

Sam had spoken several times about Jake getting started on the mosaic. In the meantime, Jake had eaten a month's worth of bread that was supposed to go toward the trade. By the time he worked his way up to the front of the line, Jake was feeling guilty that he had not yet begun his part of the bargain. Now with the kiln in a questionable state of functionality, he felt even guiltier for taking Sam's bread.

"Good day to you, Jake," said Sam in a deep, solid voice. "What'll you have?"

"A loaf of the Sunflower Bread," said Jake.

Sam wrapped the loaf in paper and handed it to Jake.

"When do you want to talk more about that mosaic? I feel bad taking your bread without following through on my part of the deal."

"It would probably be better if it weren't during rush hour," Sam responded with a smirk. "Drop by sometime after work. Just come to the back door if we're closed up front."

Jake nodded and thanked Sam for the bread. He walked quickly back to the apartment and ran up the stairs, not wanting to be late for his date with Amy. He sliced the bread into healthy slabs and slathered them with peanut butter and honey. He packed the sandwiches into his backpack and was swinging it over his shoulder when he caught a whiff of himself. He hadn't showered after sweating all morning near the hot kiln. He set his backpack aside and jumped in the shower as fast as he could.

His hair was still dripping onto his neck as he neared the glass doors of the department store in a fast jog. He hadn't even taken the time to dry off after his shower. He was propelled by his excitement in seeing Amy, so focused that he was oblivious to the world around him.

"Where ya goin', potter boy?"

He turned to see her sitting on the bench at the base of the stone wall opposite the stores. She smiled at him and he blushed like a school boy.

"Hey," he said walking toward her. Still unsure of himself, he hoped he didn't seem too anxious, but was eager to be near her.

"Hello," she said, with a big smile. She remained sitting as he approached, the sun reflecting off her auburn hair.

"Did you forget we were going to meet here?" she asked, with a wink.

"I guess I did. I'm glad you called to me. I might have gotten to your counter and wondered if you had gone to lunch with someone else." He grasped her outstretched hand and pulled her from her seat.

"No," she said, looking him in the eye. "I've been looking forward to this all morning."

"Me too."

"I hope you have sandwiches in that pack," she said teasingly, reaching behind him to heft the pack from his shoulders.

"And milk this time," he added.

"Ah, Jake, you really know how to get to a girl." A broad smile spread across her lips.

He couldn't help but smile back. "Ready?"

"Yeah," she said, touching his hair. "What did you do, go through the car wash on your scooter?"

Jake laughed. "No, I just got out of the shower. It's been a crazy morning. It started at three when I woke up and realized I'd forgotten to turn the kiln off last night. I'm afraid it might be ruined."

Amy gasped. "What did you do?"

"It's probably best not to talk about it. I just finished a marzipan therapy session with Father Thomas and I'm feeling a lot better."

They climbed the stairs to the courtyard while Jake briefly explained, trying to be as optimistic as he could.

"Father Thomas has led a much more interesting life than I ever would have imagined."

"Like what?" she asked doubtfully.

Jake took a seat on the bench and looked thoughtful for a moment. "For starters, he was engaged once."

"To be married?" she asked incredulously.

"That's right."

"So what happened?" she asked, her interest piqued.

"She was killed in an accident."

"Is that why he entered the ministry?"

"Indirectly, I guess, but he isn't really a bona fide priest."

"What?!"

"Yeah. He has a couple of jobs. He works for Sam in the bakery and he said he's a part-time plumber."

"I guess that would explain why he showed up to unclog my aunt's sink after I washed some potato peels down it the first week I was here. I thought he was just helping out."

"He's really a good guy. I enjoyed my visit with him."

"You'll have to tell me more about it sometime," she said as she tugged Jake's backpack impatiently. "I've been waiting for this sandwich all morning."

Jake smiled, pleased that he had found a friend who could be happy with so little.

"It's good to see you too," he said, teasing her.

"Hey," she said, slugging him in the shoulder. "I've eaten plenty of peanut butter sandwiches in my life, but I realized this morning there is something special about your sandwiches that I've never had before."

"Oh really," he said turning to her with mock surprise. "And what would that be?"

"It's you!"

This completely disarmed him and set a flock of butterflies loose in his stomach. I love you, he wanted to say, but caught himself. He bit his tongue and handed her his backpack with a wordless smile that seemed more appropriate.

She stuck her hand into the bag and groped around before pulling out the sandwiches. Having felt something else in the bag, she returned her hand and pulled out Jake's sketchbook.

"This looks like a pretty special book. I've seen a lot of different sketchbooks over the years, but this one's really nice. Before the picnic last Sunday, I wasn't even aware that potters used sketchbooks and I've been meaning to ask you about it." She ran her hand over the tree that had been embossed on the rich leather cover. Jake watched as she thoughtfully rubbed on a white spot that had come from contact with clay.

"So you don't think potters keep sketchbooks because ... what, we're not real artists?" he asked with raised eyebrows.

"Of course not," she said, looking up at Jake with wide eyes.

"It's ok. You're not the first to tell me that pottery is substandard art."

She elbowed him softly in the ribs. "Don't try to put words in my mouth. I was glad to see you use a sketchbook. It suggests to me that you're thoughtful about what you do."

Jake raised his eyebrows and nodded his head cynically.

"Ok," she said, "let's start over." Before he could respond, she had begun again. "Wow, what a great sketchbook! Wherever did you get such a beautiful book?"

Jake looked at her and nearly started laughing as she continued to fondle the book's cover.

"My mother gave it to me the Christmas before she died." He reached for the book and Amy handed it to him. He unwrapped the leather thong that was tied around the pewter button and opened the book. "It's really just a cover for those plain sketchbooks that you can buy at bookstores."

He turned to the front page, and she moved closer to him, sliding her hand through his arm to get even closer. He had not anticipated this and was surprised at his strong reaction as a current shot through his frame. Jake looked at her and watched her carefully. He had always been protective of his sketchbooks. They contained not only his sketches and ideas, but also his deepest thoughts. For some reason, though, he did not feel threatened.

OFFICIAL SKETCHBOOK
OF
JACOB HENRY KIMBALL
— POTTER —

IF FOUND, PLEASE RETURN TO
HUDSON UNIVERSITY CERAMICS LAB

She read the first page. "That's a good idea," she said. "Have you ever lost one?"

"I never let it get out of my sight long enough, but I put it in every sketchbook just in case."

"You mentioned yesterday that part of your job was to cover this bench with memories of Isaac. Have you come up with anything yet?"

Jake nodded. He flipped through pages of notes and sketches until he opened to the page where he had been drawing the day before, recording the ideas that had come to him while reading the New Testament. He showed her the candle he had drawn and explained how Christ taught about candles in the Sermon on the Mount.

"From all that I have heard about Isaac, I believe he was one who took to heart the notion of letting your light shine before the world, but he did it in a way that was different than anything I've heard of."

She looked at him inquisitively.

He looked back at her and paused for a moment before he explained. "I've known a lot of people in my life who have talent, who have been successful and are at the top of their game. Most of those folks do little but toot their own horn, day in and day out."

"I know what you mean," said Amy. "A few of my professors at school did little but boast about their successes. My dad and brothers have been much the same way. We all do that to some extent, don't we?"

"Yeah, we do. That's part of human nature, but Isaac didn't seem to do that. Yesterday as I reread the Sermon on the Mount, I realized there was a difference in what I've seen myself and others do, and the way I've heard that Isaac lived his life. Funny, but I never understood what was meant by the candle or the light until I stopped and looked at it with Isaac in mind."

Amy took the sketchbook from him and traced her finger over the lines on the candle he had drawn. "So what was different about Isaac?"

Jake turned the page of the sketchbook as if to reveal the answer. He had copied down the sixteenth verse of the fifth chapter of Matthew. "Let your light so shine before men that they may see your good works, and glorify your Father which is in heaven." She read it aloud.

14. YE ARE THE LIGHT OF THE WORLD. A CITY THAT IS SET ON A HILL CANNOT BE HID

15. NIETHER DO MEN LIGHT A CANDLE, AND PUT IT UNDER A BUSHEL, BUT ON A CANDLESTICK , AND IT GIVETH LIGHT UNTO ALL THAT ARE IN THE HOUSE.

16. LET YOUR LIGHT SO SHINE BEFORE MEN, THAT THEY MAY SEE YOUR GOOD WORKS, AND GLORIFY YOUR FATHER WHICH IS IN HEAVEN.

"Anything stand out to you?" asked Jake.

She screwed up her eyes and read it again. "Yeah," she finally said after reading it a third time. "The last part...it's not about you, it's about God."

"Exactly! So many of us spend our life trying to be someone in the eyes of the world and we usually give God only superficial credit, if any at all."

"I think I know what you mean, but go on."

"I'm still trying to figure it out, but yesterday, when Father Thomas suggested that I spend some time looking at the parables of Jesus, I read the Bible looking for symbols to include on this bench. This was really the first one that came to me and when I read the last part of that verse, it hit me pretty strongly as I read over it again and again. If I understand this verse the way Jesus wanted me to, I should want to show off whatever light I have. He says that we should not hide our light—our gifts and talents—but put them on a candlestick so that everyone can benefit." She nodded, encouraging him to continue.

"As I thought about the things I've learned about Isaac, I recognized that he didn't brush over the last part of that verse. Somehow, the part about giving the glory to God for all that was good seems to be at the very heart of all he did. You'd have to hear some of these stories yourself to understand it, but that was the magic behind the man. This scripture seems to be the creed he lived by. He lived in such a positive and unselfish way that everyone who knew him wanted to be a better human because of his example. He didn't do it for the glory, he did it to help people discover the love God had for them."

Amy looked down at the sketchbook again and reread the scripture. "There's a lot of power in this verse," she said, looking up at Jake.

"I know." He handed Amy a sandwich before unwrapping his own. They ate in silence for a few moments as they passed the milk back and forth. He couldn't help but smile at her as he imagined what they must look like to anyone passing by. A beautiful woman, talented, lovely, sophisticated....drinking milk from a canteen and eating peanut butter and honey sandwiches with a potter in work clothes in the middle of a graveyard. And yet she seemed to be enjoying herself.

Amy handed the bottle back to Jake and slid to the far side of the bench, still holding her sandwich in her left hand. She leaned toward the middle of the gray concrete slab and rubbed her hand over the top of it.

"So, do you want some help with this project?"

"I'd love it," he said without hesitation.

"Good, then I'd love to help, because you're a great sandwich maker, but you could use some help with your sketches."

"Ouch!" He clutched his heart and rolled back on the bench as if he had just been shot.

She smiled broadly.

"What is that supposed to mean?"

She moved closer to him and picked up the sketchbook, turning back to the page where Jake had drawn the candle. "Take this candle, for example."

"What?"

"The perspective is all wrong. It's not bad for a beginner, but it really needs some work."

"Is that right?" he said, pulling the sketchbook out of her hands, continuing his mock defense.

"Hey, I'm a painter. I work in two dimensions. No one would expect a potter working in three dimensions to be able to draw this correctly."

"Unbelievable!" He tried to keep from smiling while continuing to act hurt.

"I like the idea of the candle," she said, moving back toward the end of the bench, freeing up the middle for closer inspection. She looked at the bench as if she could envision the finished project. Then she stood to look at the whole of it. The bench was six feet long and eighteen inches wide. The top slab was more than four inches thick and was rounded slightly on the corners. She looked at it intently, like she was in a museum and trying to discover every square inch of a painting that hung before her.

"What do you see?"

"This is going to be a lot of fun," she answered, not moving her eyes from the bench.

Jake stood, moving beside her, hoping to see what she was seeing.

"This is going to be great."

"Right," said Jake, staring at the same bench she was, but seeing nothing beyond a gray concrete slab.

"I think it would be great if the candle was in the middle. I can imagine it sending out beams of light in all directions that might tell a different story with each beam."

And suddenly, there it was before him and Jake too could envision what she was seeing, or at least hoped it was the same picture she was seeing.

"Do you think it would be good to include any script in the mosaic, outside of his name and birth and death dates?" he asked.

"What do you mean?"

"Well, I've just been wondering if there are some things that can be said with words that can't be expressed in any other way."

She took another bite of her sandwich and folded her arms, looking expectantly at Jake.

He wanted to sound like he had thought about this, but the ideas were still fresh in his mind and he was worried it might come out in a stuttering stammer of mumbo jumbo. He took a deep breath. "Just off the top of my head,... I wonder if it would be good to include some script like some Bible verses, or poetry, or some form of explanation. I know that we as artists like to have our work speak for itself, and though this bench will be a work of art, it is not entirely mine or yours. It's a memorial for a man who was loved by a whole community."

She leaned back and looked up at the clock tower of the chapel. "I see what you mean, but you still want to make it beautiful, right?"

"Of course. I've spent a little time looking at the other benches and there are elements of each that I can imagine being incorporated in Isaac's. This bench needs to have information on it and the prettier, the better."

"Do you have any other ideas yet?" she asked, taking a step towards his sketchbook sitting on the bench.

"Not really as far as visuals. There are a lot of ideas that need to be expressed somehow, but I need to work on both imagery and verbiage. Everyone who has come to visit me has shared a story that has prompted all sorts of images in my mind, but I need some help working through those ideas. There are a few that I think are really important, but I am not sure how to put them into an image that might mean something to everyone who comes to visit Isaac's grave."

"Like what?"

"Well, like the idea that people came to share a cup of tea with the old man and always left feeling challenged to become something better and encouraged to believe that change was possible."

"That's a lot to put into a picture. It sounds like this will require a lot of thought."

Jake nodded. He sat down again next to Amy and picked up his sandwich.

"I really want to help with this," she said, as she looked at Lily's grave marker.

"Thanks. I need your help and ..."

"And, what?"

Jake blushed, not knowing how to say what he was feeling. He fumbled with his sandwich, but Amy didn't let it go.

"What?" she asked again.

"It's just comforting to know that you want to help."

"And?" She looked at Jake who was now smiling as he chewed on his sandwich.

"What?" she said, louder than she meant to.

Jake turned to her, not sure he was ready to spill all of his guts just yet.

"I'm really glad that you want to help," he said, as he took another bite of his sandwich. He immediately recognized how his lukewarm comment seemed to deflate her spirits. He swallowed quickly and added, "I really enjoy being with you."

She smiled and squeezed his arm. "I enjoy being with you too." She reached over and pulled off a piece of his sandwich.

"Hey," he said as he watched her stick the stolen piece into her mouth. She smiled as she chewed and Jake laughed, grateful for her companionship and her fun, teasing ways.

Jake finished his sandwich and moved to kneel on the ground next to Lily's gravestone to pull a few weeds. A blanket of short green plants with tiny blue flowers had spread across the front of her grave marker and seemed to be migrating to the dark earth that was mounded above the still-fresh grave.

"I wonder what this is?" he asked out loud as he picked a small bunch of the blue flowers and leaned back on the heels of his shoes. Amy stood and took a step towards him before stooping to look at the tiny flowers.

"They're so tiny." She reached for the bunch and pulled them closer to her face to examine them.

She lowered her nose and breathed in their sweet fragrance. "They're beautiful." She pinched one of the tiny blossoms from the bunch to take an even closer look. She counted each of the five petals and smiled at the sunny yellow ring in the center. "They remind me of the summer sky, with the sun in the middle."

Jake turned to take a closer look, their noses almost touching as they examined the tiny flower on the tip of her finger.

"Wow, they really are beautiful." Amy's other hand still held the small bunch he had picked and he raised it to his nose and breathed deeply. Their scent was intensely sweet. "I've never noticed these before."

Amy looked at him and then at the patch growing on the ground, encircling Lily's gravestone. "I wonder if they just started blooming. I didn't notice them yesterday." She stood, still looking intently at the tiny flower. "Have you ever seen Georgia O'Keefe's paintings of flowers?"

"Yeah, I mean not the originals, but in books."

"Me too. I was always amazed at how nature could inspire her to paint such monumental pictures of the smallest details of life."

Jake looked up at the clock tower and sighed.

"What's wrong?"

"Oh, nothing, except that your lunch break ends in four minutes."

She looked up, startled. "Where did the hour go?"

"I'm not sure." He reached for his backpack and put his water bottle and sandwich wrappers inside.

"Can I use your sketchbook to press these flowers?"

"Sure," he said, handing the book to her.

"I'd like to paint an O'Keefe-inspired painting of these." She opened the book to a blank page and pulled a small cluster from the bunch of flowers, placing them flat in the center before closing the book and wrapping the thong around the pewter button.

Jake tossed his pack onto his shoulder and they walked quickly out of the graveyard. When the bells chimed the half hour, they bolted through the courtyard and down the stairs to Hauptstrasse

"So do you want to go painting tonight?" asked Amy, panting.

"No," lied Jake, with a big smile, "I'm out of bread. Maybe tomorrow."

"Ok, then I'll bring the picnic tonight. I get off at five," she said as she began walking backwards, toward the front doors of the department store. "Meet me with your bike at the barber shop at 5:30 and we'll figure out where to go."

"Ok," he said, smiling as she disappeared through the doors.

33

River Pirates

Jake's head wasn't in the game after lunch and the rest of the day was less than productive. He tried to ignore his negative thoughts about the kiln, but the warm studio kept reminding him of it.

A small flurry of customers stopped by late in the afternoon and purchased several of his newest pieces. This both excited and depressed him as he continued to think about the kiln. Fortunately, thoughts of an evening with Amy helped to chase the negative reality away.

Jake took a seat on the bench outside of the barber shop and pretended to be inspecting the tires on his bike. He didn't want to seem too anxious to Amy's uncle who was still working inside the shop, finishing up the last cut of the day. The bell tolled the half hour just as the barber shop door opened and the customer left.

Jerry was just saying hello when Amy came around the corner, pushing her aunt's old bike and struggling with the heavily-laden basket on the handle bars and the French easel strapped to her back.

"Where are you kids off to?" asked Jerry. Amy put down her kickstand and took a deep breath before she looked her uncle in the eye and winked.

"It's a surprise."

Jerry looked at Jake and raised his eyebrows.

"Well, I suppose it would have to be a surprise to keep the interest of two kids who have picnics in the graveyard." He smiled warmly.

"How'd you hear about that?" asked Amy.

Jerry just smiled. "Women talk everywhere, but when men talk, it's at the barber shop. Being the town barber keeps me pretty well informed with what's going on."

Amy shook her head and smiled. "You ready, Jake?"

He nodded and stood. "Can I help you carry any of that?"

"No thanks. I think I got it."

He threw his leg over the leather saddle of his bike and extended his hand to the well-informed barber. "It's good to see you, Jerry."

Jerry shook his hand and smiled at Jake before winking at his niece. "You kids have fun now. You better hurry if you're gonna be home before dark."

Amy smiled. "Don't wait up for me." She mounted her own saddle and they were off.

Instead of heading for the hills, Amy led Jake down the hill towards the river. They rode in silence for a time, Amy staying ahead of Jake as if she had a race to win. His backside was sore from the ride the night before and  though he was pedaling hard, he continued to fall behind on his heavy bike with only one gear.

Jake pushed as hard as he could, but the distance between them remained until the road turned and she was out of sight.

When he reached the turn in the road, he saw her waiting for him on the other side of a narrow bridge that spanned the wide river. The temperature dropped rapidly as he neared the river and entered the shade cast by the tall trees on both sides. She was smiling when he coasted up alongside her.

"Are you ready?" she asked, with a broad smile.

"Ready for what?" he asked, still out of breath.

"I wanted to show you a place my dad used to bring us when we came here in the summers."

"So how far away is it?" he asked, leaning over on his handle bars, feeling nauseous. When she didn't answer he looked up to find her shaking her head.

"I'm ready," he said with a nod. The hills were much steeper on this side of the river and the forest was thicker, filled with ancient trees that had never been felled to make way for farming. They rode on, over the narrow paved road until they reached an even narrower dirt path that climbed the hill to their left.

"This is where we walk." She parked her bike and unloaded the cloth bag from the basket on the handlebars. She handed this to Jake once he had parked his own bike and they headed off up the trail, Jake leading the way.

The giant trees blocked out most of the evening sunlight here, making it seem much later than it really was. As they climbed the steep, damp trail, Amy slipped a couple of times. When she slipped the third time, Jake turned to offer his free hand. She was appreciative of the gesture and took his hand as he pulled her up. He held her hand longer than was necessary as they continued, but she didn't protest.

"It's just over here," she said, pointing to the right. Sunlight filtered through the canopy overhead, casting sunbeams through the branches and painting a mosaic of light on the dark forest floor.

"It's beautiful here."

"I'm glad you like it. This has always been one of my favorite places."

They walked until they came to an old picnic table, whose dark wood planks looked like they had seen few picnics of late.

"My dad used to bring us here when we came to visit Aunt Bev. He and my brothers built this table before I was born. It kind of became a hideout for all of us."

She slid the easel from her back and set it on the bench. "Come here," she said, grabbing the bag from his hand and setting it on the table, "I want to show you something."

She took him by the hand and pulled him back into the thicker part of the forest where no sunbeams could penetrate.

"Where are we going?" he asked, smiling at her adventurous spirit.

"This is the surprise." When they had walked about a hundred yards, she stopped and looked from side to side.

"Are you lost?" he asked, grinning.

"Of course not, it's just been a while since I've been here and I lost track of my steps back there."

"What does that mean?"

"Did you see the tree back there with the ribbon hanging from the branch?"

"No," he said hesitantly.

She turned and looked at him. "From that tree, it was fifty two paces ahead and then after turning to the river, it's supposed to be twenty-seven paces." Jake imagined buried treasures and grinned, caught up in the same spell of creativity that had imagined whatever this was.

"So where do we go from here?" he asked, genuinely excited. She lifted her hand and pointed.

"That way, twenty seven paces. I'm sure my paces are a little bigger than they used to be but that ought to get us in the general area at least." They counted their paces as they quickly walked across the soft forest floor, covered thick in decaying leaves. As they neared twenty seven, Amy's stride quickened and she lifted her head to the dark canopy overhead. "It's still here!" she cried out in joy. Jake finally saw the object drawing her attention.

They stood at the base of the tree and looked up at the platform suspended by branches and a series of braces. Amy wrapped her fingers around one of the makeshift rungs of the ladder that climbed the trunk. Without a word, she began climbing. Jake followed. Soon, they both were high above the ground, climbing toward the platform built of logs, scrap lumber and driftwood. The platform was covered with several inches of leaves. Together, they moved the leaves to the edge of the platform and kicked them off.

Jake kicked the last pile over the edge before turning to see Amy standing on the opposite edge. Her arms were folded across her chest as she looked out across the valley. Jake crossed the rickety platform and stood next to her, amazed at the sight before them. From here, they could see the river and then the road, the town of Niederbipp and the hills that rose above the town.

"Wow!" he said.

"You like?"

"It's incredible! How did you know this was here?"

"My brothers built it, several years before I was even born. They worked on it every summer when we came to see Aunt Bev. My dad built a smaller version of this, in this very tree, when he was boy. My brothers told me that some of the wood from his tree house went into building this one. We used to spend as much time here as we could get away with. My dad would bring us here to 'let the women folk visit and have their peace.' I don't remember him ever coming here to the tree house with us. He normally brought work to do and stayed back at the table while we played around over here.

"My brothers built that swing too," she said, pointing off, down the hill to where a log had been lashed in between two parallel trees.

Jake squinted. "I don't think there's a swing there anymore," he reported.

"That's fine with me. I hated that swing. It must have been a twenty foot drop from the top and I'm sure it caused me to lose control of my bladder more than once." Jake laughed at her comment.

"What's so funny?" she asked, turning to him, ready to fight.

He shook his head, but continued to smile. "I just can't imagine you being afraid of anything."

"I put on a pretty good show. When you're the only girl in a family with five older brothers, it's pretty important to never show fear or weakness."

"It must be nice to have brothers," he said thoughtfully.

"There were lots of times that I hated it, but as I've grown up, I've begun to realize how good I had it."

"What do they think about your art?"

"Oh, most of them think it's a silly dream and are waiting for me to grow out of it and get a real job. I spoke to one of them last night. I hadn't spoken to him in several months and from the very beginning of the conversation, I felt like he was on a mission to get me to come to my senses. He regurgitated all the crap my dad's been telling me for the past four years. Mike is my closest brother, both in age and in friendship, and it felt pretty awful to recognize that I no longer have him on my team."

"That's pretty heavy stuff," he said.

She nodded and silence fell between them for several moments.

"So why did you bring me here tonight?" he asked, taking a step closer to her.

She looked up and shook her head but said nothing. When she finally spoke, it came out in a torrent of emotion.

"I had to see that this place still existed. It doesn't look like much now, but this place was once a castle. This is where my imagination was born. We fought battles with river pirates and had pine cone wars with crusading armies." She reached behind the tree trunk and pulled out  a collection of faded carnival beads and baubles hanging from a rusty nail. "These were the family jewels," she said smiling, though the dams holding back the tears in her eyes were beginning to burst. "We created this world with our own hands and minds. We spent hours here, escaping reality for something so much better. I had to see this place tonight to prove to myself that my brothers once knew the joy of imagination." She leaned her back against the trunk and slid down into a pile on the floor. "They've forgotten it all and I feel like I'm the only one who hasn't."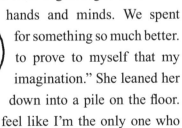

Jake moved toward her, kneeling in front of her as she cried.

When she was done, several minutes had passed. She looked up, her eyes red and swollen. "You probably think I'm an idiot," she said, shaking her head. Jake put his hand on hers and she looked at him.

"I don't know much about how boys are supposed to react in situations like this."

She pursed her lips and nodded. "I'm really sorry," she said. "I didn't mean to bring you here to listen to me sob."

"I'm really glad I could see it."

She looked at him surprised.

"I can't tell you how intimidated I've been by you."

Her look of surprise only increased.

"You seem to have all the confidence in the world, as well you should. You're talented and athletic and beautiful."

She began to laugh, so he continued. "I'm intimidated every time I'm around you, and normally I would run away from such intimidation. But with you, it makes me crazy. It makes me want to be near you, to understand you and figure out what makes you tick. Part of me still wants to run from you, but most of me wants to wrap my arms around you and not let go, hoping some of your essence will rub off on me."

Her face had turned from tears to smiles. He wasn't sure what he had just said, but he was grateful that it seemed to console her the way he hoped it would.

The forest was already dark, but it was getting even darker now. "I'm sorry you're not getting any painting done."

She started to laugh. "I'm not a painter, Jake. I'm just a dreamer, and I'm becoming a failure at both."

Jake shook his head. "Amy, I know it's not up to me what you do, but I can't sit back and watch you not paint. You have a passion for this. I've seen it every time I've been with you, but probably never as much as I have tonight. Forget your brothers. Forget your parents. You're an artist and you know it and you'll never be happy doing anything else."

She raised her eyebrows and shook her head, but said nothing.

"What does your heart tell you?" he asked with intensity.

"I don't know anymore."

"Amy," he said calmly, until she turned and looked him in the eyes. "What does your heart tell you?" She tried to look away, but he put his hand on her knee and she turned back to look at him. She looked at him intensely until her eyes once again began to fill with tears.

"I'm supposed to paint."

Jake nodded. "Last night, I knew that you knew what you were supposed to do with your life. You can't forget that." She pursed her lips again and began to nod, tears still in her eyes.

She took Jake's hand in hers and looked deep into his eyes before busting up laughing. "What?" he asked.

"You know how I told you my father would hate you?" Jake nodded.

"Well, I think my brothers would hate you too."

"I hope that's a compliment," he said with a wide grin.

"It most definitely is." She leaned forward to give him a hug.

They held each other for a long moment.

"Are you hungry?"

"Yeah," he said, letting her go.

"We better get out of this forest before it's too dark to see."

"We could have our picnic on my kitchen table if you want."

She nodded. "I'd like that."

Jake pulled himself off the floor before offering Amy a hand up. She returned the family jewels to their resting place on the rusty nail and they climbed down the tree slowly in the growing darkness. Once they were both down, Amy slid her hand into Jake's.

"Thank you," she said.

"For what?"

"For keeping the dream alive."

Jake nodded and they walked back the way they had come, hand in hand, counting out their paces in the darkness so they wouldn't lose their way.

When they came to the picnic table and could see the sky again, they stopped and marveled at the darkening red heavens through the trees. Jake threw his back pack over his shoulders before helping Amy with the easel. He grabbed the dinner bag and they walked back down the trail the way they had come. After a few strides, Amy slid her hand back into Jake's and he smiled in the darkness, feeling the tenderness of her hand in his.

They biked back to Niederbipp much slower than they had come, being careful to stay on the narrow road in the near total darkness. By the light of the first streetlamp they passed, Jake could see the goose bumps on Amy's arms and calves.

"Do you have any of that tea left?"

"I was just thinking the same thing," he said as they parked their bikes under the stairs. Jake flipped on the lights as soon as they entered the apartment. He dropped the bags and went into his room, returning with an old patchwork quilt from the closet. He draped it over Amy's head and shoulders.

Jake put the kettle on to boil and turned to find her eyes roaming the shelves full of pots.

"This is a cozy little place," she said, turning her attention to Jake.

"I thought the same thing. It's pretty humble and plain, but it's comfortable."

"So give me a lesson in pottery. What makes all of these pots so special?"

Jake shook his head. "I'm not sure if there is anything special about these. Everyone I've looked at is a second."

Amy raised her eyebrows. "What does that mean?"

"It means that each of them is flawed."

"They look pretty good to me."

The kettle whistled and Jake stood to make the tea, returning to the table with the teapot and two mugs.

"So if all of these are seconds, why are they here?"

"I've wondered the same thing. Some of them still function. Take this mug for example. The handle is really crooked, but if you're careful, it still works." He walked to the largest shelf. He pulled several pieces of pottery from the shelves, setting them down on the table. While he continued to pull pots from the shelves, Amy picked up a pitcher. She turned the pitcher over to discover it was chipped and the glaze was puddled near the bottom. "How did this happen?" she asked.

Jake turned to her and picked up the pitcher. He recognized that  it was the same glaze that had run off of his bowls, ruining the bowls and damaging the shelves. He turned the pitcher over to find the chip and the puddled glaze. He sat down, shaking his head.

"What is it?"

"It's something I wish I would have seen a few weeks ago. It might have saved me some frustration and a couple of good bowls."

"How?"

"This glaze obviously runs when it's too thick. I found that out the hard way."

"Do you think Isaac was trying to warn you about the glaze?"

"I was just wondering the same thing." Jake let out a long breath, shaking his head. "I just thought this was a bunch of junk."

Amy pulled a straight-sided vase from the collection on the table and began examining it. "There's something in here," she said, reaching her hand inside. She pulled out a yellowed piece of paper and unrolled it.

Jake looked over her shoulder. The paper was dusty and Amy brushed her hand over the surface, removing the dust and flattening the paper.

It was dated November 12, 1972. Amy read it aloud.

November 12, 1972

— Don't be discouraged by failure. It can be a positive experience. Failure is, in a sense, the highway to success, inasmuch as every discovery of what is false leads us to seek earnestly after what is true, and every fresh experience points out some form of error which we shall afterwards carefully avoid. —— John Keats

I found this quote tonight in my reading and thought it applied well to the pots on the shelf.

Jake looked at Amy. She looked back at him.

"Things aren't always what they seem," Jake said, feeling humble.

"What are you thinking?"

"I think I'm a fool. Thomas told me that today."

"Thomas told you you're a fool?"

"No," he said, shaking his head. "He told me that things aren't always what they seem." He looked away, thoughtful. "I feel like I've been wasting my time, cursing these crappy old pots and this dumpy old shop." He let out a long sigh and ran his fingers through his hair. "Isaac's will said that this collection was the most valuable part of the estate. When every piece I picked up was flawed, I assumed it was just a bunch of junk."

"And now?" Amy asked, looking a little confused.

Jake took a deep breath. "And now I'm beginning to realize that I am a fool." He looked around the room at all the pots, hundreds of pots in all colors, shapes and sizes. He shook his head.

"Tell me what you're thinking." She put her hand on his knee, causing him to turn and look at her.

"I'm thinking about our conversation from last night. I think I've been so set on making my own mistakes, following my own dream, that I've missed what's right under my nose." He picked up the pitcher. "If I had seen this….. Man, I have been so blind." He looked at the pots again, shaking his head. "If I lived for three hundred years, I might be able to make as many mistakes as the last seven potters made, but maybe these pots are here so I don't have to."

"So how do you make sense of what these pots are supposed to teach you?"

"I'm not sure. But this pitcher would have been a dead giveaway if I had taken the time to look at it instead of cursing it." He let out another long sigh.

Amy looked at all the pots around the room. "I am sure there is wisdom that can be gained from looking through the mistakes others make, but it has to be somewhat depressing to be surrounded by your mistakes all the time. I'd hate to live with only my bad paintings."

Jake poured the tea and leaned against the back of his chair. "I know what you're saying, but if you could learn something from a bad painting that could help you paint a better one, would it be worth keeping it around?" "Maybe, but after I learned whatever I needed to learn, I think I'd rather get rid of it."

"That's fair, but what if you hoped that your kids might someday pick up painting? Would you want them to be able to learn from your mistakes, from the lessons you learned so they wouldn't have to make the same ones?"

"Doesn't that bring us back to your argument from last night that we all have to crack through our own shells if we ever hope to be strong?"

"Yeah, it does," Jake said, looking thoughtful. "I know the struggle is important." He lifted up the pitcher. "But maybe I don't have to learn everything from experience. Maybe these pots and whatever secrets they hold could save me some time."

Amy took a deep breath and smiled. "I'm starving."

Jake pushed all the pots to the far side of the table and grabbed two plates from the drying rack. Amy unwrapped two huge turkey sandwiches and placed them on the plates.

As they ate, they continued to talk about the pottery collection. Amy suggested that they write a note to any future potters, warning them that the glaze on the pitcher was runny. While Jake cleaned up, she tore off a piece of brown paper bag, scribbled the note and dropped it into the pitcher.

"Do you ever eat anything besides sandwiches?" Amy asked when they were done.

Jake thought for a moment. "I had pancakes with Kai and Molly last week. Why do you ask?"

"I just wondered if you might want to try something else. I thought it might be fun to cook dinner together sometime... like tomorrow night."

Jake raised his eyebrows. "When are you ever going to paint?"

"I could paint you cooking!"

"So do you want a sandwich or maybe some pancakes?"

"Ok, so maybe that's not a good idea. How about if we cook quickly and then I set up a still life painting here on the table? I could paint while you do the dishes."

"I'll do it on one condition."

"Ok?"

"If you promise to paint and stop stalling."

"Me, stall?" she said with a wink. "I think this would be a good place to paint. There's decent light and good company and I could paint later than if we went somewhere outdoors."

"Ok, but if you don't have a painting done by the end of the night, I'm not going to let you hang out with me anymore. You came here to paint and so far you have what, a half a painting done in nearly a month?"

"So I'll cook something simple. Let me surprise you. I'll pick up some groceries after work and meet you here."

"Fine, you twisted my arm. You might as well just leave your easel here then." She nodded as she looked up at the clock.

"How'd it get to be so late?"

Jake shook his head. "I have no idea."

"I better get home. I have inventory starting tomorrow at eight."

She put the canvas bag in the basket and Jake pushed her bicycle as they walked back towards the barbershop. After a few paces, Amy reached over to take his hand. He turned to look at her and she smiled at him.

"Thank you."

"For what?"

"For letting me dream, but making me face what I came here to do. You're making me do the hard thing, but it feels good."

"You're welcome." They neared the back steps that led to her apartment.

"So are we doing lunch tomorrow too?"

"You don't think you'll get sick of me?"

"No, I'm really enjoying the time we spend together. It makes work bearable to know that I'll see you in a few hours."

"I feel the same way."

"Besides that, you still have a lot of sandwiches to go to work off that painting."

"And at this rate, it may take a couple of years for you to get around to painting it," he chided. She slugged him the best she could with her arms wrapped up in the old quilt. He grabbed her and hugged her to keep her from slugging him again and when he let her go, she was smiling.

"Walk me to the door and I'll give you your blanket back." They climbed the stairs to the small porch where she removed the blanket from her shoulders and handed it to him. She hugged him again and said goodnight.

Jake turned and wrapped the blanket around his own shoulders as he descended the stairs. He smiled all the way home, embraced in the warmth she left in the blanket.

(34) DARLING

Jake was slow to get out of bed the next morning. The quilt that Amy used to warm herself lay at the foot of his bed and he lifted it against his face, breathing in the scent of her hair. He was reminded of the day he met her, how her auburn hair brushed across his face as he pushed her on the swing. He inhaled deeply again with the blanket pressed against his nose.

None of his memories were as poignant as those from the evening before when she cried for the first time in his presence. It was in those moments that he saw her for who she was. It was as if he knew her then for the first time, and in that moment, as she allowed her truest feelings to show through, he knew he could love her.

He made himself breakfast and while he was at it, decided to make sandwiches for the picnic too. He was about to make himself a cup of tea, but the canister was nearly empty and he knew he needed some to do his taste testing.

Jake had been watching as the young peppermint plants on the stairs sent out new life. They were growing bigger every day. He had also seen several other plants growing wild around town. He figured he might be able to collect enough that afternoon to begin his first experiments with the tea.

When he finally left his apartment, he felt hurried to get the studio open. He continued to think of Amy. She had to be to work at eight for inventory. He wondered what that meant for her...probably counting lipstick tubes and mascaras. He busied himself, cleaning up the trimming scraps on the floor from the previous day.

Just before 10:00, the bells on the front door rang as the door opened.

He looked up and shouted over his shoulder, "I'm back here if you need anything."

"No problem," said a male voice. Jake heard the door close and he went on pretending to work as he listened to the customer's feet shuffle across the floor. When Jake finally looked around the corner, he saw a young man who couldn't be much older than himself.

"Hello," he said.

The man turned to him. "Hello, you must be the new potter."

"That's right, my name's Jake," he said extending his hand to the stranger.

"Paul Darling. Nice to meet you."

"Paul Darling, as in the Bluegrass Darlings?" Jake asked, his mouth agape.

"That's me," he said with a grin.

"Wow! I love your music. I've listened to it since I was a freshman in college. I always had it playing in the studio while I worked."

"Thanks," he said with a proud smile.

"And I was happy to find that Isaac had all your CDs here in the studio when I got here. I met Kai and Molly last week. They told me you used to practice right here."

"That's right. Isaac hosted us for the last three and a half years of high school. I have a lot of memories here—a lot of laughs and good times."

"So what brings you to town?"

Paul reached into his back pocket and produced a ticket, which he handed to Jake. "We're here to do a benefit concert on Saturday."

"You're kidding! This is the first I've heard about it."

"Yeah, the guy who was in charge of publicity really dropped the ball this year so we came out early to visit our folks and spend a couple of days getting the word out."

"How can I help?"

"Well, if you don't mind, I'd like to hang a poster in your front window."

"No problem," he said looking down at the ticket Paul handed him. "Wow! I've always wanted to see you guys in concert."

"It's a good seat. Isaac came every year since we started doing the concert a few years ago. It will be hard to look down and not see him there, but seeing another potter in his place will make things a bit easier."

"Thanks. Hey... um... I just remembered that I've kind of been hanging out with someone. I'm not sure if she likes bluegrass, but do you think you could spare another ticket?"

"I think I can manage that," Paul said with a big smile, producing another ticket from his back pocket.

"How about if we trade this ticket for a cup of tea every time I come to town?"

"Of course," said Jake with a grin. "You're always welcome here."

"Oh, and do you think we might be able to come and practice here tomorrow night? None of our folks have rooms big enough."

"You don't even need to ask," said Jake, grateful to have something to offer one of his heroes. "Please, bring anyone you want."

"Thanks a million. I know the boys will be glad to know we have a place to practice, especially when they hear where it is. Is 8:00 ok?"

"Fine," said Jake.

"Great! We'll see you tomorrow then. I've got a hundred posters to get up as soon as I can. It was nice to meet you."

And with that he was gone and the door closed behind him.

Jake sat in silence for a minute, looking at the tickets. He could hardly believe what just happened. He looked around the studio, realizing how much work he had to do before the band would have room to practice. He was also excited to talk to Amy about the arrangements he made and hoped she would be available for the concert on Saturday night.

GATHERING WEEDS

Just before noon, Jake locked the doors and packed his bag with the sandwiches and his sketchbook. He walked quickly to the plaza, thinking about the concert. He reached the bench across from the department store with a few minutes to burn, so he took out his sketchbook and recorded some of his thoughts. As he began to write about Amy, he paused to think.

Could it really have been only four days since Sunday? So much had changed in his life. Somehow, his cynicism for the town and his circumstances had abated. Each day's rendezvous with Amy consumed his thoughts and much of his time. They were a welcome and happy addition to his days. Everything else, his highs and his lows, were being eclipsed by his budding friendship with her.

"I hope you're thinking about me," she said, waking him from his daydream. He blushed, speechless, wondering if she could see his thoughts.

"Just working out some ideas for Isaac's bench," he lied, closing his book quickly to hide any evidence.

She sat down next to him on the bench, looking tired.

"Are you ready?" he asked.

"Yeah, just give me a minute. I've been running since early this morning. My boss had me running up and down the stairs to the storeroom in the basement. I've hardly had a chance to catch my breath. If he didn't know Daddy I might not be so diligent. I just don't want to give Daddy any more ammunition."

Jake shook his head, feeling Amy's frustration.

"Working on the inventory gave me a good idea though. I found a whole bunch of old lipstick tubes that were either returns or are all dried up. The cases on several of them are really cool. I was just about to throw them away, but I thought they would be fun to set up as a still life painting. I think I'll start on it tonight."

"I thought you didn't even like make-up," he chided.

"I don't, but most women do. It may be a crazy idea, but it inspired a painting so I think I better run with it."

She stood from the bench. "Come on, potter boy. I only have an hour."

He swung his bag onto his shoulder as they walked up the familiar stairs to the cemetery. Jake opened the gate and stepped inside, pointing to the benches over in the corner, under the shade of the crabapple tree.

They zigzagged through the crooked rows of tombstones to the corner. Amy took a seat on one of the benches and looked up through the leaves. Jake sat down on the bench next to hers and emptied his bag of its contents, handing one of the sandwiches to Amy.

As they ate, Jake told her about the visit from Paul, expressing his own love for bluegrass music. Amy looked surprised and teased him, suggesting that he didn't look like someone who would be into country music. He tried to explain that there was a difference between bluegrass and country, but Amy only continued to tease.

"Well," he finally said, "Paul gave me two tickets to their concert on Saturday night. If you don't want to go, I'll have to find another date and give you a chance to do more painting."

"Oh, I think I might be able to endure a concert," she said, backpedaling. Jake smiled broadly.

"I don't know anyone who doesn't want to dance when they hear their

ALEGHEN
SAW BACK C

music. They're coming over tomorrow night to practice in the studio. You can get a preview and then you can make your final decision if you want to come to the concert or not."

When they were finished with their sandwiches, Jake stood and pulled Amy up from the bench.

"I've already looked at these, but there are three others I wanted to look at more closely." He picked up his sketchbook and walked to the one closest to them, near the old iron fence. Amy followed. This was easily recognizable as the oldest of the benches, as its edges were chipped and several pieces were missing. Many of the shards matched the tiles of the church roof and floor. Jake explained how he had learned from Brian that Abraham Engelhart had made all the tiles with the help of his sons and some of the town folk who wanted to help out.

Jake knelt down on the ground to more closely examine the carved tile which recorded the dates of Abraham's life. As Jake wrote down the information, Amy knelt down the best she could in her summer dress. She ran her fingers over the face of the bench, reading the words carved there in an old fashioned script. "Rob not God, the source of all good gifts." [6]

She looked at Jake and asked if he knew its meaning. Jake recalled Brian's words again, how Isaac taught him about the law of tithing. He explained how Isaac's wife Lily taught him the lessons that had been passed down through the generations. Amy was unfamiliar with the law and the blessings. As Jake explained, he also told her that part of his agreement when he took over the studio was to give one tenth of his income to God.

The next bench was also very old and they quickly recognized that the familiar patterns of the chapel floor were scattered about on the top of this bench in the form of broken mosaic. On the middle of the bench was a tile that read:

Gabriel Abraham Engelhart
August 13, 1735-
October 6, 1795
Son of Abraham and Eva Faber Engelhart
Husband of Eloise Bennion Engelhart
Father of Zebulon, Gina, Johann and Muriel

This tile was glazed in a simple honey brown that accentuated the lettering. Like the first bench, the legs were also covered with a mosaic of potshards, but more colorful and refined.

Amy read the writing on the face and found that it wrapped all the way around the bench. "Come unto me, all ye that labor and are heavy laden, and I will give you rest. Take my yoke upon you and learn of me; ... For my yoke is easy and my burden is light. Matthew 11:28."

Jake was smiling when she finished. "What?" she asked.

"It just reminded me of what you told me Tuesday when we went out painting, something about you feeling the love of God every time you painted. It seems to me that the yoke of painting and the love of God are far less burdensome than the yoke you've carried as you've tried to figure out what to do."

Amy nodded, reading the verse again. "You know that scripture?"

"Yeah. It's one of my favorites. I read it in a card Mr. Williams sent my mother after she was first diagnosed with cancer. I remember asking a lot of questions about what it meant."

"What did you learn?"

Jake was distracted, brushing off the surface of the bench when he saw it. It was a carved tile whose recesses had filled with dust and dirt from its years of standing in the weather. He brushed it off with his hands to find a beautiful depiction of Christ standing in front of what looked like the world. In His hands, He held a double yoke.

"I feel like I've seen this before," he said, perplexed. "Remind me tonight to look at Isaac's bible. I wonder if this might have come from an etching in it." Amy nodded as she glanced up at the clock.

"I need to go."

Jake nodded. "I'll walk you back."

He gathered up his stuff and they walked quickly back the way they had come. When they reached the plaza, Amy turned to Jake.

"I get off at five. I just have to pick up a few things from the store and I'll be over after that."

"Sounds good," said Jake.

"What are you doing this afternoon?"

Jake thought for a moment. "I have to start collecting peppermint. I only have a few cups' worth of tea left. And I need to clean up the studio so there's room for the band tomorrow night."

The bell chimed and Amy said goodbye, walking slowly to the door. Jake watched her go before climbing the stairs to begin collecting. His thoughts took him back to the night before, holding Amy's hand as they hiked up the hill and through the woods. Never before had a girl given him that kind of attention.

His thoughts distracted him from his purpose and out of habit he was nearly at the gates of the cemetery again before he remembered where he was going. He walked past the church and into the yard of the adjacent apartment that had served as the home for Father Thomas for the past several years. He found his way to the back through the thick grass and overgrown bushes to the place where Thomas said the gooseberries grew. He had never seen gooseberries before or the bushes. He picked one of the berries from its stem and held it in his palm as he examined it. Its green flesh looked much like a grape, but it had a bit of the dead blossom on the end opposite its stem. Tiny hairs protruding from its skin glistened in the sunlight.

He swept aside some of the foliage and immediately jumped back in pain. He looked at the palm of his hand and pulled a thorn out, causing his hand to bleed even more. He sucked away the blood before returning back to the bush with new respect. Under the foliage, he recognized that the berries were mostly found on the top part of the bush and he decided he would do his leaf collecting on the lower part, leaving the berries shaded and hoping to avoid any more thorns.

Having no idea how many of the leaves he would need, he took more than he figured was necessary. When he had a sizable stack balanced in his hand, he stood and walked out of the yard. He found an old galvanized pail under one of the shrubs, filled with the leaves of more than one autumn. He set down his pile of gooseberry leaves and emptied the contents of the pail under the bush. The bottom of the pail was dirty and in some places had rusted all the way through. Jake knew it would not be missed. He tossed the gooseberry leaves into the pail and began his search for wild peppermint.

Thomas had two large patches of peppermint growing in his yard and Jake broke off several of the stems and added them to the pail before moving on. His walk back to the studio was much slower than normal, as he stopped frequently to gather peppermint wherever he could find it growing in places he knew it wouldn't be missed. He had just plucked one stem from an unkempt garden, when he looked up to see he was being watched by an old woman from an open window.

"Hope you don't mind if I take some of your peppermint?" he asked.

"Take it all," she said without expression. "It's a damn weed."

Jake smiled, wondering if this might have been one of the patches Isaac planted on a piece of neglected ground. He quickly broke most of the stems away and smiled at the old lady in the window thanking her.

"I'll be back later to get some more," he said, cheerfully.

She raised her hand to dismiss him, but her face remained expressionless.

"She needs some good tea," he said to himself as he moved on.

By the time he returned to his apartment, the pail was overflowing and he had yet to cut any growing in the planters on the stairs. He placed the pail in the sink and began making bunches by binding handfuls of the stems together with rubber bands. He rinsed the bunches quickly under the faucet and hung them to dry from hooks over the sink. When he got to the gooseberry leaves, he washed them as well, but since they didn't have a stem to tie together, he spaced them out on a cookie sheet to dry. He looked at the clock on the wall. He was already late in opening the front door and he hurried from the apartment to get back to work.

As he unlocked the front door, he noticed a woman waiting just outside. He swung the door open and apologized for being late.

"No, no," she said, "it's not a problem on a beautiful day like today." She followed him into the shop and Jake moved quickly to flip on the light in the showroom. The woman was carrying a basket which she set on the counter. She pulled from the basket an old bowl with a broken lip. Jake stood behind the counter and looked at her, wondering what she might want.

"I've been watching your new work fill the windows, and I decided it's finally time to replace this old bowl with one of the new bright ones you've been making lately." Jake nodded with a smile, moving to the other side of the counter.

"Is there a color you were most interested in?"

"A couple of days ago, you had a beautiful blue and green bowl in the window with a star in the center."

Jake smiled. "I sold it on Saturday, but I have a couple in the same glaze over here and I'll be making more." The lady looked disappointed until she looked at the others and found them to her liking. Jake left her to browse and make her selection while he returned to the counter to examine the bowl she had brought with her. It was old and the tiny craze lines that had formed in the glaze had darkened with its years of use, looking like dark spider webs. In addition to a large portion of the lip missing, there were several smaller chips on the lip. He held it in his left hand and flicked it with his right index finger. The life was gone out of the bowl and when he flicked it, it sounded like it would fall apart at any moment. He flipped it over and recognized Isaac's stamp.

"It looks like this one has had a lot of use," he said. "My best guess is that it's probably between forty and fifty years old."

"Well, now it can't be that old. It was a wedding gift and I've only been married thirty-six years."

Jake blushed and smiled.

"Looks like it's seen some good use in those years."

"Every day," she responded thoughtfully. "It could tell a lot of stories of good meals and family gatherings. My son was playing with a ball in the kitchen twenty years ago when the rim broke off but I couldn't bring myself to throw it away. I didn't know until recently, but he thought I had been keeping it to make him feel bad. Two weeks ago on my birthday, he gave me some money to buy myself a new one so I'd get rid of the old one, once and for all. I'm just afraid that this new one will meet the same fate with all my grandchildren running around."

"Well, ya know, folks need to break stuff every thirty-six years or so to keep us potters in business." She nodded and laughed.

Jake wrapped up the new bowl and set it in her basket.

"Would you like to keep the old one?"

She looked at it with a furrowed brow. "It's been a good friend, but now that I have a new one, I'm not sure what I'd do with it. No, you better keep it. I don't have the heart to throw it away." She set her purse on the counter and withdrew an envelope. She reached inside and pulled out a greeting card with cash sticking out of the ends. "How much do I owe you?" she asked.

"Forty dollars." She handed him two twenties, keeping an additional two bills for herself.

"It seems twenty years of guilt made him so sorry that he sent enough to buy two bowls."

"Maybe he's just planning on his sons doing the same thing and paying you up front for it."

They laughed together as Jake put the money in the old register. He thanked her and she turned to leave, but after she had closed the door, Jake saw her looking back in at the broken bowl on the counter, like she had just dropped off the loyal family dog at the vet to be put down. Jake lifted the bowl and motioned for her to come and get it, but she waved, more to the bowl than to him, and was gone.

He returned to his work, more focused than before as he realized all he had to do. He dropped one of Isaac's CDs into the dusty boom box and resumed cleaning, dancing while he worked.

36
THE DISCOVERY

Shortly before closing time, Amy came in through the front door with a grocery bag in each arm. The Bluegrass Darlings were still playing in the background and Amy looked past Jake into the studio. "Is that the music you were talking about?"

Jake turned his head, nodding. "Isaac has autographed copies of all their albums."

"I like it. I was afraid it would be a bunch of twangy hillbilly stuff."

Jake smiled and shook his head.

"Are you ready to cook some dinner?" Amy asked.

"I sure am. I'm starving. I just have to lock up and grab a few things. Do you want to go on up?"

"Sure," she said, walking past him with the bags. Jake noticed she had changed into jeans and a college sweatshirt and looked more comfortable, but no less pretty than she did in her summer dress. She walked out the back door and up the stairs as Jake locked the front door and removed his apron. He grabbed the tea tin with its precious last bits full of the dried peppermint. On his way up, he pulled additional stems from the pots on the stairs to add to those already hanging above the sink.

As he entered the kitchen, Amy was at the counter, chopping. He set down the tin and washed and hung the new peppermint next to the others. The room was filled with the strong aroma of peppermint and Amy smiled as she watched him work.

"You've got quite a collection here," she said, looking at the drying peppermint. The leaves on the bunches Jake had collected earlier were already wilting.

"How long do they take to dry?"

"Your guess is as good as mine. I just found out yesterday from Father Thomas how this all works. He made it sound really easy, but he also told me that he had tried many times to duplicate the taste of Isaac's recipe and still hasn't figured out his secret ingredient. I brought the last of the tea up to see if we could figure out what it might be by taking a closer look at the dried stuff. It occurred to me that no one has ever had access to the dried tea."

"Sounds like a good idea. I meant to tell you that I spoke to Kai and Molly at the grocery store. They said to say hi. I told them I was coming over for dinner and Kai had a jealous look in his eye when he asked if you were making pancakes."

Jake guffawed. "I've never seen anyone eat as many pancakes as he did. We'll have to have them over sometime so you can get to know them better."

"Molly said that she and Kai were planning on coming over tomorrow night for the band practice. She said Paul had dropped them off some tickets too and hoped we might go together."

"That would be great...that is if it's ok with you."

"Sure."

"I didn't know you knew those guys," said Jake with a puzzled look.

"I just met them on Monday. Aunt Bev asked me to pick up something after work."

"Aren't they a hoot? I really like them. They told me they're hoping to finish a kitchen remodel before the baby comes. They said they might need some help hanging cabinets in the next couple of weeks. Remind me to ask them tomorrow."

"Speaking of reminders, you wanted to look something up in your Bible, didn't you?"

"That's right," said Jake. He went into the bedroom and returned with the old German Bible with the thick leather cover. Amy glanced up from her dicing and, seeing the etchings, stepped away from her work to look over Jake's shoulder.

"That's an Albrecht Dürer!" she said with excitement.

"Yeah, there are a lot of them in here by him." He flipped to Matthew chapter 11 and there, as he had supposed, was the picture of Christ holding the double yoke that they had seen that afternoon in the graveyard on Gabriel Engelhart's bench.

"You were right," she said.

"It's a great picture, but the idea of it is even better. You asked about it earlier today and I didn't tell you what I like about this picture. A yoke is used around the necks of cattle and horses to enable them to pull heavy loads. I really like this picture because the double yoke implies that Jesus is willing to share our yoke."

Amy nodded, looking thoughtful. "How do you know so much about this kind of stuff?"

Jake shook his head. "I really don't know much. The stuff I do know is only because I've asked a lot of questions. If it hadn't been for my mom's cancer, I'm pretty sure I wouldn't know anything about the Bible at all." Jake trailed off, becoming quiet and reflective.

"What are you thinking about?" Amy asked.

"I was just thinking about something Josh Adams told me the other day. From all he said, his life was pretty messed up when he came to Niederbipp. He said something about how sad it is that some of us have to be compelled to be humble before we'll have anything to do with God. It just occurred to me that maybe it was the same way for me. I never needed God until I needed some answers that arose from the reality that my mother could die." He looked at the pots on the table from last night. "I wonder if there could be answers around us all the time that we can't see until we ask."

Jake was thoughtful for a long moment before closing the Bible gently. He turned to Amy. "What are you cooking?"

"It's a surprise."

"Can I help?"

"You can get a big pot of   water boiling."

Jake sprang into action,   motivated by his stomach and his desire to show himself   helpful and capable in the kitchen, even though he   knew he wasn't.

Amy finished chopping   the red onions, peppers and mushrooms and sautéed them   in a copper frying pan. Soon the aroma of peppermint was   being drowned out by the aroma of the vegetables and spices.   She added heavy cream and flour and set it aside to simmer   while she cooked the chicken breasts.

In an effort to be useful,   Jake decided to set up Amy's easel. It took   him the better part of fifteen minutes and all   his concentration, but he accomplished the   task just as the noodles were done. He put   away the pots and set the table as Amy made   a simple salad. She asked him to slice the   baguette and soon they were sitting at the table surrounded by   the food she had made. Jake felt foolish that he had tried to   impress her with peanut butter and honey sandwiches.

He said grace and   they served each other from the different pots and dishes   on the table.

"I thought you said you   didn't cook much."

"I don't, but that doesn't mean I don't like to. I don't know how to follow a recipe. I just throw the stuff together that I like to eat and it usually turns out well. My mom was a good cook and she spent a lot of time teaching me about spices and what sort of things work well together. I thought I was a pretty good cook until I spent a week at Aunt Bev's. There's a lot I'd like to learn from her, but she's usually almost done by the time I finish with work. By the way, she asked me to invite you over for dinner on Sunday evening."

Jake smiled as he took his first bite of pasta and white sauce. It was hot and he breathed carefully through his mouth while moving the food around inside, trying not to burn his tongue. "I've never seen anyone use more than one of the burners on the stove at a time," he said, when he could speak again.

"Your mom didn't cook?"

"Oh, she did, but it was simple fare. She worked a lot and often got home too tired to put on much of a spread. I never remember her getting more than two pans dirty for a meal."

"I guess I never cared too much about using lots of pots because my roommates were always happy to clean up if I cooked."

Jake grimaced, knowing what his job would be once the meal was finished. They ate the delicious food, laughing and talking together as if they had been friends for years.

All too soon, they both were full. Jake knew he needed to get started on the dishes and give Amy space so she would have time to paint. As Jake cleared the dishes, she draped one corner of the table with a yellow cloth and set up the tubes of lipstick in an interesting composition. Jake watched her as he began to wash the dishes. By the time he finished and wiped down the counter and the stove, she had begun to block in the colors on the canvas. He stood behind her for a moment, admiring her ability to record in paint what she saw in front of her. The painting was playful and whimsical thanks to the bold primary colors of the table covering and the lipstick cases.

Not wanting to distract her, he moved on to his project for the evening. Sitting down at the opposite end of the table with the tea tin, he turned the can over on a plate, emptying the dried leaves. With two toothpicks, he began separating the tiny pieces of crushed leaves. Feeling like an archeologist on an important dig, he sorted through the tiny details, looking for clues. The leaf fragments were very small and angled. Some of the pieces were darker than others and he separated these with the toothpicks.

Before long, he was excited to discover a small piece with an unusual shape and color. It was a tiny, gray-blue, flat piece that was nearly round. It looked altogether different from the color and shapes of the rest of the ingredients on the plate. Knowing now what he was looking for, he quickly found five more of the tiny blue things. Volumetrically, the blue circles made up only a tiny fraction compared with the other material, which he knew was peppermint and gooseberry leaves. The darker leaves, he believed, were the gooseberry leaves and he figured these made up no more than five percent of the whole. He had gathered peppermint from less than ten gardens, a far cry from the hundred gardens Isaac's peppermint was rumored to be derived from, but he wondered how different the peppermint really could be in the other gardens.

He separated out the tiny gray round things. Only six had been found in about two spoonfuls. He wondered if something so small could make such a big difference.

"Did you find anything?" asked Amy, peering around the edge of her painting. Jake nodded.

"I'm not sure what it is, but it's definitely something unusual." He licked his index finger and dabbed it on the plate over the six blue circles. When he lifted his finger, they had all stuck to it. He stood and walked to where Amy was sitting. Kneeling down at her side, he raised his finger to her face so she could take a closer look.

"It's definitely organic, but I can't think of what it could be."

"It's too flat to be a seed," he said. "I know some teas have seeds in them, but this can't be a seed."

"What else do people use to make tea?" she asked.

"Obviously leaves, but I think sometimes people use bark of certain plants."

"Ok, but this is definitely not any of those. I've heard of ginger tea, and that's a root. My aunt fixed me some chamomile tea when I was sick. What's in that?"

"I've only seen the boxes at the store, but I think chamomile tea is made out of flowers."

Amy looked up with a smile. "Where's your sketchbook?" she asked. Jake looked at her oddly but brought her the book. She turned to the page where, just the day before, she had pressed the tiny flowers they had found on Lily's grave. She pulled it from the center of the book and lifted its flat and wilted structure.

"Didn't those blue circles look a lot like these?" she said, delicately plucking one of the petals from the flower and holding it lightly in her palm.

Jake smiled. "Congratulations. You just found the secret ingredient!"

Amy beamed.

"What do you think this flower is called?" he asked.

She shrugged. "I told you yesterday that I had never seen one before, at least that I can remember. Of course, they're so small, they'd be easy to miss."

"Tomorrow, before we go up to the cemetery, I want to introduce you to some friends of mine, Gloria and Joseph, the folks who run the flower shop. If anyone knows, it would be them. And if they don't, I know she has a bunch of field books that would have a picture of it."

Amy set the rest of the small bunch back in the center of the sketchbook and closed it before handing it to Jake.

"How's the painting coming?" he asked as he moved closer to her so he could see.

"It's coming."

Jake was amazed. She had taken creative license in adding many other colors that were not in the model, making it look far more interesting. The painting was small, but cheerful, the paint thick and shiny. He complimented her and she flashed a proud grin. "I had a feeling it would turn out well," she said, "but it's even more exciting than I imagined."

"I agree. When you told me about it at lunch I imagined it being kind of boring but this is really exciting."

She looked at the clock. "Do you mind if I paint another one?"

"No, not at all."

"I thought it would be fun to try another composition."

"Sure. I'm glad you've found your groove."

Jake put the tea stuff away while Amy moved her painting and replaced it with a fresh canvas board. He went to the bedroom and returned with a book he had discovered the night before. It was a small leather-bound book whose edges were worn. Jake flipped through the pages full of poetry and quotes, stopping at a dogeared page. He read the same John Keats quote that Amy had read the night before and continued to read aloud to Amy as she painted.

By the time she finished her third painting, Jake was nearly asleep. It was well after midnight as they left the apartment to walk Amy home, leaving the paintings and easel in the kitchen.

He hugged her when they reached her front steps and she hugged him back. They both were tired and he let her go without pursuing further discussion. She had gone inside and Jake was at the bottom of the stairs when she appeared again.

"Where are we meeting for lunch?" she whispered. Jake turned back to her.

"I think the flower shop might close at noon for lunch. I'll try to get there before then and you can meet me there as soon as you can."

3.7 THE SECRET

Jake felt unmotivated and hungry the next morning as he milled about the studio. In his idleness, his thoughts returned to the kiln and the disaster he knew he would face when he was finally able to open it. The pyrometer had not been working since the firing, so he held a piece of paper to the peep hole and it immediately began to smolder, indicating the kiln was still over 450° F. He wished someone would drop by with a pastry or a story to share and distract him from his thoughts.

Jake hadn't planned on throwing on the wheel today, but with no outside distractions coming in, he knew he had to create his own or go mad worrying about the kiln. He cut and wedged the clay into three pound balls. Before he sat down at the wheel, he turned on the music as he had so many times before and got to work throwing bowls. The morning was mostly quiet and he only got up once to help a customer. She had seen one of his new vases in the window and had to have it. When she came in and started looking around, however, she took a liking to two of them. Unable to decide, she bought them both when Jake suggested she could give the other one as a gift.

Before noon, Jake had thrown two dozen bowls and filled all the available space. He washed his hands and hung up his apron before hurrying to his apartment to make the sandwiches. He put them in his backpack and carried his sketchbook to Gloria and Joseph's flower shop.

Gloria was at the counter finishing up with a customer when he arrived. She winked when she saw him. He turned his back on the two women to let them finish their business while he examined the flowers in the front window.

Finally, the woman at the counter took her arrangement and Gloria walked her to the door. Turning to Jake, she smiled warmly.

"Hello, young potter."

"Hello," he said, flashing a grin.

"I've thought a lot about you since I saw you last. I'm really glad to see you. I was afraid I was too tough on you with my straight talk."

"No," said Jake, shaking his head. "I should be thanking you. It has made me think a lot of things. Thank you."

The door opened and they turned to see Amy coming in. "Excuse me a minute," she told Jake as she turned her attention to Amy. "How can I help you, Miss?" she asked with a warm smile.

"She's with me," said Jake before Amy could answer. Gloria looked back at Jake and then again at Amy.

"You must be Amy, Jerry and Beverly's niece."

Amy smiled and nodded, surprised.

"I was wondering if you would be bringing her to meet me," she said, turning to Jake.

Jake blushed immediately. Amy just smiled, extending her hand to Gloria.

"It's nice to meet you," she said.

Gloria pulled Amy closer to Jake and looked at the two of them. "What a handsome pair you make," she said. "Rumor has it the two of you have been spending a lot of time together." Jake went from red to scarlet while Amy let out a nervous laugh.

"Now," said Gloria, ignoring both the laugh and the blush, "tell me what I can do for the two of you." Jake was speechless so Amy took the sketchbook from him and opened it to the dried bunch of tiny blue flowers.

Amy looked at Jake, but seeing he was not yet ready to speak, turned to Gloria and asked, "Do you know what flower this is?"

Gloria took the tiny bunch in the palm of her hand. She looked at Jake and took a deep breath, tears beginning to well up in her eyes. "Where did you find these?" she asked softly.

"We found them on Lily's grave," said Amy.

Gloria nodded and locked the front door, walking towards the counter. She took a deep breath before looking up to see that Jake and Amy were looking at her intently. She looked back at the small, flattened flowers and handed them back to Amy before she spoke.

"What would you like to know?"

"I don't know anything about flowers and neither of us had ever seen this flower before. We don't even know what it's called," said Jake.

Joseph came through the swinging door, dressed in his apron and smiling broadly at Jake. "Well, who's this?"

Jake knew he needed to talk fast to avoid any more of Gloria's hullabaloo. "This is my friend Amy," he said, as Amy extended her hand to him.

A smile spread through his graying beard. "Are you two joining us for lunch?" he asked.

"No," said Jake. "We were just on our way to a picnic and stopped in to get some information about a flower."

Joseph looked down at the flower in Amy's hand and nodded without uttering a word.

Gloria pulled the field book out from underneath the counter and opened it to a dogeared page near the beginning of the book, turning it so they could see. There on the page was the same flower Amy had in her palm. The caption read Myosois alpenstris, Forget-me-not.

They looked up and found Gloria smiling as tears flowed down her cheek.

Jake smiled at her warmly. "What do you know about this flower?"

Gloria dried her eyes. "We've spent the last twenty years trying to learn everything we can about this flower.

"There is an old legend that comes from the childhood of Christ. As the legend goes, He was walking one day with His mother when He bent over, picked a bunch of these and gave them to her. He told her that there would come a time when his body would be laid in a tomb, but then He took the tiny flower and lifted it closely to her eyes. The blue, he told her represents the heavens and the yellow represents the sun. He told her although he would not be able to be with her always, as long as the sun rose in the heavens, he would love her and be near her.

"There is another legend that is much newer," Gloria continued. "Somewhere during the middle ages, a knight was preparing to leave for battle and took a short walk along a stream with his sweetheart. They sat for a while and spoke of their uncertain future, not knowing when or even if he would return. As they said their goodbyes, he reached to the ground and plucked a tiny flower, giving it to her with the promise that as long as the flower remained alive, so would his love for her. He left for the war and the flower remained alive. After many years, the war ended and all the knights returned home. The woman waited for her love, but he never came. Finally, she learned he had been killed several years before. She went away heartbroken, but returned to see that her flower was brighter than ever. Though many others sought her hand in marriage, she would not accept, knowing that her true love still loved her."

"It sounds like Isaac's love for Lily."

Gloria pursed her lips and nodded. "This was an important flower to Isaac. Twenty years ago, it became an important flower for Joseph and me. Amy, I'll let Jake fill you in on the details, but I was never able to deliver a healthy baby even though I was pregnant four times. I became very depressed and spent a lot of time by myself, refusing to be comforted. I'm ashamed to admit that I lost three years of my life by locking myself away from the world. If it hadn't have been for this flower, I might still be in that dark place."

She paused and tried to smile through her tears. "And then one spring day, I looked out my window and saw a tiny flower growing from the crack of the old stone windowsill. A seed must have blown in on the wind and landed there. I was amazed that there was enough dirt and nourishment to offer it a chance at life. It's silly that after three years of pain, such a small flower could mean so much to me, but it did. I felt like the heavens were reaching out to me, giving me hope where I had none. It wasn't more than a few days later that Joseph asked me to pick that pie plate for his mother and I got to know Isaac.

"Jake, those clay hearts I made were just the beginning of my healing. Isaac taught me the joy that comes from sharing my life with others. When I had filled several jars with the clay hearts, Isaac encouraged me to seek out other opportunities to help people. He told me that the school was always looking for people to help tutor kids, so I began spending time at the school several days a week, helping kids learn to read. I knew I couldn't be a mother, but I was amazed at the joy I felt when I became a child's friend.

"After a year of tutoring at the school, Joseph asked me if I was ready to come back to work at the shop. I hadn't realized how much I had missed working with flowers until I got back into it. I've never met anyone who didn't light up when they saw a bright bouquet of flowers, and I began filling up my memory with the smiles of my customers. I still spend a couple of hours every morning at the school, helping kids learn to read."

"We can't go anywhere without running into young people who know and love Gloria," interjected Joseph. "We'll always be sad we never had children of our own, but the love we feel from generations of children has sustained us through our sorrows."

Gloria smiled. "So far, we've done the flowers for over forty weddings of school kids I learned to love as my own.

"I have one last story to tell you about this flower. We invited Isaac to our apartment for dinner one evening, shortly after I began volunteering at the school. When he arrived, he brought with him one of his homemade planters filled with the little flowers. Shocked, I asked if he knew what they were. He explained that soon after his wife died, these flowers began growing wild over her grave. Those flowers gave him all the hope he needed to believe their love would last forever. I still have the pot on my windowsill, in the very place I found the one that had given me hope. Every spring, they bloom again and my hope is renewed. Since the day I saw the flower growing on my windowsill, I can't look at a flower without feeling the love of God. And when I see flowers going out my door, being delivered to those in pain, in love, or in sorrow, I pray that those who receive them will feel that love too."

Gloria smiled and dried her eyes. She grabbed one of Amy's and one of Jake's hands and squeezed them firmly. "Thank you for helping us remember the tender mercies of God."

Joseph nodded. "Are you sure you don't want to join us for lunch?"

"Can we take a raincheck on that offer?" asked Jake. "I made Amy a picnic lunch and we both have to get back to work pretty quick. The Bluegrass Darlings are coming over tonight to practice."

"That's right. The concert's tomorrow night," said Gloria.

"Are you guys going?" asked Amy.

"Of course," responded Joseph, enthusiastically. "Gloria's known those boys since they were in grade school. Paul dropped some tickets by yesterday. We never miss that concert. It's not exactly Woodstock, but it's a close second."

"Are you ready for lunch?" asked Gloria, poking Joseph in the stomach with her finger.

Joseph smiled and embraced her.

Jake and Amy watched the graying couple act as if they were high school sweethearts.

"It was nice to meet you both," said Amy.

"It's nice to see who Jake's been hanging out with," said Gloria with a teasing smile. "If you two don't mind hanging out with a couple of middle-aged hippies, we'd love to have you over for dinner sometime."

"I'd like that," said Amy, before Jake had a chance to think.

Gloria walked to the door and unlocked it to let them out.

"Thanks for coming," she said. "I hope you found what you were looking for."

Amy walked out first and Jake followed, only to be grabbed by Gloria who was holding the door open. She had him by the arm and pulled him back in to whisper under her breath.

"She's beautiful," she said with a broad smile. "I am very happy for you." Jake blushed again, but smiled. He wondered what she had heard about them; if she knew something that he didn't.

Amy was waiting for him a few steps into the plaza. "They seem really nice," she said, as he caught up to her.

Jake nodded.

They walked toward the stairs that led from the plaza to the courtyard, their minds full of the things they had just heard.

"What did you think about all of that?" he asked as they climbed the stairs.

"It's more than I ever imagined it would be—such a simple little flower that has so much meaning."

"Yeah, who would have thought? I guess we know now why it's part of Isaac's tea. It seems the hope he found in the flower was the perfect symbol of his love for his wife. And knowing the deep faith he had, it seems the flower was a sort of tie that brought everything he cared about together."

Amy pulled him over to sit on a bench in the quiet courtyard. "Go on," she said.

"I'm just thinking out loud, but all of the people who have come to visit me so far talk about the tea Isaac shared with them. I don't know, but it seems like there is some kind of magic in his tea. It gets people talking, sharing, and loving. Somehow, it seems to open up hearts and minds. I've heard how it heals sorrows and pain and suffering. When it was just peppermint tea, it was good, but now that we know what's in it, what's really in it, the meaning behind it all, it seems even more…I don't know, miraculous, if that doesn't sound too cheesy."

"It sounds like we need to keep the tradition of the tea alive," she said.

Jake didn't miss the subtlety of her being included in the deal.

"Tell me about Gloria's children," she said. "It's hard to believe that such a beautiful, wonderful woman could have so much pain in her heart."

Jake briefly recounted the story Gloria had told him in his shop a week earlier. "I don't doubt that she still feels that pain, but it seems to me that most of it has been replaced by hope and love and joy. There is a beauty about her that seems to fill her whole body."

"I know what you mean. It just sort of oozes out of her, almost like a magnetic aura that brings you in and fills your lungs with whatever it is she has."

Jake just nodded, not knowing any words that could better describe her.

They sat in silence for a moment, thoughtfully enjoying the peace of the afternoon as they ate. "I told you on Sunday that I'm jealous that you get to make art all day long, but maybe that's just a small part of the reason I'm jealous."

Jake looked at her.

"You get to hear all these stories. You get to know people in a way no one else can. I've been working here nearly as long as you have and no one has come to my makeup counter and shared anything even remotely as interesting as the stuff you get to hear every day."

Jake didn't know how to respond, so he didn't.

The silence continued until Amy was done with her sandwich. "Will you tell me the rest of the stories about the people you've met?"

Jake nodded. "There are some good ones. Where do you want me to start?" he asked, just as the bell rang, chiming the end of Amy's lunch break and sending them scampering down the stairs.

"I want to know the secrets of this place," she said as she turned to say goodbye.

Jake nodded and smiled. He watched her go and stayed, staring, long after she was gone.

(38) DISCOVERING LILY

That afternoon, while cleaning up the studio and trimming the bowls he had made that morning, Jake reflected on the things he had learned in Gloria's shop. He wondered if Isaac had known the legends she shared with them about the forget-me-not, and decided he probably did. He also considered the many possible reasons for Isaac to include the flower in his famous tea.

As the work day came to an end, he realized how his thoughts had inspired him and his work. He had learned to respect Isaac ever since he first discovered his work in the showroom, but this new understanding increased that respect exponentially. Isaac's thoughtful nature seemed to be an essential part of everything he did. These inspired thoughts gave Jake's work a gravity he had not felt before.

By the time Amy arrived, the studio was nearly ready for the band. The bowls were set to dry on the shelves near the kiln and things were moved away from the back door, opening up a decent amount of space on the floor.

Jake was just putting away the logbook when Amy walked in through the back door.

"Wow, you clean up good."

Jake turned and smiled.

She looked at the cluttered shelf and pulled a small gold frame from the mess. "Who's this?" she asked. "Should I be jealous?"

Jake turned and looked over her shoulder and then moved next to her so their shoulders touched. "That's Lily," he said softly, "Isaac's wife."

"She's beautiful," Amy said, rubbing the dust off the glass with her fingertips.

"Yeah, kind of gives you an idea why he was never able to forget her."

Amy nodded thoughtfully. "I've been thinking about that since lunch."

Jake raised his eyebrows, urging her to continue.

"Putting forget-me-nots in the tea was a very conscious and deliberate thing for Isaac to do, almost like the memory of her sweetened his life with every cup he drank, or shared with his friends."

"Do you know anyone who has that kind of love for their husband or wife? My parents certainly didn't have anything remotely close to it."

Amy shook her head. "Neither do mine. Do you think it's possible to have that kind of love if both people are alive? I mean, so often people get sick of each other and grow apart. Maybe it's only possible to have true love when your spouse is dead."

Jake looked pensive.

"It seems like marriage is a lot more difficult than most people expect. 'Happily ever after' lasts about as long as the honeymoon, and then reality settles in. Lily died when they were still in their honeymoon phase and Isaac probably only remembered her and their relationship in the most positive light because that's all he knew.

"I don't know. I want to believe his love for Lily was as real and lasting as it seems to be. I have a hard time imagining him enduring the loneliness he must have felt if he didn't have any hope. I can't imagine him going through the effort of putting forget-me-nots in his tea and spending time every single day near her grave, if he didn't believe in his core that their love was real and somehow eternal."

Jake looked up at the clock before taking Amy's hand and leading her out the front door. "It seems like what we found out today about the forget-me-nots was more than just a clue about the secret ingredient in his tea. It was a clue about his life, what made him tick."

Amy squeezed Jake's hand and he looked at her. "The only things I know about Isaac are the things you've told me, but seeing that picture of his wife makes me want to discover who he was."

"Can we sit over there on the bench?" Amy asked, as they rounded the corner of Hauptstrasse. She didn't wait for a reply, leading Jake to the vacant bench carved into the side of the fountain. "I remember walking down this street one evening with my parents when I was just a kid and seeing the benches occupied with teenagers and twenty-somethings, paired off. It was so romantic."

They sat in silence for a minute, watching the fancy-dressed people waiting in line to be seated at Robintino's.

"What are you thinking about?" she asked.

"I was just wondering what it would be like to get dressed up and go to that fancy restaurant."

Amy watched a couple, not much older than themselves, dressed in expensive, stylish summer clothes, waiting in line.

"Pretentious," she said after a moment.

Jake looked at her, surprised.

"What?" She asked when she saw his questioning eyes.

"I just assumed girls liked that kind of stuff."

"There was a time that I did. I was always happy for a free meal and I'd even dress up, but I learned quickly that when a guy takes you to a place like that, he wants something from you. I don't know if I've ever met a guy who didn't consider a dinner at a fancy restaurant an investment, a way to woo and impress with the hopes he would get something in return."

Jake squirmed a bit, but nodded his head, grateful his scooter had run out of gas on Monday. After her comment, he wondered if he would be sitting here now if he had made it back in time to ask her to dinner as he had planned.

Amy slid closer to Jake and smiled. "Jake, this last week has been awesome for me. It's really nice to be with a guy who isn't trying to figure out what I'm thinking in hopes of positioning himself for his next move. You seem too honest for that, too sincere to play games."

Jake smiled and shook his head. "I just don't know how to play. I feel like an imbecile around you. I don't know how I'm supposed to act. It's not that I haven't thought about trying to impress you, I'm just too dumb to know how."

She smiled broadly.

"I feel like a poor, grubby potter hanging out with a beautiful, talented, amazing girl who has to be blind not to see how inept I am."

She smiled again and put her hand softly on Jake's forearm. "That's just what I'm trying to say. You're not pretentious; you don't try to be

someone you're not. You'd
those guys over there
want to hang out with
Jake furrowed his
"Jake, I can't tell you
with you, to know what
you, not some chameleon
wind and the weather or
dinner sitting on this
anyone else in the world
Jake was speechless
"It's really nice to
smile.
"I don't know where
been hanging out for a
good enough friends
"Games?"
"I'm just saying
each other. If you'd
with someone else,

look stupid dressed up like
and I don't know if I'd
you if you did."
brow, confused.
how refreshing it is to be
I'm looking at is the real
who changes with the
whoever he's with at the time. I'd rather eat
bench with you than anywhere else or with
because I know you're real."
for several seconds.
hear what you think," he said with a huge

this friendship is going to lead... we've only
week, but it seems to me that we're already
that we can avoid playing games," she said.

that I hope we can always be honest with
rather not see me, or would rather hang out
I hope you'll tell me."

Jake raised his eyebrows. "And if you finally open your eyes and realize what kind of a dud you have for a friend, I hope you'll just tell me straight up that you've come to your senses and are moving on."

She laughed, slid her arm through his, and leaned her head on his shoulder, smiling.

"I think you should know that I really like it when you grab my arm or hold my hand...that is, if we're being honest with each other." Amy responded by squeezing Jake's arm and moving a tiny bit closer.

The smell of the kabobs reminded Jake of his empty stomach. He and Amy strolled to the café, still arm in arm, and bought a couple of kabobs before returning to the bench to eat. They laughed and talked together for an hour as they enjoyed the evening, watching people coming and going and waiting to be seated at the restaurant.

"I love being with you," she said smiling up at him, "but..."

"But what?"

"But I think we better get back to the studio to meet the band."

Jake was both relieved and disappointed. He had never been this honest with a girl before, and to use Amy's word, it was "refreshing." As they stood to leave, Jake felt like he stood a little taller, his self-confidence elevated well beyond any previous level.

They walked back toward the studio quickly, hand in hand.

No sooner had they entered the studio than there was a knock at the back door and Jake rushed to open it for the four musicians with their instruments in tow.

PRACTICE

"Hello!" Jake beamed, standing aside so the musicians could enter. Once they had all filed in, accompanied by a pretty girl, Paul introduced each of the guys to Jake and Amy. Adam introduced his fiancée, Pam. Jake, in turn, introduced Amy. Kai and Molly showed up a few minutes later and the studio was abuzz with greetings and hugs as the old friends caught up with each other. Jake smiled when he saw John put his hand on Molly's growing belly, congratulating her and Kai.

Soon, the band was tuning up their instruments and getting ready to play.

Paul cleared his throat when the tuning was complete. "Jake, we really appreciate you letting us come and practice here. We have many years worth of memories from this old shop."

The others nodded their heads.

"We're planning on dedicating the concert to Isaac tomorrow night and we'll open with two of his favorite songs. The first one is 'Mud On My Pants,' an instrumental inspired by something that happened one night when we came to practice."

Jake knew the song, but had never fathomed it was inspired by the band's time in a pottery shop. Though he had liked the song before, he knew it would have a deeper meaning from now on.

"The second song is one we wish we had written. Jim, you found this one, didn't you?"

Jim looked up from his bass and nodded.

"It's called *'Potter's Wheel,'* written by Bill Danoff and recorded by John Denver. The rest of the concert will be a mix of songs from our new album and a bunch of the old ones. We won't practice most of the old songs tonight since we know them by heart."

And then without any additional explanation, Paul lifted his violin to his chin and his bow to the strings and lit out on a lighthearted melody. By the time the others chimed in, the small studio was rocking and everyone was smiling. There was no room for dancing, but that didn't stop them all from tapping their feet and wiggling their bodies as much as they could without knocking stuff over. When the first song ended, the non-musicians clapped and hooted.

Jake looked at Amy to see what she thought and she winked at him.

The second song was new to everyone except the musicians. They had obviously played the music before but had never recorded it. Jake listened closely to the lyrics as Paul and Adam sang. The tune was catchy and the lyrics meaningful, but it was the last verse that most interested Jake:

Earth and water and wind conspire,
With human hands and love and fire.
Take a little clay, Put it on a wheel,
Get a little hint how God must feel.
Give a little turn, Listen to it spin,
Make it in the shape you want it in. [7]

Jake looked up at Amy, who was watching him. She raised her eyebrows but said nothing. The music was fun and lively, but it caused Jake to think about what he had learned about Isaac and his work with both clay and people.

Laughter, clapping, and exciting music filled the evening. Kai joined in several of the songs with his harmonica. Time passed quickly and, before they knew it, they were yawning through their smiles. Though they were tired, no one wanted to leave. It was an evening of memories and

healing for those who had spent so much time in this place. For Jake and Amy, it was an evening of insight and understanding as well as a night to make new memories.

Finally, the music ended when John broke a string on his mandolin. Before leaving, each of the band members took turns shaking Jake's hand and thanking him for allowing them all to come.

Paul handed Jake one of their new CDs, signed by the whole band. "This is to add to the old dusty collection," he said. "I don't think any of us realized how much we lost when Isaac died. It meant a lot to be able to play here again."

Amy walked Kai and Molly to the front door while the band loaded their instruments into their cars behind the shop. Paul took his time putting away his fiddle as Amy helped Jake move the tables back into place and put away the chairs.

"I want to thank you for your music," Jake said as he turned to Paul. "When I discovered your music in college, I felt like I discovered the soundtrack for my life. For several weeks, it was the only thing I listened to. It made me dance."

"Hearing stuff like that makes it all worth it. It's been a lot of work getting to this point."

"Did you always want to be a musician?" asked Amy.

"Yes, but I didn't start out playing bluegrass. I was trained in the classics and my parents hoped that someday I would tour the world as a guest musician for the finest symphonies. I began performing regionally when I was nine and had my first international performances when I was eleven. When I was in town, I was often invited to play at church. That's where I first saw Isaac, sitting on the back row in his overalls."

Amy looked up at Jake before turning back to Paul. "This shop is a little different than the symphony. Why did you decide to make the change?"

"Because this is the music I heard in my heart. That... and I was fifteen years old and rather impetuous. I thank God every day that I was and that Isaac was around to believe in me, even when my parents tried to send me to the conservatory to keep me from ruining my life."

"So how did it end up working out? You guys have been playing together for what, ten years?" asked Jake.

"It'll be eleven in October. Do you know the song, 'Fight for the Dream'?"

"Sure, that's one of my favorites."

"That was the second song we ever performed together. We performed it as the encore when we won the Kinzua County Talent Show ten years ago. We were only fifteen. I don't know if you've ever listened to the lyrics closely, but that song is my story. Maybe it's every kid's story who has to go against his parents' will to fight for his own dream."

Jake turned to Amy and began reciting the lyrics to her. He didn't get very far before Paul joined in.

There is more to a boy than what his mother sees.
There is more to a boy than what his father dreams.
Inside every boy lies a heart that beats
And sometimes it screams, refusing to take defeat.
And sometimes his father's dreams aren't big enough
And sometimes his mother's vision isn't long enough
And sometimes the boy has to dream his own dreams
And break through the clouds with his own sun beams

And you want to be loved and you want to be true
And you want to do what you know you should do
But the truest truth comes from your own heart,
So listen my friend, or it will tear you apart.

Because a boy is more than what his mother sees
And a boy is more than what his father dreams
Inside every boy lies a heart that beats
And if you let him fight, he'll laugh at defeat,

For dreams are for lovers and dreamers and boys
Who'll fight for their share of good times and joys.
For surely a boy must dream his own dreams,
And fight his own fights and beam his own beams.

And you want to be loved and you want to be true
And you want to do what you know you should do
But the truest truth comes from your own heart,
So listen my friend, or it will tear you apart.
So listen my friend, or it will tear you apart.

"That song started a civil war at my house. I actually performed in two acts at that talent show—a solo where I played something from Vivaldi and then the instrumental piece we played with the band.

My parents made me perform the solo that night when they found out the grand prize was a recording session at a new music studio in Warren called Allegheny Records. When I lost, but the band won, they were furious and locked up my violin. That night they began making plans to send me to the conservatory.

"I had led a pretty sheltered life as far as music goes. I didn't even know about bluegrass until I was about fourteen. While I was away at a Mozart festival in Austin, Texas, I followed my ears to a practice room where four old guys were playing this crazy music that made me want to dance. They invited me to play with them and I was hooked.

"When I came home with the music still playing in my ears, I knew I had to do something. One evening, on my way home from my violin lesson, I saw Isaac walking up the hill carrying a violin case. I didn't know him well, but hoped if he played the violin, he might know something about bluegrass, so I followed him.

"I was very surprised when I saw him enter the cemetery and sit down on a bench. He sat his case next to him and opened it. I expected him to pull out a violin and play, but instead, he pulled out a napkin, a sandwich, and a book and began eating as he read. I stayed to watch him, wondering what else he might have in the case.

"He looked up and invited me to join him, offering me some of his sandwich. I asked if he played the violin and he laughed, telling me God had given him an ear for good music, but none of the talent, except for the harmonica which he stored in the violin case.

"When he told me I should be proud of myself for the talent I had developed I admitted I had become bored playing the music my parents wanted me to play. He asked me what I would choose if the choice was entirely up to me. I was reluctant to say, fearing that I might jinx myself and be stuck doing what I was doing for the rest of my life.

"He told me that in order for my dream to become a reality, I needed to shout it from the rooftops and then move boldly toward that dream with all the passion I could muster. His words got me really excited and I confessed that I wanted to play bluegrass music.

"To my surprise, he told me he grew up believing bluegrass was the only music there was. His father played in a band with some of the men at his church and his mom took him to all the practices from the time he was a baby.

"He encouraged my dream, telling me that too many lives are wasted, with people wondering what might have been if they had taken a chance and followed their hearts. He told me if I followed my passion, I would always be happy, even if I never found the security I might find by doing what was safe.

"He told me if I kept my mind and ears open, I would find the friends I needed. Over the next few weeks, I came here often to borrow bluegrass tapes. Before long, I was beginning to compose my own music, but still didn't have anyone to play with. When school started again in the fall, I met Jim Davis, our bass player. I brought him over to the Pottery to let him listen to Isaac's collection of bluegrass music. John and Adam joined us later that year. Adam was in the jazz band at school, but was tired of never getting a chance to play guitar the way he wanted to play. He brought in John whose father taught him to play the mandolin when he was just a kid.

We began playing together during lunch just a few weeks before the end of eighth grade.

"I hoped the boys would keep playing while I was away on my summer music tours, but I was surprised when I returned home to find they spent several hours every day working on the new songs I wrote and were ready for me to jump in and play. It was at that point that we began practicing here in the Pottery.

"By the end of the summer, we were sounding really good together. That's when the boys decided we ought to enter the county talent show that fall.

"I'll always remember the bolt of electricity that ran up my spine when John started us off with a mandolin solo he had been practicing for months. People got off their chairs and started dancing and clapping so loud, the energy of the crowd almost drowned us out. As each of us joined in, the crowd got even louder and more excited, whistling and clapping long after the curtain fell."

"What did your parents say?" asked Jake, breaking his silence.

"They told me I was born to play in Symphony Hall, not Hee Haw."

Jake and Amy looked at each other and laughed.

"So what did you do?" asked Amy

"Well, after reminding me that they had spent all of their free time in the last ten years helping me develop my talent to become a world performer, they told me they weren't going to allow me to ruin my life. When they threatened me with the conservatory, I decided I didn't need parents anymore. I ran away the next afternoon."

"That's crazy," said Jake. "I can't imagine how happy my mom would have been if I had half the musical talent you have."

Paul nodded. "It took me a couple years to understand that my parents believed the only way I could ever become a world renowned musician was to stick within the parameters they had set."

"So, how were you able to change their minds?" asked Amy.

"It didn't happen overnight. We all had to change. I planned on running away to Nashville, but only got as far as the river when I got hungry. I set up camp under a big willow tree and began imagining my parents finding my dried bones lying on the banks of the river."

They all laughed together.

"I imagined my father holding my mother as she cried out loud that she wished they would have listened to me. I realized it was actually pretty good fodder for a bluegrass song. I pulled out a notepad and wrote the words to 'Down by the River,' while the crickets kept time. By the time I finished, I knew I didn't want to die; I wanted to live to sing that song and a zillion others."

"So did you go back that night?" asked Jake, enthralled by the story of teenage drama.

"Yes, but not right away. To make a long story short, I was just finishing up that song when I heard someone approaching. I looked up river and saw Isaac walking along the bank. He sat down on the gravel next to me and told me he was inspired by my passion, adding that I could become whatever I wanted to be if I could channel my energy in a positive direction. He told me he didn't know how I was going to do it, but suggested I use some of my fervor to win my parents over to my cause.

"Before he left, he told me the guys planned to practice at his studio at 9:00 and that I was welcome to join them if I got tired of camping out. I already knew what I wanted to do, but I also knew Isaac was right. My parents were being morons, but I knew they loved me and wanted the best for me. I needed a way to make all of us happy.

"Before I went home that night, I stopped by the shop to check on the guys. I listened to them play from the open doorway and was excited about how good they sounded. As I listened, I knew this was what I wanted to do with my life.

"Isaac came out of his apartment carrying an ancient fiddle and bow. He told me it hadn't been played in more than forty years, but that it once made the sweetest sound he had ever heard. He told me it had been played by all the potters over the last two hundred years until it came to him, whose attempts at making music made the village cats scream.

"He handed me the fiddle and told me he had been waiting forty years to hear it sing again. I looked into his eyes and thought I saw tears as he told me that his father-in-law used to play it for him and his wife to dance to.

"That night I learned that all of the guys had been dealing with some level of the same crap my parents had given me, so we decided to make Fight for the Dream the title of our first album.

"I went home that night and stood my ground as my parents listened to me unfold my dreams. They saw the passion I had for the music and we agreed on a compromise. I could continue to play with the band if I kept my grades up and consented to tour one more summer. I reluctantly agreed. The CD came out a week later and sold out in three days. Allegheny Records signed us to a three album contract over the next three years and we were up and running. My parents withdrew their demands the next summer when our agent had us booked solid for one month of tours on the State Fair circuit.

"To use a trite phrase, the rest is history. When we came home at the end of the summer, we were stars. Our agent tried to rent us a nice studio where we could practice, but we felt so welcome here at the Pottery, that we decided to stay as long as we could. Many of our early songs were either written here in the studio or inspired by Isaac and our time here. You might know 'Old Man' or 'The Refining Fire' for example?"

"Of course! You mean to tell me those were written right here?" asked Jake, looking surprised.

"That's right," said Paul. "Isaac actually performed on a couple of albums with us, playing back up harmonica, but he never let us give him credit. He said he couldn't handle the fame."

Amy shook her head. "Paul, I love your story but it sounds too easy."

Paul nodded. "You're right, Amy. This business is definitely not for the weak hearted. It's been a crazy ten years. We've worked our tails off and we still are, but it's often easy to forget the struggles when you're having so much fun. Most times, it doesn't even seem like work. There is something amazing about doing what you love to do that makes you forget your troubles."

Amy furrowed her brow and nodded slowly.

"I better get going," said Paul. "Thanks again for hosting us tonight."

"I hope you'll always feel welcome," responded Jake. "When's your next visit?"

Paul shook his head. "Nothing is definite yet, but we always start out the touring season by playing here for the folks who gave us our start. If you don't mind hosting us again, we'll take you up on your offer. All of our parents are still here so we'll be home for the holidays. Maybe we could visit again then."

"Absolutely! Like I said, you're always welcome."

Paul nodded his thanks. "We'll see you guys tomorrow night. Don't be late. Your seats are right up front and we hate it when it looks like the best seats didn't sell."

"Don't worry," said Amy, "we'll be there."

Jake smiled at her. "Thanks again for the tickets," he added.

"It's my pleasure," said Paul as he picked up his violin case.

They all walked out together and said goodbye as Paul got into his car.

Amy reached for Jake's hand as they walked.

"Tell me about John and Molly," she said. "I caught on that they used to date, but what's their story?"

Jake pulled Amy to the bench where they had been meeting for lunch and sat down. "Do you know why Kai knows how to play the harmonica?" he began. He then proceeded to lay out the events of the past several years as he remembered the details. Because part of the Mayor's tale overlapped with Kai's story, Jake told her about Isaac's response to the Mayor, the part about us all being beggars.

Jake told her next about Gloria and Joseph and the thousands of hearts she had made as she watched Isaac work. They laughed together as Jake told Amy about the Mancinis and the thirty-nine year old great-grandma, and Thomas' trip down the river.

By the time he finished, the lights at Mancini's Ice Café were dark and the streets were completely deserted.

"There's still so much to tell you, but I'm really tired."

Amy smiled, but her eyelids were heavy. "Let's do this again, tomorrow," she said weakly.

Jake held her hand and walked her all the way to the door before he stopped.

"Thanks for lunch and dinner and a really fun evening," she said. "I was with you longer today than I was at work."

"Is that good?" asked Jake.

"It's really good," she said groggily, putting her arms around his neck and giving him a hug. He held her for a long time, until he wondered if she might be asleep.

"Are you awake?" he asked.

"Just barely. I better get to bed before I fall asleep in your arms." Jake couldn't think of anything as wonderful as that, but he nodded and let her go.

Jake said he planned to spend some time the next afternoon at the cemetery looking at the last two benches. Amy agreed to meet him there as soon as she could.

He walked back to his own apartment, taking the middle of the deserted street, thinking about Amy. It was the first day she hadn't punched him. Or was it the second? Their week together had been full and amazing and all the days were beginning to fade together in a blur.

40
ISAAC'S STAMP

Jake was dusting the shelves the next morning when the first customer came in. She was a tall, well dressed woman in her mid fifties. She was looking for a wedding gift for her friend's daughter and had heard the pottery shop was open again. After struggling to make a decision, she finally settled on one of Jake's bowls for the bride and one of Isaac's colanders for herself. Jake struggled with the gift wrap again. It was far better than his last effort, but he wondered if Amy might be able to give him a gift wrap tutorial so he could do a better job and not feel so stupid. The woman was pleased with his efforts and promised to be back soon.

The day was busy with customers stopping in to see the new wares. Hildegard, who had teased Jake about his shoes the previous Sunday, stopped in around noon with a basket hanging on her arm. Jake was busy helping another customer when she entered. He looked up and greeted her with a smile, which she returned genially and moved to the counter, pulling a small package from her basket. Jake wrapped the other customer's purchase before turning his full attention to Hildegard.

"Hello, I was wondering when I might see you again."

She smiled and pushed the small package towards him.

Jake unwrapped the newspaper to reveal a small broken bowl. He looked up into her kind eyes. "What happened?" he asked cheerfully.

"My naughty kitty happened," she said, with a devious smile. "This was her bowl. I found she had broken it this morning."

"Does she do that a lot?"

"About once a month, but it gave me a chance to visit with Isaac regularly and now it's given me a chance to visit you. I've wanted to drop by sooner, but I'm afraid I didn't trust myself to keep my emotions under control. It seems our generation is all dead or dying now and I'm afraid I miss Isaac more than most of those who have left me."

The door opened again and a middle-aged couple wandered in. Hildegard looked disappointed. "Do you have any bowls about this size?" she asked. Jake nodded and came around the counter to show her what he had.

"I had a problem with the kiln this last firing. I might have some more bowls in there, but I won't know until later. You could check back on Monday."

"Ahh, but aren't you closed on Mondays?" she asked.

"You know my schedule better than I do. Tuesday then."

"It's no rush. I'd like to see what you have in the kiln so maybe I'll come back around on Tuesday morning."

Jake nodded. She hadn't looked at the other bowls and seemed anxious to be on her way.

"If you don't mind," she said, touching him on his arm, "I'll bring some treats."

"I'd like that."

"Then I'll see you later," she said and turned towards the stairs and the door. Jake smiled as he watched her go, wondering what her story might be.

He turned his attention to the customers that continued to file in all day, distracting him from the kiln. He was pleased to see the shelves emptying as they bought wares for their own homes or gifts for friends and family.

Just before closing, Jake cracked open the door of the kiln. He had been trying to put it off all day, trying to avoid the heartache he knew awaited him. It was still hot inside and waves of heat escaped from the top. He closed his eyes and took a deep breath before opening the kiln enough to see inside. The top shelves were badly warped and the bowls resting on them looked much like the Dali paintings he had imagined. He reached in to touch one of the bowls, but instantly recoiled, shaking his hand in pain. They were still too hot to touch.

He turned his attention to the pots on the lower shelves. These were much cooler. As he sorted through the shelves, he found that at least twelve of the bowls were good enough to sell in the showroom. The glazes were much different on these than they had been on the pots in the previous firing, much smoother and shinier. But they weren't broken and only slightly warped.

Jake stepped back from the kiln and wiped the sweat from his brow. From what he could tell, at least ten of the shelves were so badly warped that they would need to be replaced. But Thomas was right about the bricks. They showed no sign of damage and Jake was relieved. He felt a rush of happiness and gratitude wash over him.

As he began to close the heavy kiln door, he noticed that the thermocouple sticking through the bricks was also melted. This sensitive instrument was connected to the pyrometer; together, they performed the task of measuring temperature inside the kiln. He hoped that the melted thermocouple alone was the reason the pyrometer was not functioning. The thermocouple would need to be replaced, but Jake knew it was all a small price to pay considering all the things that could have gone wrong.

Breathing a sigh of relief, he closed the door and walked to the cash register. He knew it was finally time to open a bank account as he looked at the till overflowing with bills. On Monday, he told himself, he would visit Mr. Smoot at the bank and open an account.

He pulled some grocery money from the till before closing the doors and locking up.

Molly looked up when he walked through the door of the grocery store.

"Hey, Jake," she said with a smile.

"How ya feeling, Molly?"

"Tired. I already told Kai I need a nap before the concert tonight."

"I could use one too."

Molly raised her eyebrows. "Late night last night?" she asked, teasingly.

Jake shook his head. "This town is too small! I've never known my grocer on a first name basis and I'm sure they've never asked me about my love life."

"Is that what it is then?" she asked, mischievously.

Jake realized he'd walked right into that one. "I don't know Molly," he said, trying to keep from blushing, but knowing he wasn't fooling anyone. "She's a really great girl."

Molly took a deep breath. "I know my opinion doesn't matter, but I really like her too. The other day when she was here, Mrs. Torkelson was leaving at the same time and Amy insisted on helping her carry her groceries. She seems like a really good person." Jake pursed his lips and nodded.

"So how was dinner the other night?" she asked.

Jake gave her a funny look.

Molly laughed. "She stopped here to get what she needed before she came to your place, remember? We got to talking, as girls do, and she told me she was making dinner for a boy. When we found out it was you, Kai went off about how good your pancakes were."

Jake smiled and shook his head. "It was the best meal I've had in years. She's a great cook."

"And?" asked Molly.

"And what?"

"Well, are there any sparks?"

"I really enjoy being around her. She has become a great friend."

"So, nothing romantic yet?"

Jake smiled and shook his head again. He leaned closer to her and lowered his voice. "I've never kissed a girl. I wouldn't even know where to start with all of that stuff."

"Well, you know she likes you, don't you?"

Jake looked at his shoes. "I think so."

Molly thumped him on his chest. "Jake, wake up! I'm no rocket scientist, but anyone can see that she likes you."

"I need some groceries," he said, picking up a plastic basket and heading for the aisles without giving Molly any further satisfaction.

As he was picking out some apples, Kai came out from the back room. "Dude," he said, patting Jake on the shoulder.

"Hey man," responded Jake coolly, not wanting to hear anything else about Amy.

"Hey, I was thinking earlier, we should meet somewhere and walk over to the concert together. How about if we just meet in front of the store at about 6:45. It's only a five minute walk and there's no sense in getting there any earlier than that."

"That sounds good. I've been meaning to ask you about your kitchen. How's it coming?"

"Awesome. I'm supposed to pick up the new cabinets on Monday."

"Do you need some help?"

"Dude. That would be totally cool. My father-in-law has an old van he'll let us use, but Molly isn't much help with heavy stuff right now."

"It's my day off. I'd be happy to help."

"Cool. I'll call the cabinet shop on Monday morning and let you know when we can go."

Kai helped Jake find the last of the items he needed before he returned to the back room. Molly checked him out at the register, biting her tongue about Amy, sensing it was not yet a subject Jake wanted to talk about. He thanked her and told her he'd see her later and hurried off to his apartment. He unpacked the groceries quickly and glanced at Amy's paintings. He was envious of her talent. It seemed to come so naturally to her.

Remembering all the things he still had to do, he grabbed his sketchbook and headed out the door to the graveyard. When he arrived at the rusty gate, he was surprised to find it already open and several people milling about, tending to the graves of loved ones. At first he wondered what was going on, but then remembered that it was Memorial Day weekend. He had never seen so many people in the graveyard. He felt as though his private space was being stampeded by strangers. This had been a place of quiet reflection for him since he had arrived in Niederbipp and now there was talking, laughter and activity that didn't allow the same peace and solitude he had enjoyed.

Instead of going straight to the unfamiliar benches as he had planned, he went to Isaac's bench to avoid the crowds. He was surprised to see the ground covered with several bouquets of flowers. Many of them had cards attached and he was curious what these would say. He wanted to read them, but wondered how that might look to the other people in the cemetery, few of whom he recognized. He thought he might stop by on Monday and take the notes back to his apartment where he could read them in private. His curiosity was nearly overwhelming, so he opened his sketchbook and began sketching the ideas he had been thinking about since the day before.

After a few minutes, his thoughts returned to the kiln. He knew he was lucky that things were not any worse, but still he knew his mistake would be costly. He began figuring what it would cost him to replace the shelves and the thermocouple. The shelves would be at least $50 a piece and at least another $50 for the thermocouple.

He wouldn't know for sure until he could unload the kiln, but he hoped the mistake would cost him less than a thousand

KILN SHELVES 12+ @ $50⁰⁰ = $600⁰⁰

100R

THERMOCOUPLE $50⁰⁰ = $50⁰⁰

SHIPPING ?

dollars. He was thus consumed when Amy sat down next to him.

"Hey," she said, startling him.

"Hey back." He looked up to meet her eyes.

"Have you ever seen this many people here before?"

Jake shook his head. "It makes it kind of hard to do what I wanted to do."

"What are you working on?" Amy asked, turning her attention to Jake's sketchbook.

"Oh, just figuring how much it will cost me to replace the kiln shelves. I just opened the kiln. The top shelves looks like Salvador Dali broke into the shop—they're really warped."

"Is the kiln ruined?" she asked, looking anxious.

"No, Thomas was right. Isaac was planning for my mistakes. He replaced the bricks about fifteen years ago and spent the extra money to buy the old fashioned kind of bricks. They're not as efficient as the new type, but they're more durable and apparently handle higher temperatures much better than the new style."

Amy smiled and nodded, looking down at the pile of flowers on Isaac's grave. "I'm really glad he was looking out for you."

Her words surprised Jake and he remained silent for a long moment as he considered them.

"So, have you had any more ideas about the bench," she asked, breaking the silence.

Jake nodded and flipped the page, handing it to her. He had drawn the top of the bench, spread out across both pages. In the middle was a chubby candle that had Isaac's name along with birth and death dates. The rays went out in a 360° motif, like the rays of the sun on a cloudy day. Each of the rays contained images of the stories Jake had heard from those who had come to visit. In the four corners he had drawn forget-me-nots. She smiled as she looked at it.

"What do you think?"

"I think it's great. I was hoping you'd include the forget-me-not somewhere, but I wonder if the corners are the best place for them."

"What do you mean?"

"I just wonder if it's too obvious. It seems like he tried to keep it pretty well hidden. I don't think anyone would wonder if that might be his secret ingredient in his tea by seeing it on his bench, but I wonder if it might not be better to make it smaller and put just one of them on the candlestick."

"I like that. It reminds me of a book I read in high school, The Scarlet Pimpernel, I think it was called."

"Hey, I read the same book. 'Scarlet Pimpernel' was a code name for the man who saved people from the guillotine and he used the sign of a tiny red flower to seal all of his letters."

"Yeah, and if I remember right, the man's own wife didn't even know that it was him who was helping people until she started looking around and found pictures of the pimpernel everywhere she looked."

"That's right! I can imagine people finding the forget-me-not on the candlestick and then finding the ground covered with them. They might consult a field book like Gloria's and find the name and begin to ask questions as we have, coming to a realization of what this man was all about."

Amy started laughing. "Or maybe they'll just think he liked blue flowers."

Jake took the sketchbook from her and in the corner of the page, he drew Isaac's stamp. Amy had seen it before in the shop, but hadn't thought much about it. It was the design he had stamped into all of his pots, a B with six lines coming away from it like flower petals.

"Do you know what this meant?" she asked.

Jake shook his head. "I know enough about pottery to know there is meaning in every stamp a potter puts to the clay. It's the thing that identifies it as his. I know there has to be something behind it."

Amy took the book again and looked at the picture of the stamp. "Maybe it's about letting your light shine," she said, "like the candlestick."

Jake nodded. "It could be, but why only six rays? There is room for more."

COME UNTO ME, MATT. 11:28:30
ALL YE THAT LABOR
AND ARE HEAVY LADEN.
TAKE MY YOKE UPON YOU.
MY YOKE IS EASY AND MY BURDEN IS LIGHT.

SWEET
IS THE PEACE
THE GOSPEL
BRINGS

AS FOR ME AND MY
HOUSE, WE WILL
SERVE THE
LORD
JOSHUA 24:15

OWNERSHIP
VS
STEWARDSHIP

ISAAC AA
BING

ARE
WE ALL BEGGARS

WHERE YOUR TREASURE
IS, THERE WILL YOUR
HEART BE ALSO.
MATT: 6:21

LAY NOT UP FOR YOURSELVES
TREASURES UPON THE
EARTH WHERE MOTH DOTH
CORRUPT AND THIEVES
DO BREAK THROUGH
AND STEAL - MATT: 6:19

- 414 -

...UT SEEK YE FIRST THE
KINGDOM OF GOD..—
AND ALL THESE THINGS
SHALL BE ADDED UNTO
YOU! MATT 6:33

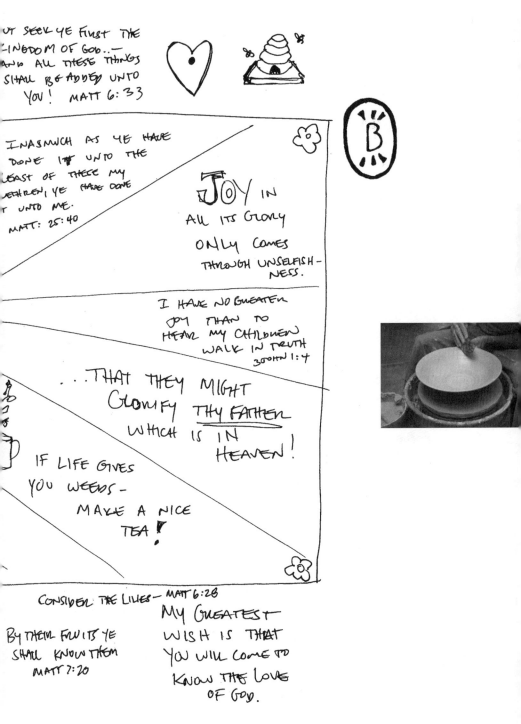

INASMUCH AS YE HAVE
DONE IT UNTO THE
LEAST OF THESE MY
BRETHREN, YE HAVE DONE
IT UNTO ME.
MATT: 25:40

JOY IN
ALL ITS GLORY
ONLY COMES
THROUGH UNSELFISH-
NESS.

I HAVE NO GREATER
JOY THAN TO
HEAR MY CHILDREN
WALK IN TRUTH
3 JOHN 1:4

...THAT THEY MIGHT
GLORIFY THY FATHER
WHICH IS IN
HEAVEN!

IF LIFE GIVES
YOU WEEDS —
MAKE A NICE
TEA!

CONSIDER THE LILIES — MATT 6:28

BY THEIR FRUITS YE
SHALL KNOW THEM
MATT 7:20

MY GREATEST
WISH IS THAT
YOU WILL COME TO
KNOW THE LOVE
OF GOD.

"What else has six rays?" she asked.

"The Star of David has six points."

"Yeah, but Isaac was a Christian."

"That's true. What's the name of a six sided shape?"

"A hexagon, I think,"

"That's right. I think it was Thomas that told me he was a bee keeper for a while. Isn't honeycomb in the shape of a hexagon? There's a beehive on one of the benches too."

Amy looked at the stamp again, doubtful. "If he was referring to bees, it seems it would be easier to put his B in the middle of a hexagon."

Jake nodded, knowing she was right.

They both sat silent for a moment, repeating "six" in their minds. "What about a sixth sense?" she asked. "You said he had a way of understanding people. I've heard that some people consider ESP the sixth sense that gives them the ability to communicate without words."

This time Jake looked doubtful. "Do you believe in that stuff?"

"I don't know. I don't really know much about it."

Jake shook his head. "That can't be it. Remember, Isaac was not one to toot his own horn. I don't think he'd go about making a stamp to show he somehow had extra powers, even if he did."

Again there was silence as they thought. "People are buried six feet underground," he said, shaking his head, knowing that had nothing to do with it.

"Wait a minute," she said, excitedly. "How many benches did you say there are in the graveyard?" Jake raised his eyebrows, finally seeing where she was headed. "We're sitting on the seventh one. That would be more like Isaac to give credit to all the potters that came before him. This was their shop. He was the first non-blood relative to take over the shop, and he lived surrounded by the pots of all of the previous generations. That has to be it," said Jake. "You're brilliant, Amy."

"I was just thinking how dumb we were that we didn't get it earlier."

Jake laughed. "I'm still tired from last night."

"Me too."

Jake looked up at the clock. It was ten minutes to five. "I promised Sam I'd talk to him about the mosaic."

He noticed that the people who had been near the bench he wanted to examine were gone now. "Let's look at this bench real quick," he said, grabbing her hand and pulling her up. They hurried to the bench near the stone wall that marked the property line of both the church and the cemetery. This was the only bench that stood alone and as they approached it, they realized much of it was missing. The tiles had fallen off or been pulled off by vandals and many of the spaces where the tiles had been were left rough from the mortar that once held the tiles in place.

"I wonder what happened to this one?" asked Amy. The name and dates were still there and Jake read them as he copied the information into his sketchbook.

When he looked up, he saw that Amy was busy reading the many different tiles filled with words of poetry

JOSEPH ALVIN ENGELHART
APRIL 12, 1814
JANVARY 6, 1898
HUSBAND OF ANNA STUSSI ENGELHART
FATHER OF ANNA, GABRIEL, ALVIN, & PAUL

and scripture. Unlike the other benches whose surfaces were covered primarily with shards and assembled fragments, this one looked like it had been covered at one time with new tiles that had been cut square in many different sizes. Even the holes that had been left by the missing tiles were square. Many of the tiles that remained were chipped and broken along the edges, as if someone had tried to pry them off.

He looked at the name tile again. "Oh, this bench was made by Alvin. He was known for his tiles. Maybe you've seen the tile over the front door?" He asked Amy.

She shook her head.

"It says something about God is love, if I remember right."

She turned back to the bench and pointed at a tile in front of her. "You mean like this one?"

He took a closer look. The tile was badly chipped and weathered with lichen growing on it, but it was otherwise identical to the one in the shop and he read the quotation aloud.

"That's the same one," he said. "A man stopped by a couple of weeks ago asking if I had seen any tiles made by Alvin as I was cleaning up

"BELOVED, LET US LOVE ONE ANOTHER: FOR EVERYONE THAT LOVETH IS BORN OF GOD AND KNOWETH GOD... FOR GOD IS LOVE."

1. JOHN 3:7-8

the shop. I told him I didn't know what he was talking about and he left, telling me he would check back with me in a few months. He said even the smallest of the tiles he made were fetching hundreds of dollars these days. Apparently, some of his tiles were shown on the Antiques Road Show and it sparked a lot of interest."

"That's probably why these tiles have been stolen," she added.

Jake shook his head. "It's hard to believe someone would steal something from a cemetery."

"Look at this one," she said, pointing to one that was upside down from their point of view. She stood and cocked her head so she could read it.

She looked at Jake. "Have you ever heard that before?"

Jake smiled and shook his head. "No, but I like it. Does it say where

" BUT NOW *O* LORD, THOU ART OUR
FATHER; WE ARE THE CLAY, AND
THOU OUR POTTER; AND WE ARE
ALL THE WORKS OF THY HANDS."
I SAIAH 64: 3 or 8 ?

it comes from?"

She looked again. "It says Isaiah 64: 3....or 8, it's been chipped in the corner." Jake asked her to read it again while he copied it in his notebook.

"You'll like this one too," she said, pointing to a blue tile that had many chipped edges.

"That's really good," he said.

"There's another here," she said.

" HATH NOT THE POTTER POWER
OVER THE CLAY ?"
ROMANS 9:21

Jake wrote this one down as well. "I had no idea that potters were even spoken of in the Bible, but these have a lot of deep

" BEHOLD, AS THE CLAY IS IN THE
HANDS OF THE POTTER, SO ARE
YE IN MINE HAND."
JEREMIAH 18:6

meaning. That last one from Jeremiah is pretty incredible, that we're becoming something in the hands of God—that is if we will let Him shape our lives."

"And what if we don't?" asked Amy. Jake thought for a moment.

"Well, then maybe He'll have to do with us as potters do with the clay. When I try to make a pot and I mess up or the clay is tough or resistant to becoming what I want it to be, I usually cut it off the wheel and wedge it up again."

"What's that?"

"It's about like kneading bread dough. After I wedge a stubborn bit of clay forty or fifty times, it is usually more cooperative. It seems like there's probably a lot more to understand about this. I'll have to look it up in the Bible when I get home. The Old Testament has always intimidated me, but I suppose I need to give it a chance, especially if it talks about potters."

She looked at the other tiles. Many of them had art nouveau designs of stylized flowers and birds and were brightly colored, but nearly all of them were chipped.

"I really like these tiles," she said. "He really had an eye for design."

Jake knelt on the ground, in awe of the beauty of each tile. "It's sad that so many of these are chipped or missing, but I still think this is my favorite bench."

Amy nodded and then got down on her knees to look at the face and the legs of the bench that were also covered with the tiles. Few of them had any writing, but one caught Amy's eye. She reached her hand out to brush away the dirt.

Jake wrote the words in his sketchbook next to the other quotes.

"GOD GAVE TO ALL PEOPLE A CUP OF CLAY, AND FROM THAT CUP, THEY DRANK THEIR LIFE." ?

Amy sat down next to him, dusting off her knees. "What are you thinking?" she asked.

"I'm not sure I'd use any of these on Isaac's bench, but I think some of these quotes are really good and they've given me more homework to do with the Bible."

Amy nodded. "Maybe you can tell me what you learn."

Jake looked at her and smiled, "Sure. Maybe I'll wait to look them up until the next time you paint so we can talk about them."

Amy nodded and yawned just as the bells began to ring, tolling five times.

"I'm supposed to be at Sam's," he said, looking very disappointed.

"That's fine; I need to take a power nap before tonight or I'm going to fall asleep at the concert."

"Maybe I'll try to catch a short nap too," He stood and offered Amy his hand, lifting her from the bench.

As they walked towards the gate, they passed the two benches in the middle of the graveyard: Isaac's and Henry's.

"We haven't spent any time looking at this one," she said

"I was kind of saving this one for the last. It's the one Isaac made and I figured I might learn more about both of the men if I understood those who came before them."

Amy nodded and yawned again. "Maybe we could look at it closer tomorrow after church."

"What? And give up our reason to get together next week for lunch?"

"You have a painting to work off," she said, poking him in the belly. "We have a reason to meet for lunch for the next three years, just so you can pay me all those sandwiches you owe me."

"Don't you think you'll get sick of peanut butter and honey?"

"I haven't yet, but I'll let you know if we need a change."

They walked through the courtyard and stopped at the top of the stairs where their paths diverged. "So what's the plan tonight?" she asked.

"I told Kai and Molly we'd meet them out in front of their store at 6:45 and we'll walk over together. Maybe you better eat dinner at home and meet me at my apartment at 6:30."

Amy yawned and said goodbye, and Jake hurried to the bakery.

41 THE DEAL

Jake knocked on the back door of the bakery a few minutes later and Sam's booming voice invited him in. He turned the knob and stepped into the large whitewashed room. It reminded him of the restaurant kitchen where one of his roommates worked as a cook in college, and where Jake had frequented after hours, picking up the unserved food to supplement their meager groceries at home.

He couldn't see Sam, but he could hear him whistling and shuffling about in the adjacent room. Jake found him standing near a large stainless steel counter covered with small ceramic jars, adding flour and water to the white liquid at the bottom of each jar.

Curious what he was doing, Jake asked several questions and Sam explained how sourdough starts had to be fed and maintained in order to keep them working. Jake was surprised to learn that some of the starts were over a hundred years old and had been passed down through Sam's family of bakers. He was even more amazed to learn that some of the bakeries in Europe had  sourdough starts that were over three hundred years old and were guarded like family heirlooms.

Jake noticed an old family picture on the wall, covered with a thin layer of flour dust. Sam told him about each of his three children and how they had scattered to the wind—a daughter on each coast and his only son, the president of a corporate bakery in Pittsburgh. Jake noticed that Sam's demeanor changed when he spoke of his son and the conversation ended quickly.

The work was done quickly and Sam removed his white cotton apron before he asked Jake to follow him to the front of the store. The bakery looked much different than it did during the day when the shelves and displays were full of bread and the shop was full of hungry customers. He walked to the entrance, just in front of the glass doors, to the patch of unfinished gray cement.

Sam folded his arms across his large belly and leaned one shoulder against the wall. "I made the mistake of tearing this apart before I had a good plan. Isaac told me he'd help me and then he died. I have the first part of the mosaic that he worked on in the back room, but unfortunately, no one really knows how this is supposed to work. I helped clean out a bunch of his stuff in the apartment after he died and hoped I would come across the plan, but I've been thinking lately that he probably just had it in his head. Have you ever done any of this kind of work before?" asked Sam.

"I helped make a mosaic on a wall at college with all the unclaimed pots at the end of the semester, but I've never really worked on tile for a floor before. To be honest, I don't even know where to begin."

Sam looked out at the rest of the floor: white honeycomb tile. "I laid all of this several years ago. It's really not too difficult. I know I could lay this with your help, but I can't make the tile."

Jake swallowed hard. The challenge was interesting, but also overwhelming. "You say there are some tiles already made?"

Sam nodded and walked back towards the kitchen, to the storage place under one of the many large counters. He stooped down and grabbed hold of a small cardboard box, hefting it as if it was very heavy. He walked to a chair next to a round table and set the box down on it before folding back the top to reveal the tiles.

"I haven't looked at these in a few months," he said, as he began lifting out pieces of the tile and laying them on the table. Jake fumbled with the pieces, trying to put them together like a puzzle, but without a picture to use as a guide.

Once all the pieces had been removed from the box, Sam set about assembling them the best he knew how and soon the picture was much clearer than the mess Jake had made of it. The round design covered most of the table. "Gottlieb Bakery," written in bold block letters, surrounded the top of the circle. Below, several loaves of bread decorated the middle and the words "Established 1717- Niederbipp" rounded out the bottom. Jake was surprised at the fine craftsmanship and detail and thought Isaac must have spent several days making the tiles and then glazing and decorating them.

"I don't understand what it is you want me to do. It looks really good to me."

"But it's too small. I asked Isaac to create a design that would fill the whole space in the front. This is nice, but it was to be only part of the design. A rather small part, as I recall. He said he wanted to design a landscape motif somehow with lots of colorful paints."

Jake looked up, knowing that he meant glaze, but decided not to waste his breath trying to explain the difference. "Do you have a tape measure?" he asked.

Sam turned away, returning with an old fashioned folding stick measurer. Jake unfolded the sticks and laid it across Isaac's tile. It was thirty-two inches in diameter. He wrote this on his sketchbook and then walked back to the front of the bakery and measured the space there. Ninety six inches by sixty. He wrote this down in the sketchbook too.

Sam was standing behind him. "Do you have any ideas?" he asked.

"Maybe. A couple of weeks ago, I was down by the river and looked up at the town and the hills behind it. I was impressed by its beauty. If you want to include a landscape motif in the design, it seems to me our own local landscape might be exciting to replicate in tile."

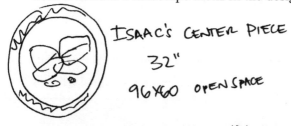

ISAAC'S CENTER PIECE
32"
96x60 OPEN SPACE

"And how would you use the pieces Isaac made?"

"I imagine his piece right in the middle," responded Jake, as he took a step into the center of the space he had just measured. Jake could tell Sam was having a hard time imagining what he was talking about, so he opened his sketchbook and quickly drew out the design he had imagined in his mind.

Sam looked at the design and nodded. "I like it. How long do you think it would take?"

Jake bit his lip as he thought about it. "Depending on the shape of tiles, it would probably take two days to cut out all the clay that would be needed. I think the tiles would need at least four days to dry out and then the bisque firing and glazing and then the high fire. I'm guessing a month. I don't know if Thomas told you about my last firing, but I have to do some repairs before I can fire anything. That could put things off for another week or two."

Sam's smile turned into a frown. "I'll tell you what; if you put this first on your list of things to do and have the tiles ready to lay in three weeks from today, I'll make sure your next three years' worth of bread are on me." Jake ran his fingers through his hair and looked over his sketch again. It was possible to do what he had been asked, but he knew it would be a challenge.

"Ok," Jake said, taking a deep breath, "I'll give it a try."

Sam's smile returned to his face. "We would have to lay the tile on Saturday afternoon so it would have the weekend to dry and then maybe we could grout it on the following Monday night."

Jake nodded, extending his hand to shake the baker's.

"Now come and get some bread before you go."

Jake followed him back to the kitchen where Sam had already prepared a large brown bag of full of bread.

"I understand you're having dinner with Beverly and Jerry tomorrow and their niece. You might consider taking a loaf with you. If you wrap it in plastic tonight, it will be fresh enough tomorrow." Jake nodded and thanked Sam.

"Oh, and before you go, I thought you might want to look through this," he said, handing him an old leather book. It was held closed with a wide rubber band and its edges were worn. "I took this from Isaac's apartment when we cleaned it out. I was hoping to find his plans for my floor, but I didn't find what I was looking for. Isaac often carried this with him. I thought you might find it interesting."

Jake was amazed and curious. He wondered what treasures and secrets he might find inside the book. He thanked Sam and walked back to his apartment, in need of a nap.

THE CONCERT

Jake woke with a start when the knock came at the door, worrying that he had overslept and missed the concert. He answered the door with his shoes in his hands, looking confused. Amy stood in the doorway and smiled when she saw his disheveled hair.

"Did you have a good nap?"

Jake smiled, still half asleep.

She came in and wrestled with his hair as he tied his shoes. It had been years since anyone had touched his hair, and he realized how nice it was to have someone care if it was out of place. He knew he had needed a trim since before he had arrived in town, and now, a month later, it had grown a little wild.

"We better hurry. I think Kai and Molly are probably waiting."

Jake nodded, still groggy from his nap, and they left the apartment, Amy leading out in a rush. He noticed that Amy had changed out of the skirt and blouse she had worn to work and was now wearing blue jeans and a white cotton dress shirt that made her hair seem even brighter than usual. As they neared the corner, they could see Kai and Molly, looking for them.

"Hey," said Kai, grinning happily.

"Hey guys," said Amy.

"We were just wondering if you decided not to go," added Kai

"No, I just fell asleep," said Jake.

"We better hustle," said Kai. "The concert starts in ten minutes."

They headed off toward the carnival grounds at a brisk pace until Molly began complaining of side aches as she braced her belly.

"Maybe you guys should go ahead," suggested Kai.

"We're in no hurry," said Jake. They moved behind Kai and Molly to allow her to set their pace and continued forward, a little slower than before. Soon, they were joined by others on the sidewalk who were hurrying quickly toward the concert. Jake was disappointed when he saw the long line at the gate, wishing they had left sooner, but Molly steered them to a different gate.

"We have VIP passes," she said as they headed to a smaller gate with no line. After they surrendered their tickets to the man at the gate, they were ushered quickly to their seats by a tall freckled young man who threw a flirty smile at Amy. She didn't seem to notice, but Jake did.

As soon as they were seated, Jake turned around and looked behind them at the bleachers rising high above. There were people of all ages in the audience. He was glad to see children and families as well as gray-haired people. Very few faces looked familiar and he wondered how so many people had heard about the concert.

"We have some great seats," said Amy, turning around and looking at the stage, just ten feet in front of them.

The stage had been set up in front of the permanent bleachers and had a tall frame that soared overhead to hold the lights. Jim's giant bass stood in a stand in the middle of the stage next to two smaller stands that held Adam's guitars. The crowd was noisy in anticipation and erupted in cheers and whistles as the guys came out on stage and approached their mics. Paul carried his fiddle by his side, holding it by its neck. In his other hand, he held his bow high above his head, waving it to the crowd. John had his mandolin strapped over his shoulder on a thin cord.

"H-e-l-l-o Niederbipp!" shouted Paul into the mic and the crowd erupted again, sending electric shocks through everyone present. When the cheering died down after a full minute, Paul looked down to the front row and winked at them before he spoke.

"It's great to be home," he said, and again, the crowd was on its feet and cheering loudly. "Ya know, ten years ago when we first played here, we were pretty nervous. Bluegrass music was still new to all of us, but you liked us then and have liked us enough ever since to make us want to come home and play for all our friends." The crowd cheered again.

"We were just talking backstage, wondering if anyone was there ten years ago. If you were there that night, please stand up." Jake and Amy turned around to see that at least a hundred people were standing. Some of them looked like they were probably children at the debut concert.

"Now, how many of you have been to one of our concerts before?" Again the crowd roared and nearly everyone was standing. Paul smiled broadly. "It's good to be among friends," he said to the generous crowd.

"Many of you know that we're hometown boys. We grew up here, went to school here, and began playing our music right here in town. Many of you probably don't know that we got started because one man believed in the passion we had for our music. He gave us a place to play and let us borrow his bluegrass tapes until we wore them out, listening to them hundreds of times. For the first time since we began playing here ten years ago, that man is  not with us. He passed away two months ago and this world lost one of the finest men any of us have ever known."

He lifted his fiddle to the crowd. "For the last ten years, I've been playing this fiddle that had been passed down from his wife's great-great grandfather. Many of you know who I'm talking about. Perhaps he touched your life in a similar way. Maybe you drink from the cups he made or eat from the plates he created. Maybe he shared his wisdom with you and loved you like a son or a daughter." Paul got choked up and stopped for a minute to regain his composure.

"This concert tonight is a fundraiser for the hospital, but we'd like to dedicate it to this wonderful, humble man, Isaac Bingham, the wise old potter of Niederbipp, who deserves more credit for our success than anyone else. He believed in us when no one else did and taught us to fight for our passions."

Jake turned to look at the crowd who had erupted once again in cheers and shouts.

"Fortunately for all of us, the old man's wheel is still spinning. I want to personally welcome Jake Kimball, the newest potter of Niederbipp." Jake had not expected this and was instantly blushing as the crowd clapped. "Stand up," said Paul, walking to the edge of the stage and motioning for Jake to stand with the wave of his bow. Jake stood and turned around to wave at the crowd, scarlet-faced and embarrassed. The crowd clapped and cheered harder. Paul went back to the mic as Jake took his seat.

"We felt it was fitting in a concert dedicated to an old potter to begin with a song we wrote one night in his studio where we practiced for more than three years. This song has some interesting history. Many of you might be aware that none of our parents were very supportive of us striking out on our own to make music."

The crowd responded with boos.

"At one point, I was banned from ever playing again. I would often have to sneak away and tell some whopper stories so my parents would allow me to leave our house for practice. The night we wrote this song, I told my parents I had to go to Jim's house to work on a science project. Anyway, Isaac had been recycling his clay that afternoon and had huge piles of mushy clay all over the studio. Needless to say, I got a little clay on my pants as we danced around the studio to the new song we were writing. When I got home that night, my mom immediately saw the clay and asked what I had been doing. I would like to take this opportunity to publicly apologize for lying that night. Mom, Dad..." he looked into the audience near where Jake and Amy were sitting "...I'm sorry, but I never really made that volcano I told you I was making." The crowd laughed. "But we did make a really great song and named it 'Mud On My Pants.'"

With that, Paul put the bow to the strings and began the song in a feverish tempo as the crowd erupted once again. There was much more room on the stage than there was in the studio and the members of the band, except Jim, took full advantage of the extra space and danced as they played. The dancing was contagious and soon the whole audience was standing and dancing the best they could in the stadium seats.

When it was over, Paul again stepped to the mic, pausing to catch his breath. "This next song was one that Jim found. We wish we could claim it, but we feel we've done a lot to make it our own and as soon as we get copyright clearance, we'll record it. When we heard this song, it reminded us all of the nights we'd practice in Isaac's studio. He would often be finishing up his work as we played and we all learned to love watching him work at the wheel. The song is called 'Potter's Wheel.'"

Again, Paul started them out with the fiddle as he had the night before. The tempo was much slower on this one and most in the audience stayed in their seats as they heard the lyrical story of the potter's wheel. Amy cuddled up against Jake's arm and shoulder and he looked at her, wondering what kind of heaven he had come to. Good friends, good music, and a beautiful evening. He doubted it could be any better than it was right then.

The next song had the audience back up on their feet, dancing. Jake and Amy laughed at each other as they watched each other dance. Jake had never really danced in public before. The one dance he had attended in high school had been such a fiasco that he decided to never dance again. Before long, Jake had put aside all his inhibitions and they both danced like they didn't care who was watching, Amy's red hair a blur in the motion. She laughed out loud at some of his dance moves that were unrefined and semi-coordinated, but sincere and natural. They looked up into the bleachers and saw that everyone was dancing, old and young, male and female, enjoying the joyful sound. Even Molly with her giant belly was dancing as if she had forgotten her pains. Amy tapped Jake on the shoulder and pointed to Kai who was dancing with his eyes closed and moving smoothly like seaweed in a tidal pool.

At intermission, Molly asked Amy to go with her to the ladies room to "powder their noses." Jake laughed when Kai leaned over to him, once they had gone, and explained that "powdering noses" was code for having a small bladder that was being kicked by a baby. While they were gone, he moved over and talked to Jake like an old friend.

Jake liked Kai. He was a simple and straight forward sort of guy who was easy to read and easy to get along with. Jake asked how Kai felt about being a dad and was surprised to learn he was far more excited than nervous or scared of the responsibility that would soon be his.

The girls returned a few a minutes before the end of intermission, each toting a cup from the concessions stand.

"Hope you like lemonade," said Amy, as she handed Jake the cup. He took a drink and handed it back to her. It was such a small thing to share a cup of lemonade with a friend, but at that moment, it meant the world to him. Molly too had brought back just one cup for the two of them to share and Jake felt endeared to Amy for this small and simple gesture that made him feel....what was it? Wanted? Accepted? He knew he shouldn't read into it—after all, they had shared several drinks together at lunch—but this somehow felt different, more friendly, more deliberate.

Jake was confused by these thoughts. He didn't want to make it a big deal, but as his lips again touched the straw where Amy's lips had just been, he felt a small shudder course through his spine. He was embarrassed by this for some reason and handed the cup back to Amy as the band reappeared on the stage.

They played all the songs they had played the night before at the studio, as well as many of the old songs from previous albums. They took turns commenting on the songs and their relationship with them, talking about some of them as if they were old friends. At one point, John stepped to the mic and asked Mrs. Hewlett to stand. She was just down the row from where Jake and Amy were sitting.

"This is the woman who taught us how to sing together in eleventh grade boys choir." The crowd applauded loudly and the old, gray haired woman beamed. "Even after we moved on to twelfth grade, we still practiced together during lunch in her classroom and she taught us all how to sing like we meant it." She blew them all kisses and sat down again as they began another set of songs.

Before they were ready for the show to end, Paul stepped to the mic. "It's always nice to come home. We're going to end with the song that got us started, a song that debuted right here, ten years ago. We've ended every concert that we've done here since with this song. Most of you probably know it, so if you want, you're welcome to sing along."

Like it had been recorded on their first album, Paul started out with his violin solo, playing 'Twinkle, Twinkle Little Star,' but was quickly joined by John on the mandolin.

Adam and Jim joined in and many in the audience began to sing the words along with the musicians.

There is more to a boy than what his mother sees.
There is more to a boy than what his father dreams.
Inside every boy lies a heart that beats
And sometimes it screams, refusing to take defeat.
And sometimes his father's dreams aren't big enough
And sometimes his mother's vision isn't long enough
And sometimes the boy has to dream his own dreams
And break through the clouds with his own sun beams

And you want to be loved and you want to be true
And you want to do what you know you should do
But the truest truth comes from your own heart,
So listen my friend, or it will tear you apart.

Because a boy is more than what his mother sees
And a boy is more than what his father dreams
Inside every boy lies a heart that beats
And if you let him fight, he'll laugh at defeat,
For dreams are for lovers and dreamers and boys
Who'll fight for their share of good times and joys.

For surely a boy must dream his own dreams,
And fight his own fights and beam his own beams.

And you want to be loved and you want to be true
And you want to do what you know you should do
But the truest truth comes from your own heart,
So listen my friend, or it will tear you apart.
So listen my friend, or it will tear you apart.

When they finished, the crowd was once again on its feet, whistling and clapping and yelling for an encore. Jake turned to see tears in Amy's eyes. He reflected on how the words of the song matched her situation. He hoped they would be inspiring to her in her quest to become a painter. Jake put his arm around her and gave her a squeeze, letting his arm linger.

The musicians left the stage and shouts of "Encore!" rang out over the applause. A minute later, they reemerged from back stage to the deafening delight of the audience and took up their instruments once again. John spoke this time as the crowd calmed down and took their seats.

"About five years ago I made a fool of myself and proposed to a girl who was in love with another guy. Needless to say, she broke my heart. Last night, we were all together as we practiced in the old pottery studio. I looked at her and her husband and her round belly and realized how lucky that son-of-a-gun is. Molly," he said, looking at her, "you're beautiful. Kai, you're a great guy and I want to congratulate you both on the upcoming birth of your child. We all hope you'll raise him on bluegrass music and when he's old enough, tell him how you broke my heart and inspired this song."

The crowd applauded as John fired up his fingers on a complex mandolin solo to start off 'Allegheny River Blues.' The others joined in, with Paul offering an echo on the fiddle to John's picking that was sad and moody. Then Paul and John harmonized as they sang the sad words.

I went down to the river,
To add my teardrops to the flow.
My heart is cracked and bleeding
And my head's about to blow.

Not long ago, she loved me
And promised she would wait
But in my long-time absence
She found another mate.

And so I sit upon the rocks
And wish it were not so.
Her ring is in my pocket
Her heart, I no longer know.

The blues are pouring o'er me
And kicking at my soul.
She's gone and left me standing
To cry and cry alone.

So listen to my song, my son
And learn the tale I know
For love and pain and sorrow
Go hand in hand, I know.

So if your love should leave you
And bring you to your knees,
Remember there's a river
For duds like you and me.

Again the crowd went wild as shouts and whistles rang out through the night air. They all took a bow and waved to the audience and disappeared back stage, taking their instruments with them this time.

Amy looked at Jake and smiled. "I like bluegrass."

Jake laughed. "These guys are great."

Kai and Molly were busy visiting with a middle-aged couple, who, from the sounds of it, were good friends with Molly's dad. They waited a few minutes for them to finish up their conversation, waving to Gloria and Joseph and Father Thomas as they were leaving the stands.

"Dudes, was that awesome or what?" said Kai. Jake and Amy smiled broadly and nodded in agreement. "I can't believe John actually dedicated a song to you and our baby," said Kai, enthusiastically. "We're totally gonna have to tell him about this when he's old enough to understand."

"And what if it's a girl?" asked Molly.

"Then, you'll have to teach her how to break hearts," he said, throwing his arms around her and squeezing her tight.

Jake and Amy just laughed.

"Let's get these kids home," said Molly. She was only a few years older than Jake and Amy, but she had assumed a role of maturity: part mother, part matchmaker, part love councilor.

Jake took the cup from Amy and dropped it in a nearby can. But before he did, he slyly pulled the straw from the cup and slid it into his back pocket, feeling silly and sentimental.

Molly's stride got faster as they neared Hauptstrasse and Jake and Amy had to hurry to keep up.

"What's wrong Molly, do you need to powder your nose?" asked Kai. They all laughed, and Molly swatted Kai on the chest with her free hand.

"Don't make me laugh," she said, "these are the last pants I have that fit."

This only made them all laugh even more.

"See you tomorrow at church," said Amy.

"Sounds good," said Kai as he unlocked the door, which Molly immediately pushed open, disappearing into the dark store.

"Goodnight," he said with a wink.

43 MAGIC

Jake and Amy continued to laugh as they walked toward her apartment. They had been holding hands since they left the stadium, but now Amy dropped Jake's hand and wrapped her hands around his arm, trying to get closer. Jake responded by putting his arm over her shoulder and pulling her close. His hand rested on the top of her arm and he was surprised how cold she was.

"Are you ok?" he asked.

She looked up at him. "Just cold, but I'm always cold. I should have brought a sweatshirt."

"I guess we better get you home."

Amy looked up at the clock tower whose whitewashed walls glowed from the lights projected on it. "I don't want to go home yet. It's too early and my paints are at your house."

"Do you want to go back and get your paints?" he asked.

"No, I want to get a sweatshirt and hang out a little longer."

Jake smiled.

"I'll be right back," she said as she ran up the stairs and into the apartment. Jake took a seat on the stairs to wait for her. It had been a wonderful day, the end of a wonderful week full of fun and excitement and learning. He marveled that it had been only one week since they had really begun hanging out. He leaned against the railing and his nose caught a whiff of peppermint. He turned to see a peppermint plant growing in the small patch of dirt at his right, and his mind returned to the leaves drying in the kitchen. He plucked a long stem filled with peppermint leaves and lifted it to his nose.

The door opened behind him and he turned to see Amy coming down the stairs, wearing a dark hooded sweatshirt with college lettering printed on it. She was carrying a plastic sandwich bag and as she sat down next to him, he saw it was filled with cookies.

"Aunt Bev must have made these tonight," she said, offering one to Jake. He grinned and took one from the bag. "How's the peppermint drying?" she asked when she saw the stem in his hand.

"I think the leaves are ready to be crushed. We could probably start working on it tomorrow after church."

"Did you get some of the secret ingredient?" she asked.

Jake stopped chewing and looked at her. "No, I forgot. I was planning on picking some today when we were there, but I got rushed trying to get to Sam's and I spaced it."

"Well, why don't we go get some now?"

Jake swallowed and looked at her. "I suppose we could."

Jake had been near the cemetery once before after dark, a month earlier at the May Day celebration when the courtyard was strung with lights and lanterns. The only light now came from the lights reflecting off of the church and a thick slice of moon hanging overhead.

Away from the trees of the courtyard, the cemetery was a little brighter, but even then they were both a little skittish as they opened the rusty gate and made their way to Isaac's bench. They sat down and Amy pulled the cookies from her pocket.

"We can use the bag to collect the flowers," she said, offering Jake another cookie. He happily took one and they sat together, eating cookies in the graveyard by the light of the moon.

"You know, the thing I was most impressed with tonight was the dedication of the encore to Molly and Kai and their baby," Jake mused. "I liked what John said, but the thing that impressed me the most was the fact that Kai thought it was cool. It's pretty obvious that John still has feelings for Molly, but Kai either didn't see it, or is secure enough with Molly's love to know he has nothing to worry about."

Amy nodded. "They really love each other. I was thinking the same thing. When I've seen them working together at the grocery store, I've noticed that they're very secure with each other, like they're best friends first."

"Yeah, I don't know if I've seen a better example of that. In many ways, they act like they're still dating, but it's been about four years, I think, since they got married, and they're about to bring their first child into the world. I don't think my parents ever had that kind of a relationship."

"I'm sure my parents have never had the friendship that Kai and Molly do. Now that my dad is getting close to retirement, I'm not sure my parents have anything in common besides their kids. They can go for days without having much to say to each other. I've never seen them be hostile toward each other, but sometimes it seems like they're strangers living together in the same house. They don't share much of anything, other than a bed, and even that is just two twin beds, pushed together with separate sheets and covers. The last time I was home, they didn't even eat together. I'd never want to live that way. Lots of my friends at school had parents who were getting divorces after twenty-five or thirty years of marriage. It's great to see Kai and Molly and the marriage they've made together. It gives me hope for the future."

A long silence fell between them. Marriage had not really been on either of their minds or agendas and talk of it now seemed suddenly awkward.

"So, how was your meeting with Sam?" she asked.

Jake perked up, grateful to have a more comfortable topic to discuss. "Isaac made a great center piece for the floor, but Sam wants me to fill in the tiles all around it. I was thinking about the sketch you did when we were down by the river on Mother's Day, you know, the one of the town with the hills in the background."

Amy nodded.

"I thought it would be fun to do a landscape like that surrounding the centerpiece. I told him I'd get started right away. I was thinking, if you wanted, we could work on the project together. You've seen my sketches, and when you make something permanent like this, you want to make sure it looks decent. Besides, I figured it would give us some experience before we start on Isaac's bench."

"What's in it for me?" she asked with a teasing smile.

"Well, he promised me if I could get it finished within three weeks, he'd give me three years' worth of bread. I'll split it with you."

"I'm not even sure where I'm going to be in three years," she said, "let alone by the end of the summer."

Her words caused Jake to become sullen as he considered the temporary nature of their circumstances. Surely, she wouldn't be able to live at her aunt and uncle's house forever. Sooner or later, she would have to move on. Jake's own future wasn't any clearer.

"Amy," he said, breaking the silence.

She looked at him and waited for him to continue, but his pause was long as he searched for the words he wanted to say.

"I don't really know what I'm feeling and I know I don't have the words to express whatever feelings I have."

Amy smiled softly.

"I was going to say that I'm really grateful for our friendship, but that sounds so lame… and really only half of what I'm feeling."

She put her hands behind her and leaned back, listening intently to his words.

"I could say that I really like being with you, but I feel like that's only a small part of it. I guess… I don't know…. I've never felt this way about anyone. I've never woken up in the morning and thought about someone all day long. I've never been so distracted that I couldn't work. I've never wished there were more hours in the day or days in the week so I could spend more time with anyone. And then this week happened and I feel like I'm no longer the same person I was before. I can hardly work because I just want to be with you every minute. I just want to breathe your same air and be near enough to touch you and look at you and talk with you and.......' "

He was afraid to look at Amy whose eyes he had been avoiding since he began his monologue. Again there was silence for a long moment and Jake feared he had ruined everything.

"Jake," she finally said, then paused. She took a deep breath. "The last thing in the world I wanted when I came here was a romantic relationship. I came here to paint and, so far, I've finished exactly three paintings. I hate my job. My parents think I'm wasting my life and the money they paid to educate me. I started to doubt myself and wonder what I was doing here. Until this week, I was miserable. But you've helped me get over my doubts and my discouragement. Even my job has become somewhat tolerable as it helped pass the time until I could be with you. Your friendship has given me hope again. You're the most sincere guy I've ever dated."

She shook her head, waiting for the right words to come. "It just seems I can't be around you enough. When you drop me off at night, I stay up thinking about you, wondering… well, hoping you're feeling the same way I am…whatever it is I'm feeling. When I hug you, even the very first hug, I just felt like…I fit—- for the first time in my life. I've tried to make things work with other guys in the past, but the more we tried to make it work, the worse things got. I don't know what it is that I'm feeling either. I feel like I'm in a dream and I hope I never wake up."

Jake looked up, a smile spreading across his face. He tried a couple of times to say something but just shook his head and bit his tongue. She put her hand on the back of his head and ran her fingers through his shaggy hair.

"What?" she asked with a nervous smile.

Jake shook his head again. "I don't know what to say. I...this is amazing. I feel like I want to climb up to the top of the clock tower and yell for the whole town to hear. I'm not sure what I'd yell," he said with a little laugh, "but I just feel like I could do anything right now. I've never been happier, never been better understood, never had such a great friend, never been so in love."

Amy smiled and threw her arms around his neck. "This is so crazy," she said. "We've known each other for two weeks and already I feel like you know me better than anyone ever has." Jake pulled her tighter against him and then let go a little. Amy too pulled back so their noses were nearly touching. Jake had never been in this position before and he cowered, not knowing what to do. For the longest time, they just looked at each other in the light of the moon.

Finally, Jake spoke. "Amy."

She looked at him, smiling softly. "Yes?"

"Can I kiss you?"

"I don't think I've ever been asked that before," she said with a broad smile.

Jake shook his head. "I'm sorry, I've never done this before."

"I know. Molly told me tonight."

Jake looked surprised.

"It's a small town." She pulled him closer. "Just follow my lead," she said as she closed her eyes, turned her head slightly, and kissed him gently on the lips.

Jake started laughing softly.

"What?" she asked, pulling away so their noses nearly touched again.

"I just wondered if this would ever happen to me and never imagined it would be in a cemetery when it finally did." He pulled her closer and kissed her again, softly on the lips and then embraced her, holding her tight.

"I've never said this to a girl before," he whispered in her ear, "but I love you."

Amy squeezed him tighter. "I love you too, Jake," she whispered. And they held each other a long, long time. When they finally let go, they looked at each other and began laughing.

"Jake, never ask me again if you can kiss me. Just know that your kisses are always welcome."

Before leaving, they knelt together, filling the cookie bag with small blue flowers—the secret ingredient to a balm that had soothed a thousand hearts.

As Jake walked back to his apartment, he considered how his life had changed in the matter of a week. He was in love and he couldn't help but smile. He smiled as he pulled the blue flowers from the plastic bag and rinsed them in the colander. He smiled as he placed them on a baking sheet to dry. He smiled when he saw Isaac's book, considering all the things he and Amy would discover together. He smiled as he brushed his teeth. And when he finally lay his head down on his pillow, he fell asleep with a smile across his face.

TO BE CONTINUED
IN...
DISCOVERING ISAAC

DUE OUT CHRISTMAS 2009

-END NOTES

All biblical references listed below and those found throughout Remembering Isaac are from the King James Translation of The Holy Bible.

1. By Mary Ann Morton. 1826-1897 Sweet is the peace the gospel brings (From page 94)
2. By Thomas Hastings and Hugh Stowell The Mercy Seat Circa 1850. (From page 96)
3. Luke 12:48 (From page 269)
4. James 2:20 (From page 289)
5. Isaiah 2:4 (From page 291)
6. Inspired by Malachi 3: 8-11 (From page 365)
7. By Bill Danoff Potter's Wheel Recorded by John Denver in 1992. (From page 394)

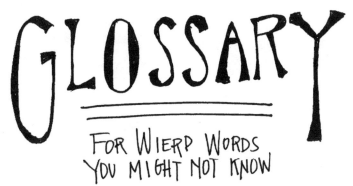

GLOSSARY

FOR WIERD WORDS YOU MIGHT NOT KNOW

Bat : In ceramics, a bat is a disc made of wood, plaster or plastic. It is attached to the wheel head, allowing a potter to make a pot and then remove the pot from the wheel by removing the bat on which it was made.

Bisqueware: Ware that is unglazed and has been fired to about 1800°F. Most pots are bisque fired before they are glazed, making them harder and more durable. See Bisque Firing for more details.

Bisque Firing: The primary reason for bisque firing is to prepare the ware to be glazed. Submerging a piece of greenware in glaze would cause it to break down and fall apart. A bisque firing, usually to about 1800°F, hardens the clay to a state where the glaze can be applied without the ware breaking down. Because ware in a bisque firing is not glazed, pieces can be stacked on top of or inside of other pots without fear of the pots fusing together. Because of this, many more pots can be fired in a bisque firing than in a glaze firing.

Burner: The kiln at Pottery Niederbipp has six burners, three on each side of the kiln. These are venturi burners that run on natural gas. All six burners are controlled by one valve, allowing the same amount gas to each burner. Gas passes through these burners and ignites on the top end, heating the kiln. See picture on page 61.

Candling: Also known as preheat. Candling refers to a small flame that is introduced to the kiln, warming it and drying out the pots inside.

It is critical to make sure all the moisture is drawn out of the pots before the rapid temperature rise of the firing begins or the pots with be blown to pieces by the inability of the water vapor in the clay to escape quickly enough.

Damper: Similar to a damper on a fireplace. It allows the heat to escape from the kiln and is the primary way to regulate the amount of reduction present in the kiln. This is adjusted throughout the firing using a long iron pole. See picture on page 61.

Glaze: Glaze at Pottery Niederbipp is applied only in liquid form by pouring onto bisqueware or by dipping bisqueware into the buckets of glaze. Glaze is made of a variety of materials that when melted at high temperatures, form a surface like glass. Some common ingredients include feldspars, clays, silica and metallic oxides.

Glaze firing: After the bisqueware is glazed, it is placed in the kiln and a second firing follows, firing the pots to 2360°F. This matures the glaze, vitrifies the clay and makes the ware functional. All glaze firing at Pottery Niederbipp are high-fire, cone 10, reduction firings.

Greenware: Unfired pottery. Term can be used for pots that have just been made and are still wet or to pots that are bone-dry and ready for a bisque fire. At this state, the pots are very fragile and extreme care is taken when handling them.

Kiln: In the ceramics world, there are hundreds of different kinds of kilns. The kiln at Pottery Niederbipp is gas fired and made of firebrick. It is used to fire pottery, making it first into bisqueware and then after the ware is glazed, it is used to used to fire the pottery to about 2360° F where the glaze matures, making it functional and non-porous.

Peephole: also called "spyhole". A small hole in the door of the kiln where a potter can look into the kiln to take a "peep" at the pyrometric cones inside and thus determine the temperature of the kiln. The kiln at Pottery Niederbipp has two peepholes, one on the top of the door and one near the bottom. The peephole is usually plugged with a piece of firebrick and removed only when the potter is checking on the pyrometric cones or to increase the cool-down speed after a firing. See page 61 for picture.

Porthole: Also known as burner holes. The holes in the floor of the kiln through which the flame from the burners enters the kiln to heat it.

Pyrometer: A high temperature thermometer that uses a thermocouple, or probe, placed in the door of the kiln with leads that are attached to a reader that helps a potter determine temperature inside the kiln. The one used at Pottery Niederbipp is an old fashioned analogue pyrometer with questionable accuracy. Because of that, pyrometric cones are always used.

Pyrometric Cones: Heat indicators made of ceramic materials similar to glazes that bend and melt in the firing, helping a potter to know when the temperature has been reached inside the kiln. These are viewed through the peephole. Seen on page 129

Reduction, reduce: Refers to a "reduction atmosphere" inside a gas-fired kiln. In short, this is caused by either starving the flame of oxygen or introducing more gas into the kiln than can be consumed by the fire, causing it to "burn rich". Many glazes, including most copper glazes, react strongly and favorably to such an atmosphere, causing the colors to change and positive effects to happen. Copper red glazes only turn red in a strong reduction atmosphere.

Slip: Slip is one of those words that literally describes what it is, or at least what it feels like. When a potter works with clay on the wheel, he uses water in the forming process to give the clay lubrication. Water mixed with the fine clay particles collects on the potter's hands, on the pot itself, on the wheel...basically everywhere. It ranges in consistency from that of milk to that of sour cream. When a potter attaches handles, to say, a mug, slip is added to the joint, helping the two pieces to bond. It looks tasty, but its not.

Throw, threw, throwing, thrown, : Words used by potters to describe the work of making pots on a potter's wheel ie I am going to throw some pots.; I threw some pots earlier today. I have been throwing pots for ten years. This bowl was obviously thrown on the wheel. This may come from the initial act of attaching the clay to the wheel head. In order for the clay to stick, one must throw the clay with some force onto the middle of the wheel head.

Wax Resist: A mixture of wax and other ingredients that remains liquid at room temperature and is applied to pots for a variety of reasons. In chapter 23, Jake looks at the results of a firing where this is used. Basically, Jake paints it on in a design over one glaze. Once the wax dries, he applies a second glaze by dipping the pot into another glaze. The resist protects the areas where it was applied, shedding the second glaze, while the unprotected or unwaxed areas received a second layer of glaze. Because wax resist in an integral part of Jake's new designs, more information will follow in volume 2.

Wedging, wedge: Wedging is one of the acts of preparing the clay before a potter can use it. It is similar to kneading bread dough and fulfills many of the same purposes. Its main purposes include getting rid of air bubbles, rounding the lumps of clay for use on the wheel and mixing the clay so there is consistency found throughout.

Wedging Table: This can take on many shapes and descriptions. At Pottery Niederbipp, the wedging table is a sturdy wood table where the wedging takes place. Because the studio is so small, it is also the glazing table.

THANK YOU

To Lynnette, who has yet to visit Niederbipp, but believed me when I told her these stories and gave me the faith I needed to make this book happen.

To Isaac and Eve, our kids, who make me laugh and teach me the meaning of life and joy.

To my siblings, Sam, John, Katie, Abe, Joe and Nate, who listened to my stories and liked them enough to keep me talking late into the night when imagination has no limits.

To my friends who served as an extension of my family and still do: Andrew, Jonas, Kirsten, Amy, Melba, Jennie, Leslie, Adam, and Mike, who encouraged me to live my dreams, no matter how crazy they were. I could not have asked for better friends.

To Irene, my sister of soul, who introduced me to Niederbipp and to Isaac and many of the others as I worked on her wheel and dreamed of becoming a potter.

To Steve and Teresa Chamberlain, who loaned me their studio and nourished the dream.

To Gordon Moore, my first teacher of clay, who made me want it.

To Mrs. Southam, Mrs. Reynolds and Mr. Henry, who taught me the joy of expression through the written word.

To my parents, who told me becoming an artist would doom me to a life of poverty and unhappiness, which made me want it badly enough to prove them wrong.

To Nettie, Brent, Donald, Sue, Heidi and especially Melba for their help in editing my thousand page babble into a readable book.

To Bert Compton who "gets it", and was able to share the vision I had for this book.

To Zach and Levi Snarr, for the use of their haven—a quiet place where one can hear the wind blowing through the trees.

·BIOGRAPHY·

Photo by Steve Speckman

I was born, Benjamino Arostophaneus Phineus Alfonsoh Picklebreath Behuninininin, but I shortened my name when I learned that every one of my names gets underlined in red when I use spellcheck.

As I mentioned in the prelude, I am a potter, and a writer when persuaded.

I was born at a very early age in Provo, Utah in 1973. I later became the oldest of seven children. We were raised primarily in Salt Lake City, Utah, but I also lived in Ohio for a couple of years and less than that in Florida. I have always been an artist and a story teller. My siblings all remember the stories I told them at night when they were going to bed. My two children, Isaac and Eve, would rather have me tell them stories than read to them at night. Someday, when the voices of Niederbipp leave me alone, I'll work on some children's stories.

I was fourteen when I first discovered clay and my experience was much like Jake's. I was terrible. Time and persistence have a way of making you into something you're not. I am still a dreamer. Thirteen years after choosing to make mudpies for a living, I am still doing it—the best I can.

I first visited Niederbipp in 1994 and considered naming my first child after the town. Isaac, my son, is happy he has a more practical mother.

You should go there sometime. It's an amazing place. It inspired me be a village potter.

I live and work in Salt Lake City. My studio is behind my home so I can be near my kids and my wife, Lynnette.

When I'm not making pots or pretending to be a writer, I like to eat strong cheese, listen to bluegrass music and hike in the mountains near our home, not necessarily at the same time, though it wouldn't be a bad idea. I wear bow ties on Sundays. We don't have any pets, but sometimes, we pretend we do. I often dream I can fly, but that is another story.

Personalized books can be ordered at
www.benbehunin.com
Please register on the email mailing list to
Receive updates about Isaac and other publications.

Please send correspondence to:
Abendmahl Press
P.O. Box 581083
Salt Lake City, Utah 84158-1083
Or by email to
benbehunin@comcast.net

More information on this book is available at
www.rememberingisaac.blogspot.com

Ben's pottery is available at www.potterboy.com
and many fine galleries across the U.S.A.

If you would like to feature Remembering Isaac
in your book club, please contact Ben for a group discount.
www.vivaniederbipp.com

For speaking engagements, including inaugurations, bar mitzvahs, or
funerals, please call (801)-883-0146

For design information, contact Bert Compton at
bert@comptonds.com